"YOU BELONG TO ME, AURORA."

You're mine. Mine! I made you mine that night beside the pond."

"Don't speak of that night! I don't want to remember!"

"You may not want to, my love, but you cannot forget it, can you? I'll wager you remember it all too clearly, particularly at night, tucked in your maidenly bed behind your uncle's marble walls."

"Stop it!" she hissed.

"You're mine, Aurora," he vowed fiercely. "No one else can have you. No one!"

"It's a lie!"

"It's the truth," he breathed, bending toward her. . . .

"Wonderful escapist fiction. It fulfills all her readers' fantasies!"

Romantic Times

SANDRA DuBAY

WILDER SHORES OF LOVE

LEISURE BOOKS ⚮ NEW YORK CITY

A LEISURE BOOK

Published by

Dorchester Publishing Co., Inc.
6 East 39th Street
New York, NY 10016

Printed in the United States of America

PROLOGUE I

High Island, 1890

The golden warmth of the summer sun bathed the island, illuminating its lush foliage and glistening on the undulating waves of the lake that stretched away to the horizon, seemingly as endless as the oceans themselves.

The cool blue waters broke along the shore, lapping hungrily at the sun-warmed sand of the beach and the varicolored pebbles and stones that eons of waves had deposited there.

From the majestic stand of towering pines that ringed the shore, a man emerged and walked to the water's edge. Tall, bronzed by the sun, body hardened by the sheer adversity of carving out a life for himself alone in nature, he was a man to be reckoned with.

He threw back his head and felt himself warmed by the golden rays that streamed from the china blue sky above. His burnished skin glowed, his thick, sable hair gleamed with the healthy sheen of a sleek, powerful animal. His only garment, a pair of soft, well-worn trousers, was left in a heap on the shore as he walked into the cool, welcoming waters of Lake Michigan.

As he swam, the man saw a yacht gliding past in the distance. Long and low, its billowing white sails were filled with the winds that caressed the chain of islands. But the man felt no envy for the people who strolled on the decks of the graceful vessel—he felt no jealousy of the men nor any desire for the carefully coiffed, beautifully dressed women who held tightly to the parasols that protected their pampered skins. He'd once known something of the life they led, but he'd rejected it—utterly, totally—to return to the islands. This was his birthplace, and the simple cabin in which he lived was the same one where his mother had cradled him on a straw-filled tick during that first bone-chilling winter, while the coyotes stalked their prey in the snow-hushed forests surrounding them.

As the yacht sailed on and disappeared from view, memories filled his mind. He frowned, his blue eyes glinting with distaste. He'd left the life of luxury behind him—left it with the vow that nothing would ever induce him to return to it. Nothing! And no one!

PROLOGUE II

New York, 1890

The warm, nurturing light of the summer sun shone through the tall, cathedral-like window at the back of the ornate Grecian temple standing in the Moravian Cemetery on Staten Island. Built to weather the centuries, its stone and ironwork still had a raw newness about them as the two mahogany and silver coffins were borne inside.

As the mourners began to file away, a young girl of seventeen lagged behind. Standing between the twin biers, she stretched out trembling, black-gloved hands, resting one on each of the cool, smooth coffins. Standing there so alone, she seemed impossibly fragile. The sunlight filtering through the stained-glass window adorned her with jewel-hued spots, and two droplets of crimson light shone on her pale cheeks as though her tears were pure heart's blood.

A gentle hand touched her sleeve, drawing her away, leading her out of the vault so that the tall iron doors could be closed and locked, separating her forever from the parents she loved.

As in a dream, she moved toward the crepe-draped carriage in which she would begin the trip home to the great Fifth Avenue mansion her father, a self-made Croesus, had built for the wife and daughter he adored. As she sank onto the hard, button-tufted leather of the seat, her wide, cat-green eyes met the gentle gaze of her father's attorney—the man who would be her guardian until the arrival of her aunt and uncle from Chicago.

"Aurora," he said softly, with great feeling, for he was a kindly man who had raised children of his own and he thought he understood something of the grief and foreboding of this child. She was heiress to a staggering fortune, yet money could not buy the only things she truly desired—the lost lives of her mother and father. He stretched out a gloved hand toward her. "Everything will be all right; you'll see."

But as the carriage rolled away, Aurora felt the warm trickle of a tear sliding down her cheek. How could everything ever be all right again? she wondered. It seemed impossible. The future was filled with nothing but the utter hopelessness of unending grief and pain, and she looked toward it with nothing but dark foreboding.

1

New York, 1890

Aurora paused at the top of the sweeping black marble staircase as the wafting strains of a waltz enveloped her, beckoning her to descend to the columned hall that served as an anteroom to the glittering, gold and white and crystal-chandeliered ballroom of Alexander de Groate's Riverside Drive mansion.

Below her, bathed in the golden glow of the etched crystal lamp held aloft by a gilded cherub, Graham Hughston admired her. She was more beautiful than he'd allowed himself to hope. She glanced down and saw him there and the faintest glimmer of a smile curved her petal-soft, pink-blushed lips as she descended the stairs.

Graham Hughston allowed a tiny frown to crease his high brow for a moment before it was banished beneath a facade of benign imperturbability. He had been summoned from Chicago to court this young millionairess, but it was proving a far more difficult task than he had at first imagined.

As he stepped back to allow her to fall into step beside him, he caught sight of himself in one of the antique Venetian mirrors that alternated with the marble columns. His appearance was faultless. There was not a man in the ballroom who could surpass him for sheer polished elegance from the top of his immaculately barbered, caramel brown hair and carefully waxed moustache, to the polished tips of his patent leather button boots peeping out from beneath uncreased black trousers. His black tailcoat fit to perfection over his broad shoulders, and the gold of his watch chain winked across the narrow expanse of his white piqué waistcoat.

"It's grown intolerably warm in here, Aurora," he said, a hint of command in his voice. "Why don't we move closer to the veranda?"

Wordlessly Aurora slipped her hand into the crook of his arm as they moved toward the French doors. The throng parted before them, and Graham felt not a little surge of pride at being the acknowledged beau of such a beauty—and such a prize on the marriage mart.

He had come to New York at the behest of his mother and of Electra Jephson, his mother's sister, who was married to Carlisle Jephson, Aurora's uncle and guardian. After her year of mourning was over—a period that had elapsed only weeks before—it would be time for the girl, now eighteen, to think about marriage. And who, the women had reasoned, was more suited to her than their own dear son and nephew—Graham Cornelius Hughston?

And so he had set out for New York in order to be on hand when Aurora emerged from her mourning and entered society. He had come to be her escort to her debutante ball—had come expecting a mousy little creature whose only redeeming feature was the size of her fortune. Instead he had found a little diamond that had glittered for too long in darkness and silence—a gem he intended to possess long before any other greedy male had the chance to steal her away.

His dark eyes swept over her as she walked beside him, head held high, back straight, determined little chin in the air. . . .

Graham sighed. He had expected a girl as young and sheltered as Aurora to succumb quickly and quietly to his practiced charm. But he had found, to his utter exasperation, that beneath the petal-soft skin he had come to savor in the way that a connoisseur savors a priceless objet d'art, her heart was sheathed by a quarter-inch shield that was equal parts stubbornness and wariness. He didn't know if it had always been there—the iron fist beneath the velvet glove of her femininity—or if it had sprung up after her parents' deaths as a sort of protection against the grief of losing another loved one, but it was proving nigh on impossible to break down. Flattery and charm had proven useless—he wondered if passion might be the chink in her armor.

Little by little, he edged her out the door and into the concealing darkness of the veranda. The music from the ballroom was merely a seductive backdrop now, and the lights that sparkled on the dark river in the distance lent a fairy-tale quality to the night that surrounded them.

Her gown was excessively plain, sleeveless above her long white gloves, made of white tulle with ribbon rosettes decorating the shoulders and at the back of the long, pointed waist. Her hair, a deep russet red, was dressed in a thick knot. Dozens of tiny kiss-curls framed her pale face, making her cat-green eyes seem huge and guile-less. Only in her lips, which were full and pouting, bee-stung and—so Graham reflected too often for his own peace of mind—eminently kissable, and in the blossoming beauty of her figure, a perfect hourglass with no need of the elaborate, merciless embrace of corsets, was the woman within re-vealed.

A sensuous woman lurked beneath that vir-ginal facade, he felt certain. At first he had thought to use her unawakened senses against her—feeling sure that the man who brought her passions surg-ing to the surface would be the man to win her guarded heart. Now his only thought was to pos-sess her, own her, as a collector owns his treasures or a miser his coin.

His hands at her waist, he drew her as near as he dared. But as he bent to kiss her, Aurora turned her face toward the concealing shadows.

"You're leaving tomorrow, aren't you, Gra-ham?" she asked softly.

He wondered if it was only curiosity he heard in her voice or if there was a hint of relief as well.

"I am," he confirmed. "Will you miss me?"

Easing herself gently from his grasp, she took a tiny step to her right—a step that brought her into the shaft of light spilling through the French doors, a step that took her from the dark, private intimacy of the veranda into the bright, public safety of the ballroom.

"Aunt Electra, Uncle Carlisle, and I will be leaving within the week ourselves. We are traveling by train to Cleveland where we will board Uncle Carlisle's yacht and sail to Mackinac Island. Aunt Electra told me that is your destination as well— that your family also owns a cottage on the island. So I shall scarcely have time to miss you, shall I?"

Graham ground his teeth in exasperation. All that, and she hadn't answered his question! She hadn't said she would miss him. Could it be that all his courting, all his flattering, all his wooing had not made any impression on her armor-plated heart? Did she have no feelings for him at all? Damn! She was the most maddening female he had ever encountered.

Taking a moment to collect his thoughts, he calmed himself and stepped nearer to her. Her subtle fragrance stole into his nostrils and his dark eyes savored the silken perfection of her flawless throat and shoulders and the gentle swell of her bosom above the low V of her neckline.

"Aurora," he said quietly, cajolingly, "come, walk with me in the garden."

Aurora's lush lashes fell to conceal her telling eyes. "I hardly think that would be prudent, do you, Graham? Why, if we were discovered there alone in the darkness, I might be hopelessly compromised."

"I am your cousin—in a manner of speaking," he reminded her.

Her laugh was half-innocent, half-knowing.

"And the resulting scandal might force you to become my husband—in a manner of speaking."

"Would that be such a tragedy?" he asked, thinking that, for his part, she had every attribute he could possibly look for in a wife—beauty, sensuality (even if she herself was as yet unaware of it), an almost obscene fortune, and no father to keep an eagle eye on the way her husband spent it.

Again the averted look that frustrated him so, hiding, as it did, her feelings.

"When I marry," she said so softly that he had to lean close and try to block out the music wafting from the ballroom, "I want it to be for love—not for convenience and not because propriety demands it."

"Love matches are rare for people such as we," he pointed out.

"Far too rare," she agreed sadly. "I want no part of a match made for wealth or position. I have wealth enough and I don't care for position. If I cannot marry for love, I shan't marry at all." Before Graham could think of a suitable comment, she eyed him coolly. "If you will pardon me, Graham, I think I shall ask Aunt Electra if we may leave now. I have the most monstrous headache."

Turning, she left him. Standing there, half in the shadows, half in the light, Graham watched her glide across the ballroom, the focus of a hundred envious, jealous, covetous eyes. Her words echoed in his mind:

"If I cannot marry for love, I shan't marry at all."

Turning away, he moved to the stone balustrade and scowled into the darkness, his gloved hands clenched on the railing.

Damn it all! he cursed angrily, his lips moving soundlessly. He had wooed this Midas in petticoats, flattered her, played the lovesick fool, and for what? To be told by a haughty little chit that she would not marry except for love! His task was clear but the course looked like a rough one—he must, preferably during the time they would spend on Mackinac Island, make her fall in love with him!

"Graham?" Electra Jephson, both his aunt and Aurora's, was at his side. "Graham, darling, we are leaving. Are you coming?"

His dark eyes darted across the ballroom to the lush form of Caroline Denbigh. Miss Denbigh had been "out" in society for a considerable time, and though her family was a respectable one and their fortune still more so, no man would offer her the security and respectability of a wedding band. She was, so the wags—and the scandal sheet *Town Topics*—said, "fast."

Graham's eyes lingered on the puffs of feathers that trimmed the dangerously low décolletage of her gown. She was a black-haired, black-eyed beauty and he longed to discover just how true the rumors might be. But he noticed Aurora's amused, mocking gaze upon him and drew himself up indignantly.

"Of course I'm coming, Aunt," he said gallantly. "If Aurora is leaving, there is no one of interest for me here any longer."

Aurora cast a significant glance toward Miss Denbigh, who had turned away, a look of ill-concealed disappointment on her pretty, vapid face.

She said nothing, but the expression in her eyes as she laid her hand on Graham's proffered

11

arm spoke volumes—all of it maddening to his already frustrated senses.

As they collected their cloaks and walked out to where their carriage waited to transport them home, Graham vowed to make the most of the time he would have on Mackinac Island before his fiancée-to-be arrived. If he was expected to woo this exasperating creature, he would first have to sow a prodigious amount of wild oats, if only to maintain a tenuous hold upon his sanity during the long dry spell of a proper courtship.

2

"Aurora? Aurora, don't dawdle!"

"No, Aunt Electra," Aurora replied, her voice soft, meek, obedient, belying the way her eyes rolled up with weary vexation and then twinkled with roguish merriment when her maid, Bridget, a pretty girl only a year removed from her native Ireland, giggled delightedly.

Aurora rose as her maid finished hooking the dozens of buttons that fastened her high-topped shoes and stood while Bridget draped her shoulders with a traveling cloak made of satin merveilleux and designed by Worth of Paris.

Taking the bonnet of Neapolitan braid the maid offered her, Aurora twined its streaming green ribbons about her fingers as she gazed wistfully at the room that would be hers no more.

"Will you miss this house, miss?" Bridget asked softly.

"Oh, Bridey, I'm not sure," Aurora sighed, touching the pink satin brocade that draped her gilded four-poster bed and sheathed the walls. "It is the only home I've ever known and I love it. But it reminds me too keenly of Mama and Papa."

Bridget was silent, allowing her young mistress a moment of remembrance. She had not known Aurora's parents—she had come from Chicago with Aurora's aunt and uncle—but she knew how painfully she missed her own parents, long since laid to rest beneath the verdant Irish sod.

Wistful, Aurora left her room and wandered down the wide corridor toward the magnificent staircase which, like so many other features of the Fifth Avenue mansion that was her home, had been stripped from some French château or English castle or Italian palazzo. The architects who labored to build the modern palaces of New York had plundered Europe like the hordes of the Hun, stripping antiquities, treasures and artifacts from the lands of their creation and bringing them home to decorate the marble halls of American Royalty.

American Royalty. The phrase never failed to bring a weary smile to Aurora's lips. That was what the newspapers had called her in the articles following her parents' tragic deaths in a carriage accident at Newport. Sole heiress to her father's railroad fortune, she was richer by far than any other girl her age in the country.

The sudden publicity had exposed her to a world she'd never known. She had grown up sheltered by the soft, protective cocoon her parents had woven about her in their desire to provide for her a happy, carefree childhood. Then suddenly, without warning, her private grief was shattered by the ugly intrusion of a curious, greedy world. Her face, a complete account of the fortune she would inherit, her entire life became matters of public record. From everywhere came a deluge of pleas for money, outpourings of resentment, offers of marriage. . . . For a girl of seventeen who had never in her life been allowed to remain alone in a room with any man save her father, she seemed overnight to have become the most desirable of women. American fortune-hunters seeking to marry their way into the swirl of New York society, nouveau-riche provincials seeking a wife who could bring them the respectability their money could not buy, impoverished European princelings who desired the wealth to go along with their exalted rank, all offered for her hand. Her existence became a nightmare—the mansion on Fifth Avenue seemed almost an armed camp.

At last, in desperation her father's attorneys had sent to Chicago for her uncle, who had made his fortune from the copper mines of the West. He and his wife, Aurora's guardians until her majority, were requested to come and try to restore some sanity to their niece's existence.

And so Aurora Jephson, the journalists' darling, disappeared once more from the public eye. She spent her year of mourning behind the elegant walls of the mansion that, with its iron-fenced lawns and gardens, covered more than an acre of prime Manhattan real estate.

Slowly, sadly, Aurora descended the stairs to the entrance hall whose vaulted ceiling had been copied from an abbey in Provence. The mansion's architect, Stanford White, had moved heaven and earth in an attempt to obtain the original hall but, failing that, had designed a replica that surpassed the real thing for breathtaking beauty and timeless elegance.

She strolled along the corridor, one gloved hand lovingly brushing the rosewood paneling with its floral-patterned inlay of brass and mother-of-pearl, toward the gallery where the magnificent stained-glass ceiling filtered the light that once had shone down on the late Aubrey Jephson's collection of masterworks.

The paintings and sculptures were gone now, crated and stored, as would be most of the rest of the mansion's priceless antique furnishings—stored against a time in the future when Aurora would be married and the finest items in the collection would adorn the mansion her husband would doubtless build for her.

As for the Fifth Avenue palace of the late Aubrey and Consuelo Jephson, it had already been sold to an up-and-coming young entrepreneur whose fortune had but recently passed the magic fifty-million-dollar mark regarded as necessary to maintain a life amidst the glittering Four Hundred.

Aurora sighed as she sank into the soft, tufted velvet of a round, gold-fringed ottoman. How she'd loved the gallery once upon a time when she and her parents lived their quiet, loving lives within these beautiful walls. She had thought their happiness complete—had expected to live here until the inevitable day when a man of her father's choosing would make her his wife and take her away to a life as peaceful and charmed as her mother's and father's. It had all seemed like a fairy tale out of some children's storybook—but this tale had no happy ending. For the king and queen were gone, snatched away by a cruel whim of fate, and the princess was left alone in the world, prey to the vagaries of chance and the caprices of the—

"Aurora!"

Wicked stepmother? Aurora thought uncharitably as her Aunt Electra's voice sounded from the corridor outside the gallery.

She was immediately ashamed of her unkind comparison. Electra Gwynne Jephson was not a bad woman, Aurora knew; it was simply that she was as different from Aurora's gentle, fragile mother as a graceful sailing ship was from a fully armed dreadnought. Certainly Electra had taken charge of the household and freed Aurora from the worries of running the mansion—a task for which her mother had only begun to train her when death had stolen her away.

What was more, Electra had effectively stemmed the tide of marriage proposals that had deluged Aurora since the newspapers had begun to make the details of her staggering inheritance known. She protected her niece from the unwanted attentions of unscrupulous fortune-hunters with all the ferocity of a tigress protecting her cub. But for all Aurora's gratitude, there was a disturbing undercurrent of suspicion—suspicion that Electra was not merely protecting her baby-tycoon niece but preserving her and her fortune for a suitor of her own choosing.

Graham Hughston. Aurora thought of him for the first time since his departure a week before. He was handsome—Aurora freely admitted as much —and he had gone about courting her most assiduously. The son of Electra's sister, Gloria Gwynne Hughston, and the late Foster Hughston, a railroad

17

magnate, Graham was twenty-eight and, obviously, eminently marriageable. There was nothing, really, that Aurora could find to hold against him except the fact that she could not, however much she might try, fall the slightest bit in love with him.

Her lips curved in a smile rife with self-mockery. Perhaps she was asking too much out of life. She was young, beautiful, rich—was love simply one blessing too many to ask for? Perhaps, and yet she felt certain that she would rather live out her life alone than with a man she did not love.

Not that she had had much experience in that direction. Before Graham had arrived from Chicago, Aurora had never had a beau. She had not been old enough for her debut at the time of her parents' deaths and during the year following she had been immured behind her marble walls like an enchanted princess. What little experience she had, had been garnered during Graham's polished courtship of the past few months.

She frowned thoughtfully, touching gloved fingers to her lips. Although the thought of stolen kisses touched some chord inside her, actually kissing Graham had seemed to stir nothing. Why was it that the prospect was more exciting than the actuality? Was it some fault in her? In him? Perhaps—

"Aurora?" Electra repeated, sweeping down on her niece, the pearl grey ostrich plumes on her hat bobbing as she moved. "Here you are!"

"I'm sorry, Aunt," Aurora said innocently, "you should have asked Bridey where I was. She knew."

Electra's bosom heaved with exertion beneath the numberless fringes of jet festooning her cloak.

18

"Your maid's name is Bridget, my dear, not Bridey. You know I do not hold with nicknames—they make you sound like an Irishman yourself. Not that you don't already look like one."

She eyed Aurora's red hair and green eyes with despair. Why couldn't the girl have inherited her mother's golden coloring rather than the red hair and pale skin of the Jephsons? Red hair was simply not the fashion!

Thick silken lashes shielded Aurora's mutinous glare from the older woman.

Her aunt smoothed on her gloves. "You must come along. The carriage is waiting to take us to the station."

Obediently Aurora rose and fell into step with her aunt.

"Only think, my dear," Electra said brightly, mistaking her niece's silence for melancholy, "within a week we will be on Mackinac Island and you will be reunited with Graham."

"How very exciting," Aurora muttered dully.

Electra shot her a scathing glare, but the girl's face was calm, placid, almost vapidly devoid of expression. "What does that mean?" she demanded, feeling uneasy, wondering if her nephew could possibly be in danger of letting this jewel of a prospective bride slip through his fingers.

"Nothing, Aunt, nothing at all," Aurora assured her.

But as they left the mansion and climbed into the carriage that would take them to Grand Central Terminal, Electra could not quell a burgeoning sense of unease.

3

"Bridey, you cannot stay out here all night!"

"And why not, I'd like to know?"

Aurora sighed as she drew her molleton mantle tighter about her. She balanced first on one bare foot, then the other, but the brisk night wind off the lake seemed to find its unerring way beneath the trailing hems of her mantle and nightgown. Reflections of the *Sea Mist's* running lights sparkled on the jet-black waves all around them.

"You'll catch your death of cold," she argued, adding resignedly, "or I'll catch mine."

The maid, jittery about boarding the yacht at the outset and growing more fearful as their voyage progressed, eyed her young mistress defiantly.

"Beggin' yer pardon, Miss Aurora, but I didn't ask you to come out here."

"No, that is quite true, you didn't," Aurora agreed with taut patience. "But I could not bear to think of you out here in the cold night air. Won't you come into the stateroom and—"

"No!" The girl's blue eyes were filled with unreasoning fear. "It's like a coffin, it is! A floating tomb!"

An image of her stateroom flashed in Aurora's mind. Elaborate, with gilt-trimmed ivory paneling, the stateroom boasted a canopied bed, a crystal chandelier, priceless carpets, and a working fireplace. At Aurora's insistence a small second bed had been installed in the room for Bridey. She had hoped it would comfort the girl to stay with her rather than in some maid's cabin farther down the corridor. It hadn't seemed to help.

"How in God's name," she asked the maid, "did you come from Ireland? Surely you didn't stay up on deck throughout the entire voyage?"

"I tried," Bridey insisted. "But after a week I took sick and they carried me below." Her eyes rounded. "I was that near to dyin'! And did those devils give me any sympathy? They did not! God curse 'em!"

Aurora sighed. She could well imagine that Bridey's fellow passengers would have little compassion for a girl who had brought her affliction upon herself. And now she was repeating her idiocy. They had another day and night to spend aboard the yacht, and it was errant foolishness to freeze on the wind-swept deck when a warm, silk-sheeted bed awaited her in her stateroom below.

"Well, I'm going to bed. You do as you please."

Leaving the girl to her fate, Aurora hurried to the stairs that took her down to the corridor where tufted leather chairs flanked marble-topped tables and gilt-framed seascapes decorated mahogany-paneled walls.

As she passed the door of the sitting room that adjoined her aunt's and uncle's twin staterooms, she heard her name mentioned. Torn between curiosity to know what was being said and guilt at eavesdropping at the keyhole like a nosy chambermaid, she hesitated, intending to move on as soon as she garnered the gist of the conversation.

"I shall be quite relieved to reach the island," Electra was saying. "I long to see Aurora and Graham reunited."

Carlisle sighed. Aurora heard him tapping his pipe against the andiron of the fireplace. "I must say I don't think much of this scheme of yours to throw Aurora and Graham together."

"Nonsense! Aurora is eighteen. A girl of her . . . prospects . . . has a responsibility to marry young. She needs a man like Graham to oversee her fortune."

"She has a battalion of lawyers to do that, my dear. To a man they are honest and competent, hand-chosen by her father with the utmost care."

"It is not the same as a husband, Carlisle. Not the same as someone with a personal interest in her welfare."

"But why rush her into a marriage with Graham? She is only just out of mourning. Give her time—"

"Time!" Electra repeated, her voice rising. "Time for what, pray? Time for some sharp fortune-hunter, some penniless stranger to sweep her into disaster?"

Carlisle's laugh was hollow, devoid of mirth. "Better a penniless relation, is that it?"

"Graham is not penniless!" Electra shrilled. "I grant you, the family fortunes have met with reverses since his father's death, but—"

"Come now, my pet, admit it. You wouldn't be so keen for this marriage if Aurora weren't one of the greatest heiresses of her generation."

"Well . . . I'll admit I'd like to see her holdings remain . . . undissipated . . . and—"

"You'd like to keep it in the family. May as well say it plainly."

"How vulgar!" Electra drew herself up. "Graham is my sister's only child. He is my only nephew. He is like a son to me—the child you never gave me! Why shouldn't I want the best for him?"

"Aurora is my brother's only child," Carlisle countered. "Though we haven't been close, I've come to love her as my own in these past months. I want the best for her, and I'm not sure Graham is the best. I think she could do better."

"Better!" Electra was outraged. "What would you have her do? Marry a title? Marry a foreigner to become a contessa or duchess?"

"I'd have her marry for love," Carlisle said softly.

Outside the sitting room, Aurora started with surprise.

"Love! Love, indeed! And where did love get you? Oh, don't think I didn't know about that little trollop you kept in that dingy little flat above—"

Not wishing to hear her uncle's dirty linen aired with or without his knowledge, Aurora hurried across the corridor to her own stateroom. Closing the door behind her, she let her mantle slide over the arm of a Louis XV armchair.

She hadn't realized until that moment how cold she was. Her feet were freezing, gooseflesh rose on her arms, she trembled. But as she climbed into the welcoming softness of the bed and drew the quilted coverlet up to her chin, she was not precisely sure if her shivering was from the cold or from the foreboding instilled in her by the realization of exactly how determined her aunt was to see her married someday to Graham Hughston.

The *Sea Mist* approached Mackinac Island in the straits between Michigan's upper and lower peninsulas where Lake Huron and Lake Michigan met. Even at a distance, the gleaming white of the buildings shone against the lush green of the pines and hardwoods that covered the island.

When the yacht was moored at one of the island's docks, the Jephson party debarked and climbed into a carriage that took them directly to their cottage high atop the east bluff.

The three-story cottage built of clapboard and shingles had a dining room, sitting room, parlor and kitchen on the first floor and four bedrooms and a bathroom on the second. The staff of six had come from Chicago, with the exception of Bridget, and included a cook, kitchen maid, parlor maid, Electra's lady's maid—Pelton—and an uppity butler who made no secret of the fact that he disliked being transported into the heathen wilderness where on occasion one still saw Indians come to trade for money and supplies. Aurora's maid, Bridey, fast recovering from her indisposition suffered aboard the yacht, would share a small room with the kitchen maid while the other servants had their own rooms on the third floor.

"Do you feel up to a walk?" Aurora asked

Bridey after surveying her room, a pretty chamber with a bay window and furnished in brass and wicker and ruffled chintz. A balcony overlooked the manicured lawns which gave way to the towering pines surrounding the carriage house.

"A walk, miss?" Bridey asked. "And where is there to walk to?"

"Why, to the village. There are dozens of charming shops. I'm sure some of them must be open even if the summer season hasn't yet begun."

"Confectioneries mostly, by the looks of 'em," the maid sniffed. "You'd best take care or you'll pop your laces before we leave for Chicago."

"I'll do nothing of the kind." Aurora slipped on the kid gloves that completed her walking ensemble of spring green trimmed with black passementerie about the tight waist, down the front of the skirt and around the elbow-length cuffs. A black felt hat with ostrich plumes perched atop her russet hair. "It's only that after the train trip and yacht voyage, I long to tread on solid ground once again. Now, are you coming with me or not?"

"Well, you can't go alone," the maid decreed. "Herself would give me the very devil if some red Indian was to catch you and take you off to the wilds."

Aurora laughed, waiting for her maid to pull on her hat and cloak. "I'm certain no 'red Indians' will ambush us on the way. Come along now."

With Bridget following, Aurora descended the stairs. Her aunt stood at the bottom, engaged in a heated discussion with Osborne, the butler.

The conversation ceased as Aurora neared. Electra eyed her niece with bewildered indignation.

"What is the meaning of this, my dear? It is nearly time for luncheon."

The tall case clock in the downstairs hall struck eleven.

"Already?" Aurora asked. "I thought it was to be at two."

"That is only three hours from now. Why don't you go upstairs and rest rather than going out into the hot sunshine?" She eyed Aurora's gleaming curls. "With that hair, you should stay in the shade and avoid freckles. You don't want to end up looking like a dalmatian, do you?"

Aurora sighed, well acquainted with her aunt's aversion to her Jephson-red hair. "I have on my bonnet, as you see, Aunt, and I shall take my parasol as well. I promise to be back well in advance of luncheon—unspotted."

"I hope so. Graham will be here, you know. In fact, if you waited until this afternoon for your outing, he would be most happy to escort you."

"I'm certain he would," Aurora agreed, a weary glint in her eyes. "More than happy."

"And what does that mean, miss?" her aunt demanded.

"Nothing—nothing at all. Now, if you will excuse me . . . ?"

Electra watched as Aurora and Bridget left the house and crossed the wide veranda. There was something in the girl's attitude she did not like—something that made her uncomfortable. Really, it was so frustrating! She had counted upon a naive, innocent, sheltered girl like Aurora falling in love with her handsome, charming nephew at first sight. But Aurora was proving so recalcitrant. It

must be the Jephson in her. They were a stubborn
lot! God knew Carlisle wasn't the easiest man in
the world to handle. If only the girl had been more
like her mother. Consuelo Stamford Jephson, God
rest her, had been a gentle, biddable creature.
Aurora definitely took after her father's family.
Electra pursed her lips, resigned. Graham would
simply have to take a more aggressive tack with the
girl. And she'd tell him so if the wretch ever
appeared! Where was he? She'd have a few choice
words for him—he should have met them at the
dock!

In his bedroom at the back of his parent's
cottage, Graham Hughston groaned and stirred in
the brass bed that dominated his room.

A soft humming filled the air—a melodious
sound that would ordinarily have soothed him.
Today it seemed to reverberate in his befogged
brain with maddening, aching persistence.

"Can't you stop that infernal noise?" he
hissed, slitting his eyes in the dim, curtain-filtered
light that seemed blinding to his hazy senses.

The humming stopped. The maid, a pert,
pretty girl dressed in a long black gown and
starched white apron and cap, cast a coquettish
glance over her beruffled shoulder.

"Well!" she said, tossing her head to make both
her curls and the long streamers of her cap bounce.
"Look who's alive!"

"Don't be fresh," he snarled. "What time is
it?"

Twining the streamers of her cap about her
fingers, the maid went to the foot of the bed. "I

27

thought you liked me to be fresh," she cooed, pouting prettily. "You certainly have this past week! And it's eleven o'clock."

"Eleven!" Throwing back the sheet, Graham clambered out of bed heedless of his nudity. He hesitated, swaying slightly, one hand to his throbbing head. "Draw me a bath, Betsy. No! On second thought, just bring me a basin of water and some towels. I haven't time to wait for a bath. Christ! I should have been down at the docks hours ago."

"Down at the docks?" Betsy asked, taking up the pitcher from its place on the washstand in the corner. "Who's coming?"

"My aunt and uncle—the Jephsons—if you must know."

He collected his shaving equipment and rummaged in the wardrobe for his clothes while the maid went for the water.

"The Jephsons?" she asked, returning without bothering to knock. "Never known you to be so anxious to meet them before."

"They are bringing someone with them, Mistress Curiosity," he snapped, lathering his face. "Someone I am 'anxious' to meet."

Betsy's brown eyes narrowed in suspicion. "A lady?" she asked, feeling that her days as Graham's playmate might be nearing an end.

"A lady indeed." He smiled smugly at his reflection. "A lady I hope soon will be my wife."

Ignoring the chambermaid's stricken groan, he took up the wicked straight razor and began to shave.

With Bridget at her side, Aurora strolled along the boardwalks that ran on either side of the main

28

street. It was as yet too early for many of the summer residents to be occupying their grand "cottages," so in the main the islanders had their island to themselves. Aurora noticed the ladies she passed eying her ensemble. A dressmaker whose shop thrived on the summer resort trade stood in her window busily making sketches as Aurora passed. Gentlemen tipped their hats to her as did the occasional blue-and-gold-coated soldier from Fort Mackinac, which overlooked the straits from its perch high atop the bluff as it had since before the Revolutionary War.

One of the latter, a handsome blond lieutenant, followed them none too discreetly, seeming indifferent to their presence and yet pausing when they paused, moving on when they moved on. Aurora and Bridget exchanged girlish grins, taking turns casting surreptitious glances over their shoulders to see if he were still behind them like a blue and gold and blond shadow.

It was not until Aurora's parasol slipped from her fingers that he saw his opening and sprang into action.

"Allow me, miss," he said, scooping up the frilly silk and lace confection with its streaming ribbons of green and cream satin. He brushed the dust from its ruffles and presented it to her with the air of a general surrendering his sword.

"Thank you, Lieutenant . . .?"

"Braxton, miss. Kyle Braxton."

Aurora felt herself blushing. The light in his grey-blue eyes was one of admiration and more. Something in his eyes, his smile, touched something inside her and set her atremble.

"You are very gallant, Lieutenant Braxton."

"And you are very lovely, Miss . . .?"

"Jephson. Aurora Jephson."

To her surprise, there was no sudden change in his handsome countenance, no quick, avaricious gleam such as she was used to seeing. He nodded thoughtfully.

"There are some Jephsons, I understand, who come to the island every summer. From Chicago, I believe?" His smile was sweetly apologetic. "Forgive me, but I've only just been posted to the fort, you see."

"I see. In any case, you are right. My uncle and aunt are from Chicago. They have a cottage on the east bluff."

"Will you be staying long, Miss Jephson?"

She smiled at the unconcealed hope in his tone. "Unfortunately not. We are to leave in a few weeks' time for Chicago."

"How sad. In that case, would you allow me to escort you on your shopping expedition?"

"We seem to have run out of shops. Perhaps I should have dropped my parasol sooner."

To her surprise, he blushed, realizing suddenly how transparent had been his pursuit of her.

"Luncheon, then?" he suggested. "There is a charming café where—"

"Luncheon! Heavens! Have you the time?"

He consulted his watch. "It's just after one. But why . . .?"

"I'm sorry. I promised my aunt I would be back by two. She has a guest coming and—" Aurora paused, one ear cocked to the devilish voice that seemed to whisper in her inner ear.

"Lieutenant Braxton," she said softly, her tone

flirtatious, cajoling. "Would you care to join us for luncheon? I'm quite certain my aunt won't mind."

"But her guest?" he asked, ill-concealing his delight at her invitation.

"Oh, pooh, don't worry about her guest. He is a relation—my aunt's nephew. I suppose that makes him my cousin, in a way, doesn't it?"

"Why, I suppose it does," he agreed, his blue eyes laughing down into her green ones.

He offered her his arm and she laid a gloved hand in the crook of it, her fingers lying across the gold braid that decorated his sleeve. Together they started back through the village while Bridget, carrying the furled parasol Aurora had handed to her, smirked as she pictured Electra Jephson's face when Aurora arrived at the tête-á-tête she had planned for her and Graham with a beau in tow.

4

"I don't like it, I tell you! Not at all!"

Electra Jephson glared at her husband's reflection in the mirror of her dressing table. Her graying brown hair had been unwound from its customary upswept knot and lay over the shoulders of her combing mantle.

Wearily Carlisle looked up from his company reports. "You are making too much of it, my dear. The girl is having a little flirtation with a handsome young officer. What harm can it do?"

"What harm? Why, poor Graham hasn't been able to have a moment alone with her these past two weeks."

"Doesn't occur to me he's tried very hard, my pet."

"What good would it do him to try? Aurora's gone driving with that young scoundrel three evenings this week alone."

"Her maid has gone with them," Carlisle reminded her.

"Hah! Much good that will do. That Bridget is as flighty as Aurora herself. I told you we should have brought someone older for Aurora. Someone with more sense. Someone like Pelton."

"Ugh." Carlisle thought of the sour, dried-up, disapproving old spinster who had been his wife's lady's maid since just after their marriage. "Pelton hasn't more sense than the next person, my sweet; she simply hates to see anyone having a good time."

"We were not discussing Pelton," Electra reminded him sharply. "We were discussing Aurora. And if you haven't a care for your niece's morals, I assure you I have."

"Her morals?" Carlisle scowled. "Aurora is a lady, born and bred, and she is chaperoned by her maid. What harm can come to her?"

"He could seduce her! Have you noticed the way that young scamp looks at her?"

"He's a normal man, darling, and Aurora is a beautiful young woman. How would you have him look at her?"

"Oh! Why do I try? Let her run amok—I wash my hands of her. I shall leave you to deal with it when we have to take her back to Chicago with her reputation in shreds."

"She'll be fine," Carlisle argued, going back to his reports. "We're leaving tomorrow. After that, it will be up to young Hughston to shred her morals. I'm sure you'll like that better."

With a savage glare for her complaisant husband, Electra slammed the silver-backed brush down onto the tabletop and tore off her mantle.

Extinguishing all save the lamp next to Carlisle's reading chair, she climbed into her bed and yanked the covers up to her chin.

At that moment, at the edge of a tree-shaded lane, Aurora trembled in the circle of Kyle Braxton's arms. She knew that Bridget was in the carriage not far away; she knew that a single word from her would bring the maid to her on the run. She knew she should call out to her if only to bolster her sagging will, but she could not.

"I love you, Rory," Kyle breathed hotly in her ear, using the pet name Aurora's father had given her. He pulled her closer, pressed her tighter against the mossy boulder at her back. "You know I do."

Aurora did not believe he loved her any more than she believed she loved him, and yet she was here in his arms, quivering, part of her wanting something the nature of which eluded her, and part of her wanting only to flee to the maidenly safety of her chamber in her uncle's cottage.

She felt his hands in her hair, drawing out the pins that secured it—felt the heavy russet curls tumbling over her shoulders. He pressed his body to hers. His mouth slanted across her lips; one hand busied itself in her hair, holding her head. His tongue touched her tautly compressed lips and tried to part them.

"What are you doing?" she demanded, pulling away from him though her hair was still painfully entangled in his fingers. He had never been so aggressive before. "Stop it, Kyle!"

"Rory," he breathed, his voice tremulous.

"Stay with me tomorrow—don't leave me. Don't go to Chicago."

Aurora struggled, her glimmering passion banished now by real fear. "Let me go! Leave me alone!"

She fought her way free of him and stumbled away, unsure of which way to go in the darkness. One hand pushed at the tangled mass of her hair, the other wiped roughly at the tears wetting her cheeks.

"I don't want you to go, Aurora," he told her, his voice tight with grim determination. "I want you to stay here. I want you to marry me."

"Marry—" She stared at him, dumbfounded, as he approached. "Kyle, I never meant . . . we weren't . . . we can't . . . It's impossible."

"Nothing is impossible," he argued. "Not if you want it badly enough." He shook his head, dismissing her stuttered objections. "I know, your aunt wouldn't like it. But there are ways to overcome her resistance."

"But we couldn't . . . Kyle—"

"We could. If we were lovers, Rory, they'd have to let us marry. The threat of scandal—"

Aurora steadied herself against a tree. What was he talking about? Marriage? Lovers? Until tonight theirs had been merely a pleasant flirtation. They held hands, smiled, talked, laughed. Before tonight they had not even kissed. And now, without warning, he was talking of their being lovers . . . marrying!

"No, Kyle, please, you know we can never—"

The easy good humor faded from his handsome face. "I'm not good enough for you, is that it? Her Royal Highness, the Great American Heiress!"

"Oh, Kyle," Aurora breathed. Damn. Damn! Why did it always have to come down to her money!

"Perhaps I'm not good enough to be your husband, Miss High-and-Mighty Jephson, but you're not too good to be my—"

He lunged after her, and Aurora fled deeper into the forest, twigs crackling beneath her boots, tripping on stones and roots, stumbling as the branches slapped at her cheeks and caught at her skirts and sleeves.

She cried out in fear, as Kyle caught her and bore them both down into the cushion of dead leaves on the forest floor.

"Bridey!" Aurora wailed. "Bridey, help me! Help me! Hurry!"

Kyle's hands seemed to be everywhere at once; his mouth, hot and wet, was on her throat, her cheeks, her mouth. He tore at the black buttons of her basque, then at the shirred white linen of her chemisette. He pulled at her skirt, snarling, swearing when the thick folds of her skirt and the heavy lace of her petticoat impeded him.

Aurora fought like a mad thing. Her fists pounded his broad shoulders, flailed against his back. She grabbed fistfuls of his thick blond hair and yanked his head back, gasping for air as his mouth left hers.

"Bridey!" she shrieked, like a frantic, desperate animal in the throes of mortal terror.

Then suddenly Kyle's suffocating weight left her, his hands freed her, his breath, so hot on her cheeks, so rasping in her ears, gave way to the soft caress of the cool, sweet night breeze.

Aurora heard the impact of a fist on flesh,

heard the crashing of the undergrowth and the grunt of pain as Kyle landed on the ground somewhere in the darkness. She heard him growl a foul epithet as he pushed himself to his feet and fled away through the forest.

"Aurora?"

Aurora cried out, scrambling away. The voice was a man's—his grasping hands reached out toward her.

"Aurora, calm down. It's me. It's Graham."

"Graham?" Panting with fear and fatigue, she squinted into the darkness. Graham Hughston was there, arms outstretched to her, face alight with compassion. "Oh, Graham."

And then she was in his arms. Sobbing, helpless. He rose, pulling her with him. They took a few stumbling steps before his arm slid beneath her knees and he lifted her and carried her through the night-shrouded forest to the carriage where Bridey paced among the dead leaves at the road's edge.

"Oh, Miss Aurora!" she cried as the two figures emerged from the forest. "I tried to find you! I swear I did! Then Mr. Graham came along and—"

"She's all right, Bridget," Graham assured her, settling Aurora into the carriage. He gave her into her maid's care, then climbed up and took the reins.

"Poor, sweet thing," Bridey cooed, rocking her lady like a very small, very precious child. "Did he hurt you, the fiend!" She looked at Graham, whose own horse trotted along behind them, his reins tied to the back of the carriage. "Mr. Graham, he didn't—"

"No, Bridget," Graham assured her. "I found them in time."

"God be thanked," the maid breathed, crossing herself. "And he seemed like such a gentleman."

"Appearances can be deceiving," Graham reminded her.

"And that's the truth of it," Bridey agreed. "I just thank the Lord you were nearby, sir."

"We are all thankful for that," Graham agreed. "All of us who love Aurora."

Bridget looked on him with a new respect. Such a kind, gentle man, so gallant, so brave. Why, he might have saved Aurora's very life tonight! Who's to say what that fiend might have been capable of? Respectable women weren't safe with devils like that about! She looked at Aurora as she lay against her, half-swooning. She'd be certain Aurora knew just how close she had come to disaster. And she'd be certain Aurora knew how much reason she had to be grateful to Graham Hughston.

Graham returned Aurora and Bridget to the Jephsons' cottage, which was soon ablaze with lights and in an uproar of confusion. Outraged, Carlisle vowed he would speak to the fort's commandant in the morning and be sure he knew what caliber of men he had under him. But Graham calmed him. The commandant, he assured his uncle, was a friend of his, and he would call upon him first thing in the morning.

Grateful to have been spared what promised to be an extremely unpleasant interview, Carlisle agreed to leave the matter in Graham's hands. Amidst profuse thanks, Graham waited until Aurora was safely settled in bed, then took his leave, promising to be on the docks in time to board the Jephsons' yacht and depart for Chicago at mid-morning.

Within minutes he was back on the road that wound through the forest. He found Kyle Braxton sitting on a fallen tree waiting for his return.

"You didn't have to make it so realistic," he told Graham, rubbing his bruised jaw. "If I'm marked in the morning, I'll have the devil of a time explaining it."

"You'll be all right," Graham assured him, less than sympathetically. "You, may I say, were quite convincing yourself."

"My pleasure," Kyle drawled, remembering the taste of Aurora's lips, the fragrance of her skin, the warmth of her body against his own.

"No doubt," Graham remarked dryly. From his pocket he extracted a roll of bank notes and handed them to the lieutenant. "Perhaps this will help soothe your bruises."

"And mend my broken heart?" Kyle asked sarcastically. "You don't mind if I count it, do you?"

"Not at all. But it's all there. The sum we agreed upon."

Satisfying himself, Kyle pocketed the money. "And is she sufficiently grateful for your rescue?"

"She will be, in the morning." Graham's smirk reeked of confident self-satisfaction.

With a last, mutually calculating glance, the men parted company. As he climbed into his carriage and heard the hoofbeats of Graham's horse as he rode off in the opposite direction, Kyle felt a glimmering of misgiving. He had truly fallen under the spell of those enchanting green eyes of Aurora's. But from the moment he had learned who she was—from the moment his fellow officers had begun teasing him—from the moment the young captain from New York had told him of Aurora's staggering wealth, he had known he had no chance with her. And it had been plain, from that first day when Aurora had brought him home to luncheon, that the dragoness, her Aunt Electra, meant her for Graham Hughston and no one else. The old lady would move heaven and earth to secure Aurora and her inheritance for her nephew, and no one, least of all a young lieutenant from a plain, middle-class family in Ohio, was going to stand in her way.

When Graham had approached him with the plan for Aurora's "attack" and subsequent "rescue," he had at first been appalled, then insulted, then intrigued. There had been a resentment inside him, not for Aurora herself, but for the unyielding class structure that put them out of reach of one another. Graham had offered him an incredible amount of money. A lifetime in the Army would pay but a fraction of what he had earned in those few brief moments on the floor of the forest.

He reached into his pocket and felt the crisp, new bank notes. His term of service was up in a matter of weeks. He had planned to stay on, counting on a promised promotion to lift him to the next rung of the long, arduous ladder of success in the military. But now everything had changed. With Graham's money as a stake, he could leave the Army and through shrewd investments, begin to build a fortune of his own. Someday he would be a man to be reckoned with, and no sour-faced old dame would ever dismiss him as "not good enough" again!

The morning sky was cloudless, the sun a blinding orb suspended on a shield of azure blue. The lake, which took on the color of the sky, was breathtakingly blue with waves that glittered as they rolled inevitably toward the shore.

Graham Hughston paced the deck of the *Sea Mist* restlessly. He was anxious to be gone from this place—eager to be well away before someone or something could expose his ploy of the night before. He had not gone to the fort's commandant that morning—he'd never had any intention of doing so. But now, as the minutes became hours and their proposed sailing time slipped further and further into the past, he began to wonder if perhaps the Jephsons had discovered his deception somehow and would descend upon him at any moment, bloodlust in their eyes.

His dark eyes scanned the streets for some sign of them. But it was not until early afternoon that his vigilance was rewarded and he saw their carriage appear, followed by a wagon bearing their trunks. He moved forward to help them aboard, but the sight of Aurora stopped him cold.

She wore a blazer suit of white serge piped in navy blue. A straw hat trailing blue and white ribbons sat atop her upswept curls. To the unsuspecting onlooker, she might seem no different—a shade pale, perhaps, but white skin was not uncommon in a woman of her coloring. To Graham, however, the change was astonishing.

Her green eyes were wary, calculating, as if

she had aged a hundred years in the course of a night. Gone was the wide-eyed innocent of days past—in her place was a hurt, suspicious woman who would trust no one until they had proven themselves worthy of her trust.

"Good afternoon, Graham," she said softly as he took her hand and steadied her while she stepped down onto the deck of the yacht.

"How are you, Aurora?" he asked carefully.

She studiously avoided his eyes. "As well as can be expected."

Bridget appeared beside them, hovering like a mother hen around one of her chicks. She said nothing, but Aurora seemed to speak volumes in a single glance at her maid. Together the two women left Graham's side and retreated belowdecks to Aurora's stateroom.

"Why don't you go to bed?" Bridget asked after directing the stowing of the single trunk brought to the cabin. It contained the items Aurora would need during the four days of their trip. The rest of her baggage had been stowed elsewhere on the yacht.

Pulling a lethal-looking hat pin from her straw hat, Aurora laid both on a bureau beneath the twin portholes.

"I stayed in bed too long this morning as it was. We would have been under way hours ago if I had not been so lazy."

"It wasn't laziness kept you abed so long this morning. Last night—"

"Please, Bridey." Aurora held up a hand, silencing her maid. "Don't let's talk about last night." Glancing out the porthole, she saw the village and behind it the long ramp leading up to the fort perched atop the bluff. Bathed in sunshine, its whitewashed walls gleamed in the afternoon light. Aurora shivered and wrapped her arms about herself, feeling a chill even in the heat of the closed cabin. "I think I'll read for a bit."

Leaving the stateroom, she went to a small, seldom-used cabin at the far end of the corridor. Normally used as a reading and card room during bad weather, it had built-in cabinets. Behind their leaded, beveled-glass doors, fiction, nonfiction, and poetry competed for space. Volumes of ancient Greek philosophers stood side by side with frothy Gothic novels by pseudonymous bluestockings.

It was one of the latter that Aurora chose. She took it to a tufted velvet, gold-fringed fainting couch that lay beneath the portholes. Hanging her white serge blazer over the back of a chair, she took up her book and lay down on the couch.

But try though she might, she found she could not lose herself in the exploits of Miss Evangeline Whitcombe, a lovely, innocent young heiress who traveled to the wilds of Scotland at the behest of an old, previously unknown aunt only to fall prey to a handsome, charming, unscrupulous cad with a smile on his lips and seduction in his heart.

Aurora laid the book aside. While it might make entertaining reading for the public at large, it struck a little too close to home for her taste. She sighed. If only there was a man somewhere who would love her for herself, not for her fortune, not for her connections. If only someone really cared about her for herself alone. But that seemed an impossible dream.

"I may as well marry Graham," she told herself. "Surely he is no more avaricious than any other man. And perhaps, since we are family after a fashion already, he would be more inclined to kindness than some men."

"Talking to yourself, Miss Aurora?" Bridget's tone was gently teasing as she let herself into the room. "'Tis the first step to madness, so they say."

"Is that your professional opinion, then, professor?"

"Who?"

"Never mind, what have you there?"

Bridget placed a small tray on the table near Aurora's couch. "It's a cup of chocolate, nice and warm and sweet, and I want you to drink it."

"A little bossy today, aren't we?"

The maid made a pouting face. "I'm only worried for you, miss. I'm sorry if that offends you."

"Now, now, Bridey, I didn't mean to hurt your feelings. I'll drink the chocolate, if only to please you."

The maid watched with secret satisfaction as her mistress lifted the cup to her lips and drained it. She should feel guilty, she supposed, for slipping the sleeping draught into the chocolate without Aurora's knowledge, but rest was what she needed most of all and Bridey knew from past experience that Aurora was stubbornly opposed to resorting to opiates of any kind.

"There!" Aurora set the empty cup back onto the tray. "I hope you're satisfied."

"I am, thank you," Bridey replied.

Aurora sighed. "Perhaps we could go for a turn on the deck later, Bridey. Would you like that? I know how nervous you get belowdecks."

"I don't think you'll be wantin' to do that, Miss Aurora," the maid confided. "I did hear the captain tryin' to talk the master into turnin' back to the island."

"Turn back! Heaven forbid! Why in the world would we want to turn back?"

"Storms. The captain told Mr. Jephson there'd been reports of a line of storms in the north end of Lake Michigan. We're sailin', so says the captain, right into 'em."

"I take it my uncle was not convinced."

"No, miss. He said this yacht was the finest afloat and could weather any storm the lake could throw at us."

Aurora glanced out the porthole. The sky was beginning to be dotted with dark grey clouds, it was true, but that didn't mean they should panic, surely.

"I daresay my uncle knows what he's saying. He has owned this yacht for some years, don't forget, while the captain has only sailed her for a matter of months. I'm certain there is nothing to worry about." She cast a roguish look at her maid. "Then again, if it storms, you'll hardly be able to spend the entire four days on deck, will you?"

Bridey said nothing as she gathered the tray and empty cup but she told herself as she left the room that she would not be shut away in a little chamber if the boat was being tossed in the grip of a storm. The deck was where the lifeboats were and the deck was where she would be as well.

With Bridey gone, Aurora sighed and lay down on her couch once more. Surely Uncle Carlisle was right, she told herself, eyeing the darkening sky through the porthole. Surely . . . Then it didn't seem to matter somehow. A deep, warm lethargy was stealing over her, beckoning her into the gentle depths of unconsciousness. Only too willing to forget the uncertainty of the future and the miserable self-pity of the past, Aurora closed her eyes and drifted away.

By the time she awoke, the room was dark. Outside the portholes there was nothing save roiling black skies and lashing rain. Gale-force winds buffeted the sleek vessel, making it pitch and roll sickeningly. Aurora saw the book she had begun reading lying on the polished wood floor. It had been the impact of the heavy book as it fell from the table that had awakened her.

Pushing herself to her feet, she made her slow, stumbling way across the darkened cabin. In the corridor she held fast to the thick silk ropes strung through brass rings set into the wall to make her way to her stateroom.

"Bridey?" she said as she entered the cabin. "Damn you, what did you put into that choco . . ."

The cabin was deserted. Most of Aurora's toiletries had been jarred out of the specially built cases and lay spilled or broken on the floor. "Bridey?" she called again over the roaring of the wind. But she could see no trace of the girl.

A picture formed in Aurora's mind—a picture of Bridey huddled on the deck, frightened of the closed spaces below.

"Oh, Lord," she whispered. "Surely she wouldn't be foolish enough to—"

But the niggling voice of reason reminded her that if the maid was too frightened to stay below in good weather, this sickening pitching and rolling would instill a mortal terror inside her.

"Oh, Bridey," she breathed. "What shall I do?"

There seemed no room for indecision. The rain was sheeting down on the yacht—the wind seemed determined to tear it apart and send the pieces spiraling down into the depths of the convulsing lake.

As she made her ponderous way back along the corridor, Aurora tried not to remember the tales both her uncle and Graham had told her of the legendary gales that whipped across the northern Great Lakes. They were far worse on the lake to the north, Superior, but no shortage of men and ships had perished in the treacherous depths of Michigan and Huron. The sparkling waters that were so beautiful on a calm summer's day could change into a greedy leviathan that exacted a precious toll from unfortunate travelers. The bottoms of the lakes were littered with the torn, splintered remains of ships—and men.

She was halfway up the stairs to the promenade deck when she met one of the *Sea Mist*'s crewmen on his way down.

"Get back to your cabin, Miss Jephson," he told her sternly, the dark eyes that usually followed her admiringly on her strolls around the yacht devoid of any emotion save concern for her safety.

"My maid, Bridget . . . I can't find her. I think she's gone out in the storm."

"If I see her, I'll send her below. Now you must go back to your stateroom."

"Please, Geoffrey," she murmured, laying a hand on his drenched sleeve. "What is happening to us?"

He sighed. For a moment he seemed overcome by fatigue, as frightened and bewildered as she was.

"The captain pleaded with Mr. Jephson to turn back to Mackinac Island. Then he tried to convince him to put in at St. James on Beaver Island . . . to anchor in the harbor there until the storm had passed. Your uncle insisted we try to outrun the gale instead."

"Can't we turn back now?"

"We can try. If there's time."

"What do you mean?"

His eyes focused on some abstract point above her head. "We're taking on water," he said dully.

Terror clutched Aurora's heart. For an instant time stood still. "We're sinking," she breathed.

The sailor snapped back to himself. He had violated a cardinal rule . . . he had frightened a passenger, and a woman at that, without absolute cause.

"The pumps are manned," he told her quickly. "She's a sturdy ship. We'll come through. I'm sorry, now, I have to go down into the hold."

"Bridey . . . ?" Aurora reminded him.

"If she's out on the deck, you can't get to her now. When I go back up, I'll tell the others. If anyone sees her, we'll bring her to you."

"Thank you," she said weakly. Turning back toward her stateroom, she took a few halting steps waiting for the crewman to disappear down the steps into the hold.

The moment the well-meaning young sailor was gone, Aurora resumed her climb to the promenade deck. Had he known she would go anyway, he would have taken her all the way back to her stateroom himself. Had he known she was so determined, he would have told her about the two crewmen who had already been washed overboard.

The wind-lashed rain pierced Aurora's tender skin like millions of tiny needles as she emerged onto the slick, wet deck. It blinded her. The force of the howling gale took her breath away.

"Bridey!" she screamed, but the sound was drowned by the ferocious roar of the wind and the nerve-shattering crash of the surging waves as they broke over the yacht. "Bridey!"

She clung fast to the railing, squinting into the darkness, searching . . . searching . . . Then she saw Bridey huddled in a corner, head hidden, arms and legs wrapped around a fitting on the upper deck.

Relief washed over Aurora like the cold rain that had already drenched her to the skin. Bridey was found. She was safe. All she had to do was make her way to the maid and take her below where they would ride out the storm together.

Fighting the wind and the rain and the fear that the storm's savage fury evoked in her, Aurora made her slow, treacherous way toward the girl.

"Bridey!" she shouted, but her cry was reduced to a whisper by the cannonade of thunder rolling across the ferocious water.

An eternity seemed to pass before the girl heard her. She looked up, eyes huge and filled with terror, tears mingled with the rivulets of rain that spilled down her cheeks.

"Oh, miss," she sighed, her lips forming words Aurora could not hear. "Thank God! Help me, please! Help me!"

Letting go of the railing, Aurora moved toward her. Her hand reached out to the maid, who released one arm from its death grip on the fitting. Their hands stretched toward one another, their fingers brushed. And then a wave that had loomed for a moment in the darkness, a great black hulk, crashed down on them in a greedy, hungry deluge. The storm demanded more of the *Sea Mist* than the two crewmen the lake had already claimed. The pounding water swept over them with bone-shattering force.

And then it was gone and Bridey was alone. Only the mocking, growling wind heard Bridey's screams. Only the churning waves saw the ghastly look of stark dread on her dead-white face.

5

It was warm when Aurora awoke—so warm. And soft. She didn't want to wake up. A sigh slid between her lips, a sigh filled with longing for the sweet darkness that had been her home since the cold dark water had claimed her and dragged her screaming into the turgid depths.

She turned her head and something tickled her cheek. Experimentally, she moved her fingers. Something silken lay beneath her. She opened one eye—then the other. She was lying on a bed made of birch logs. At the foot she could see twin posts made of slender white saplings. The bed was covered not with the silken coverlets or fine downy quilts she'd always known, but with fur—the pelts of animals carefully joined to form a seamless expanse of caressing softness.

She pushed herself up. She was in a room such as she'd never seen. The walls were of logs stacked one on the other, with something pressed between to seal them. She remembered a tutor of her schoolgirl days showing her a photograph of log cabins. But she'd never imagined waking up in one. A fireplace of fieldstone dominated one wall; its hearth was cold and empty. The furniture in the room, the chairs and tables and bed, were rough-hewn, hand-made. Only the lamp and the rug that covered the plank floor seemed in any way familiar to her. The lamp was of ornately scrolled brass with a tall, etched-crystal globe; the rug was Oriental—worn, almost threadbare, but obviously genuine and obviously valuable.

She stood, carefully, unsteadily. Her legs gave beneath her and she sat down, then stood again. Her feet seemed made of the same lead as her aching head, but she felt otherwise unharmed. She was wearing only her chemise and knee-length drawers with their bedraggled trimmings of Valenciennes lace, and she wondered bemusedly where the rest of her clothing had gone.

A blanket hung in the doorway. Perhaps her clothes were in the other room—perhaps someone was there who could tell her where she was.

The second room of the two-room cabin was deserted as well. Here, as in the bedroom, the furnishings were handmade except for a few incongruous pieces like the rug that covered the floor, the carved rosewood table with its cracked marble top, the lamps and candelabra dripping their crystal prisms, and a portrait in an ornate gilded frame of a beautiful woman with jet black hair and bronze skin.

Curiosity overriding all other emotions, Aurora went to the stone fireplace over which the protrait hung. The woman was undeniably beautiful—her high cheekbones and long almond eyes gave her a classic beauty that would endure as long as she lived. The portrait was exquisite, obviously the work of a master artist, but the woman, by her features, her coloring, the clothing she wore, was an Indian.

Aurora gazed at the portrait, bewildered. What was this place where fine furnishings of obvious quality and value competed for space with handmade items hewn from Nature herself? Where the portrait of an Indian woman took the place of honor over the mantelpiece? Where—

She gasped, whirling around as a door opened and the room was flooded with light. A figure appeared there, bathed in sunlight, silhouetted. A man.

Aurora backed away frightened, wondering, as he entered the room and closed the door. She caught her breath as the shutting of the door revealed him to her.

Starkly handsome, powerfully muscled, yet lithe and limber as a cat, he moved across the room toward her. She backed away. Sensing her fear, her confusion, he stopped.

"So you've decided to rejoin the living," he murmured, and his voice was deep, smooth, gently amused. "I'm glad."

Aurora trembled as his azure blue eyes, so striking in contrast to his deeply bronzed skin and coal black hair, swept over her. She flushed, a hot, crimson blush that rose to stain her pale cheeks. No man had ever—ever!—seen her in such a state of undress. No man should, the voice of propriety whispered inside her, no man saving a husband.

Her hair was undone—it cascaded to the middle of her back in a riotous cloud of shimmering red curls.

She caught her breath as his eyes returned to hers. His lips—they were full, she suddenly noticed, sculpted, firm—curved. A cleft appeared in his taut cheek beneath the high cheekbone. The well-washed linen shirt he wore was open at the throat and she saw the swirling of black curls there. The cuffs were turned back and she noticed that his hands were strong. She wondered if those had been the hands that had undressed her, laid her in the fur-covered bed. An unfamiliar tightening pulled in her breast—a queer fluttering began in her belly.

She moved her lips, mind maddeningly searching for words, tongue infuriatingly tied.

"Who . . ." she managed at last as the man waited and watched. "Who are you?"

His blue eyes bore deeply into her green ones, his lips scarcely seemed to move as he replied:

"They call me Raven."

"Raven," she whispered. With his gleaming, jet black hair and unwavering gaze, it seemed curiously apt.

"And you are Aurora Jephson, late of New York, en route to Chicago aboard the yacht *Sea Mist*."

"How did you know?"

"After the storm, the yacht put in at St. James harbor on Beaver Island. She was damaged. While repairs were being made, searches were organized to look for you."

"Why didn't you tell them where I was?"

"I didn't know about them until they had left. They remained in St. James only three days while the yacht was being repaired. By the time I went there, they had already left. They instructed the authorities in St. James to contact them if your . . ." He let the sentence trail into nothingness.

"If my . . . ?" Aurora's curiosity forced her to prompt.

Some unfathomable emotion flickered in the depths of his astonishing blue eyes. "If your body washes ashore at some point."

Aurora shuddered. The thought of people watching and waiting for her corpse to be swept ashore turned her stomach.

"Three days," she mused aloud. "It's been three days since the storm?"

"It's been a week."

"A week!" She was shocked. "I've been asleep for a week?"

"Not asleep. You had a fever. Most of the time you slept, but sometimes you were delirious. You had quieted—the fever had broken—by the time I felt it safe to leave you with Sarah and go to St. James for supplies."

Aurora sank into a tapestry-upholstered chair, unable to comprehend everything he had told her. Something he said struck a chord. "Sarah?" she asked. "She is your wife?" For some reason the thought disturbed her.

A ghost of a smile played at the corners of his mouth. "She is a friend," he replied cryptically.

But from his tone, Aurora sensed that there was more than mere friendship between him and the woman, Sarah. That did not surprise her. After all, he was an extraordinarily handsome man. It would have been astonishing if he hadn't had at least one woman at his beck and call. What did surprise her, and cause her no little puzzlement, was why in the world the notion should cause such an unpleasant feeling of jealousy and envy inside her.

She scowled, glanced down at her clenched hands in her lap, and remembered that she was alone with a strange man dressed in her lace-trimmed chemise and drawers. What must he think of her? What kind of woman would he think she was?

She raised her eyes to his and saw that he had read her every thought in her face as the emotions flitted across it.

Modestly she crossed her hands over her bosom.

"Where are my clothes, Mr. . . . Raven?" she asked, gaze demurely downcast.

"I threw them away," he said blithely.

Her saucer-round eyes flew to his face. "You did what! That yachting costume was fashioned by Worth!"

"It was ruined by Michigan." He shrugged. "Be sensible, Aurora—if I may call you Aurora. You would have had pneumonia had you remained in those wet clothes any longer than you did. As it was, it is a miracle of no small proportions that you did not drown, considering how weighted down you were with your boots and stockings, your drawers, chemise, corset, corset-cover, petti-coats—"

"Enough!" Aurora interrupted, cheeks flaming. "It was fortunate that your 'friend' Sarah was here to manage all the laces and buttons since you seem to disapprove of ladies' cloth—"

"Sarah had nothing to do with it," he contradicted.

"She had nothing to—" The implications made Aurora's head swim.

"Sarah lives with her family on another of the small islands in this chain. She only comes here occasionally."

"But if she didn't, then who . . . who . . . ?" A shiver coursed through her. "Not you—"

"It would seem that you would have preferred me to leave you on the shore and let the elements —and the coyotes—finish what the storm and the lake started."

"I am not ungrateful to you . . . Raven . . ." she said, her tone cool, trying desperately to salvage what few shreds of dignity might remain to her. "It is only that one does not . . . it is not proper . . ." She sighed. "Well, at least you left me with my underthings."

"Only after they dried." An impatient frown crossed his face at her shocked gasp. "Look around you, Miss Jephson," he ordered, the ice in his voice seeming to chill the air in the room. "This is not a mansion. I cannot with a flick of a finger summon a battalion of maids to see to your needs. Since the lack of social niceties here offends your delicate sensibilities, I will take you to St. James as soon as possible. I will arrange for you to stay somewhere and then dispatch word to your relations telling them where you are and asking that they come to retrieve you as soon as possible."

Aurora shrank back in her chair. His tone had wounded her, but far less than his threat to take her to St. James and leave her there for her aunt and uncle to come for as if she were a lost piece of baggage.

"I could hardly stay in a public hotel by myself, sir," she said haughtily. "No lady would."

He seemed singularly unmoved by her grand airs. One mocking ebony brow arched.

"No lady would sit before a gentleman she hardly knows in her unmentionables, either, but here you are."

His statement was as undeniable as it was infuriating. The mere fact of their being there together, alone, was enough to ensure Aurora's ruin. If Caroline Denbigh back in New York was considered "fast" because she allowed gentlemen to kiss her in darkened corridors and drive her through the park in the middle of the day without a chaperone, what would Aurora be considered after a week alone in such intimate circumstances and with so obviously unprincipled a man? And the worst of it was that he seemed so little concerned. Didn't he realize what the mere fact of her survival had cost her? If not, it was high time he did.

She raised a trembling hand to her bosom and pressed the other to her forehead. "I'm ruined," she breathed. "Utterly, hopelessly ruined!"

With a sound that was half-sigh and half-groan, she went limp in the chair, eyes closed as if dead to the world.

Silence reigned in the room until Raven broke it to say:

"There's a spider on your foot."

With a scream Aurora shot off the chair. "Where! Where!" she demanded, skittering across the floor.

Raven's gorgeous face split into a broad grin. Aurora, huddled behind a tall fern stand, realized that he had not for a moment been fooled into believing she had really fainted. A scarlet stain spread into her cheeks. She felt foolish, humiliated, furious.

"You!" she hissed, green eyes blazing. "You . . . you . . . you are no gentleman!"

Turning with a violence that would have set her skirts aflounce had she had skirts, she stormed back into the bedroom where she had awakened. But with only a blanket in the doorway, she didn't even have the satisfaction of slamming the door. And the sound of Raven's deep, mocking laughter made her mortification complete.

6

The morning gave way to afternoon, which slipped into evening. In the bedroom of the little log cabin, Aurora thought long and hard about the situation in which she'd awakened to find herself.

Raven . . . His bronzed, handsome face danced in her mind's eye. She'd never met a man like him. Here in the middle of nowhere he lived a life that seemed to her primitive, wild, dangerous. And yet he spoke like a man with first-hand knowledge of her world—the world of the privileged. His speech was that of an educated man, but one had only to look at him to see the evidence of his Indian heritage. He infuriated and tantalized her at the same time. He touched a place deep inside her that no one had ever reached before.

Even now, after she had sought the solitude of the bedroom, she wondered where he was, longed for him to return.

She had heard the cabin door close not long after she'd stormed into the bedroom. Peering out the window, she had seen him striding across the clearing in which the cabin stood. He had disappeared into the forest. That was hours ago. Knowing so little about Raven and his life on the island, she didn't know whether to worry or not.

Her stomach growled loudly, complaining because she had not eaten all day. It was strange, she thought, that she had not been hungry when she'd awakened. Someone must have managed to get some nourishment into her while she'd been ill. And the clothes she wore (she flushed again, remembering Raven's eyes sweeping over her as she stood before him in her underthings) seemed clean enough. They must have been washed at some point during her illness . . .

She let the thought die. The notion of his undressing her was more than she could bear. She would, she knew, be better off to leave this place, this man who stirred such strange emotions inside her, as soon as possible.

A surprising pang of regret twisted inside her. Leave this place . . . travel to Chicago . . . never see Raven again . . .

"What are you thinking?" she asked herself aloud. "You've only known the man one day . . ." She disregarded the days she'd spent here after Raven had found her on the beach. "If you had any sense, you'd accept his offer to be taken to St. James to wait for Aunt Electra and Uncle Carlisle to come for you. You belong with them in Chicago. With them and—"

A frown creased her brow. With them and Graham? All her return to her family would mean was a renewal of the pressure to get her to marry Graham. She sighed. She cared for Graham. It was only that he aroused no emotions in her saving, perhaps, a feeling of gratitude that he should have saved her from a frightening, potentially shattering experience on Mackinac Island. But there was nothing in her heart for him. He didn't touch her senses, not in the way—she could barely force herself to think of him—Kyle Braxton had, and certainly not in the way that Raven made her feel when those glorious cerulean eyes swept over her.

Raven. What was it about him that touched her even after only a few minutes in his presence? There was something intriguing, mysterious, dangerous about him. She felt threatened by him—not threatened with violence, not at all, but threatened with something far more subtle. He infuriated her. At the same time she was drawn to him. She had demurely covered herself from his dark scrutiny but at the same moment reveled in the glitter that lit his gaze as it traveled lingeringly over her.

She shivered, thinking of how he must have carried her from the shore more dead than alive. He had brought her here, pulled off her clothes, cared for her, watched over her . . .

She forced the thoughts from her mind. They were too disturbing. She didn't understand the way he made her feel. It disturbed her, frightened her. And yet she found herself wanting him to return from wherever it was he had gone.

As if in answer to her desire, she heard the latch on the cabin door being pushed up. Hurrying to the doorway, she pushed the blanket aside.

"Raven, I—"

She stopped, startled into silence, for Raven

had indeed returned. But he was not alone. Standing beside him was a pretty, slightly built young woman whose golden-blonde hair was confined in a thick braid that hung past her waist.

Aurora stepped back, instinctively hiding herself behind the blanket. "I'm sorry, I didn't realize you weren't alone."

"Don't be shy," Raven told her. "This is Sarah Oates. I told you about her. She tended you while I was away."

"So you did," Aurora acknowledged. "Thank you so much, Mrs. Oates."

The woman smiled. Her eyes, though paler than Raven's were a vivid blue set in the sun-kissed tan of her small, oval face.

"I'm not Mrs. Oates," she corrected. "I am not married." Her face dimpled prettily. "At least not yet."

Aurora felt a sudden twisting inside her. Despite the fact that Raven had told her Sarah was only his friend, she had a sneaking suspicion that marriage was what Sarah had in mind for them eventually.

She forced a smile. "In any case, it was kind of you to care for me. I wish there was some way I could repay you."

Sarah's smile faded a little. "Your best payment to me would be to get well again and be happily reunited with your family."

And out of Raven's life, Aurora finished to herself. I'll just bet you'd like to see me gone, wouldn't you? You can't be happy to see me here, installed in Raven's cabin—in his bedroom—with him night and day.

"Are you feeling up to eating out here?" Sarah

was asking. "You must be ready for more than just the broth you had while you were sick. You must be hungry for solid food." She glanced at Raven before continuing. "Of course, if you're not feeling well enough, I could bring you something to eat in bed."

"No, no, I'm feeling fine," Aurora assured her, determined that Sarah would not have an intimate dinner with Raven while she was banished to the loneliness of the bedroom.

"Oh, I thought . . . maybe . . . that is to say, you didn't get dressed and—"

Aurora flushed, embarrassed by her meager attire. "I haven't anything else to wear, I—"

"What do you mean?" Sarah looked at Raven. "Didn't you give her the things I brought for her?"

Beneath their combined scrutiny, Raven's generous, sensuous mouth twitched, then curved into a smile that held in it more of the devilish boy than the deceitful man. "I forgot," he said simply, looking for all the world as if he honestly expected them both to believe such an outlandish excuse.

Sarah, with her far greater experience of him, was the first to recover.

"Of course you did," she agreed, sarcasm dripping from every syllable. "Come on, then, I'll show you where they are."

Taking Aurora's arm, Sarah led her back into the bedroom. A chest covered in tooled leather and banded with wood stood against one wall. Sarah pulled up the lid and showed Aurora a small pile of clothing. There were two skirts, one emerald green, the other a deep wine red, several blouses all of plain, serviceable cream cotton, and a selection of simple cotton underthings.

"They belonged to my sister-in-law," Sarah explained. "She had a baby and she's never managed to get into them again. They're clean," she added with a defensive air that Aurora took to stem from her feelings toward the stranger who had entered Raven's life.

"This is very generous of you," Aurora told her. "And of your sister-in-law. You must thank her for me. Perhaps one day I'll be able to thank her myself."

Sarah's face took on a closed, wary look. "We live on another island. I don't think Raven would think very much of your going there."

"But why?"

"Come on, I'll help you dress. Some of those blouses button down the back and I expect you're used to a maid's help."

Dutifully Aurora stepped out of her chemise and pantalets. She felt no embarrassment in undressing in front of Sarah. In the first place, what the girl had said was true—she was used to being dressed and undressed by maids. In the second place, since Sarah had cared for her during her illness, she doubted there was much of her Sarah hadn't already seen.

When she was dressed in the dark green skirt and one of the blouses, she picked up a brush from the dresser. As she dragged it through her thick, red curls, she asked:

"Why do you suppose Raven didn't tell me these clothes were here?"

"Likely because he enjoyed seeing you traipse around in your underwear," Sarah snapped. With a toss of her long blonde braid, she left the room.

Pausing, brush poised in her hand, Aurora

turned to watch her go. Jealousy was the girl's motivation, it was clear, but there was no reason for her jealousy. After all, she would be here with Raven long after she, Aurora, had gone back to her own life far away from this place.

Aurora laid the brush aside and surveyed herself in the gilt-framed mirror on the wall. She thought of Sarah's parting words, and a shiver of some unfamiliar but delicious sensation coursed through her. It was perfectly true—Raven had not tried to hide the fact that he enjoyed the sight of her in the lacy underthings. And if Aurora were going to be brutally honest, she would have to admit that his enjoyment tantalized some heretofore unknown and wanton part of her.

A little smile playing about her lips, she left the bedroom. Her green eyes met Raven's blue ones, and his admiration was plain to see. Perhaps Sarah's jealousy was not so misplaced, Aurora thought. Perhaps—

"Will you help me with dinner?" Sarah asked from a small room at the back of the cabin.

Aurora had seen the door before but had thought it was merely the cabin's rear entrance. Now she could see that it led to a sort of lean-to that housed a pantry and cookstove.

Cook? Aurora thought. She could not remember ever having been in the kitchen since her childhood when she had slipped downstairs in her father's house to beg treats from the indulgent cook.

She exchanged another glance with Raven and found that maddening half-smile playing about his lips once more. He knows, she thought. He knows I haven't the vaguest notion of how to cook a meal.

She shot him a venomous glare and turned with a swish of her skirt to go to Sarah's aid. Her face reddened as she heard his soft, faintly mocking chuckle.

"Why don't you clean these?" Sarah asked, pushing a sharp knife and three fresh fish toward her.

Aurora took the knife and stood there, staring at the fish that glared up at her with flat, round eyes. She'd often eaten fish before, but by the time it was set before her on a piece of priceless French porcelain it bore scant resemblance to what she saw before her now. With a hesitating finger she poked at one of the fish. The skin was cold, clammy, repulsive.

"They're perch," Sarah told her. "You like perch, don't you?"

"Of course," Aurora answered, though she was not at all certain. She nudged the fish with the tip of the blade, wondering where she was supposed to start.

"Here," Sarah said, taking the knife. "Let me get you started."

Quickly, efficiently, Sarah sliced off the head and tail of one of the fish. Then, slipping the knife into the gaping hole where the head had been, she deftly slit the fish's belly.

Aurora gasped as the fish's insides spilled out onto the tabletop. She had never in her life seen so grisly a sight.

"What's wrong?" Sarah asked, dropping the cleaned fish into a pan of water and pulling the second one toward her. "Do you want to try this one?"

Shaking her head, Aurora backed away. As

Sarah shrugged and began cutting the second fish, Aurora fled from the room, past Raven and out the door.

She leaned weakly against a tree at the edge of the forest. She felt queasy, it was true, but her overriding emotion at that moment was humiliation. How could she have acted so squeamishly? It obviously didn't bother Sarah a bit to perform such simple tasks. Never in her life had Aurora felt so helpless, so ignorant, so useless. She had never before realized that her pampered and privileged position had prepared her for nothing but the life of a rich man's wife. Her social graces were faultless—she could preside over an elegant dinner or a grand ball with scarcely a worry, but when it came to the simple facts of everyday living, she felt helpless as a babe.

"Aurora?" Raven was beside her.

Aurora averted her face to hide her mortification. "I suppose you've come to gloat," she whispered. "You're going to tell me—"

"I'm going to tell you to come back and set the table," he interrupted. "Sarah didn't realize you had never done any cooking."

"I never expected to have to learn."

Raven's gaze drifted to some point over her head. "You don't have to," he told her. "I told you I'd take you to St. James. I'll find a place where you'll be properly chaperoned until your family comes for you. Now come back in. There's no reason for you to be upset."

Aurora stared after him as he retraced his steps to the cabin. She felt like an invalid who had to be cared for because she was not capable of caring for herself. It was no wonder Raven was so eager to get her off his hands. She was a burden to him. It was not surprising that he wished to be rid of her.

Well, she would leave! And as soon as she could! She would go back to her rightful place in life where the skills she had learned under her mother's gracious tutelage were appreciated. Maybe she couldn't clean a fish, but by God, she knew her etiquette!

Squaring her shoulders, she lifted her proud little chin and marched back to the cabin, determinedly ignoring the fact that in the lives of ordinary men and women there were more important things than knowing the proper placement of silver or the correct way to address visiting royalty.

7

Raven strolled along the moonlit path that wound through the forest stretching from one end of the island to the other. He had taken Sarah to the shore where her brothers waited to take her home with them after a day of fishing.

But his thoughts were not with Sarah. He took her for granted, he supposed. For years she'd been his friend, his companion, occasionally his lover. From time to time he was uncomfortably reminded that she took their relationship far more seriously than he did. Though he had told her often that he intended never to marry, he knew she continued to hope. But fond as he was of her, he did not love her. He hoped never to fall in love with anyone, for he considered love the most dangerous of all emotions, a merciless predator stalking the heart, the mind, the soul of those unlucky enough to fall into its clutches. He considered that he had done well

70

in eluding it these past fifteen years—the years since his sixteenth birthday when he had announced his intention of returning to the islands where he was born.

In the gathering twilight, while the last mauve and purple streaks of a magnificent sunset still colored the western horizon, Raven sank onto a fallen tree and listened to the awakening night sounds of the island. The wind in the treetops rustled through the leaves and the sound melded with that of the waves breaking along the shore, creating a constant susurration that rose and fell and somehow contrived to soothe his restless heart. From some hidden marsh deep in the forest came the chirping mating calls of the frogs. The night-stalking birds stirred from their daytime lethargy, and in the distance he saw a fragile-legged heron wading among the reeds in the shallows of the lake.

Fifteen years, he thought. Sometimes it seems like yesterday. Sometimes forever. Another place . . . another time . . . another life.

For the first time in a long while he allowed himself to remember the years he'd spent away from these islands. He let himself think about the man—his father—who had come and taken him away from his mother and the wilderness he loved.

Marcus Ravenswood. The name sprang from his subconscious where he usually kept it buried. In 1858 Ravenswood had come to the island as a young man seeking adventure on the last leg of his Grand Tour of the world. He was an only child, the sole heir to a Pittsburgh steel fortune. He had fallen in love with the islands, with their wild beauty and with the hospitality of the Irish immigrants who had come here fleeing the famine devastating their homeland. And he had fallen in love with a beautiful young Ojibway maiden, Wenona, Raven's mother.

Though Wenona had never seemed bitter that her handsome young lover had sailed away in answer to a summons from his father and had left her to bear their child alone, disgraced before her people, Raven had always hated him for it. From his earliest days when he had toddled happily in the woods, learning the ways of his mother's people, he had hated the man his mother wept for in the night when she thought her child slept in his little bed covered with handmade quilts and fur wraps.

Wenona knew of her son's hatred. She tried to quell it, explaining time and again to the stony-faced little boy that his father had had no choice—that his own father, Frederic Ravenswood, Raven's grandfather, had threatened to disown him, disinherit him, if he married his Ojibway girl and gave his name to her half-breed son. Raven had listened to her explanations and for her sake had pretended to accept them. But all he saw was a man who had abandoned a woman he claimed to love for the sake of money—something the Ojibway, with their system of barter and trade, had scant use for—and a life of luxury.

Then, when Raven was eight, the man had come back. Old Frederic Ravenswood was dead and Marcus had inherited the fortune that was his birthright. It was too late for Wenona. She was ill, even then, with the consumption that would eventually kill her. But she begged her lover to take their son with him, to educate him as a gentleman's son, to make of him the kind of man

Marcus Ravenswood's son should be. And though Raven had fought and argued, he had gone, bowing to the wishes of the mother he had loved, never suspecting that she was so ill, nor that he was destined never to see her again.

He had gone with his father to Pittsburgh where he'd been installed in a bedroom three times larger than the cabin he now occupied. His playroom was every child's fantasy, and in the stables of his father's country estate, ponies waited for him to ride. His father adopted him and, since Wenona had never called him anything but "Raven," christened him Charles Edward Augustus Ravenswood. Even now, after so long, Raven had to smile at what seemed to him the sheer pomposity of it all.

He had been educated by the best tutors, gone to the most exclusive schools, dressed in the height of fashion. The fortune his father had inherited had multiplied during the Civil War years owing to the Union's need for steel. By the time Raven was ready to enter polite society, it was more than willing to receive him, more than happy to look beyond his mixed blood out of deference to the immense fortune his father possessed. But the feelings were there, beneath the veneer of cultured manners. They would tolerate him among them, for as the years passed and his father remained unmarried, it seemed more and more certain that Raven would one day inherit the steel business whose worth then stood in the hundreds of millions of dollars. They would accept his presence, but he never felt like one of them and he never ceased to long for the cool, verdant wilderness of his childhood.

By the time Raven was fifteen, his father had begun to talk of universities where Raven could learn of business and politics and law, where he could be prepared to take up the reins of Ravenswood Steel and guide the company into the twentieth century. And something else happened to Raven by the time he was fifteen—women. Society matrons who had previously only looked upon him as a potential groom for their young Charlotte or Victoria or Alice now began to see him in a new light. It was not his inheritance that attracted them but the exotic looks which the melding of his father's and mother's bloodlines had produced in him. He was dark, bronzed in the summer when he spent a great deal of time in the sunshine, and his hair was a luxuriant blue-black. From the handsome, chiseled man's face that was fast emerging from the prettiness of his youth, his amazing sky-blue eyes observed the world from beneath the shelter of lush, curling black lashes that seemed to enthrall women more used to the pale, refined, cultivated men of their acquaintance.

Most of them knew of his mixed heritage— Marcus Ravenswood's dalliance with an Indian maiden and his father's subsequent threat of disinheritance had been an open secret in Pittsburgh society. And Raven's arrival in the city and his father's adoption of him soon after had been the talk of the town. They knew he was half Indian and in those days, when not all of the Indians of the great Western plains had been driven onto reservations, that spelt danger, savagery, a cachet of the untamed, the unknown. His heritage, combined with the sensuous, somehow uncivilized good looks, made him irresistible to them.

A frown creased Raven's forehead now as he remembered the countless times when he'd been suddenly summoned away from a soirée or ball to a darkened chamber where a pair of perfumed arms had embraced him, drawn him down onto a soft, silken bed where practiced hands and lips taught him how to please these women who only moments before had been so cool, so elegant, so untouchable. It seemed they wanted his father's money for their daughters, their grandchildren, but they wanted Raven for themselves.

Throughout his years in Pittsburgh, Raven wrote to his mother faithfully and sent her gifts with which she had furnished her cabin—the cabin he now occupied. Wenona would save the letters until one of the Franciscan Fathers who were missionaries to the Indians on the outlying islands arrived. The priest would read them to her and patiently draft a reply which she dictated.

And then, abruptly, Raven's letters began returning, unopened. A letter came from one of the priests. Wenona was dead. Her body was stored until the coming spring when the ground would be soft enough to dig.

Raven's grief was boundless. He blamed his father and the mores of a hypocritical society that made it impossible for his mother to join him there in the comfort in which his father lived. Most of all, he blamed himself for not returning to her. Over his father's objections, he turned his back on the world of Marcus Ravenswood and fled back to the forests of the North. When spring came he buried his mother—buried her according to Ojibway ritual, spurning the aid of the priests whom he blamed for bowing to his mother's wishes and keeping him ignorant of the devastating progress of her illness.

He vowed he would never—never!—again have anything to do with the world he had left behind him—the world of hypocrisy and deceit where one's position was in direct proportion to the degree of one's wealth. Where the amount of respect given a man, the number of friends he could call his own, ebbed and flowed with the tide of fortune.

A flash of lightning and a roll of thunder in the distance pulled Raven out of the misty world of memories and back to the present. A storm was raging out over the lake. A storm like the one a week before that had torn Aurora from the deck of her uncle's yacht and deposited her on the shore. Like the one that had brought Raven back into touch with the world he believed he had left behind him forever.

Aurora. Raven scowled at the sky, his black frown no less thunderous than the roiling stormclouds fast filling the night sky. She reminded him too much of the girls he'd known in Pittsburgh—pretty, pampered creatures, so secure in their futures that they need only be trained in the ways of the mistress at whose beck and call a hundred servants stood waiting to grant her smallest wish. Elegant, useless women bred to decorate their husband's mansion and bear him blue-blooded heirs. He'd felt an honest sympathy for her this evening when she'd seemed so bewildered in the kitchen. It wasn't her fault—girls like her were not trained in domestic matters. Still, it only proved how unsuited she was for this life. She belonged in her world, not here in his. She would have to go back.

Rising, Raven moved along the path in the darkness. He did not need the moon, which had been swallowed by the clouds of the gathering storm. He knew his way with feline certainty. Knew it too well, perhaps, for it allowed his mind to wander where it would and it wandered all too quickly back to the red-haired girl he hoped would be long asleep before he reached the cabin.

She would have to go back, he told himself again, more sternly this time. She was a part of that world he loathed. And yet she awakened feelings inside him that had lain too long dormant and aroused emotions inside him he had long held in check. He felt by turns tender toward her, then cold, hard as the ice that surrounded the islands in the depths of winter. It had been so from the moment he had found her lying on the beach, white as the sand upon which she lay, lungs half filled with water, more dead than alive.

Having found a pulse, albeit a fluttering, fragile pulse, he had done what he could to empty her lungs of the choking water before carrying her back to his cabin. He had worked feverishly to save her and then, when he was certain she would live, had pulled off the wet clothes that had helped drag her down in the churning water, dried her and put her to bed.

He felt a tightening inside him as he remembered her lying there in the bed as he dried her. Her skin was white, so delicate that the faint blue tracery of veins showed beneath it, her breasts were crested with pale pink tips that tightened into little peaks as he passed the towel over them. Her hair was as red as fire in the flickering light of the blaze he had kindled to warm her. It caught the firelight in the thick, tangled strands that lay over the pillow and in the tight, springing curls at the joining of her thighs.

That he was the first, the only man to ever have seen her that way, he had no doubt. Whatever their morals once they had married and produced a son whose paternity could not be disputed, women of her class were guarded like the treasures of the Orient before their weddings.

He had gazed at her, lost in her beauty, until the warning voice of reason had prompted him to dress her in the chemise and pantalets he had washed and dried before the fire. After that he had been almost grateful for the fever that raged inside her, for it forced him to think of other things than merely the pale, translucent beauty of her flesh and the desire it aroused in him.

He had been grateful for Sarah's help in nursing her. It had fallen to Sarah to undress her and bathe her and dress her again once her scanty garments had been washed and dried. That Sarah's willingness to help sprang not from any wellspring of goodness within her but rather from a desire to minimize Raven's contact with the beautiful stranger did not matter to him. All that mattered was that he was spared the torment of looking upon her, touching her, desiring her when he knew it was wrong of him to do so.

But now Aurora was well again. She would cease to be merely the patient whose presence in the other room he would do his best to ignore. When he had entered the cabin that morning and found her standing there—when he had looked into the fathomless depths of her wide green eyes, the desire he had at first felt for her had swept over him like the wave that had brought her to him in the beginning.

He did not want her to leave. That thought surprised even him. But if she stayed—if he were forced into daily intimate contact with her, he felt he could not be responsible for himself. There was no solution but one—she would have to go.

And that, he told himself as the light that glowed through the cabin windows appeared in the distance and the first drops of rain fell from the clouds that now obscured the stars of the summer sky, was that. It was decided. It was settled. It was—

He opened the door and found Aurora seated in a gilded armchair, hands demurely folded in her lap. She still wore the blouse and skirt she had put on for dinner and looked, despite her incongruous surroundings, simply elegant. Her hair caught the glints of the lamplight as it spilled over her shoulders, and despite himself Raven remembered the day he'd brought her to the cabin.

"I thought you'd be in bed by now," he told her, holding tight to his convictions like a drowning man clings to a bit of passing driftwood.

"I couldn't," Aurora replied.

"Why not?"

Standing, she came to him and, turning her back, lifted her hair with one long-fingered hand. "I can't unbutton this blouse by myself."

Gritting his teeth, Raven raised his hands and began to work at the row of tiny mother-of-pearl buttons that ran from the high-standing collar down her back to disappear into the waistband of her skirt. As he worked, he hoped she was too innocent to notice the effect her nearness had upon his body and the way his shaking fingers fumbled with the buttons.

When he had finished, he turned back toward the door.

"Raven?" Aurora called after him, holding the front of the loosened blouse against her chest. "Where are you going?"

"For a walk," he answered sharply.

"But you just came back." She listened to the rain that slanted against the cabin and lashed through the trees. "It's pouring outside. You'll catch your death of cold."

Raven didn't reply and as Aurora watched, bewildered, he disappeared into the night and the chilling rain he hoped would cool his heated blood.

8

Raven had to smile the next morning as Aurora dried the last of the breakfast dishes and, with a flourish, hung the damp towel on the nail near the kitchen washbasin. Afraid of hurting her feelings, he hid his amusement by taking the basin outside to empty it.

Feeling inordinately proud of her newfound domestic skills, Aurora followed him outside into the warm yellow sunshine that filtered through the trees.

"Do you know what I'd like, Raven?" she asked.

"A maid?" he teased.

She made a face at him. "No! A bath. Would that be possible?"

"Anything is possible." An impish grin lurked at the corners of his mouth. He pointed to a narrow path that disappeared into the trees. "Follow that trail. The creek is about a quarter mile, but you can't miss it."

"The creek?"

"Hmmm." He nodded, heading back toward the cabin. "Don't worry, it's not too cold this time of year."

Brow puckered, Aurora gazed after him wondering if, hoping that, he was kidding. "But, Raven—"

He paused in the doorway. "Come on. I'll get you a towel and some soap."

"Wouldn't it be simpler to draw the water from the well and heat it over the fire?"

Raven appeared from the bedroom with a towel and a bar of soap. "That's for winter," he told her. "There's no reason to go to all that trouble this time of year."

Aurora sighed, her enthusiasm somewhat dampened. Taking the towel, she reached for the soap. To her surprise, it was a bar of French-milled, delicately scented rose soap such as she might have found at home in New York.

He smiled at her astonishment. "We have a few of the luxuries here in the wilderness. Now go. Just follow the path and you'll be fine."

Her lovely face the picture of chagrin, Aurora left the cabin and disappeared down the path in the direction Raven had indicated.

From the cabin door, Raven watched her go. His azure eyes were clouded with concern. His worry was not for her; there was nothing in the forest to threaten her safety. His concern was for himself—for the threat her very presence posed to his way of life, his happiness, the contentment he had found there in his isolated paradise. How could he have gotten so attached to her in such a short time? he wondered. Why was it that she seemed to become daily more important to him? His emotions, his desires, his hopes . . . somehow she seemed intertwined with all of them.

He remembered the way he had reacted the night before when she'd asked him to unfasten her blouse. How could she touch him so deeply? Was it simply her beauty? Was it because she was a lady—an example of that rarefied breed he'd learned to loathe during his years in Pittsburgh? Or was it more?

No! He slammed the metal basin back onto its wooden stand. It couldn't be more! He wouldn't allow it. She didn't belong to his world. She didn't know the first thing about life in such a harsh environment. Moreover, he doubted that she was capable of making the adjustment to his kind of life—he doubted she would even want to try. The time would come—and come soon—when she would miss all the comforts of her other life. She would leave him then, and any feelings he had for her would be crushed like the tender young growth of the forest was crushed beneath his heel when he stalked prey in the springtime. It was inevitable.

He passed a weary hand over his furrowed brow. Better that he should send her away now, when whatever bothersome emotions stirring inside him were in their delicate infancy. Better they should be nipped in the bud than given the chance to grow, to flower, to twine their viscid roots around his vulnerable heart. He would send her away, he promised himself, and soon!

That comforting vow uppermost in his mind if

not in his heart, he took up his rifle and strode off into the woods to hunt the fat brown rabbits that throve in the undergrowth.

Whether by accident or some subconscious design, his soundless steps took him through the forest to the steep, wooded bank of the fast-flowing creek where Aurora bathed. He did not realize he was approaching it—his thoughts were elsewhere—but then he heard the splashing of the water over the rocks and fallen trees and he knew where he was. He paused, still as the most stealthy creature of the forest. His common sense screamed a warning, begged him to turn back; his heart, his desire, drove him onward through the trees on silent feet, to the thickly forested bank overlooking the tumbling waters of the creek.

The place where Aurora bathed was a small pool in which the waters that rushed from the interior of the island seemed to pause, to rest, before resuming their headlong plunge to the open waters of the lake. She knelt on the smooth, sandy bottom while the water swirled about her waist. Her hair, cascading over her shoulders, floated on the undulating surface behind her. The droplets of water on her flawless alabaster skin and clinging to the thick, silken strands of her hair, glistened in the dappled sunlight that filtered down through the verdant canopy overhead.

Raven held his breath as he gazed at her. She was more beautiful by far than the loveliest creature that dwelt in his beloved forest. She was pink and golden and white, and as she lifted her cupped hands and let the cool, clear water run in shining rivulets down her body, Raven was stunned by the reaction of his heart, his mind, his flesh.

Unconsciously he stepped closer and his moccasined foot snapped a twig lying half buried in the carpet of crisp, brown leaves. In the water, Aurora froze. Her cat-green eyes grew wide and frightened. She looked like a tender young doe listening for the footsteps of the hunter.

"Who is there?" she breathed, her voice quavering, her arms crossed over her naked breasts. "Please, is someone there?"

Unwilling to reveal himself, Raven melted back into the forest, silent as the most skillful of woodland predators. But he could not, however hard he tried, banish from his memory the image of her there with the rushing water washing about her narrow waist and the glistening droplets clinging to the curves of her tip-tilted breasts.

She would have to go, he told himself sternly, but even as he did he was aware of the cloying aching of his flesh, of the demands of his body and his heart chipping away at his will like a sculptor chipping unyielding marble.

The image of her in the creek stayed stubbornly in his mind, dancing across his dreams, haunting his days and nights. His feelings for her, his desire for her, grew with each passing day, each passing hour it seemed, and he knew he would know no peace until she was beyond his sight, his reach. Again and again he vowed to send her away, promised himself, ordered himself, to rid his once-peaceful world of her troublesome presence, but she had only to speak to him, look at him, touch him, to turn all his promises to ashes.

"There's a storm coming," he said softly one night as Aurora emerged from the kitchen where she'd completed what had become her nightly task of washing the pans and dinner dishes.

"How do you know?" she asked. She had seen no ominous thunderclouds, heard no distant rumbling.

"I can feel it—smell it. When you've lived out here long enough, changes in the weather become as easy for people to sense as they are for the animals."

"Do you think I'll be able to sense them someday?"

Raven turned from the window, his expression unreadable. "You won't be here that long."

Stung by his tone, Aurora said nothing. She busied herself straightening the already immaculate collection of books and ornaments that stood on the shelves of a whatnot in the corner. Biting her lip, she blinked back the tears that blurred her vision.

Could he really be so anxious to see her gone? Was she really so much of a burden to him? She was quite proud of her progress in matters domestic. True, it was no more than most young girls had learned by the time they reached adolescence, but she considered that for one of her upbringing it represented an accomplishment of no small proportions.

From the corner of her eye she stole a glance at him. Bending over a piece of buckskin, he was using a horn-handled hunting knife to split it into long strips, the possible uses of which eluded her.

"I think tomorrow I'll bring in some water from the well for a bath," she said idly.

"If the weather is good, why not go down to the creek again?"

"I was frightened there the last time. Someone was there."

"Damn!" Shoving his thumb into his mouth, Raven stanched the oozing of the flesh he had nicked with his knife. "That's impossible," he told her, glaring at the injured thumb. "You must have imagined it."

"I heard someone. I heard the cracking of a twig and the rustling of the leaves."

He scowled, but his pride would not let him admit that he had been at the creek, had admired her beauty.

"It was probably a rabbit or a squirrel. The woods are full of them."

"I think it was a person," she persisted.

"There is no one else on this island—only you and me. I'm sure of that. So you either imagined it or it was an animal. All right?"

Lowering her eyes, Aurora nodded. "Yes, Raven. I think I'll go to bed now."

He didn't look up from his work. "Fine. Good night."

In the bedroom, Aurora pondered the matter as she unbuttoned the front of her blouse and stepped from her skirt and petticoat. It had not been an animal there at the creek that morning. Despite her meek acceptance of Raven's explanation, she was certain she was right. It had been a person. And if, as Raven said, there were only the two of them inhabiting the island, that meant it had been Raven.

Raven. The thought of those piercing blue eyes lingering on her sent a queer sort of shiver through her. He had seen her there in the water—had seen her as no man had ever seen her before—had seen her as (so many women of her class and upbringing believed) no man should ever see her. But if that were true—if the female form was never to be unveiled before the eyes of any male—did it follow that she was somehow lacking in morals to feel the way she did? Because, if the truth were known, the thought of Raven's being there, seeing her, looking at her, made her feel so peculiar—not bad, not ashamed, but excited in a way she was not certain it was proper to feel. Her heart fluttered, she felt warm, breathless. She felt her cheeks; they were hot, flushed, she was sure. What was happening to her? Not even Kyle Braxton had made her feel so strange. She couldn't begin to understand the stirrings of a woman's passion in her girlish heart, the awakenings of a woman's needs and desires in her young, tender flesh.

If only there were someone she could talk to, but there was only Raven. And, perhaps, Sarah Oates. But she did not believe she could bring herself to talk to Sarah even though the older woman would be familiar with such matters. After all, Sarah was, to all appearances, Raven's woman and it was Raven who had stirred these emotions inside her. She could never bear to reveal her feelings to Sarah and risk having her words repeated to Raven, who, she felt sure, would only scowl and insist she must leave and return to her family.

There was, it seemed, no answer to her dilemma. In her chemise, she climbed into the fur-covered bed and yearned for sleep to erase, if only temporarily, the troubling thoughts from her mind and the disquieting sensations from her body.

* * *

The storm Raven had predicted struck in the wee hours of the morning when Aurora was in the middle of a dream about her Uncle Carlisle's yacht. The rumblings of thunder and lashing of rain against the cabin merged with those in her dream and she was once more clinging to the yacht's railing, holding on for dear life while the thrashing waters fought to claim her.

From his place on the velvet-upholstered Louis XV sofa, Raven heard Aurora tossing restlessly and crying out as the storm howled around the little cabin in the forest. Rising, he went to the doorway and pulled aside the blanket.

"Aurora?" He could see her there in the bed, writhing, hands grasping at the birch post at one corner.

Lightning lit the room with its blue-white glow and the thunder that crashed over them seemed to shake the thick, rough-hewn logs of the cabin to the very ground. With a scream, Aurora sat up in the bed. Her eyes were wild with the terror of her dream and the fury of the storm outside. She held a trembling hand out toward Raven as he stepped into the room.

"Please!" she cried, still confused by the horrifying reality of the dream. "Raven! Help me!"

In an instant she was in his arms, her cheek cradled against the warm, smooth flesh of his chest, her arms wound about his neck, her fingers buried in the ebony curls at the nape of his neck.

She felt his chin against the crown of her head, felt his arms about her, his hands at her waist, his fingers spanned across the small of her back.

"The storm," she breathed, trembling violently. "The storm reminded me of—"

"I know," he told her. "But it was only a dream. You're safe here with me."

She lifted her face toward his. "Oh, Raven," she sighed, one small hand reaching up to touch his cheek. "I was so frightened, so—"

Her words were lost as her fear, her beauty, her nearness robbed him of the few tenuous shreds of self-control still remaining to him. He slanted his lips across hers savagely, hungrily, demandingly.

Aurora shuddered, stunned for a moment until the strange, wonderful feelings that had so confused her earlier swept down on her with a vengeance. Lost in the swirling madness of pure sensation, she returned his kiss, twined her arms about his neck, pressed her body to his in innocent invitation.

Raven's senses warred within him. The man in him wanted her desperately, madly, violently, while the fading entreaties of his common sense warned him that she was not his to take. He knew from experience the premium that men of her class put on virginity in their would-be brides. For him to take her, however sweet, however mutual the desire, would be to ruin her and the future that awaited her upon her return to her family, her home.

Still, she was there in his arms, her mouth opening beneath the onslaught of his lips, his tongue. Her body burned against his—he could feel the jutting hardness of her nipples as her firm young breasts were crushed against his chest. His hand found the silken smoothness of her thigh beneath the rumpled linen of her chemise. Slowly, as if with a will of its own, his hand stroked upward along that petal-soft skin, seeking, searching, savoring the softness, the delicacy of it until he reached its apex.

He touched her then, his fingers parting the delicate, moist flesh of her, then entering her, his breath a burning lump in his chest as he encountered the fragile barrier of her virginity.

Aurora's cry reached him as through a crimson haze. One moment she was cradled in his arms, soft, pliant, yielding, the next she was arching away, eyes wide and confused, kiss-bruised lips trembling.

"What are you doing to me!" she gasped. "Let me go!"

Raven recoiled, shocked out of the passionate spell, thrust cruelly back to reality.

"Aurora," he said gently, reaching toward her.

"No! Leave me alone!" she hissed, edging away from him.

He scowled, averting his face from her lest the lightning's flashing reveal his emotions to her.

Fool! he cursed himself. Of course she's frightened; of course she's confused. Girls such as she often went to their marriage beds with little or no notion of what sex entailed.

"I'm sorry," he muttered, rising.

Without a backward glance, he stalked out of the room and out of the cabin, disappearing into the storm, leaving her alone to wrestle with her bewilderment, her stunned senses, the moist, hot aching of her flesh that cried out for . . . for . . . for something she didn't even know existed.

9

"Raven?" Aurora hurried across the clearing, relieved to see him return after a day's absence. He had apparently left with the dawn, for he had been gone when she awakened. Now, as the sun slid behind the silhouetted wall of treetops, he had reappeared at last. "Raven, where were you?"

His startling blue eyes flickered across her face only briefly as though he feared that to let them linger would be to reveal too many of the thoughts, the emotions, behind the gaze.

"I have matters to tend to, Aurora. I am not, after all, one of your gentlemen of leisure."

Stung by the chill in his tone, she followed as he strode across the clearing toward the cabin. His far longer strides meant that she had to lift her skirts and all but run to stay near him.

"I was worried about you," she said softly, shyly.

The smile that flitted across his lips seemed to mock her. "I managed on my own quite nicely before you arrived, you know."

"I didn't mean to imply—"

"It doesn't matter."

Rebuked, Aurora followed him into the cabin. The table stood waiting, set for dinner, and Aurora smiled hopefully, praying that Raven would be pleased with the simple dinner she had concocted, turning a few vegetables and some meat left over from the night before into an aromatic stew.

"I've made dinner," she told him. "It's on the stove. I hope you like—"

"I've already eaten." He disappeared into the bedroom, oblivious to her crestfallen face. It was not until he returned with a knapsack that he noticed her chagrin.

"I'm sorry, Aurora, I had no way of knowing you'd cook dinner for us both. I thought you'd have managed something for yourself and that was that. In any case, I ate dinner with Sarah's family."

"Sarah . . ." Turning her back to hide her revealing face, she forced her voice to sound lightly unconcerned. "I thought Sarah and her family lived on another island."

"They do. That's where I went today. I'm going away for a day or two." He turned his attention to the packing of his knapsack to avoid the look on Aurora's face. "I went to ask Sarah to come and stay with you while I'm gone."

"I see," Aurora murmured as she went about clearing the table she had taken so much care in setting.

Raven noticed what she was doing. "Aurora, go on with your dinner. Just because I've eaten—"

"It's all right," she replied quietly. "I'm not hungry after all."

"Aurora—"

"Honestly, I'm not at all hungry."

He shrugged. "Suit yourself. In any case, Sarah has agreed to come, but she can't be here before tomorrow afternoon. I'm leaving in the morning. I'm sure you'll be all right here until she arrives."

"I'm sure I will," she agreed dully.

"Unless—" Though he did not look up, he could feel her expectancy as she paused in her work. "—unless you'd like to come with me."

"Where are you going?"

"St. James. It might be better if you came—"

Fighting her emotions, she dropped the handful of tableware she'd been holding onto the polished tabletop.

"If you're so eager to be rid of me, I suppose—"

"It's not that." He scowled, knowing he had spoken too quickly, too revealingly. He sighed. "It's only that you are well again, Aurora. There is no excuse for you to remain here. You should be reunited—"

"No!" She blushed. "No. Please, Raven, let me stay here. I want to stay."

"Won't your family be grieving for you?"

"My family?" She went to stand before him. "My parents are dead. They died over a year ago. All I have left are my aunt and uncle. They were taking me to live with them in Chicago. I'm an obligation to them, Raven, nothing more." Her smile wavered noticeably at the corners. "They're like you. They 'managed quite nicely without me.'"

"And there was no one else? You're what? Seventeen? Eighteen? Surely you must have had suitors." He remembered from his years in Pittsburg that it was not unusual for heiresses to be betrothed out of the schoolroom.

"My parents died before my debut. I was in mourning for a year and then my aunt and uncle came to take me away. There was no time for any serious courtship."

"I suppose they expected to match you with someone in Chicago."

Graham Hughston's image flickered in her mind's eye. "I suppose so."

"Still, it seems cruel to let them go on thinking you're dead."

"If they knew I was alive, they'd come for me. They'd make me go back with them."

There was truth in what he said—no doubt her aunt, uncle, and Graham believed her drowned. Still, the guilt of her deception did not outweigh, in her mind at least, the prospect of being taken away from the island, from Raven, and being returned to the narrow, suffocating world of society in Chicago.

"Just a little longer, Raven, please," she pleaded. "Just a little longer."

Against his better judgment, Raven nodded. "Just a little," he agreed reluctantly, unable to resist the pleading of those beautiful green eyes and unable to ignore the raw aching of his heart at the thought of watching her sail away out of his life.

Joyfully she threw her arms about his neck. "Thank you!" she cried. "Oh, I knew you wouldn't—"

Her pleasure melted away as he put her gently

but firmly away from him. "Go to bed now, Aurora," he said sternly, laying his packed knapsack aside. "It's late."

She glanced out the window to see that the sun had barely reached the horizon. It couldn't be more than ten at the latest.

"The stove," she stalled. "I left a fire in it to keep the stew hot."

"I'll see to the stove. Now, go to bed before I reconsider letting you stay."

Obediently, but with the air of a recalcitrant child, she ducked beneath the blanket in the bedroom doorway. She had displeased him in some way but she was not sure how. Did he resent her touching him? An unwelcome thought crept into her mind. He had spent the day with Sarah on the other island. Had they made love? Was his mind so full of another woman that he could not bear Aurora's touch? Oh! How she wished she knew more of what went on between men and women. How she wished she were more experienced, like Sarah. How she wished . . .

"What does it matter," she told herself self-pityingly as she pulled off her clothes and poured water into the basin to wash before she went to bed. "If it is Sarah he loves, nothing I can do will change it."

But though those words came easily enough to her lips, she knew her heart would never accept them. She wanted Raven to love her; she wanted him to accept her love in return. And he couldn't be so very much in love with Sarah, could he? After all, he had not married her.

Sitting down on the bed, she blew out the lamp on the bedside table. In the warm half-darkness of the gathering twilight, she thought of spending the next day or two in Sarah Oates' company. How could she talk to the woman, be cordial to her, all the while wondering if she and Raven had made love since the night the storm had brought Aurora to the island? Perhaps it would be better if she went with Raven to St. James. But no, it would be all too easy for him to decide to leave her there. She would have to stay behind, without him, with— she sighed with weary resignation—with Sarah.

10

Aurora stood in the cabin doorway watching Raven adjust the small pack he would carry down to the shore where his boat waited for him to sail to the neighboring island. She wavered between her resolve to stay there ensconced in his cabin and the impulse to ask him to take her with him after all.

Glancing up, Raven saw the indecision in her face and mistook its cause.

"You mustn't worry," he told her. "You won't be here alone for long. Sarah's brothers will bring her here in their fishing boat when they go out this morning."

"I'm not worried," she assured him.

"Good." He took a few steps toward the path in the forest that led to the shore. Pausing, he looked back over his shoulder. "Would you like to come as far as the shore?"

Nodding, Aurora scampered across the clearing and fell into step behind him on the narrow path.

"Are you certain you don't want to come?" Raven asked. "You must be getting tired of the isolation of this island."

Yes! Aurora's heart cried. I want to come with you. I can't bear the thought of even a day without you.

"No," she said softly, her common sense reminding her of just how simple it would be for him to leave her there in St. James. "I like it here."

The rhythmic crashing of the waves on the shore grew louder as they neared the edge of the forest and the wide stretch of sand that led down to the water's edge.

Her skirts lifted, Aurora walked across the sand. The pale, fine sand squished between her toes, turning heavier, thicker and wetter as she neared the water. She said nothing as Raven laid his pack into the boat. Nor could she bring herself to raise her eyes to his as he turned to her one last time.

Raven gazed at her standing there, barefoot in the sand, her thick, glistening hair turned to flame by the sun as it tumbled down her back. Perhaps—a small, wheedling voice whispered in his mind—perhaps it is not too much to hope that she could truly abandon the life she lived before and come to appreciate the simple, difficult life so far removed from the luxuries of the city and society. Perhaps . . .

One sun-burnished hand lifted, reaching out toward the shining, curling strands of her hair. But as Aurora lifted her head, Raven allowed his hand to fall to his side. The gesture went unnoticed.

"You will be careful, won't you?" she asked, casting a nervous glance at the turgid water and the seemingly fragile sailboat that awaited Raven. She flushed, remembering his rebuke of the day before when she told him she'd been worried during his absence. "I'm sorry. I know you're perfectly capable of—"

"I'll be careful," he assured her, his voice strangely tender. Her concern touched a place inside him that he had jealously guarded for more years than he cared to remember.

"I'll—" Aurora bit her lip. She wanted to tell him how she would miss him, but she did not know how far she could go before he would retreat and turn cool and distant once more.

"Yes?" he prompted, knowing he should be going but reluctant to part from her. "You'll—?"

"I'll see you when you return," she substituted.

His smile was wan, forced. He was not certain of what he had hoped she would say, but that was not it.

"So you will," he agreed. He gazed down at her, his cerulean eyes lingering on the fiery halo of her hair as it framed her face. The delicate pink of her cheeks, once so pale, now kissed into rose-tinged perfection by exposure to the sun, the almond-shaped beauty of her black-lashed green eyes, the tip-tilted piquancy of her nose where a freckle or two was even then beginning to sprout, and her lips—her lips—so full, so soft . . . Against his will, he remembered the feel, the taste of them beneath his own. He wanted to kiss them again and again—he wanted to go on kissing her, loving her, for hours and days and . . .

"Goodbye, Aurora," he said abruptly, forcing himself to shut out those thoughts. "Sarah will be here soon."

Turning away, he waded into the lake, the small boat pushed before him until it was well afloat.

Aurora watched, her heart aching, longing for the sweet words he had not spoken, the kisses he had not given her, until he was but a speck in the distance sailing toward the far larger island five miles to the east. To reach St. James, he must round the northern tip of the other island. Aurora watched until she could no longer distinguish him from the glare of the sun on the lake. Then, her heart sinking, she turned toward the path that would take her back to the cabin.

As she emerged from the forest, she noticed that the cabin door was standing open. Sarah, she thought, torn between relief that she would not have to spend the long, lonely time until Raven's return alone, and weary chagrin at spending the time in Sarah's company. Though Raven had not seemed so very enamored of the pretty girl, Sarah obviously considered herself Raven's woman and, conversely, Raven her man.

Aurora knew that Sarah was jealous of the time she was spending in Raven's company. Now, with Raven gone, she felt sure that Sarah would make certain Aurora knew just how intimate she and Raven were.

She stepped out of the bright sunshine into the cool, shadowy cabin. "Sarah?" Squinting, waiting for her eyes to adjust to the darkness, Aurora glanced around the empty main room. "Sarah? Are you here?"

There was no reply but only a shuffling sound from the bedroom. Aurora scowled. What was the woman doing? Rifling Aurora's meager belongings in hopes of learning more about her? Or perhaps searching Raven's things for some clue as to his doings and plans?

She crossed the floor, her bare feet making no sound on the carpet. One hand reached out for the blanket that hung in the doorway. But as her fingers brushed it, it was jerked aside.

Gasping, Aurora fell back. The man who towered over her, the sour, sweaty odor of his thick, hulking body filling her nostrils, was like no one she had ever encountered. He was dirty, his slack, jowly face was shadowed by a thick bristling of whiskers. His eyes were bulbous, a pale cornflower blue, shaded by thick, bushy brows of the same dark blond as his thatch of greasy hair. He grinned as he saw her there, backing toward the center of the bigger room, and exposed a mouth of blackening teeth.

"Sarah ain't comin'," he told her. "Sarah's got better things to do than sit with Raven's fancy woman."

"Who are you?" Aurora breathed.

"Luke . . . Luke Oates." His eyes skimmed over Aurora and his tongue flicked out to wet his lips. "Sarah told us you was pretty, but she didn't say just what a fancy piece you really was."

Stepping back, Aurora gasped as she felt the unyielding bulk of the sofa behind her. She could not circle it without taking her eyes off the man, and she was too frightened of him to do that.

"So Sarah won't be coming?" she asked.

"No, she won't." He grinned his terrible, smirking grin once more. "But if yer needin' company—"

"No!" Aurora struggled to control her fear, for some part of her sensed that he enjoyed making her tremble with fright. "Not at all," she amended airily. "I'm quite all right here. Raven should be back soon and—"

"Sarah said he was goin' for a day or two. Yer gonna be lonesome here by yerself."

"No, truly, I'm not. Please, you've given me your message. Thank you. You may go."

" 'You may go,' " he mimicked cruelly. "Listen to me, girlie. I ain't no servant to be packed off when you don't want me 'round no more. Sarah said you was a high-nosed little bitch. I can see she was tellin' the truth. But high-nosed or not, a woman's a woman and I bet you love it just like the rest of 'em when Raven lays you down and—"

"Get out!" Aurora screamed, knowing even as she did so that this was no man to be ordered about. He was not the type to be commanded by respect for the power and status of the imperious rich. Commands might work with the lower orders in New York where the rich and powerful were bowed to, but not here, not with a man like this. She fought for self-control, but her fear robbed her of caution, of reason.

"Don't be orderin' me about," he growled. "I think yer in need of a little schoolin', woman. You need to learn some respect for men. You don't know a woman's place, and if Raven ain't man enough to teach you—I sure as hell am!''

Aurora shuddered as he advanced upon her. Eyes never leaving his face, she felt along the back of the sofa with trembling hands until she reached the end. Then, whirling, she fled across the cabin toward the door.

But Luke was not hampered by the weight and bulk of a flowing skirt and petticoat. For a man of his size, he moved with surprising speed as he lunged after her.

Aurora shrieked as his meaty hands closed about her arm and nearly jerked her off her feet. The pain of his fingers digging into her flesh shot up her arm to her shoulder as he spun her around to face him.

"Don't run from me, woman," he snarled, as his hand tightened on her chin until she thought his fingers would surely break her jaw. "Don't ever run from me. You'll stay where I tell you and do what I tell you."

"Raven—" she breathed between gritted teeth.

"To hell with Raven! He's been takin' my sister when he pleases for years. He leaves her cryin' for him but he won't make her his wife. His whore! That's what he's made of her. And now—that he's found hisself a pretty new whore he likes better . . . Well, he owes me, as I see it. He owes me and I'm collectin'.''

"You're wrong," Aurora whispered, jaw grinding against the brutal, crushing strength of his hand. "It's not that way. Raven and I have never— He's faithful to your sister. He is! I swear it!"

"Hah!" Luke's eyes glinted dangerously. "He keeps you here with him, don't he? He coulda taken you to St. James and been rid of you a long time ago. But he ain't done it. Now, a woman's good for two things—cleanin' a man's house and satisfyin' him in bed. Sarah told us you don't know one end of a broom from t'other. So if you ain't takin' care of his house, he must have some other use for you."

"No," Aurora moaned, feeling sick. She could not hope to fight him—he was infinitely stronger. How, then, could she escape?

"Yes," he disagreed. His laugh was filled with dark malice—it was the most evil sound Aurora had ever heard. "Give over nice and easy and I won't hurt you. Hell, Raven don't even need to know."

"Please." Aurora felt dizzy; the pounding of her heart seemed to echo in her ears. Her stomach churned at the thought of his touching her. "Oh, please, no."

Luke's gaze darkened, hardened. "I ain't good enough for ya. That it? I ain't good enough, but you'll lay down for that goddamned half-breed. I'll show you what a real man is—"

His mouth came down on hers then, grinding, painful. Aurora gagged at the sour taste of him, the fetid odor of his harsh breath, the musty stench of his body. His fingers dug into her cheeks as he tried to force her mouth open; his tongue moved against her teeth seeking entrance.

His hand released her arm and clutched at her breast. The pain made her gasp and, as she did, his tongue thrust inside her mouth. In terror, in desperation, she snapped her teeth down on it and felt the warm, metallic gush of his blood.

Howling, Luke brought his fist slashing through the air. It caught Aurora a glancing blow on the side of the head and sent her crashing across the room to land in a heap near the fireplace; her head narrowly missing the pointed finial of the brass and iron.

She gasped for breath as she lay there, praying to stay conscious, fully aware that Luke would not hesitate to rape an unconscious woman. She spat out the blood that lay sourly on her tongue and wiped her mouth with the back of her hand. Her eyes were filmed, hazed with the pain and the fear that drove her to a desperation that was near to madness.

Luke came toward her. His chest heaved with his every coarse breath, and Aurora knew suddenly, certainly, that he intended to take her, use her cruelly, violently, and then kill her to keep Raven from discovering what he had done. Beyond tears, beyond even fear, she pressed herself against the stones of the fireplace, using them to help push herself to her feet. She was fighting now not merely for her body, but for her life.

As Luke advanced on her, her hands clutched at the stones behind her. If only one were loose, if only one would come free of the mortar that held it, she would throw it at him. Even if it did not seriously injure him, it might gain her some time, even a few precious moments, to try to flee into the forest.

The stones held fast, but her hand, feeling frantically behind her, knocked against the brass stand of implements. She grasped at one and yanked it free. Swinging it around, she brandished the long, sharp poker at her attacker.

Luke hesitated. "What're you goin' to do with that?" he mocked. "It ain't goin' to help you. In the end, I'll do as I want with you. If you'd have gave me what I wanted, nice like, in the beginnin', it wouldn'a come to this. It's yer own fault now, whatever happens. Yer own fault."

Counting on her fear to make her clumsy, Luke moved toward her. He reached out to snatch the poker from her but as he did, Aurora swung her weapon. The sharp spur caught him in the shoulder, tearing the torn, dirty cotton of his shirt and gashing his arm. A stain appeared, turning the faded blue of his sleeve to crimson. Luke growled as he jerked the poker out of Aurora's hands and threw it across the cabin.

Aurora whirled to run, but Luke's hand shot out and seized the swirling fabric of her skirt. With a short, savage movement he yanked her back, making her lose her already precarious balance.

She lay as she fell, the breath knocked out of her, the blackness of unconsciousness gathering around her. Her nails dug into the planks of the floor as she felt the brute strength of Luke's hands upon her. He pushed her over onto her back and his hands kneaded the delicate softness of her breasts. Weakly, feebly, she pushed at his hands with her own, for the pain, though dulled by the haze clouding her mind, was excruciating. Tears of pain, of fear, of impotent fury ran down her bruised cheeks. Luke's breath, coming in short, heavy gasps, blew sourly in her face as he loomed over her. His hands pushed at the trailing cloth of her skirt. He grunted as he found her skin beneath the rumpled layers; his calloused hands savored the silken flesh of her thigh, softer than any woman's skin he had ever known.

Lost, Aurora prayed now for the darkness to overtake her. Her hands moved restlessly over the floor on either side of her, searching in vain for some weapon to use against him. There was none.

Then, without warning, Luke jerked, his great body heaved upward. A muffled thud sent a vibration through them both, and Luke collapsed atop her, his weight crushing her beneath him.

Aurora moaned as he was rolled off her. Her pain-glazed eyes gazed upward, trying to pierce the fog that seemed to be enveloping her. A man was bending over her, a handsome man with deeply bronzed skin and coal-black hair. His face was filled with concern, with compassion, with outraged anger.

She reached a wavering hand toward him. "Raven?" she breathed. "Raven, help me. Help me!" And then the darkness claimed her.

11

Aurora's first thought when she awakened several hours later was that it had all been a dream—a particularly hideous nightmare from which she had, peculiarly, not awakened. Still, she was there in the cabin, lying on the velvet-covered softness of the sofa. The shadows were lengthening; it was nearly twilight.

She heard a sound coming from the kitchen and her heart leapt. The man— But no, that had been a dream, hadn't it? She sat up and the aches and pains of her bruised body told her just how real Luke Oates' attack had been. If those aches and pains were real, then the rest must be . . .

"Raven?" she called softly, almost wishing no one at all would reply, somehow hoping that the noise in the kitchen had been made by a chipmunk or squirrel or mouse that had found its way inside.

A man appeared in answer to her summons.

At first she thought he was Raven—certainly he had the same bronzed skin, the same coal-black hair. But he wasn't Raven. At second glance she saw that the jet-colored hair was arrow straight and hung down his back, tied at the nape of his neck with a leather thong. He was shorter than Raven and, as he drew closer, she saw that his eyes were as dark as glittering onyx rather than the amazing sky-blue of Raven's eyes.

Aurora shrank back onto the sofa. "Who are you?" she demanded. "What are you doing here?" Memories of Luke's attack flooded her mind. Tears smarted in the corners of her eyes. "Please—" she whispered.

"I'm not going to hurt you," he said gently, coming no closer for fear of frightening her even more.

The memory of a man she'd thought was Raven bending over her as she lay half beneath the unconscious Luke Oates stirred in her mind.

"It was you, wasn't it? Not Raven. I thought it was Raven, but . . ." Her eyes darted toward the shadowy corners of the cabin. "He's gone, hasn't he?"

"Yes, he's gone. In answer to your other question, my name is Matthew. I am Raven's cousin."

"His cousin?" Aurora's face mirrored her bewilderment.

Matthew nodded toward the portrait over the fireplace. "His mother and mine were sisters."

She sat up on the sofa, wincing at the aches of her bruised body. "My name is Aurora—Aurora Jephson. Raven found me—"

"I know," Matthew interrupted. "He told me about you."

"He did?" She leaned forward. "What did he say?"

Matthew grinned. His teeth were strong and, against the burnished bronze of his skin, very white.

"He told me he found you on the beach. He said you had been swept from the deck of a yacht during the bad storm a while ago."

"Oh, is that all?"

Aurora toyed with the cuff of her blouse. She'd been hoping for something more personal, more encouraging, more informative that might give her some insight into Raven's private feelings. But if he discussed such things with this handsome cousin of his, Matthew obviously wasn't about to betray his confidence.

Matthew watched her as she sat there, her lower lip protruding ever so slightly in an unconscious but somehow provocative pout. When Raven had told him of finding the girl on the beach, he had assumed that Raven would keep her with him only until she was able to make the trip to St. James where her relatives would be summoned to take her home. He had thought it extraordinary that his cousin, who seemed only to seek the company of a woman when the demands of his body forced him to, should of his own free will keep a woman with him long after her condition warranted it. Now, seeing Aurora, it seemed even more astonishing.

She was beautiful with her fiery red hair and amazing green eyes. Her cheeks were tinged with roses from the sun, a condition he knew would horrify her lady's maid or companion, or whatever it was that Raven had told him young women of her class kept company with. Though he himself had

111

always preferred the darker beauty of the Ojibway women to the washed-out fairness of white women, he had to admit he was touched by her combination of flaming hair and delicate ivory skin. He would almost have envied Raven possessing the girl had he not known that Raven had vowed not to touch her. Raven had said the girl must return to her people and had explained to his cousin the premium put on innocence by her class, the way she would be ostracized if it were known she had lived with any man, much less had him for a lover.

His black eyes met Aurora's green ones and her soft pink lips quivered, then curved into a small, shy smile. Matthew sighed. How his cousin could live day and night in the presence of such beauty and remain celibate was beyond his understanding. For he knew what Aurora did not—he knew that Raven had not touched Sarah Oates from the day he had found Aurora. It was that fact, Matthew suspected, that had prompted Sarah to agree to Luke's coming to Raven's cabin when he had thought the girl would be alone. Matthew suspected that Sarah had believed that once Luke had had Aurora, Raven would never wish to touch her. He would send Aurora away, and then Sarah would have him to herself once again.

Matthew wondered if he should reveal any of it to Aurora, but the thought vanished as he realized she was asking him something.

"I'm sorry," he apologized. "What did you say?"

"I only said that Matthew seems an odd name for an Indian."

Matthew smiled. "Fifty or sixty years ago

Catholic missionaries came to these islands. After that it was not uncommon for children to be given Christian names and to be baptized as Catholics."

"But not Raven?" she asked.

"Raven was named in honor of his father."

"But his father was not an Indian, was he? He couldn't have been, for Raven has blue eyes."

"No, he was not an Indian. Still, that is who Raven was named for."

"He never speaks of his father."

"I think it is painful for him."

"Why? Is his father dead?" Aurora knew it was rude to press Matthew so for information, but Raven had revealed so little and she was starved to know more about his life.

"Not that I know of. But I don't think they've written to one another since Raven came back from—"

"Yes? Came back from where?" Aurora prompted.

"I think it would be best if you waited for Raven to tell you the story," Matthew decreed.

"Raven never tells me anything about his past."

"Then I've already said too much. It is his story to tell—or not to tell." Matthew smiled to take the sting out of his words. "What about you? How do you feel?"

Aurora felt her cheeks pinkening. The talk about Raven had temporarily taken her mind off the incident with Luke Oates. She hadn't wanted to remember it; she had done her best to blot it out of her mind. But Matthew's question brought it all rushing back.

"I'm all right," she told him softly. "A few bumps and bruises but nothing serious. He's not on the island any longer, is he?"

"No, he's gone." Matthew's brows arched. "He may be gone for good when Raven finds out about it. I can't imagine what was in Sarah's mind to let her brother come here. She knows Raven can't bear any of them."

"He can bear Sarah quite nicely," Aurora muttered.

Matthew hid a smile; the jealousy in Aurora's voice was plain as day. "Raven finds Sarah convenient for . . ." He wondered how he could phrase his statement. "Well, Raven enjoys Sarah's company and her help. But he has no use for any of the rest of them."

"Are they all as loathsome as . . ." She could not bring herself to speak his name. ". . . as . . ."

"As Luke? They're no better. They're supposed to be fishermen, but most people think they make their living as wreckers."

"Wreckers?"

Matthew nodded as he sat down in the chair opposite her. "The island they live on is surrounded by a reef. It has an old lighthouse that was abandoned years ago. On stormy nights they are supposed to light the beacon and lure passing ships onto the reef."

"That's horrible! Why would they do such a wicked thing?"

"They take the cargoes and sell them. Or if it is a yacht, they take whatever is valuable. They claim salvage rights."

"But what about the people who own the cargoes and the valuables? The survivors?"

"There never seem to be any." Matthew scowled. He hoped she wouldn't pursue the subject. He didn't want to tell her the rumor that anyone fortunate enough to survive the shipwreck was finished off by one of the Oateses to prevent them from telling how the ship was lured onto the reef in the first place. After all, no one could prove anything, if there were no witnesses, and it was almost impossible for the authorities to tell if a body had been bludgeoned or battered on the rocks by a storm-tossed lake.

"Something should be done," Aurora insisted. "Surely someone could—"

"No doubt someone will, in time," Matthew assured her, anxious to get her off the subject. "But right now, it's getting late. Would you like to come with me to see if we can manage to catch some fish for our dinner?"

Delighted, Aurora accepted. Raven had never offered to take her hunting or fishing and she was curious. Together she and Matthew spent the rest of the evening fishing, and though the two fish she caught were scarcely big enough to keep, she felt proud that she, who had never even seen a fish in its natural state before arriving on the island, should have been able to catch some herself.

For his part, Matthew delighted in her company. There was something about her so innocent, childlike almost, that she made him feel more manly, more protective of her than he had felt with any woman in a very long time. He found it all the easier to understand Raven's reluctance to part with the girl. What he could not understand was how Raven had the self-control to remain with her day and night and not take her into his bed—make her his woman. Had she not belonged to Raven, Matthew knew he would surely set about seducing her.

"Do you think we have enough fish?" he asked when the sun had nearly disappeared, turning into a brilliant orange ball that colored the sky and stained the lake as it sank beneath the horizon.

"I suppose so," she admitted. She had to laugh at the sight of her two tiny trout, so small beside the three gleaming pike Matthew had deemed worth keeping. Her fish seemed so pathetic, but they were hers and she could not bear to throw them back.

He nudged one of the wriggling trout with the toe of his boot. "Are you sure you want to take those poor things home? If you threw them back, they might grow some more."

She looked up at him from beneath her lowered lashes. "They are only babies, aren't they?" He nodded and she shrugged. "Oh, all right. Throw them back. But I expect you to be my witness to Raven that I really caught them."

Taking the two little fish in one hand, he tossed them back into the water. "I'll tell him what a struggle you had with them," he promised. "I'll tell him how they almost pulled you into the lake and dragged you away."

"All right, that's enough," she chided.

Laughing, Matthew took up his catch and they started back toward the cabin. They were emerging into the clearing when Aurora noticed smoke rising from the chimney attached to the cookstove. Her heart seemed to thud in her breast.

"Do you think . . . Luke's come back?" she asked Matthew in a frightened whisper.

"He wouldn't dare." Still, Matthew handed

the string of fish to Aurora and motioned for her to remain where she was while he approached the cabin.

He was halfway across the clearing when the cabin door opened and Raven appeared. Nearly giddy with relief, Aurora dropped the fish and raced toward him, her skirts held away from her flying feet.

"Raven! Oh, Raven! Thank God you've come home!"

Whether it was the taut stiffness of his posture as he stood framed in the doorway or the piercing chill of his eyes as he looked at her, Aurora didn't stop to ponder. All she knew was that there was something about him that warned her of his anger, an intangible something that told her he was furious—and that she was the object of his fury.

She stopped, having just passed Matthew who had slowed to a near standstill.

"Raven?" she said softly, approaching him with short, halting steps. "What is it? What's happened?"

"Come in here," he muttered, turning to disappear into the shadowy depths of the cabin.

She went inside and followed him to the table. On it lay a two-week-old copy of the *Chicago Tribune*. Emblazoned across the page was a photograph of her—one of many taken at the time of her parents' deaths—and a headline in thick black type: *Reward Offered for Lost Heiress*. Another, smaller picture faced her own. The man in the photograph was Graham Hughston. Beneath it the succinct caption read: *Grieving Fiancé*.

"Twenty-five thousand dollars, Aurora," Raven told her, his voice tight and dark with anger.

"This man has offered twenty-five thousand dollars for information about you. I'm not surprised that he should want you back so badly—particularly after I read the touching details of your year-long courtship in New York."

Aurora opened her mouth to speak, but Raven went on:

"There was no one else, you told me. No one. There was no time for men after your parents died. That's what you said. And now, what do I see? Your 'grieving fiancé' is willing to pay twenty-five thousand dollars merely for information. More, so it says, if you are actually found alive and well as a result of the information. You lied to me, damn you. And as far as I'm concerned, any man who is willing to pay so much to retrieve a cheating little liar like you has my sympathy."

Turning on his heel, Raven stormed from the cabin. Matthew, standing in the doorway, looked from the tearful, stricken face of Aurora to the retreating back of his cousin. After some moments' indecision, he followed Raven toward the forest, leaving Aurora to gaze after them, her heart filled with despair, her eyes misted with tears.

She looked back down at the papers. Graham's countenance, blurred by her tears, eyed her with something that seemed close to triumph.

"Damn you, Graham Hughston, damn you! Why couldn't you leave me dead!"

12

Matthew followed his cousin through the darkening forest to the shore where Raven's boat had been drawn up into the sand near Matthew's own.

"Listen to me, Raven," he said as his cousin began pulling supplies out of the boat. "There is something you need to know. Something about Aurora."

Raven's face was grim, dark as a thundercloud. "I know everything I need to know about Aurora, cousin."

"No, you don't. Not this," Matthew argued.

Raven drew himself up and glared down at the shorter man. "You are my cousin. We share the same blood. You are also my best friend. But I warn you. Do not meddle in this."

"I don't understand you. So this man has offered a reward for her. What difference does it

119

make? She was not born the day you found her on the beach."

"The man is her fiancé of over a year. She told me there was no one. No one! And I believed her. How could I have let her make such a fool of me? I should have known that a girl of her beauty, her wealth, would not have been allowed to leave the schoolroom without having a marriage arranged for her. I wouldn't have thought less of her had she told me the truth." He drew a deep breath, his glittering eyes trained on the stars just beginning to appear in the deep blue sky above. "As soon as she recovered, I should have sent her back where she belongs. I let her lie her way into my heart." His laughter was hollow. "And I thought I had learned all those years ago not to trust women like her; not to trust her kind."

"You are her kind," Matthew reminded him.

"I am Ojibway," Raven gritted.

"Tell that to your father in his mansion with his servants and his gold."

Raven's face darkened with the mottled blood of his fury. "Get into your boat, cousin, and sail away from this island while we are still friends."

"I want to tell you—"

"And I tell you I don't want to hear it! Aurora has worked her spell on you as well. Take care, cousin, for she is like the snake I told you of seeing in the zoo—she will wrap her wiles about you like the boa's coils and crush you until your heart bleeds."

"Raven—"

"Goodbye, Matthew. I will see you again— when you have had time to recover from the sorcery Aurora has worked on your weak senses. After Aurora is gone from this place."

There was nothing more to be said. Tight-lipped, angry, Matthew pushed his boat out into the water and climbed aboard. There was nothing he could do—it was obvious that Raven was not going to listen to him. Perhaps Aurora would tell Raven about Luke's attack on her and about Sarah's treachery. Perhaps not. In any case, the attack had come to nothing, so it might be best to let the matter die. It was apparent that there were more serious matters to be settled between Raven and Aurora than how and why Luke Oates came to be there when Aurora was supposed to be alone.

Standing on the shore, silhouetted by the magnificence of the glowing summer sunset, Raven watched Matthew's boat disappear into the distance. He was angry not only about his cousin's attempt at interference, but also over what he considered Aurora's lies. And he was troubled. His was not the only copy of that newspaper to be had in St. James. Others had seen the article and the photograph. It was no secret that Raven had a woman with him—a woman who had appeared on the beach the morning after the great storm. It would not take much to connect Aurora's appearance with the disappearance of the heiress from the yacht at the same time. And the reward—twenty-five thousand dollars. Men killed for far less. A man could live out his life in luxury on these islands with such a sum and still leave a handsome legacy for his children.

How long would it be before someone decided to reach for the treasure dangling so temptingly

within their grasp? How long before Graham
Hughston appeared in answer to some letter about
a girl who had emerged from the water the morning after his heiress-fiancée had disappeared over
the railing of a storm-tossed yacht? How long,
Raven wondered, before Aurora was taken from
him as suddenly as she had been given to him?

It might have come as no great surprise to
Raven that Aurora's redemption was already in the
works. On their tiny speck of land a few miles to
the west, three pairs of greedy eyes perused a
battered newspaper.

"Yer sure it's her?" Titus Oates leaned across a
scarred wooden table, eyeing his younger son with
suspicion.

Luke nodded. "Course it's her. She don't look
so ladyfied now, but then you can't expect her to,
her wearin' Belle's old clothes an' all." He cast a
derisive look toward his brother's wife who stood
stirring a pot of watery stew by the black iron stove.
"Hard to believe that Belle ever fit into them
clothes."

Rufus, the elder of Titus's two sons, cast his
wife a sullen look. He, too, was disappointed that
she had lost her pretty figure through repeated
attempts at child-bearing. She'd failed him again
and again. And all they had to show for it was a
little row of wooden crosses—still-births and babies dead before their first year.

"Jennie!" Titus bellowed.

From the second of the two small, dirty rooms
of the cabin a tall, willowy girl of fifteen appeared.
Though her simple cotton dress, a castoff of
Sarah's, was tattered and mended, her delicate,

heart-shaped face was burnt by long hours of work in the punishing sun, and her hair, an ethereal silver-blonde, hung in ragged locks to her waist, there was about her some magical difference that set her apart from the rest of them. She was like a fairy-child among the trolls in some nursery tale.

She hovered nervously in the doorway. "Yes, Pa?"

"Fetch Sarah."

Jennie disappeared only to return in a few moments with her sister in tow.

"What is it?" Sarah asked, wiping fish scales and slime onto her apron.

"Come look at this," Titus ordered. "Is this the woman that half-breed's taken into his cabin?"

Sarah came to the table and peered at the photograph. "That's her," she confirmed. " Aurora. That's her name, all right." Her blue eyes, the legacy of her Irish mother, glinted with distaste. "Look at her, so prim and proper. I wish she'd have drowned!"

"Then yer a fool," Titus growled. " 'Cause she's worth twenty-five thousand dollars to us. All we got to do is write a letter to this man here." He jabbed at Graham's picture with his finger. "And collect our reward. He'll give us more, so it says, if we can deliver her to him."

"But how can we get her away from Raven?" Rufus asked. "She's not likely to trust any of us—not after Luke tried to get under her skirts."

Titus snarled and spat in the general direction of the corner. "You damned jackass." He clouted his younger son on the side of the head, rocking him back on his heels. "If you needed a woman so bad, you coulda found one somewheres else."

123

Luke's eyes lingered on Aurora's picture. "Not one like that," he said softly, lustfully. "Why should that half-breed have her for himself?"

"'Cause he found her, that's why." Titus laughed. "But he ain't goin' to have her for long."

"What's to keep her from coming back?" Sarah wanted to know. "She's . . . she's in love with him."

Rufus's lips curled in disgust. "What the hell has that cross-bred bastard got to make you women want to lay down for him?"

Sarah cursed and swung a fist at her brother, but their father's shout brought them both under control.

"Rufus was right to ask how we're goin' to get the girl away from Raven," he said.

"Raven ain't always there," Luke pointed out.

Sarah nodded. "He goes huntin' sometimes. And fishing. Aurora's alone sometimes for the whole day."

"Could you convince her to go to St. James with you?" Titus asked.

"After what Luke did? I was supposed to stay with her. You expect her to trust me now?"

"Think of a way. Tell her it wasn't your fault. Tell her Luke forced you to stay away. She should believe that."

Sarah shook her head. "It ain't gonna work."

She gasped as her father seized a fistful of her hair and jerked her face close to his own.

"It'd better work, my girl, 'cause if I lose out on twenty-five thousand dollars because of you, I'm gonna take it out of your hide—and I don't think you got that much hide!"

With a vicious shove he sent her stumbling

across the floor. Only the steadying hands of Jennie kept her from falling against the burning iron of the stove.

Settling her clothes around her, Sarah pushed back a lock of her pale hair. She glared at her father and her brothers for a long, silent moment before she said:

"She's got to think it's Raven's doing. You've got to make her think it's Raven who is selling her off to this man. She has to believe that he wants the money more than he wants her 'cause that's the only way to keep her from runnin' to him for help."

Seeing the sense in what she said, the men nodded and fell to plotting. Their eyes sparkled with greed, their fingers itched with avarice. It seemed they could already feel the crisp, fresh banknotes of the reward fluttering into their eager, waiting hands.

Sarah turned and left the cabin to return to the pile of fish she was gutting. She would be summoned back, she knew, when they had decided on a plan. That she would play a major role in their plot she had no doubt, and while she would not be sorry to see Aurora out of Raven's life, she found, to her own surprise, that her feelings were mixed. A part of her, it seemed, had always known that Raven would never be truly hers. And however jealous and envious she might be of Aurora, she loved Raven enough to feel compassion for the pain he was bound to suffer when it seemed Aurora had deserted him for the life of luxury that was her birthright.

13

Heartsore, Aurora watched Raven gathering his fishing gear. He would be gone, she supposed, most of the day, returning to the cabin in time to eat and fall into bed.

That had been the lonely pattern into which their lives had fallen since Raven's discovery of her supposed "treachery" two weeks before. He hardly spoke to her, hardly looked at her. She might as well have been a ghost haunting his cabin for all the attention he paid to her.

Gathering her courage, she moved to his side as he was about to leave.

"Raven?" she said softly, timidly. "May I come with you?"

He didn't hesitate. "No."

"Matthew took me fishing when he was here. I caught two fish."

"Which weren't even worth keeping." His

azure eyes rested reluctantly on her face. "We don't hunt and fish for our amusement here, Aurora. We don't kill for pleasure. We do it for our survival. I realize it might be hard for someone like you—"

"Someone like me! Damn you, I'm sick of your acting as though I were some loathsome creature because of my background! If you hate me so much—" She paused, almost wishing she could take the words back, terrified of how he might reply, then plunged on recklessly:

"If you hate me so much, why don't you write to Graham and tell him where to find me!"

Raven's eyes glinted dangerously though his dark, handsome face never lost its calm, cold expression.

"How do you know I haven't?" he asked quietly.

Aurora gaped at him. The thought had not occurred to her. She had never dreamed that he might actually wish her gone from his life. Another, even less welcome thought intruded.

"Is it the money? The twenty-five thousand dollars? Is that why—?"

Her words were drowned by Raven's derisive laughter. "Do you really think I want or need your fine Mr. Hughston's money? No, Aurora, he can have you back for free."

Turning on his heel, he left the cabin and disappeared across the clearing with long, silent strides. Behind him, framed in the doorway, tears glistening on her long, curling lashes, Aurora felt as if he had plunged an arrow through her heart and twisted it.

For the rest of the day she was torn by indecision. Part of her wanted to flee back into her former world where life might be proscribed and dull but at least she would be safe from the kind of heartbreak that loving Raven had brought to her. The other part of her could not bear the thought of parting from him even if staying meant suffering his coldness, his disdain, even his neglect. At least she would be there with him, to see him, hear him, love him if only in the lonely silence of her own heart.

As darkness fell, she left the cabin and wandered across the clearing. The path Raven had taken that morning was nearly obscured by the shadows of the gathering twilight, but she knew its twists and turns. It led to the creek where she had bathed and then, moving deeper into the interior of the island, to a small inland lake where Raven often fished.

She reached the pond where she had bathed and, sitting on its bank, pulled up her skirts and dangled her feet in the cool, rippling water. A shiver coursed through her. The day had been hot and the water felt deliciously cold as it bathed her feet and ankles. It was peaceful here as evening gave way to night; it was a good place to wait for Raven to return from his day's fishing.

She sighed. Sliding a little farther down the bank, she plunged in up to her knees, her skirts held up, bunched around her thighs. It was wonderful; she felt so free, so natural. How could she even think of leaving this enchanted place? Surely Raven hadn't meant what he'd said about sending her . . . But no, she would not think of that. She would think only of today, tonight, not of tomorrow and whatever sorrows it might bring.

Suddenly, impulsively, she was pulling at her blouse, her skirt, her petticoat and chemise, tossing them casually on the grassy bank. Gasping at the icy chill of the water, she plunged in, sinking to the sandy bottom before floating up again. She stood up and the water rippled about her thighs as the night breezes through the trees caressed her wet skin.

Casting off her worries as she had cast off her clothes, she played in the water like a child. Lacking the warning instincts of forest creatures native to the wild, she did not hear the intruder's approach above the rustling of the wind, the night breezes whispering in the undergrowth. And then she saw him, Raven, standing on the bank watching her.

"You're like a child, Aurora," he said softly, his voice dark and husky. "A little woodland sprite."

She stood before him, her hands at her sides. Her hair cascaded over her shoulders and down her back. The silvery moonlight filtering through the trees bathed her in its caressing light.

"I'm not a little girl," she told him. "I'm a woman."

Raven gazed at her, his eyes devouring her beauty. She did not have to tell him she was a woman. The aching of his yearning flesh and the desire running through his veins like liquid flame had told him that long ago. Still, he held back.

"The Irish on Beaver Island believe in magical creatures called leprechauns. Maybe that's what you are."

Aurora remembered Bridey telling her tales of

the "little people." "Maybe I am," she agreed.
"And if you catch me, I will grant your wish."

"Will you?" he asked.

A shiver ran through her that owed nothing to
the chill of the water or the rush of the night winds.

"Why don't you find out?"

His blue eyes glowed like sapphires in firelight
as he cast off his clothes. Aurora caught her breath.
He stood poised for a moment on the bank before
diving into the water and, in that moment, she
thought she'd never seen anything so beautiful.
She did not dare look at him as he crossed the
pond. When his hands spanned her waist and
turned her toward him, she shuddered, her senses
spinning.

Her gaze hovered somewhere near the base of
his throat. She dared not look into his eyes and she
could not force herself to look at his body, so strong
and tanned with the curling black hair that matted
on his chest and trailed down over the muscled
plane of his belly.

For his part, Raven could not get enough of
looking at her—at the fine, translucent skin so
fragile that the delicate blue tracery of her veins
showed beneath, at the perfect, taut breasts that
rose and fell with her quickened breaths. His eyes
followed one long, water-darkened strand of her
fiery hair as it fell over her shoulders and curled to
frame the tight, pink crest of one breast.

He lifted the lock of hair aside and, as he did,
his knuckle brushed her breast. Aurora gasped as
she lifted her eyes to his.

"I wish—" he whispered softly.

She said nothing but only raised one trembling hand to touch his cheek. Raven's eyes closed.

With a single timid touch she had torn away the last shreds of his self-control. Suddenly, inevitably, his hands plunged beneath the surface of the water, and traced the curving of her back and then went lower still, sliding beneath her buttocks.

He lifted her, her wet body sliding against his, and when their faces were level he slanted his mouth across hers in a desperate, savage kiss filled with all the need, all the hunger, all the yearning he'd fought to suppress for so long—too long. Aurora slid her arms about his neck, pulling him closer, crushing her breasts to his chest. She felt his risen manhood hard against her, but her soft moan was smothered by his searing kiss. Shuddering, she raised her knees and wrapped her legs about his waist.

Moving slowly, their bodies quivering with the force of their mutual desire, Raven carried her from the pond and lay her gently on the velvety grass of the bank.

Aurora opened her eyes and gazed into his. She was frightened, but her need, her desire, her love for him so far overshadowed her fear that she felt nothing but an eagerness for the inevitable.

"Aurora," he murmured, barely reining his desire for her, "say that you want me to love you."

Turning her head, she pressed a kiss into the damp, tanned flesh of his arm. With a shuddering moan, Raven tore asunder the delicate barrier that, though neither had realized it until that moment, had always been his for the taking.

Aurora gasped at the first, sharp pain and then, lost in the raptures of his loving, she abandoned herself completely to him.

Afterward, they lay clasped in one another's

arms unable to break the spell they had woven about themselves. Aurora, her every desire sated, slept even as Raven slipped from her arms and dressed.

Returning to her, he sat down and watched her sleep. Again and again he had to stop himself from reaching out to caress her. His eyes roved adoringly over her body. She seemed so lovely, so innocent in sleep. He noticed the crimson stain of her lost virginity stark against the ivory flesh of her thighs. Dipping the corner of her petticoat into the water, he tenderly sponged it away.

Aurora moaned softly in her sleep but did not awaken. She slept on as her lover watched, torn between loving her and cursing his own madness. What had possessed him to take her? He had never before lost control of his own emotions, his own desires. Now he had taken what he had no right to take—he had taken the innocence that rightfully belonged to the man in the newspaper photograph.

Rising, he left her side and stood gazing up at the heavens where the stars glittered brightly in an endless field of deep blue sky. He wanted to be with her now and always. He wanted her to be his in every sense of the word. But he would have to deal with her other life—her other man. He realized with something close to shock that for this beautiful woman-child he would even return to his father's world. For her he would leave everything he loved, for without her he had nothing. Without her, his beloved forest would be a desolate wilderness. With her, even the hateful world of money and society would be bearable.

He returned to Aurora and gazed down at her. There were so many decisions to make. His love for her had come as a revelation. He passed a hand over his brow. He had to think, to meditate. He had to go away if only for a day or two and search his heart, his mind, his soul for the answers he needed.

She would be safe here in his absence, he told himself. There were supplies enough in the cabin to see her through his absence. His full, sensuous lips curved into a smile. Perhaps he should send Matthew back to keep her company. It was obvious that his cousin adored her.

Gathering Aurora into his arms, he carried her back to the cabin, leaving her clothes where she had discarded them near the pond. She stirred in his arms, but he calmed her—soothed her—with soft murmurs and gentle caresses, laid her onto the fur-covered bed, and drew a fine linen sheet over her cool, smooth, beautiful body.

Moving swiftly, silently, he packed what he would need for his journey to another of the islands in the chain, the island where his mother, his ancestors, lay buried beneath their spirit houses. Before he left, he took up a pen, opened an inkwell, and wrote:

> Aurora,
> I love you. Wait for me.
> Raven.

He laid the note on the table where he knew she would find it. Then, not daring to risk another glance at her pale, beloved face, he left to sail off on the night winds in search of the answers he knew he must have before he could plan their future together.

14

Dawn was just beginning to break as Sarah made her way along the winding path toward Raven's cabin. Again and again she questioned the wisdom of what she was about to do—again and again she cursed herself for every kind of a fool. Even she herself did not know the reason why she had decided to come to Raven, to warn him of her brothers' and father's scheme to take Aurora from him, their plot to sell her back to Graham Hughston in return for a fortune in gold. Why should she help Raven? she demanded of herself. Raven, who had abandoned her for another woman. Why should she help Aurora, who had shattered Sarah's life, her dreams, by simply appearing in Raven's life? Why indeed?

The only answer Sarah could think of was that she loved Raven beyond all reason, beyond even all thought of her own happiness. She knew he would never be happy without Aurora, just as she knew that she herself would never be truly happy without him. But she knew that with or without Aurora, Raven would never be the same. He would never be hers, not in the way she had always dreamed he would be. Their free and easy relationship of the past would never return either. She had little more to lose, she supposed, whatever the outcome, and so she had decided for once in her life to do the noble thing.

Luke and Rufus had put her ashore that morning to watch, to spy, to try and catch Aurora alone and somehow lure her to the deserted stretch of wooded beach near the western bluff. There they would take her aboard their fishing boat and make for St. James. Sarah had agreed—to so much as hesitate would have meant a beating. But guilt had assailed her. It was cruel to tear Aurora from Raven and even more cruel to make her think it had been Raven's plan to ransom her back to Graham Hughston.

At the edge of the clearing she hesitated, biting her lip. Hadn't it been her greatest wish to get Aurora out of her life and out of Raven's life? Now the Fates were handing her exactly the opportunity she had wished for. Wasn't she a fool to toss it back in their faces?

Indecision wracked her. Then, squaring her shoulders, she crossed the clearing toward the cabin. Raven rose with the sun. She would see him, speak to him, gauge his feelings, and then decide what to do.

Lifting the latch, she entered the shadowy cabin. The main room was deserted. A sick feeling twisted Sarah's stomach. Were they sharing the bedroom now? She had long suspected they were lovers but she had never come face to face with the reality. Did they sleep clasped in one another's arms? jealousy asked slyly in her mind. Were they in the bedroom together at this moment?

She noticed the creamy piece of paper propped on the table. Her eyes ran over the brief message once, then again, before she crumpled the page in her fist. All her good intentions, all her compassion, all her noble resolve vanished in the hot green haze of her jealousy. "I love you," it said. He loved Aurora! Sarah felt as if something had died inside her. How she had longed to hear him say those words to her. How she had wished and cried and prayed for him to love her. But he did not—never had. In eight years she had not been able to make him love her. In eight weeks Aurora had accomplished it with effortless ease.

A new thought struck her. Raven was gone. He had left Aurora alone. He must have planned to be away for some time or he would not have asked her to "wait for me." This was a new, unexpected development. It called for an alteration in plans.

She heard a stirring in the bedroom. Aurora! In a moment she would be up and would discover Sarah there. With Raven's note still crushed in her hand, Sarah tiptoed out of the cabin and raced toward the bluff. The change in circumstances merited a conference with her brothers.

In little more than an hour, she was back at Raven's cabin. She entered, and found it deserted. In the bedroom the sheet had been cast aside. Aurora was nowhere to be seen.

"Now where did she go?" Sarah asked herself. "Where could she have—"

"Sarah?" Aurora stood in the doorway, skin still moist and dewy from her morning bath. In her arms she carried a bundle of clothing. "What are you doing here?"

"I came to see you. Raven sent me."

"Raven?" Aurora frowned, confused. She had assumed that Raven had merely gone off fishing or hunting. She would have preferred to have him stay with her this morning—especially this morning—but his absence had seemed no cause for alarm. Until now. "Where is Raven?"

"He's gone to St. James," Sarah lied. "He asked me to come here and—"

"And keep me company?" Aurora snapped. "I'm surprised you actually came. The last time you were supposed to keep me company, your brother came instead!" She turned away to hide the hurt she felt at the thought of Raven's being so insensitive as to send his former lover to her after what had passed between them the night before.

Sarah gazed at her, her expression contrite, almost mournful. "I'm sorry about that, Aurora, truly I am. There was nothing I could do to stop Luke. He's—well, you saw him. If I argue with him or my other brother, Rufus, or our father, I get a beating. If there was some way I could have warned you . . . Please say you forgive me."

Aurora's glance was plainly suspicious. She carried the clothing she'd brought back from the pond (had Raven really carried her back to the cabin naked the night before? she wondered, her cheeks flaming) into the bedroom and deposited it on the trunk. The petticoat would have to be laundered (her heart fluttered at the sight of the crimson stain marring the snowy cotton).

Returning to the main room, she found Sarah standing where she'd left her, a hangdog expression on her face.

"Oh, all right. I forgive you. I wouldn't want to try and argue with your brother myself. But I surely don't envy you having to live with them!"

Sarah ground her teeth. By now she might have been living with Raven instead of Luke and Rufus if it hadn't been for this hoity-toity little snot.

"I'm sure you don't," she said tightly. "But my brothers are not the reason I'm here."

"Then what is the reason?"

"I told you. Raven. He's gone to St. James and he's asked me to bring you there as well."

"I don't believe you," Aurora told her flatly. "If Raven wanted me to go to St. James, why didn't he just take me with him when he went?"

"There were arrangements to be made. He had to meet with—"

"With whom?" Aurora demanded when Sarah seemed unwilling to go on.

"All right, I'll tell you. You'll find out soon enough anyway. With Graham Hughston—the man you're supposed to marry."

Sarah savored the shock in Aurora's eyes and the alarming pallor of her face as the blood drained out of her cheeks.

"You're lying!" Aurora breathed. "Graham is in—"

"St. James," Sarah finished for her.

"No, it's not true! You're lying! I won't go anywhere with you! Not until I talk to Raven! I want to see Raven!"

"Then you'll have to go to St. James, because

that is where he is and that is where he expects you to be by this evening."

Aurora turned away, desperate to hide her shock from the other woman. Raven would not betray her this way—he wouldn't! Not after last night! Not after they'd become lovers! It meant so much—so very much to her and to— She looked over her shoulder at Sarah. Sarah, too, had been Raven's lover but that had not stopped him from making love to another woman. He had betrayed Sarah for her. Had he now betrayed her for a cache of gold?

Doubts, maddening, painful doubts plagued her, tore at her heart, chipped away at the edges of her trust for the enigmatic man she had so recklessly fallen in love with.

"How do I know you are telling me the truth?" she demanded softly.

Wordlessly Sarah pulled a creased letter from her pocket and handed it to Aurora. She watched as Aurora gazed at the handwriting on the envelope, then pulled out the letter and read it once, then again. It was precisely what it purported to be: a reply from Graham Hughston to a letter he had received from someone called "Raven" detailing Aurora's miraculous survival in the storm-tossed lake and her subsequent stay on High Island. Though Graham's letter was genuine, the letter from Raven had been dictated by Titus Oates and written by Sarah in her careful penmanship. But Aurora could not know that any more than she could know that mail delivery, especially to the outlying islands, was haphazard at best. It was not difficult to intercept letters to Raven—almost everyone in St. James knew of Sarah's relationship with him. It was a simple matter for her or one of her family to offer to take his mail to him on their way home. They'd been doing it for years. After all, hadn't she made it her business to see to it that none of Raven's father's letters had reached him since she'd become his woman? She hadn't wanted him to get any foolish notions about returning to the city, and the best way to prevent that seemed to be to keep him from communicating with the old man, who had long since given up writing to his son pleading for forgiveness.

Aurora closed her eyes. The pounding in her ears echoed the thudding of her breaking heart. She didn't want to believe a word of it—she would have sold her very hope of Heaven to be rid of the agonizing doubts spinning in her mind. Only that morning when she'd awakened and remembered the night before, she'd been so certain of his love for her—as certain as she was of her own love for him. And now—it seemed impossible that a mere hour or two could so change the world.

She had to see Raven, to talk to him, to hear him tell her the truth—whatever the truth might be. She looked at Sarah, who eyed her expectantly.

"All right, I'll come to St. James with you."

"I'll help you pack," Sarah offered, starting toward the bedroom.

"No." Aurora stopped her as she would have gone into the bedroom. "There's no need to pack. I'll be coming back—with Raven."

Lifting her chin, Aurora left the cabin. Behind her, Sarah's smile was grim, sly. Aurora would not be coming back—not ever. By tonight, if all went according to plan, she would be aboard the grand yacht that had brought Graham Hughston to St.

James. By tonight, she would be on her way back to the life she never should have left.

Sarah cast a last look around the cabin before following Aurora to the little sailboat her brothers had provided after Sarah had advised them of the propitious change of plans. Soon, very soon, Aurora would be gone. Then Sarah would be back to her rightful place—in Raven's life, in his home, in his arms!

15

Throughout the trip from High Island to Beaver Island where the town of St. James lay curved around an almost circular harbor known as Paradise Bay, Aurora continued to hope that it was all no more than a cruel hoax. Raven wouldn't betray her—he wouldn't! He must love her as much as she loved him. Last night had been so wonderful, so beautiful; he had been so loving, so tender. It couldn't have all been merely an act. She wouldn't believe—couldn't believe that he had made love to her knowing all the while that it was their last night together—knowing that when the morning came he was going to sell her back into the silken bondage they called Society.

She clung to her hopes desperately, frantically, until Sarah guided the little boat through the mouth of the harbor. There, long, low, sleekly beautiful and blindingly white in the summer sunshine, the *Sea Mist* rode at anchor.

"Oh, God," she whispered. "It's true. It's true."

"That your boat?" Sarah asked, trying not to show any of the awe she felt at the sight of such a magnificent craft and the knowledge that it was used solely for pleasure.

"She belongs to my uncle," Aurora replied.

"Then that's where I'm supposed to take you."

Aurora frowned as Sarah steered the little boat alongside the yacht. "Here?" she asked. "But why not into town? Is Raven aboard the *Sea Mist*?"

"I don't know any more about it. All I know is that I was told to take you to the yacht."

In short order the two women found themselves standing on the polished teakwood deck. Eager for information, Aurora turned to a familiar face among the crewmen who met them.

"Hello, Geoffrey," she said, recognizing the young crewman she had spoken with on the night of the storm. "Where are Mr. Hughston and Raven?"

"Mr. Hughston went ashore, miss. I don't know anything about any Raven."

The yacht's captain stepped forward, valiantly hiding his pique that she had spoken to a lowly crewman before he could welcome her.

"Welcome back, Miss Jephson," he said pompously, the ends of his great walrus moustache quivering. "Allow me to say—"

"Where is Mr. Hughston, Captain Winston?"

The captain's brushy grey brows drew downward. "He went ashore to meet with someone, miss."

"And my uncle and aunt?"

"Mr. and Mrs. Jephson did not accompany Mr. Hughston, miss. Mr. Jephson is indisposed."

"Uncle Carlisle? Ill?" Aurora felt a twang of guilt, wondering if his illness was caused by worry over her.

"Influenza, miss. The result, so the doctors say, of standing in the rain while watching a horserace."

"I see." Relieved, Aurora went on: "Then there seems little reason for me to stay aboard. I will go and find Mr. Hughston."

The captain stepped in front of her blocking her way. "I'm sorry, miss. My orders are to keep you aboard once you get here."

Aurora drew herself up. "Are you saying I am forbidden to leave this vessel, captain?"

"Yes, miss. I'm afraid I am."

"And if I try to leave, are you prepared to forcibly restrain me?"

The captain looked away. "I regret to say I am."

Aurora's eyes flashed. "Very well then. I will stay aboard. But you may rest assured, captain, that Mr. Hughston will find his ears ringing when I get done with him!"

Turning on her heel, Aurora stormed off across the deck. Sarah, having been told to stay aboard until it was clear that Graham had delivered the money to her brother, followed.

They descended the stairs and Sarah found herself in the wide main corridor. Trailing Aurora, she could not help staring at the gold-framed oils hanging on the mahogany-paneled walls, the chairs of fine tufted leather, the rosewood tables with their marble tops, the beautiful carpet that seemed too fine to walk upon.

But even such luxury did not prepare her for the elegance of Aurora's stateroom. She stood in the doorway, stunned, as she gazed at the canopied bed standing in the center of an Aubusson carpet, the sparkling crystal chandelier hanging from the ornately plastered ceiling, the fireplace along whose mantel stood ornaments of porcelain and filigree that even to Sarah's untrained eyes bespoke antiquity and value beyond price.

"Miss!" The high-pitched squeal came from the open door of the cabin adjoining Aurora's own. "Oh, miss!"

As Sarah watched, bemused, a girl appeared dressed in grey with an apron and beribboned cap of delicate linen and fragile lace. She hurled herself across the room and into Aurora's arms.

"Bridey," Aurora murmured, hugging her maid tightly. "I've missed you."

The girl, her riot of red curls so like Aurora's own, held her mistress at arm's length. "You're alive! Praise be to God!"

"So it seems," Aurora replied. "Did you think the lake had swallowed me?"

"That I did. And I suffered so to think you had given yer life for the likes o' me!" She wiped a tear onto her apron. "I prayed for you. I prayed to God and all the saints to save you."

"Thank you, Bridey." Aurora swallowed the lump in her throat. How strange it seemed that her return could bring so much joy to her maid and so much pain to herself.

The maid shook her head. "But look at you! What's this yer wearin'? It's . . ." Her blue eyes widened. "Sweet Mother of God! Yer barefoot!"

Glancing down, Aurora saw her toes peeping from beneath her hem. "My shoes were ruined in the water. I've gotten used to going without them."

"Oh, Lord, you'll ruin yer feet! And—oh! No! Freckles!"

"Really, Bridey, it's nothing to be so concerned about."

The maid compressed her lips. "As you say, miss, but—" For the first time she noticed Sarah in the doorway.

"This is Miss Oates, Bridey. Miss Oates was kind enough to lend me some clothing. Sarah, my maid, Bridget. I call her Bridey."

Sarah murmured a greeting but she was too lost in astonishment to register much more than that this person's primary interest in life seemed to center around Aurora's appearance. Sarah had heard of lady's maids but had never before realized what they were.

Aurora sighed. "I suppose you're supposed to stay with me and make certain I don't escape?" Sarah's downcast eyes confirmed her suspicions. "Well, then, you may as well sit down."

"Escape?" Bridey echoed, bustling about the room even as she spoke collecting items of clothing for Aurora to change into. "What a notion! As if you'd want to go back into the wilderness now that you're back here where you belong."

"What a notion indeed," Aurora agreed wearily.

Before Sarah's bemused gaze, Aurora was whisked behind a coromandel screen and stripped of her simple blouse, skirt and plain cotton under-things. Standing like a child, she was re-dressed in the finest of her lace-frothed underthings, shoes of glove-soft leather, and a gown of creamy china silk whose short, puffed sleeves ended at the elbow in a double ruffle that matched those encircling the wide, round neckline and the hem of the bell-shaped skirt. A wide sash encircled her corseted waist, its ends streaming nearly to the floor. Appearing from behind the screen, she sat on a satin-covered stool while Bridey brushed out her flowing curls and then confined them in a knot on top of her head. Pearl earrings were slipped into her ears and a bracelet of pearls was clasped about her wrist.

Sarah found that she was holding her breath. Her blue eyes swept from the top of Aurora's head to her feet and back again. Thank God Raven had never seen Aurora this way, she thought. She'd always been beautiful, but now she looked like a princess from a fairy tale.

A knock on the cabin door startled them all. Sarah rose as the door opened and a tall, handsome man in an exquisitely tailored tweed suit appeared. His hair and moustache were a rich, cara-mel brown and he moved with a grace Sarah found fascinating. He seemed not to notice her as he entered the room—his eyes were too full of the beauty of Aurora.

"I never thought I'd see this day," he said softly, crossing the floor toward her as Bridey discreetly backed away. "You're more beautiful than I remembered, darling. I—" His brow furrowed. "Good Lord, are those freckles?"

Aurora had to smile. Her eyes went to Sarah's gaping face.

"Where I come from," she explained sarcastically, "freckles on a lady's nose are a hanging offense."

Graham turned and for the first time noticed Sarah. "Pardon me, I didn't even see you there."

"Sarah Oates," Aurora said, "this is Graham Hughston. Graham, Sarah befriended me during my stay here."

"Miss Oates," Graham said. He took Sarah's hand, and all she could think of was how soft his hand was, more like a woman's than a man's. "I owe you my heartfelt thanks."

Before Sarah could think of a word to say to the elegant, intimidating man before her, he had turned his attention back to Aurora.

"I've brought you a gift, my dear, to show you how delighted I am that you have been returned to your family, to me . . ." He laughed lightly. "To the living!"

Holding out his hand, he took the small, velvet case Bridey had retrieved from the dressing table. Inside, lying on a bed of purple velvet, lay a choker of pearls with a diamond clasp. Stepping behind Aurora, he placed it about her throat. Its twelve cool strands covered her throat from base to chin. Aurora stood still as a statue as he fastened the clasp, then stepped back to admire the effect.

"Thank you, Graham," she murmured. "It's lovely."

Encouraged, he stepped forward and, spanning her waist with his hands, bent to kiss her. Subtly, firmly, she averted her face, her eyes going to Sarah who watched the scene with silent awe.

The woman rose, suddenly self-conscious. "As long as everything is settled, I'll be leaving."

"I'll walk with you," Aurora offered quickly.

The two women mounted the stairs to the promenade deck and went to the railing, where Sarah was helped into the little boat that bobbed beside the yacht.

"Goodbye," Sarah called up to her.

"Goodbye," Aurora replied. Adding: "Tell Raven that—"

"Yes?"

Straightening, Aurora shook her head. "Nothing. Goodbye, Sarah."

Aurora stared after Sarah as she guided her little boat away from the yacht. She started nervously when Graham appeared beside her and draped a short, gold-embroidered blue velvet cape about her shoulders.

"You'll take a chill standing out here," he told her.

"Why did you go ashore to meet Raven?" she asked. "Why didn't you have him come aboard?"

Graham shrugged. "It was his request that we meet ashore. It was also his request that you be brought directly to the yacht."

"He didn't want to see me?"

The tremor in her voice bewildered Graham. This "Raven" character had been a thoroughly disreputable-looking man, hulking and dirty with a lascivious gleam in his small, dark eyes that had set Graham's teeth on edge. The thought of Aurora's having spent the better part of the past two months in the man's company made him want to retch. Now she seemed upset at being parted from him. It made no sense—none at all.

She turned her head, piqued by his silence. "Graham?" she prompted. "Didn't Raven want to see me? Didn't he give you any message for me at all?"

"No, darling, none. All he wanted was the money."

Closing her eyes, she recalled the night before on the bank of the pond with heartbreaking accuracy.

"All he wanted was the money," she murmured. "He'd already taken everything else."

"What was that?" Graham asked.

"Nothing. Nothing at all."

"Is there anyone you'd like to say goodbye to before we leave?" He couldn't imagine who there could be, but Aurora was an unusual girl and it wasn't impossible that she might have made some friends in this godforsaken place.

"No, no one." She sighed as a tear welled in the corner of her eyes, then slid slowly down her rose-tinged cheek. If Raven had forsaken her, then she had no one, nothing. Nothing mattered. She would go back to her world and take up her life where she had left off. But even if she might seem like the same girl on the outside, inside she would be lost, lonely, empty, the heart and soul torn out of her forever. Raven had betrayed her—betrayed her for the same thing everyone else seemed to want most from her—money. That one single fact would color her every waking moment for the rest of her life.

Choking back the bitter, aching sobs that welled in her chest, she slipped into Graham's arms.

"Take me home, Graham," she begged. "Please, just take me home."

Delighted, Graham gave the orders and the *Sea Mist* weighed anchor and slipped out of Paradise Bay as silently as it had come.

16

At peace with himself and his decision, Raven made his way back from the beauty and solitude of Garden Island. With a clear vision of his future, he was prepared to tell Aurora how much he loved her, how he wanted only to be with her. To prove his love, he was willing to leave the islands he loved and return with her to the turmoil and bustle of the city and the primpings and preenings of Society.

The closer he got to home, the more certain he was that his decision was the right one. By the time he drew his boat up onto the sand, he could not wait to see Aurora, to touch her, to love her and to tell her that her future was with him and his with her, wherever and however she would be happiest.

He broke into a run along the path that led from the shore to the cabin. His heart pounded with excitement, his blood raced through his veins. He could not bear another moment's passing before he told her what was in his heart.

And so his disappointment was as intense as his excitement had been when he burst into the cabin and found it empty, deserted.

"Aurora?" he called, somehow knowing all the while that she was not there.

He looked in the bedroom, the kitchen. He went outside and looked all around the clearing. Though he tried to assure himself that she was likely only walking in the forest or down at the pond bathing, there was an uneasiness in the back of his mind that told him something was terribly wrong.

Running silently, swiftly, like the most graceful of the forest's creatures, he went to the pond and then, following the stream, to the lake, hoping against hope that she might have gone there to fish as Matthew had taught her.

But she was nowhere to be found, and the nagging voice inside him whispered that he could search each and every one of the island's nearly six square miles and not find her.

Confused, concerned, he walked back to the cabin in the clearing. Inside, her belongings remained intact and so did his. If she'd left the island, she'd taken nothing but the clothes on her back. But how, when, why had she gone? Their last night together had been perfection. He had left her the note telling her that he loved her, asking her to wait for him. Why hadn't she?

Questions filled his mind, and a growing sense of unease filled his heart. She could not have left the island alone, for his was the only boat. Someone had taken her away. But who? And where had they taken her? He could not begin to imagine who she would willingly go with. There were only Sarah and Matthew, for she had met no one else. But he could not imagine her leaving the island with either of them and not leaving a message for him.

"Raven?"

At the sound of a woman's voice, Raven leapt to his feet. He whirled toward the voice, his hopes soaring.

Sarah smiled uncertainly. She tried hard to ignore the look of bitter disappointment that appeared on his handsome face when he saw that she was not Aurora.

"Where did you go?" she asked. "I was worried that you had—"

"Where is she?" he demanded. "Do you know?"

"You mean Aurora?"

"Of course I mean Aurora! She's not on the island. Someone took her away and I believe it had to be either you or Matthew. Was it you?"

Sarah avoided his gaze. It didn't really matter what she told him, she told herself. Aurora was so hurt, so bitter over what she saw as his betrayal of her that she was unlikely ever to try to communicate with him. The truth was safely buried.

"Well?" he prompted.

"Yes, it was me." She fell back a step as she saw the black rage flood into his face. "She asked me to, Raven! She wanted to go!"

"I don't believe you. I told her that I—" He paused, not wanting to reveal too much. "I asked her to wait for me," he amended. "Did she mention the note I left her?"

The note. The memory of the message of love
for Aurora touched a raw nerve inside Sarah. She
remembered how the pieces of that hateful note
had floated on the surface of the lake after she'd
torn it into a hundred pieces.

"She didn't say anything about a note," Sarah
told him honestly.

Raven ran a hand through his hair. "Where
did you take her?"

"To a boat—a yacht," Sarah corrected. "It was
anchored in Paradise Bay. They were expecting
her."

"A yacht? Whose?"

"She said it belonged to her uncle. There was a
man on board waiting for her."

"Her uncle?"

Sarah feigned ignorance. "I'm not certain who
he was. He seemed too young to be her uncle. His
name was Graham Hughston."

"Hughston." His mind awhirl, Raven sank into
a chair. Hughston had come for her. Someone else
must have seen the same newspaper article he had
seen. Someone must have told Hughston where to
find Aurora so they could collect the reward. But
how had Aurora learned of the Sea Mist's arrival?

"Did she say how she knew Hughston had
arrived in St. James?"

"She didn't say anything at all about it. I took
her to the yacht. I went on board with her."

"And Hughston was there?"

"No. I guess he was meeting with someone
ashore. He came later."

"What did he say? Was she happy to see him?"

Sarah shrugged. "I don't know. He gave her a
necklace. Oh, Raven! It was so beautiful! Pearls

and diamonds. A maid dressed her in a white silk gown and put up her hair. She looked like a princess!"

"I imagine she did," Raven murmured.

"Her room in the yacht was as big as this cabin! It was all white and gold with a fireplace and—"

"What happened with Hughston?"

"I don't know. I left right after he gave her the necklace. He wanted to kiss her, but she didn't want him to in front of me. So I left. She walked with me up to the deck. As I was sailing away, I looked back and saw Mr. Hughston come up behind her and wrap a cape around her shoulders." She sighed. "They looked so grand together. Like a picture in the society papers."

"Almost as if they were made for one another," Raven muttered.

"Yes, that's right."

Raven passed a hand over his eyes. She had left him. She had returned to her world of yachts and gowns and jewels. She had returned to her fiancé.

"Was there something you wanted?" he asked Sarah impatiently.

"Not really. I was just worried because you were gone and—"

"I'd rather be left alone just now, Sarah. I'll see you soon."

There was nothing more to be said. Sarah had learned from long experience that there was no use in trying to dissuade Raven once he'd made up his mind. At the same time, she knew that once his heart was hardened against someone, it never softened. His emotions, his passions, ran deeply and wounds healed slowly. It would be a long time before he would be willing to even speak Aurora's name; it was doubtful that he would ever forgive her.

Left alone in the cabin, Raven rose and walked into the bedroom. Aurora's clothes lay strewn about the room. The sheet was twisted and tangled. They had lain together in that bed on their last night together. They had lain in one another's arms and he had thought that their hearts, their souls, were one just as their bodies had been. Obviously, he had been wrong.

The creamy pile of her petticoat lay on the floor. He picked it up. The crumpled cotton was stained with the blood he had washed from her thighs after their lovemaking on the bank of the pond. Had she known, even then, that Graham Hughston was on his way to retrieve her? Had she known even at that moment that she was going to leave him? And if she had, why had she permitted him to make love to her? She must have known the scandal, the disgrace that befell any young debutante upon her fall from the hallowed pedestal of virginity. Did she think that her fortune would cushion her from the slander, the gossip? Was Graham Hughston so in love with her—or so avaricious—that he would accept a bride who was less than pure? Or was she, deep inside, like those other grand society ladies who had willingly, even eagerly, taken him to their beds in his youth because the notion of bedding a man in whose veins ran the blood of a "savage" excited them?

With a muttered oath, Raven threw the petticoat across the room. Damn her! Damn her to hell!

he raged inside, storming out of the room and out of the cabin. He ran into the forest, but for once he had no eyes for the beauty of his beloved island. He ran on and on until he was surrounded by the verdant beauty that now failed to move him. He ran on until he reached the western bluff that rose two hundred and forty feet above the rolling blue lake.

Standing on the bluff, staring out at the sparkling blue water that seemed to stretch away to the ends of the earth, Raven cursed Aurora. He hated her, he loved her. He wept.

Aboard the *Sea Mist*, Aurora was being dressed for the second time that day. Bridey, standing behind her, fussed with the satin bows that surmounted the shoulder straps of her sleeveless gown of pale blue spotted tulle.

"I had forgotten all the dressing," Aurora mused. "Dress for morning, for tea, for dinner, for evening if there's a ball or the theater. Once it seemed so natural. Now it just seems a ridiculous waste of time."

"You'll get used to it again," Bridey predicted.

"I suppose I will," Aurora admitted, taking the long suede gloves and tasseled feather fan Bridey held out to her. "What choice will I have?"

Not wanting an answer, Aurora swept out of the room, leaving her maid to stare after her and wonder why her mistress should seem so melancholy. After all, hadn't she been rescued from the wilderness? Wasn't she going back to the glitter and grandeur of the world in which she truly belonged? She should be happy. Shouldn't she?

Halfway down the corridor, Aurora met Graham. As ever, he was faultlessly elegant in his black and white evening attire. Once she had admired it. Now his very perfection irritated her. For the first time she questioned the priorities that ruled her life as it had that of her parents and of everyone she had known in her life before Raven.

"You look beautiful, darling," Graham murmured, lifting her gloved fingers to his lips.

Aurora forced her lips into a wan ghost of a smile. Laying her hand in the crook of his arm, she accompanied him into the dining room, where the two of them sat at opposite ends of a table that could seat twenty.

After dinner, when Aurora would have returned to her stateroom, Graham took a gentle but firm hold on her elbow.

"Walk with me on the deck for a while," he asked.

"I'm very tired," she told him. "All I truly want is to go to sleep."

"Just for a little while," he insisted. "You'll sleep better if you get a little exercise before retiring."

Knowing it was useless to argue, she nodded wearily. "All right, but only for a bit."

Summoning Bridey, Graham called for an evening wrap for Aurora and then the two of them left the dining room and strolled slowly around the promenade deck.

Alone in the moonlight, Graham tried to take her into his arms. He lowered his face toward hers, but Aurora turned away, stepping out of his embrace.

"Tell me about your life on the island, Auro-ra," he asked, more than a little curious to know what had happened to her there.

She shook her head. "I can't talk about it. Please, don't ask me to."

"I understand. Perhaps in time—"

"No. Never. Don't ask me about it again."

Graham's brown brows drew together. "Was it so terrible?"

Aurora closed her eyes as the ache of her broken heart assailed her. When she opened them, she gazed up at the glowing moon. Was Raven even then gazing at that same moon? Did he think of her? Did he . . . No! She would not think of him! She would not!

Graham took her silence as a refusal to discuss the subject. Tactfully he changed the direction of their conversation.

"I don't think we should wait too long before we officially announce our engagement."

"Engagement?" Aurora gaped at him. "What engagement? I know what it said in the papers— Raven showed me the article in the *Tribune*. But we are not engaged, Graham, regardless of what you or Aunt Electra told the reporters. You have not proposed and I have not accepted."

"Then I will propose now. Aurora, will you marry me?"

She turned toward the railing, averting her face to hide her emotions. "No," she whispered.

"No? Just like that?"

"Just like that."

A muscle twitched in Graham's cheek. Gazing out at the night-black lake, he twisted the ends of his moustache.

"After I offered the reward?" he said tightly. "After I came all this way to rescue you?"

"I didn't ask you to," she retorted. "And you'll pardon me if I doubt that the twenty-five thousand dollars came out of your pocket."

"I don't believe this," he muttered. "You sound as if you'd rather have remained on that godforsaken island with that filthy, savage—"

"That is enough! Don't ever speak to me of the island—or of Raven—again!"

Head held high, Aurora stormed off the deck and down to her cabin, where she stonily allowed Bridey to undress her and prepare her for bed. It was not until she was tucked into her grand, canopied bed and Bridey had blown out the lamps and retired to her own room that Aurora's icy façade crumbled and all the pain, all the heartbreak, all the disappointment that filled her heart found vent in the sobs and the hot, bitter tears that she smothered in the softness of her satin-covered pillows.

17

If Aurora had expected to slip unnoticed into Chicago, she was quickly disillusioned. Reporters swarmed over the docks, somehow knowing when the *Sea Mist* would dock. They followed the carriage that took Aurora and Graham to the Jephsons' Lake Shore Drive mansion. They crowded against the iron gates that were opened only long enough for the carriage to pass between and then were quickly closed again and locked against further intrusions into Aurora's privacy.

As she had after her parents' deaths, Aurora withdrew behind the elegant walls of her aunt's and uncle's mansion where the pryings of the reporters pandering to the purient interests of the public could not reach her.

Day after day she tried to lose herself in the depths of the forty-five-room mansion. She visited her uncle, still bedridden, convalescing from a near-fatal bout of influenza. She sat in the library reading and re-reading some of the rare and priceless first editions her uncle collected as investments. She wandered along the picture gallery so reminiscent of the one her father had built in his New York mansion. Most of all, she tried to avoid her aunt, who had taken up where she'd left off pressuring her to marry Graham Hughston.

"Aurora," Electra said one day when she had managed to corner her niece in the Turkish parlor where the dark stained-glass windows and ancient Oriental furnishings made the chamber seem like nothing so much as a refuge of some sultan's favorite kadin. "I must insist you do not treat Graham so cavalierly. You are hurting his feelings by being so distant."

"It would take a harpoon to pierce Graham Hughston's hide," Aurora muttered.

"What was that?" Electra demanded.

Sighing, Aurora set an ornate bronze brazier back onto a low table inlaid with mother-of-pearl.

"I'm sorry, Aunt Electra. I don't wish to marry anyone. It is no reflection on Graham, I—"

"I should hope not! You could do a great deal worse, you know."

"I'm sure that's true, but—"

"You should be grateful that Graham traveled three hundred miles—each way!—simply to bring you home to us."

"I am grateful, Aunt Electra. But gratitude is hardly a reason to marry."

"Then perhaps I can give you a better reason! It may be that Graham is your last hope."

Aurora laughed. "Come now, Aunt. I hope I'm not such a pathetic case that no one will be willing to make me his wife. Without meaning to sound conceited, I am passably attractive. If nothing else, my fortune seems eminently enticing to suitors."

"There are other considerations, my dear."

"Considerations the size of my inheritance will not overcome?" Aurora widened her eyes. "I thought fortune solved everything."

"A woman's reputation is more important than her fortune. Any man suitable to be your husband will have a fortune of his own. While your inheritance would naturally be a great attraction, if you are perceived as a woman of loose moral character—"

"Loose moral character!" Aurora rose from the tapestry-covered divan. "What can you mean!"

Smug, Electra drew herself up self-righteously. "Think about it, my dear. You spent two months on your own in a remote wilderness. No one outside the family need know you were alone with a man, but I'm sure there are those who wonder what happened to you there."

"Rumor is not proof, Aunt. People can speculate all they want, but they will do that no matter what the circumstances. People in New York are always looking for fresh scandal. I doubt it's any different here in Chicago."

"Everything you say is true," Electra allowed. "But when coupled with the rest of it—"

"The rest of it? What are you talking about?"

"Come now, my dear. You did spend several days alone on a yacht with Graham."

"Of course I did! But that was obviously at your request, because it was you who dispatched Graham to—" Aurora stopped as the truth suddenly dawned upon her. "You! You deliberately sent

Graham alone to bring me home so that I would be compromised!"

"Don't be ridiculous. Your uncle was sick. I had to be here—"

"Uncle Carlisle was attended by a battery of doctors and nurses. He has told me himself that you scarcely visited him at all during the worst of his illness."

"I didn't want to risk catching his influenza and—"

"Hah! You planned it all! You planned for me to be compromised by Graham so that I would have to marry him. It wasn't bad enough that you told the reporters that Graham is my fiancé, you set out to see that it became a reality."

"Aurora! You're becoming overwrought. Perhaps you should see one of your uncle's doctors when they come to examine him."

"I don't need to see a doctor. What I need is a little less scheming! For God's sake! From the moment you came to New York after my parents died, you've done nothing but push me to marry your nephew. I want it to stop! All you are doing is making me loathe the very sight of Graham."

Electra's chins quivered. "Oh! How can you say such things to me after all I've done for you! You are a hateful, ungrateful girl! Do as you please! Ruin yourself, for all I care! I hope your money is a comfort to you when you are an old maid."

Aurora sighed. "I hardly think I have to worry about that. After all, there is always Graham, isn't there?"

The estrangement between Aurora and her aunt did nothing to lessen the tension that reigned within the white marble walls of the Jephsons' mansion.

As the days dragged by, Aurora found her thoughts returning more and more to the green forests and blue waters of the islands to the north. Inevitably, Raven figured in her broodings. His face appeared in her mind's eye with agonizing regularity. It was that torment that drove her out of the mansion. More than her fear of pursuit by dogged reporters, she hated the thought of remaining inside, haunted by her memories and heartache. She visited the museums, the galleries, the modistes, the milliners, but returned home each day no less restless and weary than she had been when she left.

The routine was broken at last when she returned home from an outing to Jackson Park with Bridey. As she was admitted into the marble foyer whose soaring stained-glass dome threw jewel-colored patterns down onto the white marble walls and floor, she was met by Electra in a flushed and obviously overexcited state.

"Aurora, here you are at last! Hurry upstairs. You, too, Bridget. Don't dawdle!"

"What is this?" Aurora demanded as she and her maid were herded up the wide curving staircase. "What's happened?"

"You have a visitor!" Electra followed Aurora and Bridey into Aurora's room, where a fresh ensemble was laid out on the gold brocade chaise. "Now hurry and change. I'll be back in a moment."

"Aunt Electra—"

"Hurry!"

Aurora frowned, puzzled, as Bridey began unhooking the back of her gown. "Now what is she up to?" she wondered aloud. "A visitor? I don't know anyone in Chicago except Aunt Electra and Uncle Carlisle and Graham. What kind of visitor could I have?"

Quickly, efficiently, she was stripped to her camisole, corset and drawers, then re-dressed in a lacy petticoat and corset cover threaded with cherry red ribbons. She stopped Bridey as the maid took up the gown from the chaise.

"Oh, Bridey, she can't truly mean for me to wear that! I wore that dress two years ago when I was graduated from Miss Vandervelt's Academy in New York. It's much too young."

Before Bridey could comment, the door opened and Electra swept in.

"Aurora, aren't you dressed yet? Do hurry!"

"Aunt Electra, this dress is two years old. It's far too childish—"

"No, my dear, it isn't. Put it on her, Bridget."

Over Aurora's muffled protests, the dress of creamy Swiss muslin was slipped over her head. The sleeves were puffed to the elbow, then long cuffs reached her wrists where they ended in ruffles. The collar was high, standing about her throat, and the bodice was pleated to conceal as much as reveal the curves of her bosom. From the tightly sashed waist, the skirt fell to a demurely ruffled hem.

"Now brush out her hair, Bridget, and tie it loosely with a ribbon."

"I'm not to wear it up?" Aurora questioned.

"No. Now listen to me, Aurora. Please."

When Bridey was finished, Aurora stepped before the gilt-framed pier glass. A schoolgirl gazed back at her.

"I don't understand this at all," she told her aunt.

"Come along and listen. I'll explain it on the way down."

As they passed along the corridor, Electra bent her head toward her niece's.

"There is a gentleman downstairs. He arrived nearly an hour ago specifically asking to meet you. I told him you were out, but he insisted on waiting. He said he has seen your photograph in the newspaper. I do believe he is smitten."

"Oh, Lord, you're matchmaking again! Aunt Electra!"

"Well? What's wrong with meeting him? What could it hurt?"

"Never tell me you've given up on a match with Graham?"

"Of course not. But this gentleman is rather advanced in years. If he married a young girl, she could easily be expected to outlive him. Then, a rich young woman could become a richer young widow. After her mourning she could, of course, marry a younger—"

"Aunt Electra!" Aurora stopped at the head of the stairs and stared at her aunt. "That's what all this is about, isn't it?" With a sweep of her hand, she indicated the girlish gown and schoolgirl coiffure. "You think I'll appeal more to this old gentleman if I look younger!"

"Well? Older men like younger girls. Don't blame me! It's the nature of the beast."

"Well, I think it's deplorable! You're already planning for me to put this old man in an early grave and then, with my money and whatever he leaves me, I'll make a more desirable bride for Graham!"

"Oh, Aurora, you do carry on." Electra laughed, more nervously than dismissively.

Together they descended the stairs. Outside the closed doors of the Louis XV drawing room, Electra straightened the ruffles at Aurora's wrists and smoothed the cascading curls of her hair.

"You're being ridiculous," Aurora told her. "What if marriage isn't at all what he has in mind?"

"What else could it be? He's a wealthy man, you're a beautiful girl of breeding and family. He could suggest nothing less and still be deemed a gentleman. Now come along."

Signaling a footman, Electra took Aurora's elbow and led her into a room decorated in royal blue and gold, across whose ceiling goddesses and cherubim disported themselves in a credible imitation of the paintings of François Boucher.

"Good afternoon, sir," Electra purred as the gentleman seated in the gilt and tapestry armchair rose to his feet. "As you can see, my niece has at last returned."

Bemused, Aurora smiled as the tall, distinguished, white-haired gentleman whose youthful looks belied his sixty years came forward and bent to kiss her hand.

"How do you do, my dear," he said, his piercing sky-blue eyes captivating her gaze. "My name is Marcus Ravenswood."

18

"Mr. Ravenswood, won't you sit down?" Aurora invited. "Please forgive me for keeping you waiting."

He waved a dismissing hand. "Not at all, my dear. You must forgive me for intruding this way, uninvited and without previous introduction."

"Let me call for some tea," Electra offered, hovering behind Aurora's chair. "Some cakes, perhaps?"

"Nothing, thank you, madam," he said coolly.

Subdued, Electra took a chair in an unobtrusive corner of the room. It was, of course, out of the question for Aurora to be left alone with the elderly gentleman, but it was clear that Marcus Ravenswood had no interest in a cozy chat with Electra Jephson.

Aurora compressed her lips, recognizing Electra's piqued expression. She could not but admire Mr. Ravenswood's ability to put her aunt in her place. He was, for all that gossip painted him an eccentric and a recluse, a forceful and, for his age, attractive man. His morning coat, striped trousers and tall silk hat were the very latest in gentlemen's fashions. It was clear that, even if he did not move in society, he kept up with its trends.

His eyes—so blue, she thought, like Raven's, then forced the troubling thought from her mind—examined her discreetly. With one gloved hand he absently stroked his full white moustache.

"My dear," he said at last, "let me get to the reason for my visit. Like everyone else, I have read the newspaper accounts of your recent stay in the islands to the north." He saw the quick flush that rose into her cheeks and the concealing of her eyes beneath the lowered fans of her lashes. "Oh, dear, I hope I'm not distressing you too badly. I thought, since an interval of several weeks had elapsed since your return—"

"It's quite all right," she assured him, smiling faintly. "Please, go on."

"Well, in any case, I have a son whom I have neither seen nor heard from in many years. When last I heard, he was living in the islands. I have written to him many times—there has been no reply. I thought perhaps . . . that is, I hoped that you might have come across him."

"I met very few people during my stay, sir," Aurora replied, sorry to disappoint him.

"I see. Perhaps you heard of him? His name is Charles."

Aurora shook her head, feeling sorry that she could not offer this kind gentleman any news of his son.

171

"I am sorry. I neither heard of nor met anyone at all named Charles, let alone a Charles Ravenswood."

The faint light of hope died in his eyes. "I see. Well . . . There wouldn't be anyone in the islands with whom you expect to be corresponding, would there? Someone you befriended, perhaps? Someone you could ask?"

"No one. I'm so sorry. There's no one at all."

"Well, then—" Rising, he took up his hat and walking stick. "I shan't trouble you any more. Miss Jephson? Delightful meeting you. Good day, Mrs. Jephson. Thank you so much."

Electra walked with him to the door and saw him out to the porte cochere where his carriage waited. She returned to find Aurora halfway up the staircase.

"I assume it's all right if I put my grown-up clothes back on now?" Aurora asked archly.

"The nerve of that man!" Electra groused, apparently not having heard Aurora's question. "Leading me to think he was courting you! Leading me to think his intentions were—"

Ignoring her aunt, Aurora climbed the stairs and returned to her room where Bridey dressed her in an afternoon gown of India silk.

"Bridey," she said as she sat at her dressing table. "Have you ever heard anything about Marcus Ravenswood?"

Bridey paused to take the hairpins out of her mouth. "No, I don't think he gets around much. Does he?"

"I don't know. I heard he was a recluse—Graham pointed out his home to me while we were out riding. Some people think he's mad, Graham

172

said. But he seemed quite an elegant and rational gentleman just now."

"Is he your beau, miss?"

Aurora laughed. "Not at all. That was all in Aunt Electra's imagination. He wanted to know if I'd met his son in the islands."

"His son?" Bridey pinned a silk rosette in Aurora's upswept hair. "How'd he come to have a son, then?"

"The same way everyone else does, I expect," Aurora said teasingly.

Bridey's cheeks flamed. "Oh, miss! That's not what I meant and you know it! But while you were downstairs, yer aunt's maid, Pelton, told me that Mr. Ravenswood's never been married. 'An old bachelor,' that's what she called him. She said that everybody's curious about him 'cause 'old scandals die hard.'"

"Old scandals? Did she say what the scandal was?"

"No, miss. I asked her, but she said it wasn't for my young ears." An impish light lit up her pretty, round face. "Sounds good, don't it?"

"Bridey! Shame on you!" Aurora chided, smiling. She gazed at her own reflection in the mirror for a long, silent moment, then said: "Maybe I'll ask Uncle Carlisle about it."

Laughing, she rose and left the room intending to seek out her uncle and coax the tale of Marcus Ravenswood's indiscretion out of him. But as she walked along the corridor, she saw her uncle's doctors being let into his room by Electra.

There seemed little she could do just then. The battery of doctors closeted themselves with her uncle for hours every afternoon. They seemed determined to draw out his recovery as long as possible. She walked on toward the stairs.

"This foyer always reminds me of Grand Central Terminal," a voice said from the foot of the stairs.

Aurora looked down and found Graham smiling up at her. "Uncle Carlisle seems perfectly all right to me," she told him as she descended the stairs. "But the doctors refuse to let him out of bed. I'm beginning to suspect that they're all being paid by the hour rather than the case."

She showed him into a parlor off the foyer and busied herself with the cascading fronds of a massive Boston fern while he sat on the settee near the stained-glass window.

"I stopped by this morning," he told her. "I was going to invite you for a drive."

"I went walking in Jackson Park with Bridey," she revealed. A new thought dawned in her head. "Graham? What do you know about Marcus Ravenswood?"

"Marcus Ravenswood? Now what makes you ask about him?"

"He was here not more than an hour ago. Aunt Electra seemed to think he was setting his cap for me."

"That's ludicrous!"

"Calm yourself, Graham," she soothed. "He wasn't doing anything of the kind. He wanted to ask if I knew anything about his son."

"Good Lord!"

"Then you do know about his son? Bridey said that Pelton told her Ravenswood has never been married."

"That's right. He hasn't."

"Then where does this son fit in?"

Frowning, Graham toyed with the brim of his bowler as he balanced it on his knee. "I hardly think Aunt Electra would approve of my regaling you with gossip of this nature, Aurora."

She snipped at a frond with her fingers. "Oh, bother Aunt Electra!"

"Aurora!"

Crossing the room, she sat beside him on the settee. Leaning close, she toyed with his silk cravat. "Please, Graham. What can it hurt? I want to know. It's not fair of you not to tell me."

Graham swallowed hard. This was a side of Aurora he had not seen. She was using feminine wiles on him he didn't even know she possessed. And they were working, he realized as she leaned against him, the fullness of her bosom pressed against his arm, and breathed in his ear:

"Please, Graham?"

"I shouldn't," he wavered. "Really, it's not the sort of thing a gentleman—"

"Have I asked you to be a gentleman?" she purred.

"Even so—"

"Oh, never mind! You ask me to marry you! How can you expect me to want a husband who won't even tell me one little story?"

She rose and started from the room, and Graham, wanting to keep her there all to himself while Electra was busy upstairs, said:

"All right, I'll tell you."

Smiling sweetly, Aurora returned to his side.

"Now, all I know are the stories I've heard, Aurora. I've never met Ravenswood myself. Few people have. It all happened years ago when

Ravenswood was a young man. He was traveling—
on the last leg of his Grand Tour, apparently—and
stopped on Beaver Island. There he met a woman
and fell in love. He wanted to marry her, but his
family, who were steel tycoons in Pittsburgh, dis-
approved. He persisted in his intentions, and his
family threatened to disinherit him. Reluctantly,
he agreed not to marry her, but he was estranged
from his parents for the rest of their lives. The
woman, he learned, had borne him a son."

"And he has searched for the son all these
years?" Aurora asked.

"Oh, no. He found the boy. In fact, after his
parents were both dead, he tried to convince the
woman to bring the boy and go to Pittsburgh where
he lived at that time. Whether he intended to
marry her or not, I don't know. If he did, she must
have refused. But she sent the boy to Pittsburgh to
be educated. Ravenswood legitimized him, gave
him his name, made him his heir. He sent him to
the best schools, introduced him into the right
circles. Then, suddenly, when the boy had grown
into a young man, he left. Rumor said that he
returned to the islands. Ravenswood, so they say,
was brokenhearted. After that, he sold his steel
business and came to Chicago, where he became a
recluse."

Aurora sighed. "How romantic! He seemed
like a wonderful man. He was elegant, charming,
urbane. He had beautiful eyes. They reminded me
of—" She stopped, frowning. "Well, they reminded me of someone else's eyes. So he's remained true to his lost love all these years. Tell me,
though, why were his parents so opposed to the

girl? I suppose she wasn't an heiress or of the correct pedigree?"

"More than that, I'm afraid," Graham replied. "She was a full-blooded Indian squaw."

"An Indian? That's extraordinary. He fell in love with an—"

Aurora caught her breath. The pieces suddenly fell into place, leaving her to wonder at her own stupidity. It was so clear—so crystal clear! The beautiful furnishings of Raven's cabin, the portrait of the lovely Indian woman, the piercing, sky-blue eyes, Matthew's telling her that Raven's father was not an Indian, that he was named to honor his father. His father—Marcus Ravenswood—Raven!

"Oh, my God!" she breathed.

"What is it, Aurora?" Graham touched her cheek. "You're pale as a ghost and you're trembling."

"Nothing," she whispered, rising. She pressed a shaking hand to her lips. "Nothing. Please, excuse me, Graham. I must go."

"Go?" He rose, brow furrowed in confusion. "But, Aurora, I thought if I told you the story, you would agree to go riding with me. I have a new carriage and—"

"I will. I'd love to," she told him hurriedly, even as she backed out of the room. "But not just now. I can't just now, Graham. I have—suddenly I have an appalling headache. Please, you must excuse me."

"I'll get Aunt Electra. Perhaps one of Uncle Carlisle's doctors can—"

"No! Don't do that. It's not necessary. Truly, I have to go—"

Without waiting for any further arguments, Aurora swept from the room and up the stairs. She needed to be alone to digest this information. What it would mean to her she didn't know; what she would or should do about it she had no idea. All she knew was that she had to think about it, try to make some sense of it, and decide what to do.

19

For days following Marcus Ravenswood's visit, Aurora brooded, pondering what course of action she should follow, wondering if she should tell the elegant gentleman that his son was alive and well or simply keep her silence, assuming that if Raven wanted to contact his father he would.

She took no one into her confidence saving Bridey who, she could see, was becoming too concerned over the reason for her restless moodiness.

"I don't know what to do," she said for the thousandth time as they strolled in the walled garden behind the mansion.

"I think you should go and tell him," Bridey said. "After all, he is the man's father and he must care to be so concerned."

"But why wouldn't Raven answer his letters?

Perhaps he'd as soon never hear from his father again."

"Then he's a wretched man! To the devil with him!"

"Yes!" Aurora agreed fiercely. "He is a wretched man! Mr. Ravenswood is better off without him! It would only hurt him to know what kind of man his son has turned out to be."

"Then again," Bridey ventured, "he must be willin' to risk gettin' hurt, else he wouldn't be tryin' so hard to find his son."

Aurora sighed. "You're no help, Bridey, do you know that?"

The maid shrugged. "I'm only tryin' to help you see both sides of the question."

"I see both sides of the question. But I don't know the answer to either side." She sank onto a wrought-iron bench. "After what Raven did, I don't care to do anything for him. On the other hand, Mr. Ravenswood seems a charming, kind man and he is the one who asked for the information. I suppose it wouldn't hurt to give it to him. He can do as he pleases with it."

"That's true," Bridey allowed.

"I'll do it! Now, the second question is how am I going to get to him? He's a recluse. I'd have to go to his home and try to get someone to let me in."

"Pelton told me he lives right down the road."

"I know. Graham pointed out his house to me. But if I go to the carriage house and ask for a carriage, there are bound to be questions asked. I don't want Aunt Electra knowing about it. I can't even ask for a horse. I could walk, but it would take a long time."

The two women sat side by side, turning the

problem over in their minds. At last Aurora snapped her fingers.

"I have it! The bicycle!"

"Bicycle?"

"You remember. It's in the storage room at the back of the stable. I think Aunt Electra said it used to belong to a parlor maid who rode it home to visit her mother on her afternoons off. Graham has a bicycle and he said we could go riding sometime. You remember? I had a bicycling costume made."

"I remember that. Filthy thing!"

"Oh, Bridey, it's not filthy. The dressmaker promised me it's all the rage in Paris."

"Well, we all know what kind of women they've got there, now don't we?"

"Parisiennes are some of the most elegant women in the world. And the most fashionable." Aurora clapped her hands. "I'll do it! It's perfect!"

That afternoon, while Carlisle Jephson suffered the attentions of his regiment of doctors and Electra Jephson met with her battery of dressmakers, Aurora donned the bicycling costume that had so scandalized her maid.

Of emerald green velveteen, it consisted of a waist-length jacket left open over a double-breasted vest of oyster-colored silk. The full cravat of oyster-colored chiffon tied about the neck then draped in rippling ruffles over the front. It made a pretty picture with the little befeathered bonnet that perched high on her upswept red curls. But what shocked Bridget were the full Turkish trousers that bloused over gaiters fastened with pearl buttons to the knee.

"I like it very much," Aurora decided, feeling

strange in the trousers that were so different from
her long skirts and swaying petticoats.

"You'll be lucky if they don't arrest you!"
Bridey chided. "Showin' yer legs like a shameless
hus—"

"Careful," Aurora cautioned. "It is fashionable."

Lips compressed, disapproving frown painted
across her pert face, Bridey followed Aurora down
to the storage room, where they extracted the
bicycle and took it out into the long, curving drive
to practice. After a few near spills, Aurora felt
confident enough to leave. Signaling the man at the
gates to let her out, she ventured out onto the edge
of the road, then steered for the home of Marcus
Ravenswood.

The mansion, long and narrow, rising four
stories to a mansard roof, reminded Aurora more
than any other she'd seen in Chicago of the
mansions that lined Fifth Avenue in New York. It
was grand, imposing, forbidding. The long years of
Marcus Ravenswood's self-imposed seclusion
seemed to have impressed themselves on the mansion, lending it an air of melancholy neglect for all
that it was well cared for. Though the lawns and
hedges were carefully manicured and the long,
winding walks neatly swept, it seemed to be waiting, dozing in the summer sun, slumbering until it
was awakened, brought alive once more.

Aurora stumbled to a stop near the tightly
closed gates. Stepping off the bicycle, she leaned it
against the brick wall and went to yank at the bell
chain hanging beside the gate.

It seemed forever before someone answered
her summons. An old man appeared in the open

door of the carriage house. He motioned her away, apparently thinking her merely a nosy passerby. She yanked again and, when he reappeared, waved for him to come to her.

Slowly, almost grudgingly, he made his way down the long drive to the gates. His eyes, behind steel-rimmed spectacles, ran quickly, curiously, over her costume before returning to her face.

"I must see Mr. Ravenswood," she told him. "I—"

"Mr. Ravenswood don't see nobody," he told her. "Now get back on that contraption of yours and get out of here."

"Wait!" she cried as the man turned to leave. "It's very important. Please, tell him—"

"I said, he don't see no one. Now—"

"My good man," Aurora interrupted, her tones icy with disdain and hauteur. "I insist you tell Mr. Ravenswood I wish to see him. I have important information for him. Now, please tell Mr. Ravenswood that Miss Aurora Jephson is here to see him."

The man eyed Aurora curiously. Marcus Ravenswood's excursion to the Jephson mansion had caused no little comment belowstairs in the Ravenswood household. The gossip and speculation had reached the carriage house where the grooms and coachmen discussed it over their dinners with as much gusto as the parlor maids and kitchen staff did in the servants' hall.

"Miss Aurora Jephson?" he repeated.

"That is correct."

He unlocked the gate and let her inside. Once the gate was securely fastened behind her, he took her bicycle.

"I'll take that for you, miss," he offered. "Just go on to the door and tell the butler who you are."

Thanking him, Aurora made her way up the winding path to the twelve-foot-high front door. She twisted the brass doorbell and waited for the butler to appear.

When at last he appeared, she was startled by his appearance. He couldn't have been more than forty. She had somehow expected all the servants in this quiet household to be ancient, if not doddering, relics of Marcus Ravenswood's more sociable youth.

"May I help you, miss?" the butler asked, wondering how the devil this outlandishly dressed young woman had managed to get past the gates.

"My name is Aurora Jephson. I would like to speak with Mr. Ravenswood."

Bowing, the butler opened the door wider. "If you will come this way."

Aurora passed him and stepped through the vestibule and into the main hall where the air was rich with the scents of lemon and beeswax polish that made the honey-colored paneling glow with a rich golden sheen. The staircase rose, twisting around a landing overlooked by a magnificent stained-glass window. Across the hall, a fireplace yawned behind its ornate brass screen. Everywhere, it seemed, in the main hall and in the chambers she glimpsed through adjoining doorways, potted palms and spreading ferns nodded in the air currents moving through the house. But what touched her most was the silence. It seemed that if the lowliest kitchen maid had sneezed in the scullery below, Aurora could have heard it.

A door closed somewhere above and footsteps

moved along an upper corridor. She heard them descending a staircase, though apparently not the one that rose from the main hall.

"Miss Jephson?" a low, masculine voice said. "My, don't you look—fashionable."

Turning, she found Marcus Ravenswood approaching through a twenty-foot-high reception room to the right of the main hall.

"Mr. Ravenswood. Now it is my turn to ask you to excuse me for appearing unannounced and uninvited."

"On the contrary. I am pleased you ventured here, alone. I must say, without meaning to offend, that I find your aunt a trifle tiring. I am surprised, however, that she allowed you to come calling sans chaperone."

Aurora blushed. "She doesn't know I've come. If she did, I'm sure I'd get a lecture on the dangers of being compromised."

Marcus chuckled. "If anyone were to accuse me of compromising so young and lovely a woman as yourself, my dear, I should be very pleased indeed."

In spite of herself, Aurora laughed. She found that she genuinely liked this man, Raven's father. In his azure eyes she saw something of Raven. For all that Raven claimed to be wholly of his mother's people, the Ojibway, the legacy of Marcus Ravenswood was clearly a part of him.

The butler who had admitted Aurora and summoned Marcus hovered in the doorway, awaiting instructions.

Marcus's blue eyes glittered as he offered Aurora his arm.

"I should like to invite you into the library

where you might find some things of considerable interest, my dear, but it is upstairs and I fear that would give poor Dawkins quite a turn. He's so damnably proper. English, you know."

"Hawkins, sir," the butler corrected.

"Who was talking to you?" Ravenswood demanded. "Go find something to do."

Offended, the butler turned and stalked off down the corridor wishing yet again he had never left the employ of the British embassy in Washington.

Smiling mischievously, Marcus led Aurora into a parlor nearly thirty-five-feet square whose twin bay windows overlooked a gazebo set in the center of an artfully wild garden plot at the end of the mansion.

The parlor, walled in rosewood inlaid with a delicate floral pattern of mother-of-pearl, was hung with gold brocade. At Ravenswood's invitation, Aurora seated herself on an ornately carved settee, part of an exquisite Belter parlor suite.

"May I offer you anything, my dear?" Marcus asked. "Lemonade, perhaps? You must be thirsty. Surely you didn't walk here from your aunt and uncle's home?"

"I rode a bicycle," she replied.

"Ah, so that explains—" He glanced pointedly at her trousers. "In any case . . . the lemonade?"

"Thank you. That would be nice."

Pressing the bell, Marcus summoned the butler, Hawkins, from wherever he had gone to nurse his snit.

"Bring up some lemonade," he ordered.

"I shall tell cook to make some," the butler replied.

"Make some? Do you mean to tell me, man, there's nothing in the house prepared for guests?"

Hawkins drew himself up. "May I remind you, sir, that there hasn't been a guest in this house for nearly twelve years."

Marcus scowled ferociously. "Don't give me excuses, Dawkins. You're unprepared. Admit it. I'm going to write a letter to your former master about you."

"It is Hawkins, sir, and my former master is dead."

"I don't wonder. Probably starved to death waiting for you to bring him something to eat. Get on with it, man!"

The butler strode from the room, and Aurora stifled a giggle as Ravenswood threw her a broad wink.

"You've hurt his feelings," she told him, gently chiding.

"Pah! He likes it. He's damned bored around here, like the rest of us. Now, my dear, to what do I owe the pleasure of this visit?"

Aurora took a deep breath. "I have information for you, sir, about your son."

Ravenswood's eyes glowed as he took a seat opposite hers. "I had hoped you would. Oh, yes, I had so hoped you would!"

20

As succinctly, as unemotionally as she could, Aurora related her meeting with Raven and the conditions in which he lived on High Island. Carefully she omitted any reference to her personal relationship with Raven and the circumstances surrounding her departure from the island as well as Raven's part in her recovery by Graham Hughston.

When she'd finished, she leaned back and sipped at the lemonade the butler had brought to them before she'd begun her story.

"Fascinating," Marcus said. "Fascinating. But why do I get the impression there is more to this tale than you are telling me?"

Aurora studied her glass. "I don't know," she said softly. "I can't think of a reason."

"My dear, I don't mean to pry, but I sense that my son did something to hurt you. It is there in the way you speak his name—the way you describe him to me. There was more between you than merely the gratitude of the rescued for her rescuer. Am I correct?"

Cheeks flaming, Aurora set aside her glass and rose. "I must be going," she murmured. "My aunt will have returned from her dressmakers by now and—"

"My dear child . . ." Marcus rose and came to her as she stood near one of the bay windows. "I don't mean to pry into what is obviously a painful memory for you. But if I can help—"

"There is nothing you can do," Aurora assured him. "There is nothing anyone can do. Raven made his choice. He decided what was important to him." She smiled tremulously. "It is hardly surprising, really. This may sound cynical, but I've learned that most people are by nature avaricious. The gentler, more human emotions are swept aside by greed."

"Greed? Avarice? I'm afraid I do not understand. You really must tell me what you mean."

Aurora touched his sleeve. "It may not be pleasant for you to hear. It is not a very attractive story."

"Tell me," he urged.

Aurora drew a deep breath. "There was an article in the newspaper in which Graham Hughston offered a substantial reward for my recovery. Raven saw the article and, in spite of the fact that he knew I wished to remain there on the island with him, he wrote to Graham telling him where to find me. He betrayed me. In effect, he sold me like some kind of white slave for the reward money."

"How large was the reward?" Marcus asked. Seeing Aurora's curious glance, he explained: "I'm sorry, I don't read the newspapers as a rule."

"Twenty-five thousand dollars."

To her surprise, Marcus laughed. "Twenty-five thousand dollars? I apologize, my dear, but I don't believe my son did any such thing."

"How can you say that? I tell you, he did precisely what I've told you."

"For twenty-five thousand dollars? Dear child, when Raven was still a boy I set up a trust for him. It became his when he reached twenty-one years of age. I had it transferred to a bank up north so it would be within easy access for him. It is available to him on demand and should be worth by now something in the neighborhood of four million dollars. I cannot, I will not, believe he would ransom you away for twenty-five thousand." Marcus chuckled again. "When I die he will inherit my entire estate. He will be, I assure you, an extremely wealthy man for the rest of his life."

"But then why—?" Aurora was bewildered. "If it wasn't for the money—" A new, depressing thought occurred to her. "If it wasn't for the money, he must simply have wanted to be rid of me."

"I cannot believe that could be the case. There must have been another reason."

Aurora shook her head. "I can't think of any." She bit her lip. "I'd almost rather think it was for the money."

"Well, let's not think about it just now, shall we? Come with me. I want to show you something."

Taking Aurora by the arm, Marcus led her out

of the parlor and up the grand staircase. Together they walked along a long, floral-carpeted corridor. Marcus opened a door and led Aurora into the library where the walls were paneled to the height of the tall doors with wainscoting of ebonized maple. The fireplace that dominated the room was of Sienna marble. Above the fireplace hung a duplicate of the portrait that hung in Raven's cabin—the beautiful Indian woman, Wenona.

Around the room were scattered photographs in rich sepia tones framed with silver, and miniature portraits on ivory and porcelain. All of them depicted the same subject—Raven—from the ages of eight to eighteen. Touring the room, Aurora watched him grow from a pretty, black-haired little boy into a devastatingly handsome man whose long-lashed eyes seemed even at that age to have seen too much of the seamier side of life. He looked weary, disillusioned. Aurora was fascinated with the picture of him in evening dress. Unaware of Marcus's gaze upon her, she touched the image behind the glass with wondering fingers.

"Why don't you take that one with you?" Marcus asked, his voice seeming unnaturally loud in the quiet room.

Aurora started, her cheeks pinkening as she realized how much of her emotions she had unwittingly revealed to him.

"I couldn't," she said softly, though she longed with all her heart to possess the picture.

"Please, I insist. A thank-you gift for your information."

Aurora took the photograph in its silver filigree frame. Raven gazed back at her, his beautiful azure eyes no less compelling in the shaded brown photograph than in life. He was so handsome, so sensual, so strong. . . . She remembered their last night together when their passion for one another had slipped the tenuous bonds of restraint they'd tried so hard to keep on it. They had come together, making sweet love in the forest by the pond on the edge of twilight. She'd thought it was the beginning; she'd never dreamed it was the end. But how she'd loved him then—how she loved him now. She would love him, she feared, for the rest of her life. A tear slipped unheeded down her cheek as the empty, lonely years stretched before her.

"I can't," she whispered, setting the picture back onto the tabletop. "I'm sorry. I can't."

"Aurora. Aurora, wait," Marcus called as she slipped past him and headed for the door.

He caught her by the wrist and pulled her to a stop. "You love him. Don't you?"

Wordlessly, miserably, she nodded.

"And does he love you?"

"I don't know," she breathed. "If he did, wouldn't he have kept me with him?"

"Not if he thought you would be happier here than in the wilderness. I tried to keep him with me in Pittsburgh because I loved him. That was a mistake. He would remember how unhappy he was there—away from the forests he loved."

"But I told him I wanted to stay. I begged him to let me stay with him. But he sent me away without even saying goodbye."

"Then he owes you an explanation. Why don't you write to him? Tell him how you feel. Ask him why he sent you away."

"Oh, no. I couldn't. I couldn't bear it if he were cold to me. I'd rather be left with memories of—"

She looked away as the scene beside the pond replayed itself in her mind with torturous accuracy.

"What will you do?" Marcus asked.

She shrugged. "My aunt wishes for me to marry Graham Hughston, her nephew. Graham has proposed to me several times. He has promised he will be good to me." She shrugged her shoulders. "I suppose it is as good a match as most made in society."

"And is that what you want? A society match? A marriage made with as much emotion as a business merger?"

"Better that than being hurt!" she cried. "I've been wishing for the moon! It's tearing me apart! My life with Graham would be comfortable—"

"Comfortable!" Marcus scowled. "Are you willing to settle for that? I'm disappointed in you."

"At least Graham wouldn't break my heart! At least he wouldn't betray me! At least he wouldn't take what he wanted from me and then send me away without a word of explana—"

She stopped, eyes widening, aware she'd said far too much.

"Aurora," Marcus said gently. "Did Raven seduce you on that island of his?"

She tried to pull her hand free of his grasp. "Please, I have to go."

"Tell me," he insisted. "Did my son seduce you while you were in his care?"

"Let me go. Please," she begged.

"Not until you tell me."

She hung her head wishing desperately that she had never gone there. "Yes," she murmured, so softly that he wouldn't have heard were it not for the preternatural silence that reigned inside the great house. "Yes."

"Oh, my child," he breathed. He pulled her into his arms and held her gently, tenderly, as though she were a very small child.

Aurora wept. The secret that had gnawed at her very soul ever since she'd left the island was a secret no more. She could only trust in Marcus Ravenswood's sense of decency, of gentlemanly discretion, to keep it unknown to anyone else.

As he held her, Marcus frowned. None of it made any sense to him. Raven would not have betrayed a woman he loved for money—not for any amount—and he would not have taken something so precious as this lovely girl's innocence unless he loved her. There was something missing —some essential piece of information. And unless he discovered what it was, a great wrong would be done to two people. He wondered how Raven truly felt about Aurora's leaving. Did he also feel betrayed?

Marcus dried Aurora's tears and, taking her downstairs, called for his carriage to take her and her bicycle home. Alone once more after her departure, he returned to the library and stood gazing up into the beloved face of his Wenona.

"History is repeating itself," he told the portrait of Raven's mother. "I can see it happening before my eyes." He shook his head sadly. "I did nothing all those years ago—I let us be torn apart. I cannot stand by and let that happen to our son. I have to try—"

Moving to the desk, Marcus Ravenswood took up pen and paper and began yet another letter to his son. Whether Raven had received and read those other letters, he didn't know. He had never acknowledged them—had never answered them. For years Marcus had wondered if Raven were alive or dead. Now he had the answer. His son was alive and well. He had heard it from the lips of a woman whose love for Raven was obvious every time she spoke his name, every time her eyes found his image in one of the paintings and photographs. Marcus could not help believing that Raven must surely love Aurora. Whatever had caused him to send her away must have been some sort of misunderstanding.

Marcus began his letter. He had seen how a star-crossed love affair could blight the lives of those it touches. His beloved Wenona was dead. His own life was no real life at all—he moved through his days caring little about what was happening to him and to the world around him. The son they had created out of their love had come to him reluctantly and had left hating him because of the years he had spent in the luxury of his father's world while his mother suffered with her last illness alone in the wilderness.

Now, it seemed, it was happening again. Fate seemed to have dealt Raven the same hand it had dealt his parents. Marcus did not know, as he wrote to his son, if he could change the future—if he could alter fate—but he was damned determined to give it a fighting try!

21

Day by day, week by week, Raven began to cope with the shock, the anger, the pain of Aurora's leaving. Though he knew his life would never be as simple or as contented as it had been before she'd become a part of it, he believed that in time he could learn to push the heartache of her going into the dimmer recesses of his mind and go on.

He wondered, on occasion, what she was doing. He wondered if she had married Graham Hughston. Probably not yet, he told himself, for he knew that weddings of that magnitude took months of planning. Were they happily engaged, then? he wondered. Did he squire her to all the right places, all the fashionable soirées? Did he lead her proudly about on his arm displaying her to all his acquaintance? Was she playing the blushing, demure maiden all the while knowing in her heart that she belonged to another man in another place by right of possession? Was she such a hypocrite that she would go to her marriage bed pretending an innocence to which she had no claim?

A lopsided, cynical smile curved his lips. She wouldn't have been the first society belle to have discovered the delights of married life long before the ceremony. Although generally they confined their experimenting to the man to whom they were betrothed.

It was that knowledge, more than anything else, that had shocked Raven. If she had truly come to him, given herself to him, knowing all the while that she would be leaving him for another man the very next day, then she was infinitely more cunning and cold-hearted than he had ever imagined.

If that were true . . . Raven frowned as he paused in his work—chopping wood for the winter. Leaning his axe against the chopping block, he used the back of his arm to wipe the sweat from his brow.

"Raven!" Matthew appeared in the clearing, coming along the path from the boat landing. "I'm glad you're here. I've come from St. James. There was a letter for you. I told them I'd bring it."

"A letter?" For a brief, bittersweet moment, some flickering ray of hope gleamed inside Raven, but he cruelly quashed it. Aurora would no more write him a letter now, after so much time had passed, than she would return to him from the luxury and pampered comfort of her uncle's home.

Matthew held it out and Raven took it, but what he found in his hand bore little resemblance to any letter he'd ever received. The envelope was crisp and crackling, wrinkled and puckered where it had been soaked and then dried over a pot-bellied stove.

Matthew shrugged at the questioning look Raven gave him.

"Old Ben Harding went to Mackinaw for the mail again. He had a few too many in one of the saloons and fell into the lake. Unfortunately, he was holding the mailbag at the time." He nodded toward the letter. "Is it from Aurora?"

"What would make you think that?" Raven demanded.

"The postmark. You can just make it out. It's from Chicago."

Sitting on a log, Raven opened the letter. The ink was, for the most part, a water-smeared mess barely legible in a few isolated places. Tipping the letter this way and that, he tried to decipher enough of the pale blue smear to discover who had written it.

"It's from my father."

"I thought your father lived in Pittsburgh."

"So did I. I wonder when he moved." A wry smile flitted across his face. "It seems like everyone ends up in Chicago sooner or later." He scowled, leaning closer to the paper. "It says . . . there's something here about Aurora."

"Has he seen her?"

Raven shrugged. "I don't know. Most of the paragraph is gone. But there is something here about Aurora and . . . Jephsons . . . Lake Shore Drive. . . . Apparently my father is a neighbor of the Jephsons—Aurora's uncle and aunt—and he—" He shook his head. "I can't make out anything else until down here where it says—" He scowled. "Graham Hughston."

Leaning back against a tree, he shook his head. "They must be the toast of Chicago, Graham Hughston and his lily-white fiancée."

"I've never known you to be so bitter," Matthew remarked. "At least not since you came back from Pittsburgh."

"I haven't dealt with this kind of people since I came back from Pittsburgh," Raven reminded him. He sighed. "Oh, what the hell. I hope they're happy together."

"Do you really?"

He nodded. "I do. Aurora wasn't meant to live here in these backward surroundings any more than I was meant to live as I did with my father. It was a mistake for me to go there, and it was a mistake for Aurora to try to live here. She was right to leave. It's only that—"

"Only that?" Matthew prompted. Now that Raven had at last opened up about Aurora, Matthew didn't want him to retreat into his shell of stoic silence again.

"It's only that I don't understand why she left the way she did. If she knew Hughston was coming for her, then why—" He broke off, unwilling to reveal to Matthew that he had been Aurora's lover. "—why didn't she tell me," he substituted for what he had been about to say. "Why didn't she warn me that she was leaving? I wouldn't have stopped her. I wouldn't have tried to keep her here if she wanted to leave. Hell, I offered to send her back more than once." He shook his head. "It just doesn't make sense. It doesn't seem like the Aurora I knew. Then again, maybe I didn't know her as well as I thought."

"But you'll always wonder, won't you?" Matthew asked.

"I suppose I will," Raven admitted.

"Then why don't you ask her?"

Raven eyed him curiously. "Ask her? What do you mean? Write her a letter?" He laughed. "I wonder if that aunt of hers would let her have it. From what Aurora said, it was her aunt who first got the notion of a marriage between Aurora and Graham Hughston. Hughston is the aunt's nephew —her sister's son. Apparently she likes the idea of her sister's son marrying her brother-in-law's daughter."

"No doubt she likes the idea of her sister's son marrying a girl with all that money, as well," Matthew added slyly.

Raven shrugged. "I don't know anything about the Hughstons—I never really heard much about Chicago society in Pittsburgh—but I suppose he's wealthy enough himself. Or his family is, at any rate. He'd have to be what is known as a 'suitable mate' for Aurora before the match would be considered."

Matthew's laugh was filled with disdain. "It sounds like they're breeding cattle."

"They are. Very rich cattle."

His eyes met his cousin's and he saw the question in them. "You weren't really serious, were you?" he asked.

"About asking Aurora why she left? Of course I was. Why not?"

"As I told you. Her aunt would probably see to it that she never got any letter I wrote to her."

"Then why write? Go there yourself."

Raven's rich, deep laughter rumbled forth. "Appear on the doorstep, hat in hand, and ask humbly for the reason Aurora deserted me? I have my pride, cousin. She wanted to go—let her go. Good luck to her. And good riddance."

"Raven—"

"Just let it go, Matthew. Thank you for bringing me the letter. But as for the rest, it's over, finished, bury it and get on with the future."

"I would if I really believed you cared as little as that," Matthew told him. "But I don't believe it. You'll always wonder about Aurora's leaving; it'll eat you up inside in time."

"I'll get over it," he predicted, squinting at the ruined letter, wondering what the illegible parts said.

"You don't mind that she'll belong to another man? It doesn't matter to you that she'll be his wife? Bear his sons? Can you really—"

"Christ!" Raven thrust himself to his feet. "Will you let it go!"

"No!" Matthew rose as well. He was nearly as tall as Raven and the two men stood there, glaring at one another. "I don't want you to live out here all alone this way for the rest of your life. I had never seen you happy—not truly happy—until those weeks with Aurora. I had never seen you so near to contentment. I don't want you to give that up without a fight."

"I have my pride," Raven said again. "And it's taken one hell of a beating lately. If I went to Chicago to see Aurora and she—"

"Then don't go to see Aurora," Matthew interrupted.

"But you just said—"

"Go to see your father. He's in Chicago now. He's written to you. Even if you can't read that letter, he wouldn't have written to you if he didn't want peace between you. Go to see him. While you're visiting him, you can find out the situation between Aurora and Hughston. If she's happily engaged to him, you'll have made peace with your father and you can come back here with nothing lost and no injury to that damned pride of yours. If Aurora's not happy, you can step in and, maybe, clear the air about why she left the way she did. It's a chance, Raven, a second chance for you and for Aurora."

Raven gazed thoughtfully into the dark eyes of the cousin who had always been more of a brother to him. A second chance for him and for Aurora. Was it possible? Or would a trip to Chicago bring only heartbreak and disappointment? He frowned.

"I wonder why my father wrote to me now, after all these years," he murmured, little suspecting the dozen and more letters that Sarah Oates had managed to intercept and destroy over the years.

"It's fate," Matthew told him blithely. "The spirits are smiling on you."

Raven smiled. "I wish I could believe that. I'd be bound for Chicago on the next boat."

"Go anyway. You can't lose. Even if Aurora is truly going to marry this Graham Hughston, at least you'll be reunited with your father."

An image of Marcus Ravenswood as Raven had last seen him formed in Raven's mind. How much had he changed over the past fifteen years?

How much had each of them changed since the grief and bitterness of Wenona's death had torn them apart? The passing of time had softened the anger and animosity Raven felt for his father. In a way, he understood what his father had done. He'd been torn between his family, the only way of life he'd ever known, and the woman he loved. At the time, Raven had only been able to see that Marcus had chosen his family's wealth over Wenona. Now, Raven could see that the choice had not been so clear-cut. The situation with Aurora was similar, although Raven told himself that he would have been willing to return to a way of life he loathed if it had been what Aurora wanted.

"Well?" Matthew asked, watching the play of emotions across his cousin's handsome face. "Are you going or aren't you?"

"I'd like to see my father again," Raven admitted. "It's been too long. I hadn't even realized that I missed him."

"And Aurora?"

"Aurora. If I happen to see her, that's fine. If I happen to hear that she's unhappy with Hughston, that's better."

"And if she happens to have discovered that she truly loves you and wants nothing in the world more than to come back here with you, that's the best!" Matthew finished, laughing.

Raven laughed as well, but in his heart of hearts he was worried that just the opposite would turn out to be the case. Still, that was a circumstance he would have to deal with when the time came. In the meantime he would tell himself—and his troublesome pride—that the only reason he was even considering a trip to Chicago was to be reunited with his father. Aurora, and whatever the future might bring with regards to her, was a worry he need not concern himself with just yet.

22

As the carriage Raven had hired drove along Lake
Shore Drive, he leaned forward and tapped the
driver's shoulder.

"Which is the home of Carlisle Jephson?" he
asked.

"Comin' along in a minute, sir," the driver
replied. With his whip he pointed to a handsome
white marble mansion whose four massive fluted
pillars held up a classical portico that spanned the
front of the nearly square home. "That'll be the
Jephsons' now, sir," the driver told him.

Raven studied the mansion as they passed. It
was an elegant home, bespeaking wealth, luxury,
success. A small smile filled with irony curved his
lips as he realized that his beloved cabin tucked
away in the forest on High Island would easily fit
into one corner of that impressive front porch. He
remembered his reaction to the manses of Pitts-

burgh when, as a boy, his father had taken him to live with him. All those rooms, all that space, so much that the people who lived within those imposing walls had to hire other people to care for them. He hadn't seen the sense of it then, and now, over twenty years later, he still couldn't see much sense to it.

"Mr. Ravenswood's house, that is what you said, ain't it, sir?" the driver questioned.

"It is," Raven confirmed.

"Here we are, then."

The driver guided the carriage between the opened iron gates of Marcus Ravenswood's curving drive. Newly graveled, it swept up to the side of the mansion and beneath a pillared porte cochere.

"Here you are, sir," the driver said, hauling at the reins to bring the horses to an halt. "Need help with that?"

He nodded to the single suitcase Raven had brought with him. He had purchased a single suit before setting out in order to be presentable upon his arrival. There was no guarantee that he would want to remain long in Chicago, but if he wished to stay, Raven knew he would have to buy a new wardrobe. The suitcase, nearly empty, contained the plain, simple clothing he had worn from the island and his toiletries.

"Thank you, no," Raven answered. Climbing down from the carriage, he paid the driver, then mounted the half-dozen steps to the carriage entrance of the mansion.

After ringing the bell, he waited for someone to open the door.

"May I help you sir?" Hawkins asked brightly. In the days and weeks since Aurora had first turned up on Marcus Ravenswood's doorstep, the gates had begun to be left open. Visitors and tradesmen had begun to call, and the previously reclusive Mr. Ravenswood had begun going out again. The house was coming to life just as Hawkins had always hoped it would.

"Will you tell Mr. Ravenswood that his son is here?" Raven asked.

"His . . . you wouldn't be . . ."

"Charles Ravenswood."

Stunned, Hawkins opened the door. "Come in, please, sir," he murmured. He could hardly believe it, and yet the resemblance between this handsome, self-assured man and the photographs, paintings and sketches that littered the library upstairs was unmistakable.

The butler reached for the suitcase. "Let me take that for you, sir."

Handing him the suitcase, Raven perused the handsome vestibule with its oak paneling and rose brocade portieres. Beyond the arching doorway he could see a salon decorated in royal blue and gold.

"How long has my father lived in Chicago . . . er . . . ?

"Hawkins, sir," the butler supplied. "He moved here from Pittsburgh twelve years ago."

"Twelve years," Raven murmured thoughtfully. "I had no idea."

"If you will follow me, sir. Mr. Ravenswood is out at the moment. Shall I show you to your room while you wait?"

"Yes, thank you," Raven replied.

The two men mounted the stairs to the second floor. As they walked along the corridor, Hawkins pointed to door after door.

"That is Mr. Ravenswood's room, sir, his dressing room, the library, the lavatory, the backstairs, the elevator, down at the end, the billiard room." He stopped at a door. "Here we are. I hope this room will be satisfactory."

Opening the door, Hawkins led Raven into a bedroom walled with a cream and blue striped paper. The windows were hung with blue brocade and a brass canopy bed stood against one wall, its foot pointed toward a yawning marble fireplace.

"Will this room do, sir? There are others upstairs. I could show you—"

"This will be fine," Raven told him.

"Very good, sir." Hawkins set Raven's suitcase down and crossed to a second door on the far side of the room. "Your dressing room and lavatory are through here. The bell is there next to the bed if you require anything."

"Thank you, I'll ring," Raven promised.

The butler moved toward the door. He was nearly to it when Raven stopped him.

"And Hawkins?"

"Sir?"

"When my father returns, don't tell him I've arrived. I'd prefer to surprise him."

The butler smiled. "A pleasant surprise indeed, sir. I'll not say a word and I'll caution the other servants to say nothing either."

"Thank you, Hawkins."

Bowing, the butler left and Raven explored his room. The bed he remembered—it had been in his father's home in Pittsburgh, and Marcus had told his son that it had come from the home of a famous madam in one of San Francisco's most notorious brothels. The rest of the furniture was unfamiliar.

The wing chairs, marble-topped tables, the paintings—he wondered what had become of the fine old family pieces that had decorated the mansion in Pittsburgh. Likely relegated to the upper floors, he thought, too valuable to be discarded but too unfashionable for the lower floors.

Opening his suitcase, he took his clothes and toiletries into the bathroom and dressing room. Feeling dusty after the drive from the docks, he undressed, bathed and shaved, then shook out the dust from his vicuna frock coat, double-breasted white brocade waistcoat and striped trousers. The tall silk hat and grey suede gloves that were required dress for a gentleman he had discarded in the other room with pleasure, but there was no escaping the hateful embrace of his tie and he scowled into the mirror as he retied it into a neat bow over the stiff collar of his shirt. As he polished the fine leather of his black boots, he resigned himself to a trip to his father's tailor.

Then, with nothing more to concern him in the dressing room, he left his suite and wandered along the corridor.

Passing the ornately scrolled brass cage of the elevator, he opened the door Hawkins had pointed out as the library. What he found there astonished him.

The room was nothing so much as a shrine to the memory of Wenona and the son she had borne Marcus thirty-three years before. Raven stood before the fireplace looking up at the lifelike portrayal of his mother's beautiful face. Her gentle, deep brown eyes gazed down at him, and somehow he felt she knew he was there and was pleased that he had come at last to make peace with his father. Wenona had loved Marcus until the day she died, and Raven knew it would have broken her heart to know of the deep and bitter strife that existed between her lover and their son for so many years.

Touring the room, he examined the dozens of depictions of himself at various ages. Oddly, for he had not thought of those years in Pittsburgh for a long time, he found he could remember the circumstances in which each and every photograph had been taken, each miniature painted, each sketch drawn. He felt transported back to that other place, that other time. The memories that were revived in him were not all happy ones.

Leaving the library and its storehouse of memories, he moved down the hall toward the billiard room. Inside, the table stood beneath a Tiffany lamp, its green baize top alight with the sunshine that flooded through the twin bay windows— duplicates of the windows that adorned the parlor at the mansion's opposite end. Club chairs stood in each of the bays. On the wall opposite, a polished mahogany rack held the billiards accessories, and on a third wall a carved oak fireplace held neatly stacked logs awaiting only the match to set them alight.

Sitting in one of the chairs, Raven stretched out his legs and wondered at the wisdom of his setting out so impetuously from the island. He looked forward to seeing his father again. Clearing away the old, gnawing rancor between them seemed like a good idea now that he had arrived. But he could not help feeling a certain nagging apprehension about Aurora. Did he want to see her? Speak to her? Would she want to see him? He sighed. Whatever the outcome of his trip, at least the wondering would be over. He intended to find out why she had left when she did, and how she had done it. Beyond that, he would take his cue from her. If she was happy here, he would leave her to her happiness and return to the islands. Heartsore, to be sure, but willing to relegate her and his love for her to the back of his mind and go on with his own life.

The sound of carriage wheels and horses' hooves on the gravel drive caught his attention. Glancing out the bay window, he saw a smart open landau drawn by two gleaming white horses approaching the carriage porch whose roof jutted out beneath the billiard-room bays. In the carriage, behind the handsomely liveried driver, a woman in a plain straw bonnet sat with her back to the driver. Facing her on the opposite seat were a white-haired man and another woman, dressed more fashionably than the first.

The man, Raven knew, was his father, although he was startled by the white hair—when he'd left, his father's rich brown hair had only begun to be tinged with wings of grey at the temples. The woman beside him, dressed in a long jacket and skirt of brown Silesienne, the satin ruffled at her throat framing her delicate chin, the ribbons of her jacket and decorating her befeathered straw bonnet streaming out behind her, her parasol characteristically furled and abandoned on the carriage floor, was unmistakable.

"Aurora," Raven whispered. He gazed at her as she turned her head to speak to his father and the sunshine picked out the bright golden highlights of her upswept titian hair.

He was stunned by her beauty and by the fierce possessiveness that swept over him. He knew suddenly, unquestionably, that he would not give her up without a fight.

At the same time, he was filled with anxiety. It was too soon to see her—he wanted to speak to his father first, learn what Marcus knew of Aurora's circumstances. More specifically, he wanted to know of the status of her relationship with Graham Hughston.

He heard the carriage stopping below the roof of the porte cochere and held his breath until it rolled out on the other side, turning in a wide arc to begin retracing its path back down the drive. Aurora and the other woman—her companion, he guessed, knowing how indispensable chaperones were considered for young, unmarried women— were still in the carriage. Raven's eyes followed the carriage, and Aurora, hungrily until it turned back out between the iron gates and disappeared in the direction of the Jephsons' mansion.

Remembering his father, Raven left the billiard room and descended to the first floor. Hawkins stood in the downstairs hall and silently pointed to a small parlor at the back of the house.

"Shall I announce you, sir?" he asked softly, his eyes bright with excitement.

"Please," Raven replied.

Laying his master's hat, gloves and walking stick aside, the butler went to the parlor door and rapped lightly.

"What is it?" came the voice from within.

"Excuse me, sir," Hawkins said, opening the door partway. "You have a visitor."

"A visitor? I didn't hear anyone arrive."

"The gentleman arrived while you were out."

"While I was out? Well, who is it? Send him in here."

The butler moved away and Raven pushed the door wide. For a long, silent, disbelieving moment, Marcus stared at his son.

"My God," he breathed at last. "Is it you? It is you! I can't believe it!"

"Good afternoon, Father," Raven said softly. "I got your letter."

Marcus raised a shaking hand to the son he never thought he'd see again. Tears blurred his vision as he started forward, and he stumbled on the edge of the Persian rug.

Moving swiftly, Raven crossed the room and caught the older man before he could fall. They stood there gazing at one another and then they embraced, silently, warmly, tearfully.

23

After luncheon, over which Raven explained about the accidental defacement of Marcus's letter and Marcus recounted to his son what the missive had contained, the two men set out for Marcus's favorite haberdashery.

"I'm sorry Aurora didn't come in this morning," Marcus said, facing his son in the carriage. "I should have liked to see the look on her face when she saw you there."

Raven shook his head. "I'm not ready to see her yet. And there was another person in the carriage. Perhaps Aurora would not like our meeting witnessed by a stranger."

"A stranger?" Marcus was for a moment perplexed, but then his brow cleared. "Ah, Bridey!"

"Bridey?"

"Bridget O'Shaughnessy. Aurora's maid. Aurora calls her Bridey. They're devoted to one another."

"I see." Raven scowled, brooding. "The one thing I cannot understand in all this, Father, is why Aurora would tell you that I was the one who sent for Hughston. I knew nothing of his arrival until they were already gone. Anyone could have written to him—half the island saw the article in the Tribune."

Marcus gazed at his son. He could not seem to get enough of looking at him—could not, even now, quite believe that Raven had come back to him.

"Perhaps," he suggested, "whoever wrote to Hughston told him she was living on High Island with you. Hughston may have made it seem as if you were at fault deliberately. He may have wished to discredit you in Aurora's eyes."

Raven, still stunned by the tale of seduction and avaricious betrayal that Aurora had spun for his father, had begun to wonder if he could have been wrong all along about her true character.

"Perhaps," he allowed. "Then again, it may be that Aurora is simply a scheming little liar after all."

"I don't want to believe that of her," Marcus told him sadly.

"You've become very fond of her in these past weeks, haven't you, Father?"

"Very fond." Marcus's blue eyes twinkled. "With my son at my side and that pretty little creature for a daughter-in-law, I should be supremely happy."

"I can't promise you either of those things,"

Raven told him honestly. He was unsure of Aurora, but he knew beyond doubt that he would return at some time to his home in the islands. "I may know more after tonight. Are you certain Madame Beauchene will not mind my accompanying you to her soirée tonight?"

"Knowing Louise Beauchene, she will be thrilled. Your arrival in Chicago will cause a sensation. She will be in ecstacy to have you as a guest before any other hostess in town."

"She is a widow, is she not?"

"How do you know?" Marcus's eyes narrowed mutinously. "I suppose that damned Dawkins has been telling tales again."

"Hawkins, Father," Raven corrected. "And he did mention to me that you had met the lovely Widow Beauchene a few weeks ago. He said you have been to dinner with her several times."

"Twice," Marcus grumped. "That doesn't mean I'm courting her. She's a pretty woman and good company."

"Perhaps you should court her. After all these years—"

"I'll never marry, if that's what's in your mind. It is the least I can do to honor your mother's memory."

"She would not have wanted you to spend your life alone for her sake," Raven told him. "She was not so selfish."

"I won't be alone if you'll stay, marry, and give me grandchildren to make my old age happy."

Raven laughed but said nothing. Mercifully the carriage was even then drawing up before the tailor shop and he was more than happy to lose himself in discussions of the clothing he would need for his stay in Chicago and, more immediately, for the soirée that night.

In the beautiful dining room of the Jephsons' mansion, Aurora recounted the events of her drive with Marcus Ravenswood earlier in the afternoon.

"Are you certain he isn't interested in you, Aurora?" Electra asked.

Aurora laughed. "Quite certain. If anything, he looks upon me as a daughter or, perhaps, a favorite niece. Nothing more. In fact . . ." Leaning forward as if imparting a confidence, she told them: ". . . I understand he is quite partial to Madame Beauchene. He will be at her soirée tonight."

"You must promise me all your dances," Graham said from the doorway where he had appeared unannounced.

"Surely not all," Aurora replied coolly. "What of all the other handsome men in Chicago? If I dance only with you, won't they become discouraged?"

"All the better for them. They will be discouraged in the end at any rate."

Aurora said nothing, but as soon as she could she excused herself from the table and went upstairs to begin preparing for the soirée at Madame Beauchene's North Side mansion.

Darkness was falling earlier now that summer was giving way to autumn. It was nearly complete by the time the Jephsons' carriage drew up beneath the porte cochere of the magnificent Astor Street mansion that had been Louise Beauchene's domain since the death of her husband in California had sent her East in search of culture and sophistication.

There was a great deal of speculation about the beautiful widow. Some went as far as to whisper that there had never been a Monsieur Beauchene and that Louise's fortune had been earned through shrewd investment of moneys she received from a string of rich paramours. But nothing could be proven against her, and her behavior since moving to Chicago had been so faultlessly correct and circumspect that the jealous hostesses had at last given in and opened their ranks to her.

The mansion she had purchased upon her arrival was small by some standards, only twenty-five rooms, but it boasted a glass-walled conservatory where a triple-tiered fountain played. On nights when she entertained, it was lit with candlelight and became a popular and romantic trysting place for young—and not-so-young—lovers.

Aurora's entrance on the arm of Graham Hughston generated less attention than it would have a month before. The sensation of her rescue from the "northern wilderness" was beginning to pall, much to her relief. Still, her beauty and her fortune were both considerable, and more than one admiring would-be suitor looked eagerly toward the door as she entered. She was with Graham Hughston, as usual, but as no engagement had been announced, the other young men—and their hopeful mamas—continued to hope.

She entered the ballroom smiling, confident that her gown of leaf green damask sewn with thousands of tiny pearls on the bodice and in a broad garland of flowers around the tightly laced waist and hem, suited her to perfection. More pearls had been laced through her upswept curls and decorated the sticks of her sweeping feather fan.

After greeting their hostess, Aurora and Graham circled the dance floor. Purposely Graham maneuvered them toward the conservatory.

"We shouldn't be alone this way," Aurora chided as he drew her into the shadows behind some tropical greenery.

"Nonsense. In everyone's eyes we're as good as betrothed."

"But we are not betrothed," she reminded him stubbornly.

Reaching into his pocket, Graham drew out a tiny, leather-covered case. Unfastening the silver clasp, he opened it. Inside, a thumbnail-size ruby glowed like a drop of purest heart's blood.

"It was my grandmother's engagement ring," he told her. "She left it to my mother, who wishes me to give it to you. Marry me, Aurora."

Aurora closed her eyes. What was she waiting for? Marcus had told her he had written to Raven but received no answer. It was obvious that Raven had washed his hands of her as he had of his father years before. She knew that Graham was as good a choice as any of the fawning suitors who had vied for her attention since she'd come to Chicago. Perhaps he was the best choice, considering that her aunt was also his aunt and his mother was her aunt's sister. If he mistreated her, it would be a simple matter to bring familial pressure to bear on him.

"I . . ." She opened her eyes and found him watching her breathlessly. "I need more time."

"But Aurora," he began.

"Please." She laid an entreating hand on his arm. "Not here. Not now. Let's go back."

Followed by a petulant Graham Hughston, Aurora made her way back to the ballroom. She stepped into his arms and they joined in the waltz as, together with a hundred other couples, they circled the cavernous chamber.

A hand tapped Graham's shoulder. Aurora knew he hated to relinquish her to another partner, but good manners dictated that he must. He stepped aside, and Aurora found herself in Raven's arms.

The blood drained from her face as the shock of recognition shot through her. Her knees turned to water. Only the strong support of Raven's arm at the small of her back kept her from falling to the gleaming parquet floor.

As they circled the floor silently, Raven's sky-blue eyes glowing as they bored into Aurora's bloodless face, Aurora felt dazed, faint, giddy. She was only faintly aware of the eyes of the room upon them; she was not at all aware of the whispers, the murmurs of how beautiful they were together; she knew only that he was there, holding her in his arms, moving with her in the rhythmic, sensual movements of the dance.

"Why are you here?" she breathed over the last fading notes of the waltz.

His eyes glimmered, a muscle twitched in the bronze plane of his smooth cheek. "I've come for you, Aurora," he said softly.

"No." Shaking her head, she backed away. Only when she was out of reach did she turn and disappear into the watching throngs on the dance floor.

"Aurora?" Electra was at her side. "Aurora, what is it? You look as if you'd seen a ghost!"

Aurora raised a trembling hand to her cheek. It was cold, clammy. "I want to go home, Aunt. Please!"

"Are you ill, my dear?" Louise Beauchene was at her side. "Perhaps you should lie down."

"No, I think I should go."

"Nonsense." Electra's mouth was set. "We are not leaving yet. Not over an attack of the vapors or whatever it is. Go with Madame Beauchene and lie down for a few minutes."

Unhappy, Aurora followed her hostess out of the ballroom and down a short staircase to a pretty pink and gold room.

"Here is my boudoir, my darling," the beautiful widow cooed. "Lie down. If you need anything, ring that bell and my maid will come to help you." She caressed Aurora's cheek. "Don't stay here too long. The gentlemen will be quite disappointed."

Left alone, Aurora sank onto a gold-fringed, rose velvet fainting couch. Raven. She could hardly believe he was there, and yet he had held her, danced with her, spoken to her. He said he had "come for her." What could it mean? She covered her face with her hands. What did he want of her!

The door opened and closed. Footsteps, muffled in the thick carpet, approached.

"I didn't ring for you," Aurora said, assuming Madame Beauchene's maid had come in. "I—"

She opened her eyes. Raven stood over her. Her breath caught in her throat. She had always thought him handsome, but nothing—nothing—could have prepared her for the sheer masculine perfection of him in his elegant evening clothes.

She pushed herself up ready to rise, but he sat on the edge of the couch and leaned over her, one restraining arm across her hips, one hand resting on the opposite edge.

"What do you want?" she breathed, eyes captivated by his.

"You," he replied simply.

"No," she whispered. "Go away."

"You told my father I seduced you."

"You did."

He smiled. "I'd say we seduced one another."

"It's not true!" she declared. She knew it was, but she could not admit it, even to herself.

"You told my father I turned you over to Hughston for the reward money."

"You did."

"Then why didn't he recognize me when I cut in while you were dancing with him?"

Aurora thought quickly, desperately. "You probably had someone else masquerade as you to collect the money."

"You're a fool if you believe that."

Confused, frightened, Aurora tried to escape, but Raven refused to let her go.

"You'll leave when I say you can," he hissed. "You belong to me, Aurora. You're mine. Mine! I made you mine that night beside the pond."

"Don't speak of that night! I don't want to remember!"

"You may not want to, my love, but you cannot forget it, can you? I'll wager you remember it all too clearly, particularly at night, tucked in your maidenly bed behind your uncle's marble walls."

"Stop it!" she hissed.

"You're mine, Aurora," he vowed fiercely. "No one else can have you. No one!"

"It's a lie!"

"It's the truth," he breathed, bending toward her.

His kiss was hard, savage, punishing. Aurora pressed herself back into the yielding cushions of the couch, trying to escape the plundering mouth that bruised her tender lips. She trembled, shuddered, and when at last he leaned away, she thrust herself to her feet.

"Stay away from me," she whispered, backing toward the door. "Stay away! I hate you! Do you hear me! I hate you!"

Swift and graceful as one of the sleek predators of his beloved forest, Raven left the couch and crossed the room to bar her way to the door.

"You hate me?" he asked, his voice low, soft, dark with the same smoldering desire she saw so clearly in his black-lashed eyes. "You don't hate me, Aurora, and you know it. That's what frightens you. You love me, only me, and you want me, even now, at this moment. Admit it."

"I don't," she insisted, her voice quavering, her body trembling with emotions she dared not examine too closely.

"You don't what?" he taunted. "You don't hate me? Or you don't want me?"

"I don't . . . I mean, I do! Oh, God, I . . ." She

223

swallowed hard, befuddled by the relentless weight of his heated stare. "I don't know!" It was a wail of despair as she buried her face in her hands.

"Let me go, Raven," she entreated, tears shimmering in her cat-green eyes as she ventured a timid glance over her trembling fingers.

"I couldn't," he said simply, "even if I truly believed you wanted me to."

"I do want you to. Oh, Raven, can't you see? It was a mistake—our being together. An accident of nature."

"An act of fate," he disagreed. "Of destiny. If we hadn't met on the island, it would have happened somewhere else. Perhaps here. After all, my father lives here—you were on your way here when the storm brought you to me. Our paths were meant to cross, Aurora."

"To cross, perhaps, and then go their separate ways," she said, grasping at any thin thread of logic that presented itself.

"Why does it frighten you so?" he asked. "It terrifies you, doesn't it? This love, this desire, that was between us from the first."

She shook her head slowly, silently, wanting to deny his words, but in the end she could only hang her head, tears glistening on her lashes. "Yes," she admitted brokenly.

"Aurora?"

"Yes!" She pressed her fingers to her lips as though she could take back what seemed a foolish, even dangerous admission.

Raven gazed at her, torn between triumph at her admission and compassion for her heart-rending distress.

"Why?" he asked, moving toward her. "Why does it frighten you so?"

"Because it's wrong!"

"Oh, Aurora." His lips, his tone, his voice caressed her name. "Nothing has ever been more right. You know that. If not in here—" He touched her temple with one gentle hand. "—then in here—" His fingertips grazed her breast above the edging of her neckline. "Why deny yourself your heart's desire?"

As he would have taken her into his arms, she backed away. Her senses were whirling madly. She was confused and dazed. She had learned to loathe him in those dark, unhappy days when she'd agonized over his betrayal—she'd hated him even while she'd longed for him with every fiber of her being. She'd told herself her life would be better without him, for she knew that no one else would ever arouse the disturbing passions in her that he had—no one else would ever touch her as he had—no other man would ever make her as happy. Or as miserable. It was that power she feared—that mastery of her senses. And now, after all the days and nights when she'd vowed to hate him till the end of her days, to have him reappear and show her that she was his to command at the sound of his voice, the glance of his eyes, the beckoning wave of his hand . . . It was too much! And yet—

She trembled as he reached for her yet again. Her lips parted, glistening moistly, as she drew a harsh little breath. Again she backed out of his reach. Her eyes were wide and filled with foreboding.

Raven stopped. His eyes, so darkly blue they

looked like rare and precious sapphires, bore into hers, gauging her mood, her fear, the depth of her desire, reading her thoughts which were as open to him as his own.

He took a step back, then another. The gulf between them widened. His eyes never left her face as he moved across the room, returning to the fainting couch where he had first found her. Sinking onto the tufted velvet cushions, he held out a hand to her.

"Come here, Aurora," he commanded, sinking back onto one elbow as he held out a hand to her.

Aurora's tongue darted out to wet her lips. Her eyes went from him to the door. Unguarded now, her path of escape was clear. All she had to do was leave. But she couldn't—she couldn't take that first small step toward—

"Aurora," Raven repeated, his voice soft, caressing, inviting. "Come to me."

She shook her head slowly, but even as she did, her body as though of its own accord swayed toward him. Her feet moved woodenly, her knees, strangely weak, threatened at any moment to buckle under her as she took one step, then another, toward him.

"Come to me, Aurora," he insisted, his heart pounding, belying the casual attitude of his body.

Helpless to refuse, she approached him. She didn't understand it—she couldn't analyze her own actions. But she was drawn irresistibly toward him as though he were a magnet and she steel. She reached out a hand to him and gasped as flesh touched flesh. His fingers threaded through hers, closed, and he drew her down beside him on the softly yielding couch.

Aurora gazed up at him with something close to awe. Her fingertips trailed across the smooth, strong planes of his face, brushed across his parted lips. She closed her eyes, catching a ragged, shuddering breath as his hand caressed her breasts through the leaf-green damask of her gown. He bent toward her and his lips touched her cheek, her jaw, her throat, the throbbing hollow of her shoulder, the alabaster curve of her breast. Arching toward him, Aurora sank her fingers into the ebony silk of his hair. The tantalizing heat of his hands, his mouth, was intoxicating and Aurora felt herself sinking beneath its spell. Her fear was giving way to desire—to passion—his caresses became more intimate, his kisses more urgent, but still she craved more of him. In a moment, surely no more than two, they would be—

"Aurora!" The pounding at the door shattered the heated spell they had woven about them. "Aurora? Are you in there?"

"Electra!" she hissed, fighting her way out of his arms.

Electra rattled the latch, and within the boudoir Aurora's breath caught in her throat. But the latch held fast. Raven had locked the door.

"I'm here," she called back, her voice strained, sounding like a stranger's.

Her eyes went to Raven, who sat on the fainting couch. His eyes still smoldered with unslaked desire. A faint glimmering of perspiration dotted his brow and top lip.

"My God," she breathed, realizing what had

been about to happen. Another minute would have found them making love—she'd wanted him—her need had been like a desperate, ravening hunger inside her. He had moved away from her. The way of escape had been open. And yet she had gone to him willingly, even eagerly. She was stunned by his command of her senses, her desires—stunned and terrified. She gazed at him with horrified fascination.

The latch rattled again. "Aurora?" Electra persisted.

Sidling past Raven as though he were some demon incarnate, she stumbled to the door and, fumbling, managed to unfasten the lock.

She opened the door just enough to squeeze out. Then, lifting her skirts, she ran away along the corridor leaving her aunt to gape after her.

As she entered the ballroom, her eyes sought out Graham Hughston. She drew him into a secluded corner and whispered to him tearfully. His handsome face reflected his astonishment. Taking her hand, he led her to her uncle and aunt.

Raven made his way back to the ballroom wondering if he had gone too far. He had acted impulsively, he had frightened her, shocked her by showing her how easily he could command her senses. Well, it was too late to change things now. He would have to wait and see what happened next.

He didn't have to wait long. By the time he reached the ballroom, he found the room abuzz as waiters circulated with trays of champagne. Carlisle and Electra Jephson stood on the bandstand flanking Aurora and Graham. Lifting his glass, Aurora's uncle stepped forward.

"I should like to propose a toast," he said loudly. "To my dear niece and ward, Aurora, and my dear nephew, Graham Hughston—may their marriage be long and filled with happiness."

Aurora, still trembling, lifted her glass to her lips. On her hand, Graham's heirloom ruby glowed in the lamplight. Over the rim of her glass she saw Raven, and all the maddening, frightening emotions she had felt in Louise Beauchene's boudoir were nothing compared with the foreboding that filled her heart at the sight of the murderous fury in his cerulean eyes.

24

Having left Madame Beauchene's soirée soon after Aurora and Graham's startling announcement, Raven and his father sat in the library on the second floor of the Ravenswood mansion.

"You seem surprisingly unconcerned about that little scene at the soirée," Marcus commented as he stared into the swirling depths of the brandy in its crystal snifter.

Raven, in shirtsleeves, the stiff collar of his shirt opened, smiled wryly. "I see no reason to be overly alarmed."

"You don't?" Marcus was clearly astonished. "The silly girl has gone and gotten herself engaged. It's all a mystery to me. She seemed utterly opposed to the marriage her aunt was trying to push her into. Now, out of the blue, she not only accepts Hughston's ring, she announces it publicly. I'm disappointed in her; she is not what I thought her to be."

"No? Well, she is exactly what I thought her to be," Raven told him. "She is headstrong, stubborn, impulsive and willful. Unfortunately, she is also as beautiful as an angel and more desirable than any woman I've ever known."

He laughed, and his father eyed him curiously and not a little crossly.

"I'm glad you find this all so amusing," Marcus said. "I must say, though, that I don't share your amusement. In fact, I'm beginning to feel as if I'd been used by some sly little schemer."

"How so?" Raven asked.

"She came to me, told me that she loved you. She seemed utterly heartbroken at having been parted from you. I wrote to you thinking that if you knew how she felt—and if you felt the same—you would come here and the two of you could be happily reunited. Instead, the very night you arrive she announces her engagement to the man who took her away from you. Now, I ask myself, was it all a charade on her part? Did she use me merely as a means of getting you here to Chicago so she could humiliate you? Force you to witness her betrothal?"

"No, not at all," Raven assured him. "If you recall, you said she knew nothing of your letter. My arrival in Chicago was a complete surprise to her."

"Not a pleasant surprise, by the looks of things."

"I don't know about that. A shocking surprise, to be sure. No, Father, you must not judge Aurora too harshly. I frightened her tonight—frightened her into doing what she did."

"But how?"

Briefly, Raven recounted his conversations with Aurora on the dance floor and in Madame Beauchene's boudoir. He did not tell his father how he had kissed her—how frightened she had become of her own feelings, her own emotions.

"And so she ran back to the ballroom and told Hughston she'd marry him?" Marcus shook his head. "It would appear that the only victor in all this will turn out to be Graham Hughston."

"He has not won yet," Raven cautioned. "A betrothal, after all, is not a marriage."

"You seem confident, even after the engagement has been announced."

"I am confident. And determined. Aurora will not marry Graham Hughston, Father. Aurora belongs to me. I made her mine and no other man will have her—not ever!"

Marcus was clearly unconvinced. "I wish I could be so positive, my son."

"Believe me when I tell you that, even as we speak, Aurora, wherever she is, is more sorry than you or I about what she did this evening."

Not so very far away, in the moonlit garden of the Jephsons' mansion, Aurora sat slumped on a bench in some Chicago architect's version of an ornamental Greek temple.

"What have I done!" she asked the cool, fragrant darkness. "What have I done!"

She clasped her hands tightly, and the ruby of Graham's ring bit into her finger as though in protest of her thoughts. Scowling, she held out her hand as if it had suddenly become a traitor to her.

"Aurora!" Electra's voice cut through the night as it echoed from the veranda at the back of the house. "Aurora? Where are you? Come inside at once!"

Aurora leaned back on the bench, determined to pretend she had not heard her aunt's summons. Graham was in there. He wanted to take her home to his mother so they could tell her the good news. Aurora had begged for a few moments of solitude in the garden before setting out. That had been at least an hour before. She wished they'd all just give up and leave her alone.

Despairing, she covered her face with her hands. She was lost in her hopeless misery, so much so that she did not hear Graham approaching on the flagstone walk.

"Aurora?"

She cried out. Dropping her hands, she found him standing over her.

"My God! You scared me to death!"

"I'm sorry. I thought you'd heard me coming." He sat down beside her. "What were you thinking about?"

Raven, she thought to herself. She said: "About you—and me. Graham—"

He took her hand and raised it to his lips. "You've made me so happy, Aurora. And I will make you happy. I swear it."

Aurora closed her eyes. You can never make me happy, she cried to herself. Because you are not Raven. Damn him. Damn him! He owns me, heart, soul and senses, and he knows it!

"You don't believe me?" Graham asked, seeing but not understanding the anguish on her beautiful, pale face.

"I believe that you mean what you say," she assured him. "It is only that . . . that . . ."

"That you don't love me," he finished for her. He went on, cutting her off as she was about to speak: "No, you needn't deny it or try to make me feel better. I know it's true. But we can be happy together. Few marriages between people such as you and me are based on love. Perhaps—" His expression softened, his dark eyes lingered on her lips. "—perhaps it is merely that you do not understand what it is to love. You are so innocent."

With a gasp, Aurora tore her hand out of his and thrust herself to her feet. She was about to flee the temple when Graham caught her skirt and brought her to a sudden stop.

"Aurora, wait, listen to what I say. I'm older than you and I know more of such things, which is as it should be. Once we're married, I will teach you—"

"Let me go!" She struggled in his grasp, but his hands held tight on her wrists. She didn't want him to touch her. What Raven had said was true. She belonged to him. She felt it as much as he did. She could not imagine letting another man touch her as he did.

"Aurora, Aurora! Calm yourself. I won't hurt you. I promise."

"I don't want you to touch me! Take your hands off me!"

"Only if you promise not to run away. Promise me that and I'll let you go."

She nodded grudgingly, and cautiously he

released her. She stood before him, head bent, one balled fist rubbing away the tears that had begun slipping down her cheeks.

"Aurora," he said softly. "You must not be afraid of the physical side of love."

"I'm not," she whispered. It is only you, her thoughts continued. The physical side of love with you!

"I think you are. That is only natural and proper. But once we are married—"

She turned her back. "I don't wish to discuss this, Graham."

Thinking she meant the subject of lovemaking, he nodded. "As you wish. It is early yet. In time I will help you overcome these fears." Pulling out his ornate gold watch, he looked at the time. "I'm afraid it's too late for us to call on my mother. It will have to wait."

Turning back to him, Aurora seized her chance to say: "Listen to me, Graham. I'm afraid we've been hasty in announcing our engagement and—"

"Hasty?" he interrupted. "But you accepted my proposal."

"I know. But I acted impulsively."

"Nonsense. Now, Aurora, you're just overtired and overexcited."

"No, I'm not. Please, listen to me."

"I won't listen to such foolishness. Now, go upstairs like a good girl and let your maid put you to bed. After all—"

"Damn it, Graham! Stop talking to me as if I were a child! I am trying to tell you something!"

"I'm sorry, darling, what is it?"

Aurora ground her teeth in exasperation. "I

think we should call off our engagement. I was foolish tonight to tell you I would marry you."

The maddening half-smile on his lips never wavered. "You weren't foolish at all," he disagreed. "In fact, it is only now that you are being foolish. You're frightened; it is understandable. But I will not call off our engagement merely because of these useless schoolgirl qualms of yours.

"I'll say good night now since it is obvious that you are in no condition to discuss the matter rationally."

With a little half bow, Graham left her in the temple at the end of the garden. She squinted into the shadows, watching as he made his way back toward the veranda where the yellow light spilled through the French doors. She saw his silhouette as he opened one of the doors and disappeared into the house.

"Oh, Lord," she breathed, sinking back onto the bench and into the depths of her despair. "Why wouldn't he listen to me?"

But in the back of her mind she thought she knew the reason. Graham was determined that she would be his wife—as determined in his own way as Raven was that she belonged to him.

How had this happened? she asked the star-filled night sky. If she had never met Raven, would she have given in eventually to her aunt's and Graham's pressures and agreed to this marriage? She didn't like to think so. Even before Raven, she had dreamed in her innocent heart of a lover who would want her for herself and not merely because she was a "suitable" wife for a man of breeding and an heiress into the bargain.

Was that how Raven wanted her? For herself?

If what Marcus had told her was true, Raven was a wealthy man in his own right. He would not need a woman simply for her inheritance. He wanted her—he said she was his—but if that was the truth, why had he sent her away? And if he had been the one to send her away, why hadn't Graham recognized him at Madame Beauchene's soirée?

Hopelessly confused, she dropped her head into her hands. She didn't know which way to turn. She loved Raven, but she didn't know if she could trust him. She neither loved nor trusted Graham. But she was engaged to marry him. And on top of all that, Graham thought her aversion to his advances was simply a case of maidenly trepidation.

What would he think, she wondered, if he knew she could not bear his touch because her traitorous flesh cried out for the caresses of another man—a man who had already taken that which Graham believed belonged to him and him alone?

"What will I do?" she whispered. "I wish I could run away! I wish . . . I wish . . ."

She sighed, knowing how futile such an action would be. No matter where she ran, no matter how many miles she put between herself and Raven, his face would always haunt her dreams and her heart would always be his.

She looked down at her hand and at the great ruby that looked black in the darkness. She could not break her engagement to Graham. He would not let her and her aunt would not let her. And yet she had believed Raven when he said she was his and no one else could have her. Could she make Raven see that she had no choice—that Graham would never let her go? She laughed disdainfully at the folly of such a thought. Raven would never see that, and she—in her heart of hearts—knew she could never be a proper wife to Graham. How could she share a bed with him? Let him touch her as Raven had touched her? Bear his children? All the while mourning the loss of the most magnificent man she'd ever known. How could she ever hope to enter into such a union? It was madness to even think of such a thing. It was—

"Aurora!" Electra loomed over her like a great avenging angel.

"Good God!" Aurora breathed. "That's the second time tonight I was nearly scared to death!"

"What is this I hear about your wanting to end your engagement to Graham?"

Aurora stood, taking a deep breath. "I think, Aunt, that it was impulsive of me to accept. And I think—"

"You think! You think! I'll tell you what I think, my girl! If I hear one more word about breaking this engagement, I'll lock you in your room without so much as a crust of bread until you come to your senses!"

"You wouldn't dare!"

"Oh, wouldn't I? Try me!"

With a savage scowl, Electra turned and stormed back toward the house, leaving her niece to stare after her in stunned silence.

25

On the morning after Madame Beauchene's soirée,
Aurora came downstairs to find that her worst
fears had been realized. She had hoped to keep the
news of her engagement a secret until she could
find a way of breaking it. Those fond but foolish hopes died a quick death when she found
the newspapers on the table in the downstairs
hall.

Emblazoned across the front pages of both the
Chicago Tribune and the larger *Chicago Daily News*
were photographs of her and Graham taken by the
hordes of photographers who had met them on the
dock after their return from the islands. The
journalists, so it seemed, found the tale of her loss
overboard in the storm, her survival in the "wilderness," her "rescue" and now her betrothal to her
"rescuer" irresistible.

Electra swept into the hall and found her

there, gazing balefully at the headlines. "All this interest in the betrothal," Electra said with smug satisfaction, examining the papers through the gold-filigree lorgnette that hung on a long chain about her neck. "Your wedding will be the social event of the year!"

Aurora glared at her, and Electra's rouged cheeks flushed an even darker shade of red.

"Now, don't start being difficult again, Aurora," she warned. "I've had quite enough of that foolishness after last night. Preparations for the wedding will go forward, and you will not—will not, do you hear me?—do one thing to hinder them. I was perfectly serious last night. Any more of your ridiculous objections and I will see to it that you are shown precisely how little you can do to foil this marriage."

"My parents would not have forced me into a loveless marriage!" Aurora retorted.

"How do you know? You were too young for such considerations when they died. At least Graham is an American. There are many, many heiresses these days being sold off to impoverished European princelings. Oh, no, I am not the villainess you paint me to be, my dear. I am only concerned for your best interests."

"And with your nephew's finances!"

"How dare you?" Electra's eyes bulged; her cheeks flushed scarlet. "You horrid little wretch!" Before she could stop it, her hand lashed out, catching Aurora on the cheek and gouging her pale, translucent flesh with the edge of her emerald-cut diamond.

Gasping, Aurora staggered back, her hand raised to her injured cheek. When she looked at her palm, it was stained with crimson. Horrified, Electra started toward her, but Aurora, tears smarting her eyes, ran from the hall, retreating up the stairs to her room.

"It's not a deep cut," Bridey told her as she tenderly bathed Aurora's cheek. "I don't think it will leave a scar. But it's going to show for a time."

Taking the damp cloth from her maid, Aurora held it against her cheek to stanch the steady trickle of blood.

"I don't care about that," she said dully.

"Don't care? Miss Aurora! To be scarred! Ah, yer sweet face—"

"What difference does it make? Graham would marry me if I were a two-headed hunchback with a nose like a cucumber!"

Bridey giggled. "Of course he would. He loves you!"

"Oh, not you too," Aurora groaned, rolling her eyes.

"Well? Doesn't he love you?"

Aurora shrugged, frowning at the stained cloth before pressing it to her cheek again. "I don't know if he does or not. I don't really care. I don't want to marry him, but I don't know how to get out of this engagement. Aunt Electra, as you can see, goes insane if I even suggest it. Oh, God! Why did I ever agree to marry him?"

"Why did you?" Bridey asked, having been curious about it herself.

Aurora looked at the maid and in spite of herself smiled at the curiosity on the girl's face. She shook her head.

"I don't know," she answered, much to

Bridey's disappointment. That was not, strictly speaking, the truth, but the truth was something she could share with no one, not even her maid. She rose.

"Find something for me to wear, Bridey. I've a mind to go out."

An hour later, dressed in a gown of soft grey wool over which was worn a tailored jacket of black silk, Aurora straightened her black and grey bonnet in the mirror.

"You look like you're in mourning," Bridey said with a grimace. She preferred the brighter, gayer gowns in Aurora's extensive wardrobe, but Aurora had rejected them all.

"I feel like I'm in mourning," Aurora replied sourly. "Get your cloak. We'll go shopping."

Calling for a carriage, the two women drove through the city, strolled through the park, visited milliners, dressmakers, stationers. The shopkeepers fawned on Aurora, recognizing her from the morning's papers. They were, Aurora speculated to Bridey, hopeful of sharing in the bounty of her aunt's elaborate and expensive "wedding of the year." Occasionally an enterprising reporter, recognizing Aurora, would respectfully—sometimes rudely—demand a statement. To them, respectful or rude, Aurora refused to comment.

At last, plagued by the whispers and stares that followed them everywhere, they took refuge in a small bookshop tucked between a French perfumery and a gentlemen's club.

The proprietor, a small German gentleman who squinted through a pair of thick spectacles and whose gnarled fingers were permanently stained with the ink of a thousand books, was occupied with a customer at the back of the shop. He bent to take a volume from a bottom shelf, and Aurora saw that his customer was Marcus Ravenswood.

Relief swept over her. A friend! After all the gawkers and gossips in the street who had made her feel like little more than some new specimen on display in the zoo, it was a pleasure to see a familiar face.

She watched as Marcus examined the book and then, shaking his head, returned it to the bookseller. He came toward the door, and Aurora smiled as he looked up and noticed her there.

"Hello, Mr. Ravenswood," she said. "It's so very nice to—"

Marcus's sky-blue eyes swept over her quickly, coldly, dismissively. Reaching up a gloved hand, he tipped his hat to her and then, without a single word of greeting, was gone.

Aurora stared after him. His disdain hurt her more than Electra's slap. What had she done? Why had he turned against her?

He had been present at Madame Beauchene's when her engagement was announced, of course. And no doubt he had seen the newspaper articles. She supposed he thought her betrothal was a betrayal of his son.

She clenched her fists. In that one moment of panic—in the single instant of impulsive foolishness—she had ruined everything.

"I may help you, Fräulein?" the little bookseller asked, standing at a respectful distance. "I have many new novels; stories of romance and intrigue that the ladies like."

"What was that?" Aurora turned to him, for a moment nonplussed. "Oh, yes, thank you."

Without thought she allowed the bookseller to sell her a small stack of novels she neither wanted nor expected to read. Giving him her uncle's address, she told him to have the books sent over by messenger. Then, followed by Bridey, she climbed back into her carriage and asked to be taken home.

Listlessly she picked at her lunch, ignoring her aunt's attempts to enlist her in a conversation about wedding preparations. She was thankful that Graham had not been invited. Or had he? Has he had some convenient excuse to keep him away from another boring luncheon at his aunt's table? Before, he had been so attentive, so eager to spend every possible moment in her company. But now— now they were engaged. She was his—or so he thought, she reminded herself—and perhaps he felt that he needn't play the part of the ardent swain quite so assiduously. Either way, she was glad of his absence.

"What are you going to do this afternoon, Aurora?" Electra asked.

Aurora pushed a bit of meat across her plate with her fork. "I thought I'd ride my bicycle," she replied. "This beautiful weather isn't going to last forever, summer is all but over. Soon I won't be able to ride any longer."

Electra grimaced. "I know it's fashionable, but somehow riding a bicycle seems so unladylike."

"It's no worse than riding a horse," Aurora pointed out.

"Yes, I think it is. After all, a lady rides a horse

sidesaddle. A bicycle is ridden—" She shuddered delicately. "Astride."

Despite her aunt's misgivings, Aurora dressed in her green velveteen cycling costume and left, bound for Marcus Ravenswood's mansion, determined to win back the friendship she had jeopardized by her foolishness.

Hawkins opened the door. "Ah, Miss Jephson," he said. "Please come in."

"Is Mr. Ravenswood at home?" she asked.

"He is in the library, miss. I shall tell him you are here."

"That won't be necessary. I know the way."

Before the butler could say more, Aurora was on her way up the stairs. She strode down the hall, trying desperately to think of what she would say when she and Marcus were face to face. How could she explain her sudden about face? How could she make him understand that although everything she had told him about her feelings for his son were perfectly true, it might prove necessary for her to marry Graham Hughston? How could she convince him that that just might prove to be the wisest course after all—particularly when she couldn't begin to convince herself of it?

Hesitating outside the library door, she tidied her hair—upswept beneath her little green bonnet —and arranged her ruffled chiffon cravat. Rubbing the toes of her shoes on the backs of her pearl-buttoned gaiters, she removed the road dust from them. Then, very lightly, she tapped at the door.

"Come in?" The words were muffled by the thickness of the door.

Aurora opened it and stepped inside. "Excuse

me for barging in this way, sir, but after this morning I wanted to see you and try to explain—"

She stopped just inside the doorway. Lounging in an armchair, a book opened on his lap, was Raven.

He rose with the easy, feline grace that had always fascinated her. In shirtsleeves, the front of his shirt opened, the long, French-cuffed sleeves rolled back, he looked devastatingly masculine. The white silk of his shirt was a startling contrast to the sun-kissed bronze of his skin.

"Aurora." His azure eyes swept over her. "What a wonderful surprise."

She stared at him, stunned. The thought that he might be here had never entered her befuddled mind.

"I didn't come here to see you," she blurted, her heart pounding in her chest as he approached.

"How sad," he murmured, his eyes never leaving hers.

"I . . . I . . ." She gazed into his eyes, mesmerized, fascinated, unable to force herself to move even as he crossed the room toward her. "I came to see your father."

"He is not at home at the moment, I'm afraid."

"But Hawkins said Mr. Ravenswood was in the library."

"And so he is," Raven said softly. And his cerulean eyes glittered like blue fire as he moved past her and closed the library door.

26

He made her a little half-bow that mocked them both.

"Mr. Charles Ravenswood, at your service." He circled her slowly, his glorious, long-lashed eyes perusing her cycling costume. "Very fetching, my love," he said. "It reminds me of those pretty, lace-trimmed little drawers I saw you in on the island."

Aurora felt her cheeks flushing hotly. "Really, Raven! You have no business even remembering such things."

"It's damned hard to forget!"

"You're no gentleman!"

He laughed. "I've never claimed to be, remember?"

Aurora clasped her hands in front of her. Suddenly the room felt so close, so warm. Why did he have to stand so close to her?

"I came to see your father," she repeated.

"So you said. Why?"

"I ran into him in a shop this morning. He seemed angry with me. He didn't even say hello."

"He thinks you lied to him. He feels you've used him."

"But I didn't! I—"

She cried out as Raven took her by the arm. His fingers were gentle, but his blue eyes were stormy as he touched the scarlet scratch on her cheek.

"Who did this to you!" he demanded. "Did Hughston strike you?"

"No. No! It was an accident."

"If he ever touches you—hurts you—I'll kill him!" Raven snarled.

His vehemence frightened her. She trembled. "I told you. It wasn't Graham. It was an accident."

Raven looked unconvinced but he released her. "I mean it, Aurora. If he ever harms you—"

"He wouldn't," she told him coolly. "And anyway, it's not really your concern."

"I protect what's mine."

"I'm not yours. Haven't you read the papers this morning? Weren't you at Madame Beauchene's last night?"

His smile betrayed not the slightest concern. "I don't always believe what I read in the papers," he told her. "And I know what caused you to act so impulsively at Madame Beauchene's."

"You think you know so much," she taunted, infuriated by his cool self-confidence, his maddening arrogance. "Well, you don't know anything. I am going to marry Graham Hughston! I am! Aunt Electra has already begun the planning."

"A waste of time," Raven murmured.

Aurora glared at him. How dare he! He was so sure of himself, so certain of his hold on her heart, her senses. She wanted more than anything to extricate herself from the senseless entanglement of her engagement to Graham, but at that moment she would have endured the tortures of the damned before she'd let Raven know it.

"A waste of time?" she asked. "But it's not, I assure you. My Aunt Electra has promised me that my wedding to Graham will be the social event of the year."

Raven's eyes flashed with sudden anger. "That is not amusing, Aurora."

"It wasn't meant to be amusing." She held out her hand. The ruby that covered the first joint of her finger glowed with a fire all its own. "This is hardly a joke, would you say?"

"Do you want to know what I think of that?" Raven snarled.

Smiling, she gracefully inclined her head. "By all means."

She cried out as he seized her wrist in a viselike grip. Before she could react, he had wrenched the heirloom gem off her finger and strode to the open window.

"Raven, don't!" she screamed. "Please! I—"

Her eyes were wide and horrified as he threw the ring out the window toward the broad, rolling, shrub-dotted lawn.

She ran to the window. "Oh, my God," she breathed. The lawns seemed to go on forever and here and there they were ornamented with tangled beds of bushes and vines. "What am I going to tell Graham?"

Leaning on the window casement, Raven smiled lazily. "Send him to me," he offered. "I'll explain."

"Explain?" She stared up at him. "Explain what? How could you possibly explain throwing away an heirloom engagement ring? That ruby is worth tens of thousands of dollars."

"I'll simply tell him I don't appreciate other men trying to lay claim to what is mine."

"I'm not yours, damn you!"

He touched her cheek. "You are. You're just too damned stubborn to admit it." Leaving the window, he strolled across the room. "Graham Hughston is not the man for you. Even if you had never met me, he wouldn't have been the man for you. He's weak. And you—you're stubborn, headstrong, spoiled and willful. You need a strong hand—applied to your backside if necessary."

"How dare you!" she hissed. "No one speaks to me that way!"

"I'll speak to you any way I please, Aurora." His voice was soft, grim. "And I'll dare a damned sight more than that if I want to."

The dangerous glitter in his eyes told her precisely what he meant. Aurora felt fury rising inside her like a scorching flame—fury at him for his arrogance and at herself for the burgeoning glimmer of excitement he kindled inside her with such effortless ease.

"You're insufferable," she snapped, green eyes glowing.

His smile was slow and sensuous. "And you're beautiful." His eyes traveled over her, lingering on the full Turkish trousers of her cycling costume. He stretched out a hand toward her but she jumped back out of his reach.

"Don't touch me!"

His eyes narrowed. "Is that what you say to Graham?"

She lifted her chin and regarded him scornfully. "Graham is my fiancé," she reminded him. "He has the right—"

"Damn you!" Raven snarled. Lunging, he caught her by the arm before she could flee. "Damn you! Have you let him touch you? Have you?" He shook her. "Tell me!"

"It's none of your business!" she snapped. "Let me go!"

Jerking herself free, she ran toward the door but he was faster. Before she could reach for the latch he had seized her about the waist. With his superior strength and greater weight, he pinioned her against the gleaming oak panels of the door.

"Answer me, God damn you!" he snarled into her ear. "Has that bastard touched you? Have you let him into your bed!"

"You have no right to ask me that!" she whimpered. "No right!"

"I have every right! You gave me the right on the island when you gave yourself to me."

"I didn't! You took what you wanted! You—"

His derisive laughter silenced her. "And you didn't want it? The way you don't want it now? That must be why you're trembling. Is it?"

She gasped as he pressed his body to hers. Without the cushioning layers of petticoats between them, his desire for her was all too evident. He chuckled softly as she laid her forehead against the door and a little moan escaped her.

"Please, Raven," she breathed. "No, I can't—"

His hands were at her hips, his mouth at the tender nape of her neck. Her fingernails scratched at the polished door panels and, instinctively, she pressed back against him.

"Aurora," he whispered, his lips moving against the back of her neck, his hot breath caressing her skin. "Tell me that you want me."

"No," she moaned. "I don't want you! I hate you! Hate you!"

His hands slipped between her body and the door and he freed the buttons of her jacket and caressed her breasts through the soft, thin fabric of her blouse.

"Tell me," he murmured, his fingers teasing their taut, aching crests until Aurora wanted to scream.

"I hate you!" she sobbed, shuddering, buffeted by a hunger like nothing she could ever have imagined existed.

He opened her blouse and one hand slipped inside and found its unerring way beneath the beribboned chemise she wore underneath. His other hand slipped down over her belly to the joining of her thighs.

"Tell me," he insisted, his voice low and husky with his own desire.

Aurora wept. Her body burned for him, ached for him. Turning in his arms, she buried her head in his shoulder even as her traitorous body strained against him.

He cupped her chin with one hand and lifted her face toward his. "Tell me," he demanded, his eyes dark and smoldering with his desire for her.

Tears crept down Aurora's flushed cheeks. She

was beaten, helpless, her will was his to command. She had no choice but to accept defeat.

"I want you," she sighed, her lips scarcely forming the words.

Sweeping her into his arms, Raven left the library and carried her down the corridor to his room where the brass four-poster, gleaming in the muted sunlight of the late afternoon, waited.

He stood her on her feet in the shadowy chamber where the blue damask draperies dimmed the glow of the sun. Slipping a finger beneath her chin, he tilted her face toward his. Her eyes, wide with wonder and dark with desire, fluttered, then closed as he kissed each corner of her trembling mouth. A tiny sigh escaped her as he traced the full, pouting curve of her lower lip with the tip of his tongue. One small, trembling hand touched his cheek as she pressed her lips to his. The time for pretense, for reluctance, was past.

She stood like an obedient child while he undressed her. Her lips parted, she breathed quickly, shallowly, lightly while his hands lovingly traced the tempting curves of her legs, her hips, through the soft, clinging velvet. She giggled when he cursed the high-buttoned gaiters, sighed when he freed the pearl fastening of her blouse and his hands found the quivering softness of her breasts.

Then, after an eternity, she stood before him, the muted sunlight highlighting the lush beauty of her body. His hands were in her hair, freeing it from its pins, spreading it over her shoulders, letting it cascade down her back.

"Aurora," he moaned softly, burying his face in its fragrant, fiery mass.

Her fingers fumbled with the buttons of his

shirt but his hands closed over her wrists, pulling them away.

"Later," he rasped.

His need was too urgent, too sharp, to wait another moment for her. He worked at the fastenings of his trousers and then, lying back on the coverlet of the wide brass bed, drew her to him, over him.

"Raven!" Aurora gasped. There was something deliciously wicked about being naked while he was clothed.

But then all thoughts of right and wrong, of goodness and wickedness, were forgotten as he pulled her to him, astride him. Surrendering her will to him, she let him guide her, lower her, until her body, her mind, was filled with him. His hands at her hips taught her the motion, set the rhythm. Through slitted eyes, Raven watched her as she loved him, pleasuring them both. He pulled her closer, kissed her lips, her throat, the tight, aching, exquisitely sensitive tips of her creamy breasts.

Desire became passion and their passion flourished, growing apace, rising, soaring, raging, becoming a kind of madness, swirling around them, within them, a maelstrom of pure sensation, whirling higher, faster, until at last it released them in an exquisite, shattering ecstasy that left them weak, exhausted, sated.

Aurora awoke to find herself in Raven's arms. His clothes lay in a tangled heap on the floor beside the bed. He lay behind her and his body curved about hers protectively, possessively. She felt his breath, hot and sweet, against her ear.

It had been madness, the voice of reason

whispered to her, but what sweet, what rapturous madness! She cursed the part of her mind that told her she should leave him—that she must leave him.

As gently as she could, she slipped out of his arms, but as she would have left the bed, his fingers closed about her wrist.

"Don't go," he asked softly.

"I have to."

"Not yet."

Impossible as it seemed, she felt the heat of desire rising in her once more. What was it about him, what magic did he possess, to make her need him so? Want him again and again?

Heedless of the voices of reason and warning that whispered inside her head, she turned and slid back into his bed, back into his arms, and reveled in the touch of his skin against hers.

27

Buried in the snowy mounds of rose-scented bubbles that filled the walnut-paneled, rose-painted porcelain tub in the upstairs bathroom of her uncle's house, Aurora hid her face in her hands. It seemed she didn't know herself any more. Hadn't she proven that this afternoon?

Lying back in the tub, her eyes closed, she remembered how he had touched her, stroked her, kissed her. It seemed there wasn't a square inch of her body that he hadn't kissed, caressed, tasted. And she had been helpless to resist. Resist! She had to smile at the thought. After those first few paltry protests, she hadn't even tried to resist. She had wanted him, needed him, and in the end, when his continued teasings had become a kind of exquisite, sensual torment, demanded him. He had become her teacher and she his eager pupil. He had taught her things, shown her pleasures, she'd never dreamed existed. She'd wanted to stay with him forever and never venture beyond the confines of that gleaming, dimity-draped bed.

But the time had come, as she'd known it must, when she'd had to put on her clothes and leave. Raven had lain on the bed and watched her dress. When she had been about to leave, he'd caught her wrist and stopped her.

"I'm leaving Chicago," he had told her. "In one month. I am going back to the island and you're coming with me."

"Raven," she had whispered, loath to allow reality to shatter the dreamlike spell that had enveloped them. "I can't—"

He had silenced her protests with kisses before unlocking the door to let her go. "One month," he had repeated before closing the bedroom door behind her.

Dazed, Aurora had gone downstairs, bade goodbye to Hawkins (who, like the perfect butler he was, gave no clue as to whether he knew what had happened upstairs or not) and took her leave.

Now, scarcely two hours later, she was at a loss to explain the fevered, passionate hours she had spent locked in Raven's arms.

But the memories of those sweet hours made her tremble all over again. Her tender breasts ached for his touch, his kiss. Her body seemed to grow warm with the mere thought of his caresses. With trembling fingers she touched her breasts, her belly, her thighs. Shyly, tentatively, she touched herself, flushing as she remembered Raven's dark hair on the white skin of her thighs as he had kissed her there where she had scarcely ever even touched herself.

"Miss Aurora?" Bridey was peering around the door.

Aurora sat up in the tub, her cheeks scarlet. "What is it?" she asked, her voice strangely tight and strained.

"Your aunt wants to know if you'll be much longer in here. Mr. Graham is downstairs waitin' to take you to dinner."

Graham. After this afternoon, she was going to have to spend the evening with Graham and pretend that nothing at all was wrong. Well, what did she expect? After all, she had accepted his proposal. She had accepted his ring.

His ring! She held up her bare hand before her face. The ring! She had completely forgotten it.

"Oh, Lord!" she breathed.

"What's wrong?" Bridey asked, entering the room.

"Nothing!" Aurora plunged her hand beneath the sudsy surface of the water to hide it. "Nothing at all. I'll be out in a moment. Are my things laid out?"

"Everything's all ready and waitin'," Bridey assured her.

"And my gloves? I told you I want the black gloves to wear with that gown."

"The long suede ones? But how will you wear your engagement ring?"

Aurora shrugged one bare, soapy shoulder. "I won't be able to, I suppose. Graham will simply have to understand."

The maid left and Aurora heaved a sigh of relief. She would have one night's grace. But she would have to get that ring back tomorrow if she

258

had to go over to Marcus Ravenswood's house and search the lawns herself with a fine-tooth comb!

Forty-five minutes later, dressed in an evening gown of yellow satin embroidered with jet and trimmed around the hem and over the shoulders with black marten fur, Aurora smoothed on the twenty-button gloves of black suede and took the black-lace fan Bridey offered her. She stood, tucking a stray curl into her upswept coiffure while the maid draped over her shoulders an evening cape of black satin trimmed with black marten and creamy guipure lace.

"All ready?" Bridey asked, hurrying to open the door for her.

"As ready as I shall ever be," Aurora answered, resigned.

The look of genuine admiration on Graham's face as he watched her descend the marble stairs brought no rush of answering warmth into Aurora's heart. She resented his intrusion into her day—she would much rather have spent the evening lying in the beautiful bed upstairs dreaming of Raven's exquisite lovemaking.

"You look ravishing," he murmured, dropping decorous pecks on both her cheeks. "You're positively radiant. Isn't she glowing, Aunt Electra?"

Their mutual aunt appeared from an adjoining salon. "She is," Electra allowed. "It's not surprising—"

Aurora's heart thudded in her chest. Had her aunt somehow discovered where she'd been all afternoon? Had she discovered what she'd been doing?

"She's in love with a handsome young man."
Electra patted Graham's arm. "Why shouldn't she
be radiant?"

A sick feeling twisted inside Aurora. How long
could this go on? How long . . . ? She realized her
aunt was saying something.

"I'm sorry. What was that?" she asked.

"I said, where is your ring?"

Aurora gritted her teeth. Trust dear Aunt
Electra to draw Graham's attention to its absence.

"These gloves are very tight," she explained. "I
couldn't possibly wear the ring under them."

Electra's lips tightened into a narrow, disapproving line. "I hope you've put it somewhere safe.
We wouldn't want someone to steal it, would we?"

"Aunt Electra!" Graham objected. "Who
would steal it? Don't you trust your own servants?"

"Believe me, Aunt," Aurora replied. "It would
take a miracle for anyone to find that ring."

Electra shot her a suspicious glance, wondering what she meant, but Graham insisted they
leave. Aurora was only too pleased to accompany
him out of the mansion and into the carriage that
waited in the drive.

"Where are we going?" she asked as they
rolled out from beneath the porte cochere.

"Some friends of my family are having an
intimate dinner party. They have a daughter who
made her debut some years ago. They haven't
managed to procure a husband for her yet, despite
a very respectable dowry."

"Sounds like your little friend from New York.
What was her name? Oh yes, Caroline Denbigh."

"I scarcely knew Caroline Denbigh," Graham
objected. And it was true. Electra had kept such a

tight rein on him in New York that he hadn't the opportunity to do more than make the acquaintance of the delicious, scandal-tarnished Miss Denbigh.

"Well, what seems to be this girl's problem? I thought a large dowry overcame any obstacle."

"How cynical you sound. I don't like it, really, Aurora." Graham glanced out the window unaware that, as he did, he displayed the greatest flaw in his otherwise handsome face—his weak chin.

"Have you ever considered growing a beard?" Aurora wanted to know, studying his chin critically.

"What?" Graham glanced at her curiously. "A beard? No one wears beards these days, except, perhaps, very old men and sailors."

"Pity," she murmured.

Silence reigned until Aurora brought the conversation back to their hosts' daughter.

"Well, what is wrong with her?"

"Wrong with whom?" Graham asked, bewildered by the sudden change of topic.

"With this girl—the one with the respectable dowry."

"Now that you mention it, it is rather like Caroline Denbigh."

"She's fast?"

"Aurora! No! At least not that I've heard. The scandal concerns her mother. The rumor is that she was not fathered by her mother's husband but by a Chinese houseboy they once employed."

"The Chinese houseboy!" Aurora laughed. "That's ridiculous!"

"Wait until you see her. She has a rather Oriental look about her."

"So have some of the Vanderbilts; no one ever slandered them that way."

But Aurora's interest was piqued and when they arrived at the strange, castlelike home of Colonel and Mrs. Alton Armbruster, she took Graham's arm and made her way almost eagerly into the house.

Their host, a distinguished white-haired man with an impressive set of side-whiskers, and his wife, a bejeweled pouter pigeon of a woman, greeted them effusively and apologized for the tardiness of their daughter who was still upstairs dressing. They expressed their best wishes for Aurora's and Graham's marriage, and Mrs. Armbruster cooed her disappointment that Aurora had not worn the famed ruby she had heard so much about.

"Come into the salon, dear," she invited when Graham and the colonel launched into a discussion of the War Between the States in which the colonel had earned his rank and nickname. "I shall send someone up to hurry my daughter, Abra, along. She is not usually so late, but I'm afraid she wishes to be especially pretty tonight."

"I see," Aurora murmured, scarcely hearing a word her hostess said. Try though she might, she could not imagine this formidable, jewel-bedecked, silver-haired, oh-so-proper matron writhing in ecstasy beneath a Chinese houseboy.

She flushed then at her own thoughts. Raven was turning her into some sort of wanton, she told herself. Or was it just that she was discovering her own true nature under his expert tutelage?

"You must be looking forward to your wedding," Deborah Armbruster said, leaning forward, blue eyes gleaming, as if she expected Aurora to confide something scandalous to her.

Aurora hesitated. She couldn't tell this woman the truth—that she wanted nothing more than to wave a final fond farewell to her dear fiancé—so she only smiled.

Fortunately, at that moment a tap on the salon door heralded the arrival of the tardy Miss Abra Armbruster.

"Abra, dear," Deborah Armbruster said, holding out a gloved hand to her daughter. "Do come and meet dear Graham's fiancée, Miss Aurora Jephson."

Abra Armbruster was nearly twenty-five. She was short, dark and slender, with blue-black hair and a complexion like old ivory. Her eyes, Aurora had to admit, had an exotic Oriental tilt to them, but, as she had pointed out to Graham, that didn't prove the houseboy story. She was likely merely a throwback to some long-forgotten ancestor, but scandal-hungry society was making her pay for it.

"How do you do," Aurora murmured.

"So nice to meet you," Abra replied. Sitting down on the sofa beside her mother, she arranged her gown of cream broché satin and pleated chiffon around her.

"You're looking lovely tonight, my dear," Mrs. Armbruster said to her daughter. She turned to Aurora, her blue eyes twinkling. "Abra and Graham were courting before your aunt summoned Graham to New York, you know."

"I didn't know that," Aurora murmured. Inwardly she cursed Graham for bringing her here to spend the evening in the company of a girl he had jilted in favor of Aurora's larger fortune. "I'm sorry it didn't work out."

"No matter," Deborah assured her airly. "There's no dearth of eligible young men in Chicago. In fact, our other guest—who is also tardy—is a new beau. We have high hopes of a match between him and Abra."

"Mother," Abra whispered, her cheeks flushing to a dusky pink that was very becoming. "He isn't a beau. His father and Father are friends. I'm sure he hasn't the slightest interest in me."

"I'll hear none of that," Mrs. Armbruster hissed, irritated at being contradicted before a guest. "That is why you are twenty-five without a husband in sight, my girl! With your moaning and moping, you drive the men away!" She turned to Aurora, who was passionately wishing she were somewhere else. "How old are you, my dear?"

"Eighteen," Aurora replied, thankful for once that Electra was her aunt. It could have been this dragoness!

"Eighteen! Do you hear that?" Deborah demanded of her miserable daughter. "Eighteen and making one of the most dazzling matches of the year! I'll wager she doesn't belittle herself that way you—"

Mercifully a tap at the door cut off Mrs. Armbruster's tirade.

"Yes?" she called, her voice suddenly cheery and musical.

Colonel Armbruster stuck his bewhiskered head around the door. "Dinner is served, m'dear. And our other guest has arrived."

"Oh, my! We're coming. Come along, children."

After tugging her daughter's gown into what she considered a more satisfying drape, Mrs. Armbruster led the girls out of the salon and toward the dining room that lay at the other end of a dark stone corridor.

"Smile," she cautioned her daughter. "This may be last chance to catch a husband!"

"Ah, here they are," the colonel said as the three women trooped into the room.

The three men stood behind their chairs as Deborah directed Aurora and Abra to their seats. Aurora's chair faced Graham's across the table. Her host and hostess sat at either end. As she took her seat, her eyes lifted to the face of the sixth member of the party.

"Miss Aurora Jephson," Deborah was saying, "have you met Mr. Charles Ravenswood?"

28

"Yes," Aurora said softly, unable to tear her eyes away from Raven's smiling face. "Of course. Good evening, Mr. Ravenswood."

"Charles, please," he corrected. His voice was cool, polite, a stranger's voice.

They took their seats, each unaware of the presence of anyone else in the room. Then, prompted by a sharp kick delivered by her mother under the table, Abra Armbruster bestirred herself to say:

"What a very handsome tie pin that is, Mr. Ravenswood. Is it a family heirloom?"

"So I'm told," Raven replied, smiling blithely.

Aurora's eyes, like everyone else's, were drawn to the creamy folds of Raven's cravat. There, fastened into the carefully tied foulard ascot, Aurora's ruby glowed in the light of the chandelier above the table.

Her eyes, wide and horrified, flew to his face. His azure eyes twinkled back at her, sparkling with amusement.

"I'm told," he said, his eyes never leaving her face, "that your engagement ring also boasts a ruby of exceptional size and quality, Miss Jephson. May I see it?" He glanced pointedly down toward her hands.

Aurora longed to untie the precise folds of his cravat and strangle him with it. But, aware that all eyes were upon them, she forced a convincing, if less than bright, smile to her lips.

"Unfortunately I was forced to leave it at home tonight, sir. My gloves, you know."

"How sad," he murmured.

Their eyes locked and sparks flew between them. Deborah Armbruster, sensing the inexplicable tension between her guests, jangled the bell to summon her servants with the first course of dinner.

Though she refused to look at him again, Aurora was all too aware of Raven beside her. She could feel the warmth of his body, smell the heady, spicy fragrance of his cologne, hear, during lulls in the Armbrusters' banal dinner conversation, his breathing. She knew without looking that he glanced her way again and again. She could feel his maddening amusement at her expense. She was also aware of the doggedly admiring eyes of Abra Armbruster which seemed never to leave Raven's face, even when she was addressed by another of her mother's guests.

Good Lord! Aurora thought. Surely the girl can't believe her mother will be able to match her with Raven! Surely Raven would never even think of—

But though the thought was absurd, a wave of jealousy swept over her. How dare that dreadful Deborah Armbruster scheme to win Raven for her daughter? Raven was hers! Hers! He belonged to—

Aurora closed her eyes, berating herself for her own foolishness. How could she claim Raven for her own when she herself belonged to another? She had no right to dictate to him as to what he should do, where he should go, whom he should see or court. But then, her mind argued, what right had he to berate her for her engagement? To taunt her by flaunting Graham's engagement ring under his very nose?

She glared across the table at Graham. What was wrong with the fool? Couldn't he see that the heirloom ruby he was so proud of was nestled in Raven's cravat? Couldn't he recognize the man he had rewarded for betraying her? Was he blind? Raven didn't look so very different in evening dress. Why couldn't Graham make the connection?

Graham glanced up and caught Aurora's ferocious stare upon him. He looked startled, as if he'd been caught committing some despicable faux pas of which he wasn't even aware.

At that moment Deborah Armbruster rose and, wishing the gentlemen the enjoyment of their port and cigars, led Aurora and Abra into the small drawing room next to the dining room.

"Oh, Mama, he's very handsome," Abra breathed as she sank onto the blue and gold silk of the couch. "But he didn't even seem to notice me."

"Of course he noticed you, my dear," Deborah

soothed, inwardly irritated that his attention had seemed centered on Aurora rather than her daughter. "He is too much of a gentleman to stare, that is all."

Aurora sighed, thinking them both ridiculous. If Raven was interested, they wouldn't be wondering. Surely—

"Do you know Mr. Ravenswood well?" Deborah was asking.

"I beg your pardon?" Aurora asked. "Oh! Charles Ravenswood, you mean?" Deborah nodded, and Aurora had a sudden, reckless urge to shout: Yes! I know him! In fact, I spent the afternoon in his bed! Instead she merely lifted one creamy shoulder. "We've met, of course. His father befriended me not long after my arrival in Chicago."

Deborah cooed sympathetically. "You must have had great need of a friend then, my dear. I remember all the dreadful publicity. How horrible it must have been for you. Lost in the wilderness with no one but backward clods for company."

"Actually, it was quite beautiful," Aurora defended. "As for the people—there are good people and bad people there like everywhere else."

"I'm sure there are, but still . . ." She shivered. "Savages! There are, aren't there? Savages?"

"I presume you mean Indians. Yes, there are. But I assure you they neither ambush wagon trains nor scalp settlers." Fleetingly she wondered if Deborah could be unaware of Raven's mixed ancestry. Or was it simply that she was willing to overlook anything short of abject poverty and raving lunacy in order to catch a husband for her daughter?

"I see." Her hostess seemed disappointed. "In any case, you must have been relieved to return to civilization."

"I suppose I must have been," Aurora agreed blandly.

Ignoring Deborah's sharp look, she gazed toward the French windows that led out onto the curving veranda. For a moment, an instant, another face peered back at her through the window. Then it was gone, but not before she had recognized that chiseled jaw, those piercing eyes. Raven.

Her heart pounded. He was there, in the darkness, waiting for her. Did she dare? Graham was in the next room. What if they were caught? How could they explain?

Casting caution to the winds, she lifted a hand to her forehead. "Please, Mrs. Armbruster," she said. "I suddenly feel quite light-headed. It must have been the wine at dinner. Would you think me terribly rude if I stepped out onto the veranda for a moment?"

Anxious for a few moments alone with her daughter to plan their strategy, Deborah Armbruster snapped at the bait like a hungry trout.

"Not at all, my dear. Please do. Shall I call for your wrap?"

"It's not necessary. I shall only be out for a few moments."

Smiling wanly, Aurora let herself out onto the night-shrouded, roofed veranda. It curved off in both directions, but she saw nothing save the glow of the dining-room windows some ways off to her left.

She frowned in disappointment. Had she been seeing things? Had she simply imagined she saw

Raven's face at the window? Perhaps she had been more truthful with Mrs. Armbruster than she had at first imagined—perhaps the wine she had drunk at dinner was causing her mind to play tricks on her.

Sighing, she leaned on the stone railing, her gloved fingers tapping on the grey stone banister impatiently. Lost in her thoughts, she did not hear Raven approaching. She was not aware of his presence until his strong hands spanned her waist, his body pressed against hers.

"Good evening, my love," he murmured, his lips warm and caressing on her bare shoulder.

"You must be insane," she hissed. "To come out here this way."

He chuckled. "If I'm insane, what does that make you? You knew I was here before you came out."

She ignored that. "What if we're caught?"

"What if we are? None of it will matter after we're back on the island."

"Raven—"

"Shhh. Let's save that argument for later, shall we?" He kissed her other shoulder. "You're beautiful in this gown," he told her, his hands sliding over the jet-embroidered yellow satin of her bodice to the deep curve of her breasts. "But you're far more beautiful out of it."

She quivered as he caressed her. It was madness! Insanity! But oh! So delicious!

"Stop it," she whispered, unconsciously pressing back against him.

"Say it again," he murmured.

"Stop it," she repeated weakly.

"Mean it," he challenged.

Reaching up with trembling hands, she took his wrists and held them as she turned to face him. The silver light of a three-quarter moon was captured in the glowing depths of the ruby he wore.

"My ring," she said, remembering it suddenly, reminded by its moonlit gleam. "Where did you find it?"

He touched the cold, blood-colored stone. "I didn't. One of the gardeners did."

"Give it back to me."

He laughed. "How could I? Everyone's noticed it thanks to Abra's compliment. If it suddenly disappeared, it would be missed."

"I must have it!" she insisted. "Graham, and my aunt, and even my maid have all questioned me about it. I covered for tonight by wearing these gloves, but I can't go on with that."

"Come and get it tomorrow. About three? My father will be out. He's going to Washington Park to the races. Perhaps I can convince him to take Hawkins with him."

Aurora closed her eyes, damning the hot flush of excitement that filled her. No! Not again! She couldn't! She wouldn't!

"I can't," she breathed. "It's wrong."

"It would be wrong if you didn't," he argued. "I promise I'll be good."

In spite of herself, Aurora smiled. "You'll be good?" she asked skeptically. "You promise?"

He nodded, his expression innocent. "I promise," he said solemnly, then deviltry sparkled in his azure eyes. "Even better than today."

"Oh!" Balling a fist, she punched him in the chest. "Damn you!" A noise from within the mansion startled her. "I have to go back. Graham might—" She scowled. "Graham. Why doesn't he recognize you? Why can't he see that you are the same man he paid the reward money to?"

"Because I'm not," Raven replied simply. "I've told you that."

"I don't believe you."

"That's your concern. I've told you the truth. Whether you believe me or not is up to you."

Aurora turned to return to the drawing room but hesitated as another thought struck her.

"Since you're being so honest tonight . . . Have you given the Armbrusters reason to believe you're interested in their daughter?"

He shrugged. "Not intentionally." He grinned. "But you can't fault them for hoping, can you? I'm considered quite a catch."

"And modest, above all." Aurora's green eyes glinted angrily. "You should marry her, Raven. Just think of the interesting children you'd have. Half white, one-quarter Ojibway, and one-quarter Chinese!"

She turned with a flounce of her head to return to the drawing room when his parting words, delivered in a mournfully mocking tone, reached her ears:

"Jealousy is such an ugly emotion."

Her hand on the latch, Aurora swung around to deliver a stinging retort, but he was gone, as silently as he'd come. He had disappeared swiftly, soundlessly, back into the dining room.

"Oh!" she raged. "Damn you to hell! Damn—"

"Aurora?"

Aurora started and, turning, found Deborah

Sandra DuBay

Armbruster standing in a second set of French windows further along the veranda. The woman squinted into the darkness.

"Is someone out there with you, dear?" she asked.

"With me?" Aurora repeated, the very picture of innocence. "No, of course not. There's no one else out here. I'm quite alone, as you can see. In fact, I was just coming in."

"How nice." Deborah eyed her guest curiously as both women reentered the drawing room. The girl had been speaking to someone. She had heard her plainly! But there appeared to be no one else there. If that was the case, she must have been speaking to herself. Perhaps she had addled her brains in the accident that had left her stranded on that island. Then again—she made a mental note to discover if Aurora's parents had been closely related. Perhaps, she thought just before her attention was captured by the return of the men, it was not such a good idea for Aurora to be marrying her cousin even if they were not strictly blood relations.

Later, in the carriage on the way home, Graham told her how Raven had excused himself and retreated to the veranda. The cigar smoke, he explained, made it difficult to breathe.

"Can you imagine that? Really!" Graham said, smirking.

"Well, he has lived most of his life in the country," Aurora reminded him. "He's used to clean, fresh air."

"I suppose."

"Mrs. Armbruster seems to think she may be

274

able to match Rav—Charles—and her daughter, Abra."

"It would probably be the best match either of them could make."

"That's unkind. Really, Graham!"

"Nevertheless, it's true. Ravenswood's heir or not, the man lacks breeding."

"I thought his manners were impeccable." She flushed, remembering the scene on the veranda. "In the dining room."

"Oh, he's learned all the niceties, of course," Graham allowed. "But breeding tells. That tie pin, for example. Did you ever see anything so ostentatious? It was obviously paste."

Aurora bit back a smile. "Was it really?"

"Unquestionably. I have an eye for quality, remember. It's a pity you didn't wear your engagement ring tonight. The comparison would have been quite startling, I can assure you."

"No doubt," Aurora agreed. She sighed, wondering yet again how she could ever hope to go through with a marriage to this pompous, overweening fool.

29

Listless and pale, wracked by indecision and worry, Aurora sat in a small flower-bedecked salon at the back of the mansion gazing out at the rainsoaked garden. The ticking of a long-case clock reminded her of the passage of time—of the approach of the hour when Raven expected her to come to him to retrieve her ring.

Shivering, she crossed her arms over her breasts and rubbed her shoulders. If she went . . . if they were alone as Raven seemed determined they should be . . . it seemed inevitable that they would make love. And yet, if she were going to marry Graham, she had no right to allow such a thing to happen.

She closed her eyes and heaved a profound sigh. The thought of marrying Graham dropped her into the deepest depths of despair. But each day that passed seemed to draw her further and further into the web her aunt and Graham were weaving about her. She was caught like the proverbial fly in the spider's parlor and she didn't know how to begin breaking free.

The door behind her opened, and she straightened her back, lifted her chin, raised her hand in an automatic gesture to the thick mass of flaming curls that tumbled freely past her shoulders. Glancing over her shoulder, she saw to her relief that it was not her aunt or Graham but her Uncle Carlisle who had entered the room.

"Good afternoon, darling," he said softly, moving slowly, painfully it seemed to Aurora, toward her.

Aurora watched him as he leaned heavily on the gold-knobbed walking stick he had begun using after his illness. Though he insisted frequently and vehemently that it was a mere affectation, Aurora knew better. He had been far more seriously ill than anyone had intimated, and he was not yet recovered. She wondered if Electra had known the real gravity of his illness. She wondered further if he would ever again be the laughing, charming man he had been during their year in New York.

"Why don't you sit down and talk to me for a while, Uncle?" Aurora invited, eager to see him take any rest she could entice him into.

"I must be going out soon," he told her. "Business, you know, will not wait on pleasant chit-chat."

She sighed. "Uncle, you have hundreds of people working for you. Can't they lift some of the burden off your shoulders?"

"Now, Aurora," he said sternly. "It is my

company, don't forget. I intend to see that it is run my way. To do that, I must be there."

"As you wish," she surrendered. "I can see it would do no good to argue. But I do wish you would take more time for relaxation and pleasure." She remembered an overheard conversation aboard her uncle's yacht—a conversation in which Electra was haranguing her husband about a girl he had apparently been keeping in an apartment. Aurora wondered if he still kept a mistress. She could not ask him, of course, but in a way she hoped he did.

Gingerly he lowered himself into the armchair opposite hers. His eyes were filled with paternal concern as he looked at her.

"You've been looking wan lately, Aurora. Pale. You've lost weight since you returned from that island."

She smiled. "It's only that I was sunburned when I came here. It's faded now to a fashionable pallor. As for the weight—with all the hustling and bustling about I do, I never get a chance to eat!"

He did not return her smile. "Tell me the truth. You are not happy—no, don't deny it. What's wrong? Is it Electra? Has she been badgering you? I know she can be difficult."

Aurora sighed, dropping her carefree pose. "I don't want to burden you, Uncle. You haven't been well lately and—"

"I'm not an invalid, child, nor has senility set in quite yet. I am your guardian—you should bring your worries, however small, to me."

Aurora toyed with the blue silk sash of her blue and cream plaid gown. "I'm afraid this is a rather large worry, Uncle Carlisle."

"I'm listening."

"I—"

Aurora broke off as there came a tapping at the door. A footman opened it and announced that Carlisle's carriage was waiting to take him to his office.

"Tell him to wait," Carlisle ordered. "And don't disturb me again."

Alone once more, Aurora took a deep breath and went on. "I don't want to marry Graham Hughston," she blurted out.

Carlisle's grey brows shot upward. "You're quite right, m'dear. That is a rather large worry. When did all this happen?"

"Actually, I never wanted to marry him. Not even when we were still in New York. I don't love him."

"Then why, may I ask, did you accept the man's proposal?"

"Because . . ." She paused, her eyes filling with tears. ". . . because I thought it didn't matter. I thought I would never find anyone who would love me for myself and not simply for my fortune. I suppose I thought Graham was the best of a bad lot."

"But now you've changed your mind?"

"I knew it was a mistake from the start. I—oh, Uncle Carlisle—I'm in love!"

Her uncle didn't bother to hide his surprise. "With whom, may I ask?"

"Rav—Charles Ravenswood," she corrected.

"Marcus's son? A handsome man. And does he feel the same way about you?"

"He does." She bit her lip. "Oh, Uncle Carlisle, I love him so. I have, ever since the island."

"Whoa! The island? What has he to do with the island?"

As succinctly as she could, Aurora described her meeting on the island with Raven. She told him of Raven's finding her on the beach, of his tending her, caring for her, of their falling in love. She trembled as she told him of their parting.

"I thought he had betrayed me," she finished. "I thought he had sold me back to Graham for the reward money. I thought he was like everyone else—willing to sacrifice anything for the right price. So I came to the conclusion that I may as well marry Graham. But then I saw Raven again at Madame Beauchene's soirée. My feelings for him, in spite of believing he had betrayed me, frightened me. I accepted Graham's proposal in a moment of panic."

"I see." Carlisle seemed a bit dazed by her revelations. "So you love this man in spite of the fact that he was willing to part with you for twenty-five thousand dollars?"

"That's just it. I'm not certain he was."

"Explain."

"He says he didn't. His father says he wouldn't. And Graham, who met with 'Raven' on the island to pay the reward, hasn't seemed to know him from Adam when he's met him here in Chicago."

"I see." Carlisle frowned thoughtfully. "And you, what do you think?"

"I don't think he would have left the island he loves so much to come to Chicago if he had been so willing to see me gone. He says he loves me, Uncle, and I believe him."

"And what of this counterfeit Raven on the

island? Do you think someone pretended to be him?"

"It's possible. I was taken from Raven's island directly to the yacht. I never saw the man Graham met."

"Was there someone on the island who would have wished you gone?"

"I don't know. I suppose there could have been someone who saw the reward offer in the newspaper and merely wanted to collect the reward. As far as anyone wanting me gone, only Sarah Oates—" Aurora's brow cleared. "Sarah Oates! Luke—"

"Yes?" Carlisle prompted. "Who is Sarah Oates? And Luke?"

"Sarah is Luke's sister. The family live on a tiny island to the west of Raven's island. They are a sinister clan, Uncle. There are rumors of their being wreckers. There is an abandoned lighthouse on their island, and it is widely suspected that they have lured yachts and small cargo ships onto the reef that surrounds their island in order to claim salvage rights."

"What do the survivors say?"

"There seem never to have been any survivors."

"Surely you can't mean—" Carlisle was clearly appalled.

"I don't know what I mean," she admitted. "These are only rumors."

"And you think they would have turned you over to Graham for the reward?"

"I think they would turn over their own mother for half as much. It was Sarah who came to the island that day while Raven was gone and told me

Raven wanted me taken to the yacht." She covered her face with her hands. "How could I have believed her? She wanted Raven for herself—of course she would have helped her brothers get rid of me!"

"It seems a logical assumption," Carlisle allowed.

"Oh, Uncle Carlisle, I've wronged Raven."

Her uncle smiled gently. "It would appear he's forgiven you, my dear."

"Yes!" She smiled, but her smile faded like the sun as it slips behind a stormcloud. "But there is still Graham."

"Tell him the truth. Tell him you don't love him. Give him back his ring and send him on his way."

"But Aunt Electra says—"

"Aurora." Carlisle sat forward in his chair. "You are eighteen years old. There is nothing Electra can legally do to stop you from doing as you please. You do not even need my permission anymore, although I would willingly give it to you— with my blessings."

"There will be trouble."

"I'll stand by you."

"Oh, dear Uncle Carlisle!" The long-case clock chimed two-thirty. "I'm supposed to meet Raven at his father's home at three."

"Then go. Take my carriage."

"Your carriage? But you were supposed to go to the office, remember?"

"Take it, child. I think I'll stay home this afternoon and have a little talk with your Aunt Electra."

Filled with joyous relief, Aurora threw her

arms about her uncle's neck and hugged him tightly. "Thank you. Thank you! Bless you, Uncle. I love you!"

He laughed. "Be happy, my dear, that is all I ask of you. Now go along and call your faithful Bridey. Have her dress you in your prettiest frock. You must look your best for your Raven."

Gleeful, Aurora almost skipped to the door. She smiled back over her shoulder as her uncle called to her one last time.

"And Aurora? I expect you to invite this young man to dinner. And soon. I want to get a good look at this prospective nephew-in-law of mine!"

"I will! Oh, yes, I will! I promise!"

Leaving the salon, Aurora felt as if the weight of the world had been lifted off her shoulders. Uncle Carlisle would fix everything! She would be free of Graham, and Raven would be hers—and she his—for ever and ever!

"Bridey!" she called, swinging the door of her bedroom wide. "Bridey! Come quickly! I need you!"

The maid appeared and stared at her mistress, amazed and bewildered by the difference in her. Instead of the morose, lethargic Aurora she'd seen in the past few weeks, this Aurora was radiant, carefree, filled with the simple joy of living.

"What's happened, miss?" she asked eagerly.

"Everything, Bridey! Everything! Now, hurry, I must look my best—for the man I love!"

30

In her newest gown, a snowy confection of gleaming white wool with an elbow-length cape, both bordered with ruffles of white moiré, Aurora bounced down the marble stairs of her uncle's mansion.

"Will you be wantin' me to come too?" Bridey asked, hurrying down after her, Aurora's white kid gloves in her hand.

"It's not necessary," Aurora told her, taking the gloves.

"It's rainin' somethin' fierce outside, miss," the maid said as she hovered in the doorway. "You'll ruin that dress and that hat!"

"I don't care!" Aurora called back as the coachman slapped the reins and the carriage started off. She laughed as she settled back against the leather seat. "I don't care."

In spite of the rain-swollen black clouds that

seemed determined to drench Chicago and everyone in it, Aurora's mood was light and gay. She couldn't remember ever being so happy, so filled with optimism for the future. She couldn't wait to tell Raven what her uncle had said. And although Marcus Ravenswood's mansion was not far from the Jephsons' it seemed to take forever and a day to make the trip down Lake Shore Drive.

At last—at last!—they turned between the wrought-iron gates and drew to a halt beneath the Ravenswoods' porte cochere.

A maidservant answered the door when Aurora rang the bell.

"Mr. Ravenswood, please," Aurora told her. "Mr. Charles. He's expecting me."

"Come in, please, miss," the girl invited. "Mr. Charles is in the music room. This way."

Aurora followed the parlor maid to the back of the mansion where an oval, bow-windowed room overlooked the tangle of trees and shrubbery left to grow naturally at the edge of the garden. From within the room came a rather disjointed series of notes. To Aurora it sounded rather like a kitten playing on a harpsichord keyboard.

"You needn't announce me," she told the maid, who curtsied and left her to return to her afternoon duties.

Aurora opened the door. In the music room with its beautiful frescoed ceiling and cream and gilt paneling, both taken whole out of an eighteenth-century Paris townhouse, several priceless instruments lay awaiting a hand to bring their music pouring forth. A golden harp stood in muted splendor, its reflection gleaming in the intricate parquet of the floor. A violin lay across a brocade and gilt bench. A cello leaned against a chair, its deep red-brown body catching the glimmer of the crystal chandelier above. In the bow of a set of curving windows, Raven sat. Head bent, he frowned at a yellowed sheet of music as with two fingers he hesitantly tapped out what sounded vaguely like a passage from a sonata.

Coming up behind him, Aurora slid her hands over his shoulders and down onto his chest. She kissed the back of his head lightly as he took one of her hands and raised it to his lips.

"Contemplating a musical career?" she asked teasingly.

He laughed. "Believe it or not, I had lessons as a boy. I used to be better than this."

"You could hardly have been worse," she said honestly.

"Don't you like Mozart?"

She sat on the bench beside him. "Is that what that was?"

"No doubt he's turning over in his grave about now."

Aurora snickered. "Spinning like a top, my love. Spinning like a top!"

"I resent that!" Raven protested.

"Mozart would have resented it too."

Laughing, Raven took Aurora's hand and led her to a curved loveseat fitted into one end of the bowed room just below an exquisite stained-glass window. Sitting down, he drew her onto his lap. With sure fingers he unfastened her cape and tossed it aside and, drawing out the long, pearl-headed hat pin, tossed her white-ribboned hat on top of it.

Enchanted, Aurora gazed into his magnificent azure eyes. "Something wonderful has happened," she said softly.

"Something wonderful is about to happen," he murmured, pulling her toward him.

Aurora shivered as he kissed her lips, her cheek, her throat. His hands were in her hair, drawing out all Bridey's carefully placed pins. Sighing, Aurora laid her head on his shoulder. His mouth was against her ear as his tongue toyed with the cameo earring dangling from her lobe.

"Raven, listen to me," she breathed.

"I'm listening," he assured her.

"No, you're not." She pushed herself upright. "You're not listening at all."

"I can listen and do this at the same time," he promised, his fingers working their nimble magic on the tiny pearl buttons that fastened the front of her gown.

"Raven—" she sighed as he opened her gown and in quick succession the lace-trimmed corset and chemise she wore beneath. He touched her breasts, caressing them, brushing the hardened tips with his thumbs, and Aurora knew she had to speak quickly or wait until much later to tell him her news.

Taking his wrists, she stilled his hands. "Wait," she ordered. "This is more important."

He fixed her with such a look of amazed skepticism that she had to laugh.

"Well, it is. Just now," she insisted. "I spoke to Uncle Carlisle this morning. I told him the truth."

"The truth about me?" Raven asked. "About us?"

"About everything. I told him I didn't want to marry Graham. I told him I didn't love Graham. I explained what caused me to accept Graham's proposal—what caused me to doubt your love for me."

"And what did he say?"

Aurora's smile blossomed. "He said I should give Graham back his ring and send him on his way."

"A man of rare sense," Raven decided. "But your aunt won't be so easy to convince."

"But I needn't convince her of anything. Uncle Carlisle promised to speak to her. And, as he said, I am eighteen. I don't need anyone's permission to marry. In any case, he said he would support me in all this." Tears welled into her eyes. "Do you know what this means?"

"It means you can free yourself from Hughston."

"Yes." Aurora waited breathlessly for him to go on. Surely he still wished to—surely he wanted her to—

"And you can marry me," Raven finished.

Aurora's heart leapt. "Oh, yes, Raven! I can marry you!"

She grew concerned as she noticed that he seemed not to share her unbridled joy. "What is it?" she demanded.

"I don't want to live in Chicago," he told her. "If you feel you can't give up the luxury and society of a city—"

"Dolt," she chided gently. "Don't you know I'd go anywhere with you? None of this means anything without you."

He smiled then, gently, tenderly. "And I take it

you have given up the notion that it was I who took the reward from Hughston?"

She nodded, feeling ashamed for having ever doubted him. "I think it must have been the Oateses," she said. "They wanted the reward. Sarah would have helped because, of course, she wanted you to herself."

He traced the path of a curl as it fell over her shoulder and down onto a milk-white breast where the skin was so translucent that the blue veins beneath were like a delicate, intricate tracery.

"How could you have thought I wanted you out of my life?" he asked. "Only the night before we had become lovers."

"You disappeared," she reminded him. "How was I to know where you had gone?"

"I went to Garden Island to think, to meditate, to decide what to do next. I left you a note telling you I love you and asking you to wait for me. Why do you think I did that if not to—"

"A note?" Aurora shook her head. "There was no note."

He closed his eyes, sighing wearily. "Sarah likely disposed of it. They were very thorough."

"But they didn't succeed," Aurora reminded him, caressing his cheek with the back of her hand.

"No," he agreed, capturing it and kissing it. "They didn't."

"Won't your father be pleased? It's what he wanted."

"Until he discovers we're going back to the island. We'll have to promise to come back to Chicago for Christmas."

"Oh, Raven, I'd like that. Let's tell him."

Raven smiled fondly at her giddy, childlike

289

enthusiasm. "He's not here. He went to the races with Madame Beauchene and Hawkins. We'll tell him when he returns."

"Maybe we could celebrate," Aurora suggested. "Uncle Carlisle said to invite you to dinner. Why don't you bring your father and we'll all celebrate."

"All except your Aunt Electra," Raven reminded her.

"Oh, pooh! She can go and mourn with Graham!"

They laughed, and Raven gazed longingly at the long white curve from the tip of her chin down to the beautiful, coral-tipped white breasts so temptingly near.

"Are we finished with our discussion now?" he asked hopefully.

"We're finished," she breathed, shuddering in anticipation.

"Good."

Taking her in his arms, he turned so that she lay on the loveseat. Kneeling above her, he pushed back her skirts and slipped her white doeskin slippers from her feet. His hands caressed her legs, moving up along the white silk stockings that encased them to the lacy garters that held them at mid-thigh. When his hand found the bare flesh above her garter, Aurora gasped and Raven's eyes met hers, twinkling devilishly.

"Aurora," he breathed, nuzzling her neck.

"Yes?" she asked, heart pounding.

"You're not wearing pantalettes."

She giggled, flushing. "I know," she whispered. "I'm wicked, don't you think so?"

"Shameless." His dark head bent and he

kissed the quivering fullness of her breast. "And delicious."

She sighed then and, arching her back, offered herself to him with all the eagerness that made her ache inside.

Lost in their sweet pursuits, neither heard the door of the music room open—neither noticed the inexperienced parlor maid until she announced:

"Mrs. Armbruster. Miss Armbrus—"

Raven and Aurora looked up. Standing framed in the doorway, their faces identical pictures of shocked amazement, were Deborah Armbruster and her daughter Abra. Aurora pulled her corset closed over her breasts, but it was too late—the two women had fled.

Raven smiled ruefully at the maid who stood in the doorway transfixed.

"That will be all, Lily," he said, amused.

The girl snapped to her senses and, in a flurry of black and white linen and white lace streamers, was gone, banging the door behind her.

"Oh, Lord," Aurora breathed. "We might as well have invited in a photographer from the *Daily News*." She grinned. "I suppose this will ruin your chances with Abra."

"I suppose it will." His eyes glittered. "Now, where were we?"

Reaching down, Aurora touched him and reveled in his soft moan. "Right about here," she replied.

Two hours later, Graham's ring in her possession, Aurora left Raven after making him promise not to tell his father their news until they could do it together.

She rode home in the carriage, body sated, mind at peace, utterly confident that her future was secure and her happiness assured.

But as the carriage approached her uncle's home, she noticed the people who milled about outside the wrought-iron fence. Three carriages stood in the drive. Two policemen had been stationed at the gates. Her carriage was stopped and she had to identify herself before they let her in. They refused, however, to explain the tumult.

Aurora entered the house to find it strangely quiet in comparison to the excitement and confusion that reigned outside. The hall was deserted. The house was silent but for a muffled weeping whose source she could not discover.

Unfastening her cape, she laid it over a chair. She was about to ring for a servant and demand an explanation when a door slammed somewhere upstairs and her aunt appeared at the head of the stairs.

"Aurora!" Electra's face was suffused with the hot blood of rage as she stormed down the marble steps. "There you are! By God!"

"What's happened?" Aurora asked as her aunt crossed the marble floor toward her. "There are policemen outside and report—"

She screamed, staggering back, as her aunt struck her a punishing blow across the face.

"You ungrateful, wanton little hussy!" her aunt hissed. "You're not fit to be a Jephson! You're not fit to be received by decent people!"

"What are you talking about!" Aurora demanded, her hand shielding her injured cheek. "If you mean Raven, I love him and I—"

"I don't want to hear his name! I don't want to

see you! Your complaining, your whining, your obstinacy gave your uncle a heart attack!"

Aurora's hand fell to her side. The blood drained from her face leaving a blood-red stain to mark the impact of her aunt's attack.

"It's not true," she breathed.

"It is true! And it is all your fault! You knew he was unwell but you couldn't let him have a moment's peace. You had to go to him with your nonsense, upset him. . . . He collapsed. It's all your fault! Do you hear? And I hope you are well satisfied!"

"But he seemed to understand! He didn't seem upset. He—"

"He was a gentleman. He held in his emotions. But what you told him tore out his heart. The shame of his brother's only child, little more than a common trollop." Electra daubed at her eyes with a lace-trimmed handkerchief. "It was too much for him to bear."

"No," Aurora whispered. "It can't be." Her eyes filled with tears. "It's not possible."

A tall, distinguished man in grey whom Aurora recognized as one of her uncle's doctors approached and in the most respectful of tones asked to see Electra alone. Aurora gazed after them as they disappeared into a small parlor off the main hall.

It was only a few moments later that she heard her aunt's anguished cry and knew that her uncle was dead.

31

The news of Carlisle Jephson's death sped through the fashionable salons of Chicago on the heels of the scandal of Graham Hughston's beautiful young fiancée having been found in *flagrante delicto* with Marcus Ravenswood's half-breed illegitimate son. The two stories, as was perhaps inevitable, became one, and the new tale, repeated with great relish, had it that Carlisle's fatal attack had been the result of his learning of his niece's unforgivable behavior.

For Aurora's part, the scandal that rocked the city passed over her, leaving no impression. Wracked with guilt over having been the instrument, albeit unwitting, of her uncle's death, she was plunged into the depths of depression and despair. Immured in the crepe-draped house of death her uncle's mansion had become, she spent her days in her room, her evenings downstairs with her aunt, praying beside her uncle's bier for the repose of his soul, and her nights lying awake in her room, wishing for the comfort of slumber but fearing the dreams that might come.

All the while, fashionable Chicago poured through the doors of the Jephson mansion, dutifully offering their condolences and pausing for a moment of silent farewell to the departed before moving on to the parlor where a cold collation awaited them. Most, though they might not have admitted as much, had come not so much to see Carlisle, but in hopes of catching sight of Aurora—society's favorite scarlet woman of the moment. In that they were disappointed, for Electra was not about to let her husband's funeral become a circus or her niece the center of attention. It was only after the doors were closed to all but family and the closest of friends that Aurora was summoned down from her rooms to join the mourners.

"Eat something, dear," Electra exhorted. Though she'd hoped to instill a sense of guilt in her niece, Aurora's abject despair frightened her. She couldn't remember having seen the girl take a bite of food since Carlisle's death, and Aurora's pale, thin face, the sylphlike body upon which her gown of black crepe almost swam, and the fragile, almost skeletal hands bore out her suspicions.

"I'm not hungry," Aurora told her. She leaned back and signaled a servant to remove her untouched plate. Her eyes, wide and haunted, the deep blue shadows giving evidence of her sleepless nights, darted around the table. Her aunt sat in her customary place, Graham sat beside Aurora,

Carlisle's attorney and the foremost of his battery of doctors sat opposite them. At the other end of the table Carlisle's chair sat draped in crepe, empty but for a gilt-framed portrait and a spray of flowers.

Aurora swayed slightly in her chair. Her shoulder touched Graham's and he reached out and steadied her.

"Are you all right, Aurora?" he asked softly.

She raised a trembling hand to her forehead. "Yes, I . . . it's only that . . . Please excuse me."

Rising, she left the dining room with the intention of returning to her bedroom to lie down. But she could not. Like a moth to a flame, she was drawn to that macabre chamber where the scent of flowers and hot candle wax filled the air with an overpowering aroma of death.

It was there that they found her three hours later after Bridey had come down to look for her. She was unconscious, lying on the cold marble floor. Graham gathered her into his arms and carried her upstairs. She was undressed and tucked into bed, and Carlisle's doctor was asked to examine her. Exhaustion, he diagnosed, and lack of food. Bedrest, laudanum if necessary, and nourishment even if it was only broth at first, spooned down her throat, was his prescription.

It was not until the small hours of the following morning that it was discovered that Aurora was burning with fever.

While Aurora lay in her bed, lost in the delirium of her fever, Carlisle Jephson was laid to rest with all the pomp and ostentation due a man of his wealth and status. The scandal would then have begun to die down but for a fresh tidbit that was added after the funeral: When Marcus Ravenswood and his son had arrived at the church to pay their last respects, Electra Jephson had had them barred at the door.

Alone in his carriage as he drove past the Jephson mansion, Raven seethed with impotent fury. Aurora was his—his! Legally she was an adult; they could not keep her there if she did not wish to stay. She knew it as well as he did. Why, then, was she staying? Why did she not simply pack her belongings and leave? Lastly, how much truth was there to the rumors that she was desperately ill?

Like everything else about the scandal, the stories of Aurora's illness were greatly exaggerated. She had typhoid, it was whispered, or consumption. Some said she was suffering from some loathsome disease such as any woman of such loose morals might expect to contract. She was recovering, some said; she was dying, others contended. For a while a rumor swept the city that she was dead.

In fact, she seemed to be suspended in a netherworld somewhere between those states. She was not dead, nor did there seem to be any real danger, once the fever had broken, that her illness was fatal. At the same time, she did not seem to be recovering. The doctors were at a loss, Bridey was frantic, and even Electra had begun to wonder if she had gone too far to instill a sense of guilt in her wayward niece.

By the time she had recovered enough to leave her bed, summer had given way to autumn and it was too chilly for her to sit outside on the veranda.

Graham was enlisted to carry her downstairs to a west-facing parlor one afternoon. He laid her with exquisite gentleness onto the soft, yielding cushions of a daybed and tucked a sable throw around her legs.

As he turned to leave the room, Aurora reached out and touched his arm.

"Graham?" she said, her voice a muted whisper.

He looked down at the hand that rested on his sleeve and was appalled at its fragility. He took it into his own gingerly, as if afraid it would shatter with the slightest hint of pressure.

Sitting on the edge of the daybed, he forced himself to look into those huge, blue-shadowed, cat-green eyes. The sparkle had left them. They seemed too big for her narrow, pale face. At that moment he would almost have welcomed Raven into the house if it would have brought some hint of color into those dead-white cheeks.

"What is it?" he asked. "Do you need something? Are you in pain?"

She shook her head. Even her hair, he reflected, once so beautiful, turning to fire in the sunlight, was lank and lusterless despite Bridey's diligent care. The cheery red ribbon that tied it at the nape of her neck seemed somehow a travesty.

"Why . . ." She spoke softly, haltingly, awkwardly, for she had scarcely spoken in nearly a month. "Why are you being so kind to me?"

"Why shouldn't I be kind to you?"

"Because I . . ." She lowered her gaze, unable to meet his steady stare. "Because I accepted your proposal when I had no real intention of marrying you. And because I betrayed you with another man."

Graham looked away. It was not her betrayal that had hurt him, nor even the realization that she had never had any true desire to become his wife. It was the knowledge that although he had courted her, wooed her, done everything in his power to make her love him, he had not touched her heart while a man like Charles Ravenswood—a man who despised all the conventions, all the values that ruled Graham's life—had accomplished the feat with so little apparent effort. Despite what rumor called Aurora, he knew her true nature. She had gone to Ravenswood's bed a virgin, of that he was certain, and she had been faithful to him. It was not Aurora for whom Graham had conceived a deep, lasting hatred, it was Ravenswood.

"You loved him," he said simply. "And not me."

"But I used you. Say you will forgive me."

"I already have."

"It happened on the island," she went on, feeling she owed him an explanation. "He is Raven, you see. He found me on the beach after the storm. I was with him on his island until you came for me."

"He is Raven?" Graham was astonished. "But he is not the man who claimed the reward."

"No. We have discussed that. We believe the men who sent you that letter—who forged Raven's signature—were from a family called Oates. They are loathsome, lawless people who do anything for money. Anything!"

"It is hard to imagine," Graham murmured.

"Yes. But it is a different world than ours."

"I'm beginning to understand that."

"I'm sorry, Graham—" she began.

He laid a finger on her lips to silence her. "No more apologies, Aurora. Rest now. I will come back later to take you back up to your room."

With a kiss on her brow, Graham left her to bask in the healing sunshine while he went off to search for his Aunt Electra.

Aurora was nearly asleep when one of the footmen entered the parlor bearing a letter on a silver salver.

"This message was just delivered, miss," he said, leaning over toward her. "I would have taken it to the madame, but she is closeted with Mr. Hughston and has left orders not to be disturbed." As if to further bolster his excuse for awakening the convalescing patient, he added: "And it is addressed to you."

Aurora took the letter and turned it over in her hands. "Miss Aurora Jephson" it read, with their Lake Shore Drive address. Aurora's heart seemed to turn over in her chest. A pain that had no origin other than the depths of her tortured soul shot through her. The handwriting was unmistakable: it was Raven's.

She clutched the letter in her shaking hands. Raven! She loved him still. She pressed the crisp vellum to her cheek. She would never love another as she loved him, she knew it as surely as she knew that night followed day, that autumn followed summer. But she believed that theirs was a doomed love. It had caused nothing but misery and heartache and death. For a few brief hours of pleasure, they had paid and paid and paid. Didn't he understand, couldn't he sense that their love was simply not meant to be? For them to be reunited now would be to say that her uncle's death had meant nothing.

And yet her delicate fingers longed to tear open the precious envelope and read the words he had inscribed inside. The tip of one finger traced the edge of the seal. It gave a little—a little more—

"No," she moaned. "I can't. I must not. I must put him out of my life if not out of my heart."

Weeping, she rose from her bed and took her first stumbling steps. She had to find someone, anyone, who would send the letter back—someone who would rid her of its evil enticement.

"Please," she sobbed as she reached the door, the letter crumpled in her hand. "Please, help me. Help me—"

The young footman who had brought the letter dropped the Sèvres vase he was about to place on a tall marble pedestal and ran to her. He caught her as she fell toward the hard floor of the main hall.

The crash of the vase brought Electra and Graham out of their tête-à-tête on the run. Electra moaned when she saw the shattered pieces of magnificent porcelain. But her anger quickly faded when she saw Graham take Aurora's limp body from the frightened footman.

"What happened?" she demanded as Graham carried Aurora up the stairs.

"This came," the footman said, retrieving the letter from the floor where Aurora had dropped it. "You weren't to be disturbed, so I took it to Miss Aurora."

Electra turned it over in her hands. "Who brought this?"

"A footman from the Ravenswoods'," he replied.

"Ravenswood! I might have known." She handed it back to him. "Take it to the Ravenswood mansion and tell Mr. Charles Ravenswood that Miss Aurora wishes never to see him again! Tell him—this is important—tell him that Miss Aurora did receive the letter but that she did not open it. Do you understand?"

Dispatched, the footman hurried out of the room, and Electra mounted the stairs to Aurora's room.

"She's better," Graham told her as she entered. "It was only a mild shock. No harm was done."

"Is that true?" Electra asked Aurora. "Are you all right? We don't want a relapse."

"I'm all right, Aunt," Aurora assured her. She frowned, unsure of her next move but knowing she had to do something to rid herself of the ghosts, both living and dead, who were haunting her.

She looked up at her aunt. "Do you think I could go to Uncle Carlisle's mausoleum this afternoon?"

Startled, Electra exchanged a look with Graham. "If you wish, my dear." A sudden thought struck her and she smiled gently. "I shan't be able to go with you, but perhaps Graham could accompany you."

"Of course," Graham agreed instantly. "But you should rest now if you plan to go out later."

"Thank you." Aurora smiled as Graham rose and moved toward the door with their aunt. When they were almost out, she called to them. "Graham? May I speak to you for a moment?"

Again he exchanged a look with Electra, then moved back into the room. "Of course, Aurora, what is it?"

"Please come and sit down. There is something I must discuss with you."

Curious, Graham went to sit on the edge of her bed.

It was late afternoon when Graham and Aurora made their way to the ornate Gothic tomb Carlisle had built when first he had made his fortune. The glass and ironwork doors were unlocked, and Aurora entered and laid her hands on the marble sarcophagus that held her uncle's coffin.

"Will he forgive me?" she asked Graham, her eyes darkly pleading behind the waist-length veil that fell from her black bonnet.

"I'm certain of it," Graham told her soothingly. "He loved you as if you were his own daughter."

A wavering smile appeared at the corners of Aurora's mouth, then was gone. With a last look at her uncle's final resting place, she left the tomb, and Graham nodded to the caretaker to lock it again.

Taking her elbow, Graham steered her toward the closed carriage that waited to take them home. A shadow fell across the path in front of them. Hearing Graham's muffled oath, Aurora looked up to find Raven blocking their way.

Raven was stunned by Aurora's appearance. He had heard the rumors of her illness, but now it seemed they were, if anything, optimistic.

"Aurora," he whispered. "My God."

She shook her head, feeling giddy. "Leave me alone, Raven. Let us pass and leave me alone."

"I sent a letter. Did you—?"

"I got it. I didn't open it. I couldn't. It's not meant to be. You must see that now. I will not cause any more pain—any more misery—"

"What about your pain? Your misery?" he countered.

She was trembling. Tears blurred her vision and she had to depend on Graham to steer her toward the carriage.

"Please," she whispered. "Let me pass. I want to go home."

Seeing her distress and fearing for her if he caused her any more anguish, Raven had no recourse but to stand aside and let her go with Graham. He might have found reason to hope—he might have told himself that once she had recovered her health she would come to her senses, had it not been that, as she passed, she raised a trembling hand to her lips. On that hand, worn over the black glove, was Graham Hughston's ruby betrothal ring.

32

"She's going to marry him!" Raven raged, pacing the carpet in his father's elegant library. "She is actually going to marry him! I saw the ring on her finger."

"It's hardly surprising," Marcus said, swirling the brandy in his crystal snifter.

"Hardly surprising!" Raven's handsome face was a mask of stunned disbelief. "How can you say that! We had agreed to be married, Father. We were going back to the island to live. She wanted it as much as I." He scowled ferociously. "Not surprising, indeed!"

"Well, it's not." Marcus regarded his son intently. "She feels responsible for her uncle's death. You yourself said she looked terrible."

"Terrible doesn't do it justice," Raven said, remembering Aurora's white face, the frailty of her body, the trembling she could not seem to control. "If I had seen her before, I'd have believed all those rumors that had her at death's door."

"She is suffering."

"And so she's turning to Hughston in her sorrow? Forgive me, Father, but the reason behind that escapes me somehow."

"I didn't say it made sense. I merely said that she is suffering. Guilt is a powerful weapon in the hands of those ruthless enough to use it."

"Electra Jephson," Raven hissed.

"Precisely. And Graham Hughston as well. My guess is that Electra either made Aurora believe she was responsible for her uncle's death or encouraged Aurora's own suspicions and fears that she was responsible. Either way, Aurora apparently believes it. And it is tormenting her."

"Tormenting her so badly that she will marry Hughston? How will that assuage her grief over her uncle's death?"

Setting his brandy aside, Marcus made a steeple of his fingers. "If she believes that grief over the ending of her engagement and her betrayal of Hughston with you precipitated Carlisle's attack, then I suppose it makes sense for her to try to atone for his death by marrying the man he favored."

"But Aurora told me her uncle supported her in her desire to marry me."

"At times such as these, my dear boy, clear-headed thinking goes out the window. In Aurora's state, she may not be capable of reasoning it out. All she knows is that she told her uncle she did not wish to marry Graham Hughston. The next thing she knows, he has suddenly dropped dead of a heart attack. What can she think?"

"And so she turned against me into the bargain?"

"Not at all, I should think. She loved you enough to be willing to leave everything she's ever known, all the luxuries that have always been part of her day-to-day life, and go to live with you on your island. She would not stop loving you in a moment, not for all the grief in the world."

"She won't see me. She returned my letter."

"It may be too painful for her to see you. It could be that it tears her heart out to even think of you and the life you could have had together."

"I wish I could believe that, Father," Raven sighed, sinking into an armchair. Stretching out his long legs toward the fire, he gazed into its flickering flames. "I wish to God I could believe that."

"Give her time. The shock will pass. The pain will ease. She will come to realize how foolish it is for her to hold herself responsible for Carlisle's attack. Particularly in view of the man's medical history."

"Medical history? I thought he was perfectly sound until that bout of influenza earlier in the summer."

"Sound? Oh my, no. Of course it is not widely known, but Carlisle Jephson had a history of heart ailments." He chuckled. "Influenza, indeed."

"It wasn't influenza?" Raven sat up in his chair.

"Not at all. It was merely the worst in a series of attacks he's had in recent years. This goes back, oh, five years at least. It was only a matter of time until one killed him."

"Then why tell people it was influenza?"

"Carlisle Jephson guarded that mining business of his like a lioness guarding her cubs. It was his, and no one else was allowed a hand in the running of it. If word got out that all the power, all the know-how, in running Jephson Mining was concentrated in the hands of a man living literally on borrowed time, the company stock would have plummeted on the Exchange. As it is, I'm told it's worth less than half what it was the day before his death. No one knows anything about the company's business—not even the extent of the holdings. It will be months before it can all be sorted out. Frankly, Electra will be lucky to come out of this with enough money to hold on to that marble monstrosity she lives in."

"She would have to depend on Hughston to support her."

Marcus laughed. "She'll get little help from that quarter, I assure you. Graham Hughston is known to live a rather extravagant life. And he supports his mother's household as well as his own."

"But he inherited his father's company, did he not?"

"So he did. But he pays more attention to the workings of a roulette wheel than to the workings of the Hughston railroad holdings. The Hughston family's finances have met with serious reverses since Foster Hughston's death. I should not be surprised to see it sold to a larger, more profitable firm in the near future."

Raven's eyes narrowed. "So it is important that he marry Aurora because of her fortune?"

"More than merely important. I should think it is imperative. Now more than ever."

"Damn. Damn!" Raven thrust himself to his

feet and began once more to pace. "They're using her grief, playing upon her guilt, to secure her fortune so they can maintain the life-style to which they've become accustomed."

"So it would seem," Marcus agreed.

"I won't allow it, Father." He drew himself up, magnificent in his anger. "I won't allow it! Aurora loves me! She loved me before her uncle's death and she still does. I know it! She's mine and I won't let them use her—abuse her—for her fortune!"

"Good for you! I wouldn't expect less from any son of mine. How do you intend to prevent it?"

Leaning against the mantel, Raven let the heat of the fire engulf him. The restless indecision of the past few days had drained out of him, leaving him invigorated, filled with a new determination, eager to spring into action and free Aurora from her devious, avaricious relatives.

He smiled. "I don't know. Truly I don't. I doubt Queen Victoria in England or President Harrison in Washington is better guarded than Aurora right now. She never goes out alone—she hardly goes out at all. Moreover, even if I found her alone somewhere, how could I convince her of what her aunt and Hughston are doing? They obviously have her right where they want her."

"Not a particularly optimistic prospect," Marcus pointed out.

"No, but it doesn't matter. I'm determined. I'm going to get Aurora back, and when I do I'm going to make her see what kind of people her aunt and Hughston really are."

Unaware of the plans being formulated for Aurora's delivery from the clutches of Graham and

Electra, the Hughstons were busy with preparations for the wedding.

It was to be a small affair, both out of respect for the Jephson family's mourning and to prevent it from turning into some kind of sideshow with guests and intruders gathering to gossip and ogle the infamous bride.

Fittings for Aurora's gown were held in Electra's boudoir. Though she offered no suggestions, gave few opinions, Aurora dutifully stood for hours until exhaustion overtook her.

Of ivory satin and Brussels lace, the gown was somewhat less elaborate than was fashionable, but after all, Electra reasoned, Aurora was in mourning for her uncle and frivolity would be in bad taste. Still, the draping lace-jabot sewn with iridescent beads was exquisite. In a way, the gown, with its long, tight sleeves, high standing collar and lace-trimmed hem, was more elegant for its simplicity.

The final touch, the tulle veil to be secured with orange blossoms, was placed over Aurora's head as she stood before a gilt-framed pier glass.

"Finished," the dressmaker said proudly. "And so very beautiful. I think it is a shame there will be so few guests there to see how lovely she looks."

"I don't look lovely at all," Aurora murmured, gazing at her own reflection. "I look hideous. Hideous!" She trembled and buried her face in her hands as Electra hurried to her side.

"Calm yourself, my dear," she soothed. "Bridget? Bridget!" she motioned impatiently to the dressmaker. "Summon my niece's maid."

"I think—" the dressmaker began.

"You are not paid to think," Electra snarled. "Now do as I say!"

In short order the maid was summoned and Electra dispatched her to fetch Aurora's medicine. Aurora was divested of her veil and gown, and Electra ordered the dressmaker and her assistants to help get her settled on the divan.

Secretly appalled by the frailty of Aurora's wasted body, the dressmaker's young assistants could not help staring. Electra noticed.

"Get out. Now!" she ordered, seeing the assistant exchange a look with another of the girls. "And if I hear one word of any of this repeated in public, I'll see you are ruined. Do you understand me?"

"Of course, madam. I am discretion itself," the intimidated dressmaker assured her.

"You'd better be!"

As the dressmaker and her assistants were leaving with their hastily gathered wares, Bridey returned with the little bottle that contained the medicine Electra had obtained to treat her niece's nerves.

"Here, my dear, here is your medicine. You must take it like a good girl."

Aurora struggled to sit up and swallow the medicine her aunt offered her. She knew what it was—a powerful sedative. And she knew what it would do. When she took it so late in the afternoon, she invariably slept until the middle of the following morning. And that was precisely what Aurora wanted, to sleep the deep, dreamless sleep of the drugged. To forget—to forget the past, to forget the future, to forget Raven.

Sighing, she lay down on the silken pillows of her aunt's divan and fell into a swift, sound slumber.

"Should I call someone to take her to her own room, ma'am?" Bridey asked, gazing wonderingly at Aurora's sleeping form.

"No. Leave her where she is. Just cover her with a nice warm quilt. She can't afford to take a chill in her weakened condition."

"As you say, ma'am."

Satisfied, Electra left the boudoir. She preferred Aurora under the effects of the drug. She had a tendency to be maudlin at other times. She had recently begun, alarmingly, to question the wisdom of her hurriedly approaching wedding which was to take place in Graham's mother's formal parlor.

But under the influence of the sedative— smaller doses to render her listless and malleable and larger ones to put her to sleep—she was docile as a lamb, putty in Electra's hands.

"Where is Aurora?" Graham asked, meeting his aunt in the corridor.

"She is asleep in my boudoir," Electra told him. "She became agitated during her fitting and I had to give her some of her medicine."

Graham scowled. "Good Christ, Aunt Electra! Will she at least be conscious to repeat her wedding vows?"

"I guarantee it." Electra smiled. "A little of her medicine and she will repeat anything we ask her to repeat."

"Well, I can't say I'm looking forward to having a sleepwalker for a wife."

"What do you care? As long as you have free

access to her fortune you should be satisfied. While she's sleeping, remember, she cannot object to the way you spend her money."

A slow smile crept across Graham's face. "There is always that," he agreed. "But still, a man wants more from his wife occasionally."

"Really, Graham! These baser instincts of yours. So long as you manage to produce a child or two, the rest doesn't matter. With her fortune, you could keep a string of mistresses the way other men keep a string of polo ponies."

Graham laughed. "Ah, yes, I've always said Aurora would make a wonderful wife!"

Laughing, the two of them linked arms and strolled toward the stairs. As they went, however, neither of them noticed Bridey standing in the boudoir doorway staring after them, horrified.

She had wanted to ask Electra a question and had waited silently in the doorway for an opportunity to speak. Instead, she had heard their conversation, and the revelations terrified her. At stake was the safety of the one person in the world she loved—the one person who had nearly given her life in an attempt to save Bridey's own on that storm-tossed night months before. Bridey loved Aurora, and she knew, at that moment, that the poor, drugged, defenseless creature in the boudoir needed her protection.

33

"I feel I must tell you, Mr. Ravenswood, that legally our hands are tied."

A muscle twitched in the taut plane of Raven's cheek as he stood in the office of the senior partner of the law firm that handled his father's affairs.

"But it is illegal, is it not, for a person to be forced into a marriage under duress?"

"To be sure. But duress must be proved. For that, we would have to have the testimony of the lady in question. And I take it she will not testify to duress?"

"She is in no condition to testify to anything."

Raven closed his eyes wearily. He was tired and frustrated. All the avenues to Aurora's freedom seemed irrevocably blocked.

"Then there is little we can do. If the lady is unwilling—or unable—to testify at this time, I see no way of legally preventing the marriage from taking place." He removed his spectacles and laid them on the leather-topped desk. "If, after the marriage, she were to sue for divorce, duress could, of course, form the basis for such a suit."

"The marriage must not be allowed to take place at all," Raven insisted.

"I'm sorry, Mr. Ravenswood. Legally, there is nothing you can do to prevent it."

"Then perhaps something will have to be done illegally," Raven said grimly. "For I intend to stop it, and if the law will not help me, I will help myself."

The lawyer raised his hands. "I beg you, sir, tell me no more. Formulate what plans you will, but I do not wish to know what they might be. You understand, I should not like to be called as a witness if your plans went awry. Your father has an association of many years' standing with this firm. I should not like to see it jeopardized."

"I understand." Raven took up his hat and gloves. "Thank you for your time."

Leaving the office, Raven was more frustrated than ever but no less determined to take Aurora away from a situation that, robbed of Carlisle Jephson's governing presence to keep Electra and Graham under control, was turning into a very real danger to Aurora's health, her well-being and, Raven very much feared, to her very life.

"Bridget? Bridget, where are you?" Electra called along the upstairs corridor.

"Here, ma'am," Bridey replied, appearing at the doorway of Aurora's boudoir.

"Well, come here. Don't just stand there gaping!" Turning back into the second-floor sitting room, Electra rolled her eyes at Graham. "Irish!"

"Yes, ma'am?" Bridey stood in the doorway.

"Where is Miss Aurora?"

"Sleeping, ma'am."

"As usual," Graham muttered.

Electra paid him no attention. "Bridget, I need you to go to that hat shop over on—drat! What was the street? Well, Mrs. Bellamy's, at any rate. You've been there with Miss Aurora, haven't you?"

"Yes, ma'am."

"Good. Now, I have some sketches for hats I wish made for Miss Aurora's trousseau. I want you to give them to Mrs. Bellamy and ask her for suggestions as to materials and trimmings. Can you do that?"

"I think so, ma'am."

"I'd go myself if I had the time," Electra told Graham as if the maid were not there. "One can never trust these people to do anything right." She turned back to Bridey. "Mr. Hughston is going that way on his way to his office. He will let you off at the shop. I will give you money to take a cab back. Do you think you can handle all of this?"

"Yes, ma'am," Bridey said with exaggerated patience.

"Then go and change out of your uniform and into something presentable."

Bridey curtsied, then hurried to the narrow staircase that would take her up to the attic where she had a tiny room of her own—one of the privileges of being a lady's maid. She was happy to be getting out of the house—eager even. Her duties of late consisted mostly of watching Aurora sleep and trying to coax her to eat something. She could take no pleasure in dressing her or fixing her hair, for Aurora did not seem to care how she looked— nor, now that she thought of it, did anyone else. Bridey was frightened for Aurora, but there seemed nothing she could do to help her—she was not even sure anymore if Aurora wished to be helped.

Dressed in a plainly tailored skirt and coat of black braided grey wool worn over a high-collared cream linen blouse, Bridey covered her upswept, knotted hair with a bonnet of flower-trimmed straw. After a quick, appraising look in the broken mirror hanging on the wall over her crack-legged chair, she left her room and hurried down to the porte cochere where Graham waited in a small carriage he drove himself.

"Here you are at last," he snapped. "I've seen women take less time dressing for a ball."

"I'm sorry, sir," Bridey apologized, eyes downcast.

"Never mind. Here are the sketches Mrs. Jephson wishes you to give to the hatmaker."

Bridey took them and laid them across her lap, holding them down with her grey-gloved hands as Graham cracked his whip and set his team of matched bays in motion.

As they reached the end of the drive, Graham reined in his horses to allow another carriage to pass before he turned out into the road. The other carriage slowed and a man's face appeared at the window, set and grim beneath the brim of his high silk hat. He glared at them, his eyes narrow and fierce, then disappeared as the carriage passed on down Lake Shore Drive.

"Damn!" Graham muttered. "Ravenswood!"

Bridey caught her breath. "Ravenswood," she murmured, realizing who the man was and why he had stared so pointedly at them as he passed. With her red hair and Graham at her side, he might have thought she was Aurora.

Graham heard her soft exclamation. "So you've heard of him, have you? No doubt Miss Aurora speaks of him to you."

"Oh, no, sir," Bridey hastened to assure him.

"It's a sin to lie, Bridey. Didn't all your priests in Ireland tell you that? Well, it doesn't matter if she's spoken of him or not. In a few days she'll be my wife. And there isn't a thing Ravenswood can do to stop it."

"Mr. Graham?"

"Yes?"

"I'm worried about Miss Aurora. I don't think it is good for her to have quite so much of her medicine. I don't think Mrs. Jephson should—"

"Now, see here!" Graham snarled. "Just who in the hell do you think you are? It is not for you to 'think' anything concerning your betters, my girl. You'd do well to remember that if you want to keep your position."

Abashed, Bridey nodded. "Yes, sir. I'm sorry, sir."

"You damned well should be!" Graham looked sideways at the pretty, red-headed girl sitting beside him. "Don't be upset, Bridget. I'm not cross with you. But you must not question either Mrs. Jephson or myself. Do you understand?"

"Yes, sir," Bridey whispered.

"I will forgive you, for I know you do it out of

concern for your mistress and that is commendable."

"Thank you, sir."

Graham looked at her again, noting with interest the small, upturned nose with its sprinkling of freckles and the little mouth with its full, rosebud lips.

"You know, Bridget, you're a very pretty girl."

"Thank you, sir."

"I mean that. And that's a lovely dress you're wearing."

Bridey smoothed the soft wool. "It was Miss Aurora's. She gave it to me."

"It suits you admirably." His dark eyes skimmed over her deep bosom and narrow waist. "You know, Bridget, that you will be coming to live at my house once Miss Aurora is my wife."

"I was hoping to stay with Miss Aurora, sir."

"And so you shall. And I will be your master."

"Yes, sir, that is true."

"And I hope you and I will become fast friends." With a scarcely perceptible movement, Graham pressed his thigh to Bridey's on the narrow seat of the small carriage. "Fast friends, indeed."

Bridey's eyes widened, though she didn't dare to venture a glance in his direction. Surely he couldn't be meanin' . . . the devil! And him marryin' sweet Miss Aurora in a few short days! If he thought she was the kind of woman who would . . . Well! She was Miss Aurora's lady's maid, but, master or not, she was not about to be Mr. Graham's fancy woman! The swine! He wasn't fit to touch Miss Aurora's hem!

"Here we are," Graham said, drawing the horses to a halt in front of Mrs. Bellamy's hat shop. "Let me help you down."

"I can manage, thank you, sir," Bridey said quickly.

"Stay where you are!" Graham ordered.

Afraid to disobey, Bridey sat on the seat while Graham climbed down and circled the carriage. Then, taking her by the waist, he lifted her down. His hands slid up from her waist as he set her on her feet. He released her, but not before his hands subtly but firmly caressed the sides of her breasts.

As he tipped his bowler jauntily and climbed up into his carriage to drive away, Bridey stared after him, shocked. To be mauled on a public street like a common trollop! She had an image of what her life would be like in Graham Hughston's home—the furtive looks, the stealthy caresses, the stolen kisses, the threats if she refused to comply. It was not a pleasant prospect, but she knew it was one faced all too often by pretty servant girls.

Shaking with rage and humiliation, she entered Mrs. Bellamy's shop with Electra's sketches. She would not allow it to happen to her, she thought, not if she had to starve in the streets!

Two hours later, she paid the driver of the carriage she had hired to take her home and walked up the graveled drive toward the grand Lake Shore Drive mansion. Her outrage had cooled into a kind of cold determination. No man was going to treat her the way Graham Hughston obviously planned to treat her once she lived under his roof and was subject to his orders! She might be no more than a lady's maid, a servant, but she had her dignity, her pride, and a right not to be taken advantage of by those whose position and wealth gave them power over the lives of others.

And she wasn't about to let him treat Miss Aurora that way, either! Here he was, not even her husband yet, and already planning to go behind her back with another woman! And beneath her own roof! Well, she wouldn't stand for it! If Miss Aurora couldn't defend herself, then Bridget Mary Frances O'Shaughnessy would!

She gave the doorbell a vicious twist and waited to be let in, the luscious little mouth Graham had so admired pursed with grim determination.

Raven looked up from the newspaper he'd been reading as Hawkins appeared in the doorway.

"Pardon me, sir. A young woman is asking to see you."

"A young woman? Who is she?"

"She will say only that her name is Bridget O'Shaughnessy and that she must see you on a matter of the utmost urgency."

"What matter?"

"She will not say, sir."

"Send her on her way, Hawkins. I haven't time for foolishness."

"As you say, sir."

Raven scowled as he returned to his paper. He couldn't concentrate—his mind, as usual, was filled with thoughts of Aurora.

"Bridget O'Shaughnessy," he murmured. Something about the name sounded familiar.

"Bridget O'Shaughnessy. Bridget O' . . ." The light dawned with sudden, shocking clarity. "Bridget! Bridey! Holy Christ!"

Throwing down the paper, Raven rushed out of the parlor and down the corridor to the vestibule where Hawkins had just succeeded in ejecting a protesting Bridget.

"She didn't go quietly," the butler said disapprovingly. "These modern girls . . . so forward. It's not the way it was when I was a boy, I can—"

He stopped, astonished, when Raven pushed past him and tore down the steps and out along the walk.

"Wait!" he called. "Wait, Miss O'Shaughnessy! Please, wait!"

Bridey turned and fixed him with a furious glare. "I'll have you know, I'm not used to being tossed out on my ear!" she told him sternly, her Irish temper flaring.

"I'm sure you're not," Raven agreed. "And I do apologize. It is only that I did not at first realize who you are. You are Bridey, aren't you? Aurora's lady's maid."

"I am," Bridey confirmed proudly.

"Have you brought me a message from Aurora? Did she send you to me?"

"Oh no, sir." Bridey shook her head mournfully. "Miss Aurora's in no fit state to send messages to anybody. She's that bad off!"

"Then why have you come?"

Bridey sighed, her brow furrowing. "I'm afraid for her, sir. I'm afraid of Mrs. Jephson and Mr. Graham. They don't love her like I do and it don't seem like they're takin' good care of her. I was hopin' you'd want to help her."

"I do," Raven told her. "I'd do anything I could to help Aurora." He smiled joyfully. "Oh, Bridey, I could kiss you for coming here this way!"

"Don't you do it!" Bridey warned. "I've been pawed by one jack-full-o'-money today! Two's more than I could bear!"

Raven laughed. "Very well, I won't kiss you. But come in and sit down. We'll have tea and you can tell me how I can help Aurora."

Pleased by his eagerness to help and by his charming attitude toward her, Bridey was only too happy to accompany him back into the mansion. For the first time in a long time, Bridey allowed herself to hope that things would be all right after all.

34

Ensconced in a deeply cushioned armchair, drinking tea from a priceless porcelain cup and eating pastries so delicate they seemed to melt as they touched her tongue, Bridey related to Raven and a hurriedly summoned Marcus the events in the Jephson household surrounding Carlisle's sudden, fatal attack.

"What happened to Carlisle?" Marcus asked. "Was his attack in any way Aurora's fault?"

"Oh, no, sir. He was fine after Miss Aurora left. He went up to speak with the madam and found two gentlemen from Markham and Hambleton just leavin'."

"The furriers?" Marcus inquired.

Bridey nodded. "Mr. Jephson was in a right fury to find 'em there. He went into the madam's room and gave her a royal readin' out over how

much she was spendin' lately." Softly, confidential-
ly, she went on: "I guess his business is not what it
should be."

"Were you there?" Raven wanted to know.

"No, sir," Bridey admitted sheepishly. "But
Pelton, madam's maid, and the butler were outside.
They said the master and Mrs. Jephson had a
fearful row. But then, right in the middle of it all,
the master groaned and there was the sound of a
fallin' body. Mrs. Jephson started screamin' for
help. They carried him to the bedroom and sent for
the doctor. But by then it was too late."

"In other words," Raven said. "It was not
Aurora's news that brought on the attack, but
Carlisle's rage over his wife's extravagance."

"That's right," Bridey agreed. "He never got to
say anything about Aurora not wantin' to marry
Mr. Graham."

"Then how did Electra know that Aurora had
told her uncle she did not want to marry
Hughston?" Marcus demanded.

Bridey shrugged. "The same way I know what
happened between the master and Mrs. Jephson, I
expect. Someone listened at the keyhole."

Raven scowled. "And Electra is making Aurora suffer agonies of guilt believing that she killed
her uncle. She's a fiend."

"Obviously," Marcus agreed. "And no doubt
she'll continue to use Aurora's guilt to bend her to
her will for as long as she's allowed. Anything to
get her to marry Hughston."

"She won't marry Hughston, Father," Raven
vowed.

"I should hope not!" Bridey cried.

Both men stared at her, startled by her vehemence. But the girl lifted her chin and returned their looks defiantly.

"That's right! I hope she doesn't marry him! Mr. Graham is no better than that aunt of his!"

"Has he harmed Aurora as well?" Raven asked, his eyes narrowed and dark, his voice tight, his rage ready to explode into violence.

"Not yet, but that don't mean he won't. Oh, I don't mean he'll beat her, but he'll hurt her—in other ways."

"What do you mean?" Marcus wanted to know.

Bridey flushed. "With other women." She lowered her gaze, embarrassed. "He drove me to Mrs. Bellamy's hat shop this morning and made—improper advances. He said that when I come with Miss Aurora to his house—well—" Her cheeks darkened to scarlet. "Oh! The cursed devil!"

"Christ!" Raven muttered. "Not even married yet and already planning to tumble his wife's maid." He shot a look at his father. "And these are the civilized sophisticates who would call my mother's people savages."

He leaned closer to the red-haired maid. "Bridey, I want to take Aurora away—not only away from Electra Jephson and Graham Hughston, but away from Chicago. Far away. Where she'll be safe—and happy. I promise you she'll be happy. But to do that, I need the help of someone inside the Jephson house. Someone who can tell me the details of the wedding Electra has planned. I suspect that that will be my only opportunity to get near Aurora between now and the marriage."

"She won't be allowed out until then," Bridey

confirmed. "They keep her—well, she's in no condition to go anywhere even if she was wantin' to." She brightened. "But I can tell you about the wedding. It's all they've talked about for weeks!"

"Good girl. Now tell me the details and we'll make our plans."

"There's a condition," Bridey said, glancing from Raven to his father and back.

"A condition?" Marcus asked. "What is it?"

Bridey looked away nervously. "You have to promise to take me with you." She looked up uncertainly, then went on quickly before either could object. "If you take Miss Aurora away, they'll know who helped you. I'll be thrown into the streets! Not, mind, that I'd want to stay with them if Miss Aurora was gone, but I'd not be able to get another position. They'd put it about that I wasn't loyal. And I'm afraid—afraid of what Mr. Graham might do to me."

Raven sat back in his chair. Aurora would have no need of a lady's maid on the island, but Bridey was right, it would be a cruel injustice to abandon her after she had risked so much to save the mistress she adored.

Bridey took his silence for refusal. "You won't take me, then?" she asked, her voice quavering.

"I didn't say that," Raven replied. "Of course, you're welcome to come. But I warn you, the place where I'm taking Aurora is nothing like this." With a sweep of his hand, he encompassed the grand mansion surrounding them. "It's primitive—a cabin in the forest on an island. Life there is simple. There aren't any luxuries."

Bridey fixed him with a calm, direct stare. "Mr. Ravenswood, I grew up in a house that was little more than a hut on a hillside in Ireland. In two rooms my mother and father raised eight of us. It was hot in the summer and cold in the winter and it leaked the year round. Is it worse than that where you're goin'?"

A smile curved Raven's full mouth. "No, Bridey, I don't believe it is."

"Then I'll get by." She held out a hand to him. "And so, Mr. Ravenswood, are we agreed then?"

Taking her hand, Raven shook it warmly. "We are agreed."

Satisfied, Bridey detailed the plans for Aurora's wedding, and she and Raven spent the next hour planning her rescue.

"I don't know how much help she'll be herself," Bridey told them. "They'll likely give her just enough of her medicine to keep her in line without puttin' her to sleep."

"That might be for the best," Marcus told Raven. "She won't become alarmed and upset your plans."

Raven nodded his agreement. "If the plans for the wedding are changed," he asked Bridey, "will you be able to let me know?"

"I'll do my best," Bridey promised. "That's all I can say."

Hearing the clock on the mantel chime the hour, Bridey stood. "I've got to be goin' now. There'll be hell to pay as it is because I'm so late."

"I'll get someone to drive you home," Marcus said.

"Oh, no. 'Tis only up the road. And besides, if they see me walkin' up the drive, they'll think I walked all the way. That'll make up for my bein' so late."

Raven walked her to the door. "You're a brave girl, Bridey. Aurora is lucky to have you."

Bridey flushed, pleased with his praise. "Well now, I'd say she's lucky to have both of us, wouldn't you?"

With a last smile for both men, Bridey left and began her walk home. In the doorway Marcus and Raven watched her go.

"What are you thinking?" Marcus asked his son.

Raven grinned. "I'm thinking I'm going to have to build a bigger cabin!"

For the first time in weeks, the men laughed, joyously, without reservation, optimistic that their plans would succeed and Aurora would soon be delivered from her aunt's scheming clutches.

Three days later, two plain, closed carriages drew up beneath the porte cochere of the Jephsons' mansion.

"Are the carriages ready?" Electra asked, sweeping down the stairs in a swirl of black crepe, the glitter of her jet and diamond jewelry dulled by the trailing gauze of her knee-length veil. "It's about time. I should have been at the Hughstons' an hour ago. What if they've muddled the flowers or the seating? Bridget! Drat! Where is that girl? Bridget!"

Bridey appeared at the top of the stairs. "Yes, ma'am?"

"Is Aurora ready?"

"Not quite. She's still groggy, ma'am. It's hard to dress her like that."

"Well, get someone to help you! She's got to be there at three! Pelton!"

Electra's maid appeared behind her. "Ma'am?"

"Are you ready? We have to go."

"You're only wearing one earring," the sour-faced lady's maid observed.

"What?" Electra pinched her lobes. "Good God! You dressed me, you old clot! Why didn't you notice?" She turned back toward the stairs. "Bridget!"

Again Bridey appeared on the upper landing. "Yes, ma'am?"

"Go into my room and bring me my other earring. The long, teardrop jet and diamond one. It should be on the dressing table. Pelton and I will be waiting in the carriage."

Retrieving the earring, Bridey ran downstairs. Electra and her maid were already settled in the first carriage.

"Oh, ma'am!" Bridey cried. "This is Miss Aurora's carriage!"

"What difference does it make?" Electra asked irritably, glaring at the earring and longing for the brilliantly colored jewels which her widowhood forbade her from ever again wearing in public. Black, unrelieved black for a year and a day, then a little grey trimming. It was tiresome. She saw that the maid had not moved. "Both carriages are going to the same place, Bridget. It doesn't matter which I take and which Aurora takes."

"But it does!" Bridey insisted. "Miss Aurora's travelin' clothes have been packed into this carriage, but I'm to take her case with her personal things in it with us. Now, if her clothes go in this carriage and her case goes in the other, somethin' might just get left behind. Then, when Miss Aurora and Mr. Graham leave for their honeymoon, she'll be without—"

"All right! Anything to stop this diatribe! Come along, Pelton!"

Bustling out of the first carriage, Electra and her dour-faced maid climbed into the second. As it rolled around the first and disappeared down the drive, Bridey stole a glance at the coachman sitting on the box with his turned-up collar and low-brimmed hat. He looked down at her, and for a moment her Irish blue eyes met a pair as startlingly blue as the clear, cloudless sky.

The ballroom of Consuelo Gwynne Hughston's Ashland Avenue mansion was a wonderland of flowers and candles and crystal chandeliers. White brocade draperies had been drawn across the Palladian windows to create a dim, romantic atmosphere. The dozen or so guests deemed close enough and trusted enough to keep the wedding time and place a secret from the prying press and gawking public sat on gilded chairs listening to the uplifting tones of hymns played on the late Foster Hughston's one-hundred-thousand-dollar pipe organ.

Twisting in her chair, Electra looked toward the double doors at the back of the room. A footman stationed there to signal her of Aurora's arrival merely shrugged his shoulders and shook his white-bewigged head.

"Where is she?" Graham hissed from his place near the altar that had been built at one end of the long, narrow room.

"I don't know! I told that stupid maid of hers to have her here at three. I'll kill that girl with my bare hands! I swear I won't rest until she's sent all the way back to Ireland!"

Graham brushed an imaginary speck from the silk lapels of his black frock coat. His waistcoat was of charcoal grey, his tie and trousers of lighter striped grey, the former of silk, the latter of cashmere.

"I'm beginning to feel like a damned fool up here." He glanced at the minister standing nearby. "Pardon me, Reverend."

"She'll be here any moment," Electra insisted. "I'm sure it's not her fault. I should have known better than to leave matters in the hands of that fool maid."

"Is anything wrong?" Gloria Gwynne Hughston asked, leaning across the aisle. Used to being overshadowed by her older, more assertive sister, she spoke softly, as if afraid of being out of line.

"Nothing, Gloria dear. Aurora's a bit late, that's all."

"We should have had a police escort for the carriage," Graham told her.

"We couldn't. If we had tried to arrange for one, word surely would have gotten out and the route would have been lined with curiosity-seekers and reporters. No, I still say that she will—" She scowled. "Who is that?"

An old man dressed in a shabby frock coat and battered silk hat limped down the aisle. In his hand he carried a small parcel which he handed to Graham. Then, with a tip of his hat toward Electra, he turned and, as wordlessly as he'd come, was gone.

"What is that?" Electra wanted to know. "And who was that man?"

"I don't know," Graham replied, opening the small, scuffed box. He emptied it into his hand. The blood drained from his face. His eyes widened, then narrowed. He quivered with outrage.

"He's done it! The bastard's done it!"

"Done what?" Electra demanded over the sudden buzz of shocked conversation. "Who?"

Graham stretched out his hand toward his aunt. "Ravenswood!" he hissed, and showed her the blood-red ruby ring that lay in his palm glittering in the candlelight.

35

The yacht *Viorica II* lay in readiness, prepared to sail upon Raven's and Aurora's arrival. Marcus, having managed to rent the vessel from an acquaintance of his friend Louise Beauchene, stood on the deck anxiously awaiting the arrival of his son.

"Surely nothing could have gone wrong," he said to Madame Beauchene as she stood beside him at the railing of the yacht, which, though not as modern and sleek as Carlisle Jephson's *Sea Mist*, was built to supply her passengers with every comfort.

"Surely not," Louise reassured him. "They'll be here at any moment." She consulted the elegant enameled watch that hung from a chatelaine at her belt. "If she was due at the wedding at three, they should be here in a very few minutes."

True to Louise Beauchene's prediction, the carriage appeared and was drawn up on the dock beside the yacht. At Marcus's orders, the crewmen, who had been told to keep themselves in readiness to sail upon Raven's arrival, went down to unload the items Bridey had smuggled into the carriage under the guise of packing "Miss Aurora's traveling clothes."

Inside the carriage, Aurora was conscious but groggy. Having been dosed with her medicine over a period of weeks, she seemed to be never truly alert anymore. The world looked to her as if someone had drawn a thick gauze veil over it, dulling all perceptions, clouding all thoughts. As Raven reached for her, she frowned, confused, and reached out to touch his face wonderingly.

"Raven?" she whispered. "Where . . . I thought . . . But . . ." She lifted a hand to her head, knocking askew the wreath of orange blossoms that held her veil in place. "I don't understand."

"I'll explain later," Raven assured her, pulling the tangle of tulle aside and discarding it on the carriage floor. "For now you must trust me. Let me help you."

Willingly Aurora went into his arms and he lifted her out of the carriage. Rather than setting her on her feet, he carried her aboard the yacht, past the bemused eyes of his father and Louise, and down to the darkly paneled cabin that would be hers for the duration of the voyage back to the islands.

"Stay with her," he told Bridey, who was already below, having been shown to the cabin by one of the crew. "I'll see her later, after we've sailed."

"Yes, sir," Bridey agreed, bending over Aurora lying on the high iron bed.

"And Bridey?" Raven stood in the doorway. "You did very well today. I'll always be grateful to you."

They exchanged an understanding smile, and Raven returned to the deck where his father and Louise Beauchene waited to bid him farewell.

"Goodbye, Charles," Louise said. "I know that you and Aurora will be happy." She kissed his cheek lightly. "Don't stay away on that island forever. You will come to visit, won't you?"

"We will," Raven promised. "Perhaps in the spring."

Her smile atremble with emotion, Louise tactfully excused herself, leaving father and son to say their goodbyes in private.

Marcus's blue eyes were awash with tears. "I feel as if I'm losing you all over again," he said, his voice quavering despite his best efforts to control it. "And now Aurora as well. She's become very dear to me."

"I know, Father. And you are very dear to her. But you're not losing either of us. We'll all be together again. We'll come back to Chicago, and perhaps you'll venture out into the wilds." He glanced at the lovely widow who waited near the stylish open carriage on the dock. "Why don't you bring Madame Beauchene? She's a beautiful woman, Father, and she loves you. Don't spend your life alone simply to punish yourself for something that happened long ago. Mother would not have wanted that."

"I know you're right," Marcus conceded. "Who knows? I may take your advice. Now, I'll say goodbye. Godspeed and all happiness to you both."

"Goodbye, Father. I love you very much."

Tearfully Marcus embraced the son he'd once thought forever lost to him. "And I love you, my son," he whispered.

They parted and Marcus joined Louise Beauchene on the docks as the gangway was removed and the great steam engines that drove the yacht roared into life.

Standing at the rail, Raven was sad to see the father he had at long last come to know and understand fading into the distance. He was less sorry to see the stretch of water separating him and Chicago widening by the minute.

When he could no longer see his father, he went below to see how Aurora was faring.

In a small downstairs parlor of Gloria Hughston's home, Electra and Graham sat in outraged silence. The guests had departed in varying stages of shock and amusement, and Graham's mother had retired to her suite to lie down with what she termed a "sick headache."

"How could she do this to us?" Electra asked for what seemed the hundredth time. "After all I've done for her." She touched a black-edged handkerchief to the corner of her eye. "All I ever wanted was her happiness."

"And her money," Graham sneered.

"And I suppose you didn't want her money?" Electra challenged.

"Of course I did. But I'm not such a hypocrite as to pretend I didn't." He ran a distracted hand through his hair. "Christ! Why couldn't you have been more careful? You should have known better than to leave her in the hands of that damned Irish maid of hers."

"I didn't see you there protecting her! No! You were here preening! Basking in the glory of being husband to the Great Heiress!"

Graham glared at her. "Do you think it's going to do any good for us to sit here trying to fix the blame on one another? We've got to get her back."

"We've got to find her first. Who knows where that damned savage has taken her? I'll see him thrown into prison for kidnapping!"

"Aurora would never testify against him, you know that."

"Then how are we going to get her back?"

"I don't know. I don't know! But we have to!" He sighed, hanging his head. "We have to, because if we don't . . ."

"If we don't, what?" Electra wanted to know.

"I have debts," he told her.

Her laugh was soft, unpleasant. "Who hasn't? You cannot imagine the muddle Carlisle left his affairs in. If I'd have known this while he was alive, I'd have killed him! I'll be lucky if I don't wind up here, living with your mother."

"My mother will be lucky if she's able to keep on living here," Graham replied.

For the first time, Electra looked truly alarmed. "What can you mean?"

"As I said, Aunt, I have debts. Certain . . . gentlemen . . . have allotted me credit in certain . . . transactions . . . because of my prospects. Because I was known to be marrying a great fortune. I am heavily indebted to these men. They will want their money repaid, and soon."

"They will simply have to understand that—" Electra began.

Graham's short, derisive bark of laughter cut

her off. "All these men understand is that I owe them money. They are not particularly kind or charitable when it comes to welshers."

"Gamblers!" The light dawned on Electra. "These are gambling debts, aren't they? You're a gambler just as your father was!"

"I like to make a wager now and again at cards or at the racetrack, yes. It's not an unusual pastime, you know."

"How much do you owe them?" Electra wanted to know.

"I hardly think that's your concern."

"More than ten thousand dollars?"

"A bit more," he admitted.

"How much more?"

He looked away. "Three hundred thous—"

"My God! Graham! They'll take your home and your mother's home, and your—"

"They'll take my life if I don't pay them," he told her bluntly. "If you don't see me for a few days and no one seems able to locate me, have someone go and speak to Big Mike McDonald or Prince Hal Varnell."

"Good Lord." Even Electra, whose interest seldom strayed beyond fashion and scandal, recognized the names of the two men who between them controlled much of the vice and most of the politics of the city of Chicago. "What are you going to do?"

"Get Aurora back."

"There are other heiresses."

"None of her caliber."

Electra fell silent. It was perfectly true. Even someone like Abra Armbruster whose parents would be overjoyed to have Graham Hughston as a son-in-law would have balked at being asked to hand over more than a quarter of a million dollars to pay off his gambling debts. He needed a wife with a fortune the size of Aurora's—a fortune without watchdogs guarding it.

"First we have to find her," Electra reminded him. "If only we had some clue, some notion. He can't have gone far so soon, can he? Perhaps he's taken her to Marcus Ravenswood's mansion. From there they might leave Chicago and go to—"

"That damned island," Graham muttered.

"What?"

"The island. That's where he'd take her."

"But that's out in the middle of nowhere! In the wilderness!"

"Believe it or not, Aunt, she liked it there. She was happy there."

"But how can we be certain that's where they've gone?"

Before Graham could answer, there was a knock at the door. It opened and Gloria Hughston's butler appeared.

"Pardon me, madam, sir. There is a gentleman here asking to see Mr. Hughston. A policeman."

"A policeman?" Graham shot a look toward his aunt. "Show him in."

The uniformed officer entered the room carrying a parcel. Surreptitiously his eyes scanned the elegant room, then came to rest on the people before him. He touched the brim of his hat.

"Afternoon, madam. Sir. You are Mr. Hughston?"

"I am. This is my aunt, Mrs. Jephson. What is this about?"

"A carriage was found abandoned, sir. We

believe it belongs to you. This was found inside."
He opened the parcel and pulled out Aurora's veil,
the orange-blossom wreath mangled.

Electra gasped. "Was that all that was inside?
There was nothing else?"

"Nothing, ma'am. Nothing at all."

"Where was the carriage found?" Graham
asked.

"On the docks, sir. Near an empty berth.
People nearby were questioned and they said the
people from the carriage boarded a yacht, the—"
He consulted his notebook. "The *Viorica II*. They
steamed away, leaving an elderly gentleman and a
lady behind."

"Marcus and Louise Beauchene," Electra said.

"The island," Graham replied.

"Beg pardon, sir?" the policeman asked.

"Nothing, officer. Has the carriage been returned?"

"It's in the drive, sir. I'll need someone to
identify it."

"I'll be out in a moment. May I have that?" He
took the veil. "Thank you very much, officer. Will
you wait in the vestibule?"

"Yes, sir." He touched the brim of his hat once
more. "Good day, ma'am."

"Well, that's that," Graham said as the policeman left the room.

"You'll have to go after her," Electra insisted.

"Yes," Graham agreed. "But I'll need help." He
smiled slyly. "And I may know where to find it. If
you will excuse me, I think I'll go home and begin
formulating my plans."

With a kiss on his aunt's rouged cheek, Graham left his mother's house, leaving Aurora's veil

discarded in a snowy pile on the flowered carpet at Electra's feet.

Graham let himself into his modest—by Society standards—Huron Street mansion. That the foyer was deserted was no surprise. He had expected to spend the night ensconced in comfort in a luxurious private Pullman car on the way to New York, where he had planned to spend his honeymoon inspecting Aurora's real estate holdings. The servants, accordingly, had been given a holiday and had obviously wasted no time in vacating the premises.

He walked along the wide main hall, pausing at the foot of the stairs to shrug out of his frock coat and drape it over the newel. But as he stepped up onto the first tread, a noise from within the grand front sitting room commanded his attention.

For the first time, he noticed the faint sliver of light beneath the closed sitting-room doors. A sick feeling of apprehension quivered in the pit of his stomach.

"Don't be a fool," he told himself. "It's probably one of the servants who had nowhere to go." He chuckled weakly. "With luck it's that pretty kitchen maid."

Squaring his shoulders, he pushed open the double doors and marched into the parlor where a lamp burned low on a marble-topped table.

With the gathering twilight outside and only the single lamp to dispel the darkness in the cavernous room, the atmosphere was eerie, filled with shadows. But it was not until Graham heard the two doors he had just opened swinging shut behind him that he realized his mistake in returning home alone to the empty house.

Turning, he found himself confronted by two hulking men, one in black and white check worsted, the other in grey striped flannel, both wearing bowlers.

"Well, gentlemen," he said brightly, trying desperately to hide his growing terror, "don't you look jaunty. To whom do I owe the pleasure of this visit? Mr. Varnell? Or, perhaps, Mr. McDonald."

"Big Mike sent us," one growled as they both moved forward.

"I see." Graham swallowed hard, any faint hopes dying. Big Mike was the worst. Even his wife was so tough she had gunned down a policeman in cold blood and then, a few years later, had run off to Paris with a priest. "And how is Mr. McDonald?"

"He heard a rumor that the wedding's off," the second man snarled. The cracking of his knuckles sounded like gunshots in the silent room. "He's a little worried."

"Off? Off!" Graham laughed nervously. "Oh no, it's not off. It's just been postponed. There was a little difficulty with the bride. She—"

"Postponed, eh?" the first man interrupted.

"That's right. Just postponed. But there will be a wedding. Tell Mike he has my word there will be a wedding!"

"He said to tell you there'll either be a wedding or a funeral," the man in the checked suit snarled.

Graham felt perspiration breaking out all over his body. "There's no need for that."

"You better hope not."

"In any case, you go tell Mr. McDonald that I will marry Miss Jephson and he will get his money."

"We'll tell him," the man in striped flannel promised. "He told us to give you a message too."

"He did? And what was that?"

The two men moved toward Graham in unison, their actions agile and quick despite their size. Graham's shriek of terror went unheard, and it would be the middle of the next day before a parlor maid returning from a visit to her mother would find him lying, still unconscious, his body bruised, battered and bloodied, two ribs and several teeth broken, his handsome face swollen, nearly unrecognizable, on the sitting-room floor.

36

Lying in his bed wracked with the pain of his injuries, Graham pondered the next step he should take toward recovering Aurora. He would have to go himself, he knew, eventually. But the trip would be impossible until his ribs healed enough to make movement, if not painless, then at least not as dangerous as his doctors warned him it would be for the first few weeks.

He remembered what Aurora had said about the people she suspected had forged "Raven's" letter to him telling him of Aurora's whereabouts and demanding the reward for returning her to him. They would do anything for money, she had said. For twenty-five thousand dollars they had found a way to get Aurora away from Raven. He smiled, remembering how the man he'd thought to be Raven had angrily reminded him that the article had promised a larger amount if Aurora was returned unharmed. He had shown the man the twenty-five thousand, reminded him that Aurora was already aboard the yacht, and shown him the pistol he had in his pocket. The greedy bastard had snatched up the case with the money and run.

. Now, as he lay there scheming, Graham wondered how much that same man would demand to once more capture Aurora and then do them all the service of killing Raven. Murder was an expensive business, but Graham suspected that the man he had dealt with hated Raven and would kill him with pleasure. The extra money would merely be a bonus for doing what he'd wanted to do for years.

Ringing for a maid, Graham ordered pen, ink and paper. Slowly, painfully, he set about composing a letter to the Oates family, care of General Delivery, St. James, Beaver Island.

In the letter, Graham told Mr. Oates—damn Aurora!, he thought, she could at least have given him a first name—that he'd discovered it was not Raven he'd dealt with earlier but that it didn't matter, for the result was all that mattered to him. He alerted the Oateses to the fact that Aurora and Raven were once more together and were even then steaming toward the island. Aurora was his, he told Oates, and had been abducted on the way to her wedding. Raven had no right to her, and Graham meant to have her back—at all costs. He asked Oates to help him again as he had helped him once and invited him to reply, naming his terms. The last, perhaps most important, favor, that of ridding Graham and the Oateses and Aurora of Raven forever, Graham thought would be best conveyed in person. It would be better to discuss that after they had come to terms on Aurora's abduction, and better not to leave the evidence of such an arrangement where it could be used against one if the worst came to the worst.

Signing and sealing the letter, Graham once more called for the maid and ordered the missive sent on its way without delay.

Lying back against his pillows, he calculated the time it should take the letter to reach its destination, allowed time for his offer to be considered, and added the time it would take for a reply to reach him. Yes, he thought with a satisfied smile, by the time he heard from the greedy Mr. Oates—and he felt not the slightest doubt that the man was greedy enough to accept such an offer—he would be able to undertake a cruise to the islands in the north.

In the white-painted, curlicued iron bed in her cabin aboard the *Viorica II*, Aurora's eyelids fluttered, then lifted. She scowled into the darkness; the only light in the cabin was the moonlight that filtered through the filmy curtains over the two portholes opposite her bed.

She pushed herself up in bed and covered her face with her hands. "Where am I?" she whispered, confused. She felt the movement of the ship. "Is this the train? Am I Mrs. Graham Hughston?" She bit her lip, unable to suppress a shudder of revulsion at the thought. Trying with little success to gather her thoughts, she reasoned that she could not be aboard a train for there was no noise. She had ridden the train from New York to Cleveland with her aunt and uncle and she knew how it had rocked, how the wheels on the rails had sounded with their rhythmic clackety-clack. "It's not the

train," she told herself firmly. "But . . . it feels
like . . . how can it be . . .?"

Throwing back the coverlet and sheet, she
swung her legs over the side of the bed. The cabin
swayed, a movement that was half the motion of
the yacht and half the giddiness of her befuddled
senses, dulled by weeks of Electra Jephson's "medicine." Closing her eyes, Aurora tried to clear away
the fog that seemed to have settled in her brain in
the weeks since her uncle's death. It was frightening, for she could not remember much after being
told that Carlisle was dead. The intervening time
was blurred into a bewildering jumble of sounds
and faces. And now, to awaken alone in a strange
place . . .

She pushed herself to her feet and managed
the few steps to the porthole. All she could see was
water, endless, black water, silvered in places by
the light of the moon. A ship—she was on a ship.
But how had she gotten here? Where was Graham?

"Raven," she whispered. An image of him
flickered at the edges of her mind, teasing her,
tormenting her. She saw him smiling at her, reaching down toward her, pulling off the cascading veil
of her wedding gown.

Had she dreamed it? Was it real? But why?
When? How? Stumbling back to the bed, her head
spinning, she sank weakly onto its edge.

As she sat there resting, trying desperately to
make some sense of the blur of images flitting
through her mind, the cabin door opened behind
her.

"Aurora?"

She gasped, for an instant uncertain of whom

she would find when she looked toward the door. A feeling of inexpressible relief swept over her when she found Raven framed in the doorway.

"You should be sleeping," he said gently, coming to sit beside her.

She smiled wanly. "It seems that's all I've done for ages and ages."

"According to Bridey, it is," he confirmed. "Your aunt was keeping you sedated to make sure you went through with your wedding to Graham."

Aurora's smile faded. "I had to marry him. I owed it to Uncle Carlisle."

"No, you didn't." Raven laid a finger across her lips to still her protests. "Listen to me. Bridey told me your uncle never spoke to your aunt about us. She said Pelton and Hawkins overheard him having a terrible argument with Mrs. Jephson about her extravagance, and that was when he had his attack. It was not you. It was his wife who caused his death."

"Truly?" she asked, seizing upon the hope his explanation offered. "I didn't kill him?"

"Your uncle had a heart condition for years. No one was supposed to know, because it would have affected his business. That "influenza" he had, remember? That was a heart attack. It was only a matter of time before one killed him. Electra knew that. But she knew you felt guilty about your uncle's death, and she used it to force you into the marriage."

"She was so desperate for the wedding?" Aurora was astonished. "I knew she wanted Graham to marry me, but—"

"She was even more desperate after Carlisle's

death," Raven explained. "There is going to be trouble with Jephson Mining because of the way your uncle ran his business. Oh, I don't imagine Electra will be poverty-stricken, but certainly she'd have had a far more comfortable life if she'd had access to your fortune."

"And Graham?"

"He's no businessman. His father's company is worth half what it was when he inherited it. He gambles. He's heavily in debt to some very unpleasant men in Chicago."

"All I was good for to them was money," Aurora said softly. "They didn't care about me at all."

"I can't speak for your aunt," Raven told her, "but I think Graham Hughston wanted more from you than your inheritance. You're far too beautiful for any man to dismiss you so lightly."

She averted her face. "I'm not beautiful. I remember looking into a mirror when I was being fitted for my wedding gown and I looked so pale and thin with great, dark circles under my eyes. My hands—" She held them out in front of her. "Look at them, skin and bones." She touched her ring finger. "What happened to Graham's ruby?"

"I had it returned to him at his mother's."

Her eyes widened. "Not at the altar!"

Raven grinned. "Um-hmm. In front of all the guests."

"That was wicked of you, you know."

"I know." His eyes glittered and a mischievous smile played about his full lips. "I feel so guilty."

"I'm certain you do." Reaching up, she touched his cheek. Her breath caught somewhere in her chest as he took her hand and pressed a kiss into her palm.

"Raven?"

His blue eyes met her green ones. "Yes, my love?"

"How did I get here?"

Laughing, he explained how Bridey had come to him, told him of her concerns, helped him plan to take Aurora away from Electra and Graham and the entrapment of a forced marriage.

"Why did she do that?" Aurora asked when he'd finished.

"Because she loves you, goose," he answered simply. "She knew you wouldn't be happy with Hughston."

"And she knew I'd be happy with you?"

"She must have."

"What will she do now? She'll be punished by Aunt Electra." Aurora gazed up at him, her eyes awash with tears. "She'll be turned out, Raven. Who will care for her? Poor Bridey! We shouldn't have left her there all alone to face—"

"Hush. You're upsetting yourself for nothing. Bridey is here aboard the yacht. She's coming with us."

"To the island? Bridey on the island?" Aurora laughed. "Whatever will she make of it?"

"She'll be all right," Raven predicted. "Bridey is a strong young woman. And a brave one. But I'm afraid I'm going to have trouble."

"Trouble? What sort of trouble?"

"I've lived alone for a long time. Now," he sighed, "I'm going to be outnumbered by women in my own home."

"You'll have to add a room to the cabin," Aurora reminded him. "Bridey will need a room of her own."

"And will you want one too?" he asked innocently.

The joy faded from Aurora's face and was replaced by concern. "But . . . that is, I thought . . . Raven? Won't you marry me?"

He grinned. "Why, Miss Jephson, I thought you'd never ask."

Aurora blushed. "Damn you! You tricked me! Now I suppose you'll go and tell that handsome cousin of yours that I proposed to you."

"On your knees," he confirmed. "Begged me, in fact."

"Raven! You wouldn't dare! Matthew will think that . . ." She paused thoughtfully. "Matthew! Raven, has Matthew a sweetheart?"

"I don't know. I think Matthew enjoys having women fight over him too much to settle down to one. Why?"

"I was thinking. Bridey will be there and Matthew will be coming to visit—"

"And you plan on playing matchmaker?"

"If they like one another, nature could take its course, couldn't it?"

"Why don't we let it and not try to push it along, all right?"

"Oh, very well. But I hope they do like one another. Bridey deserves to be happy."

"Yes, she does," Raven agreed. He smiled. "Now that you mention it, I hope she and Matthew do take to one another."

"You do? Why?"

"If she were to become Matthew's woman, I wouldn't have to add a room to the cabin."

"Raven! That's no reason to hope two people fall in love."

"Easy for you to say, my darling. You won't be the one cutting those logs."

"Oh, you're ter—" Her words were cut off as a huge yawn overtook her. She shook her head. "I don't know why I'm so tired. All I've been doing is sleeping and sleeping."

"It's only natural," Raven told her. "The drugs induced sleep, but it wasn't a natural, restful sleep. You're exhausted. Come on, get into bed. We'll have the rest of our lives to talk, starting in the morning."

"I don't want to get back into bed," she said, her hand on his sleeve.

"Why not? There's nothing to be afraid of."

"I don't want you to leave me. As long as I can see you and touch you, I know this isn't all just a dream."

"I don't have to leave you."

Gently, he tucked Aurora into the bed and then, casting off his shirt, trousers and shoes, slipped between the crisp linen sheets and gathered her into his arms.

"Raven?" she whispered, her cheek nestled against his chest.

"Hmmm?"

She smiled as the sound made vibrations against her cheek. "I love you."

He stroked her hair, her shoulder, held her close. "And I love you," he whispered, his lips moving against the silken crown of her head.

"I wish—" she began.

"What do you wish?"

She sighed and snuggled as close to him as she could. "I wish I wasn't so tired," she finished and then, warmed and comforted by his presence, let herself slip away into a deep, and for the first time in weeks, natural sleep.

37

It was Sarah who brought the letter to her father. None of the others ever bothered to stop and ask if there was mail for them—it seemed there never was. But Sarah always did, though she couldn't say why. It was not because she expected a letter from Raven—she had long since lost hope that he would come back to her. For him to leave his beloved island and follow Aurora to Chicago—it had sounded the death knell of all her hopes and dreams. It seemed as if something had died inside her when she'd gone to his island and found his cabin deserted. She had met Matthew in St. James and he had told her that Raven had gone to Chicago determined to find Aurora and bring her back. From that moment she'd felt empty inside—empty and cold and dead.

When she had asked if there was any mail and

had been handed the letter postmarked Chicago, her heart had thudded painfully for an instant. Then, realizing that the handwriting was not Raven's and the letter was addressed simply to "The Oates Family," she had seen how foolish this faint glimmering of hope was. Slipping the letter into her pocket, she had set out for home.

"A letter, Pa," she said as she entered the cabin and put down the pack of supplies she had brought back from the larger island. "From Chicago."

"Chicago?" Titus looked up from his meal of boiled venison and potatoes. "What is it? Raven writin' to say how much he misses us?"

Luke and Rufus laughed, but Sarah didn't bother to force a smile. Handing her father the letter, she left the room.

"Let's see what this is," Titus said. Digging between his teeth, he extracted a piece of meat, spat it on the wide plank floor, then, after wiping his hands on his dirty trousers, ripped open the envelope and pulled out the letter.

"What is it, Pa?" Luke wanted to know. "Is it from Raven?"

"I'll be damned. No, it's not from Raven. It's from that young jackass who came up to get that rich girl Raven was keepin'."

"How'd he know who we are?" Rufus demanded.

"Likely Raven told him." Titus frowned. "Says here this man Hughston was supposed to marry that girl. He was waitin' at the altar and she was on her way when Raven up and ab . . . abdu . . . Sarah! What's this word?"

Summoned from the other room, Sarah took the letter from her father. "Abducted," she said dully, having listened through the open door. "It means he kidnapped her."

Titus laughed. "Raven kidnapped her on the way to marry Hughston! Bet he was surprised!"

The brothers laughed, ignoring Sarah's pained expression.

"Don't that beat all!" Rufus chuckled. "That woman's gone back and forth between them two men so much, I wonder if she can keep track of who she's with anymore."

"Maybe she don't care!" Luke laughed.

"She cares," Sarah said quietly, sadly.

"Who asked you?" Titus demanded. "Take your long face and git on out of here, girl."

As Sarah left, Luke leaned forward. "What else does he say, Pa?"

"He says—" Titus consulted the letter once more. "He says Raven's bringin' that woman back here to his island. But Hughston wants her back and he wants us to git her for him."

"We got her for him once," Rufus groused. "It ain't our fault if he can't hang on to her."

"He's willin' to pay again. He wants us to name our price."

"We could use another twenty-five thousand," Rufus said thoughtfully.

His wife, Belle, walked into the room. "Like you used the last twenty-five thousand? A fortune! And you toss it away like it was water. Did any of us see a cent of it? No! The three of you left us to starve while you went off to the mainland and spent it on gamblin' and whores."

"You don't look like you missed any meals," Luke sneered, his eyes running over the ample form of his sister-in-law.

"Why don't you shut up?" Belle snarled.

Rufus leapt to his feet and raised his fist toward his wife. "Don't you talk to my brother like that, woman. You got no call to talk to any man like that! You hear me?"

"I hear you," Belle growled. With a swish of her tattered calico skirts, she left the room.

"That woman needs a good beatin'," Titus observed. "You shouldn't let her git away with sassin' you that way."

"She won't git away with it again," Rufus promised.

"Aw, to hell with her," Luke said. "What're we gonna do about Raven's woman?"

"I say we take her," Rufus voted. "Tell this man, Hughston to bring the money with him. Tell him we won't give her to him till we git the money."

"What's to keep Raven from comin' after her?" Luke asked worriedly. He was, had always been, more than a little in awe of Raven. For all his brute strength and ferocious appearance, Luke Oates was a coward at heart. Brutalizing women was as far as his bravery would take him. The thought of Raven descending on them, blood-lust in those blue eyes, frightened him more than he cared to admit.

"Nothin' will keep him from comin' after her," Titus said. "You can bet he will. But that's good."

"Good how?" Luke demanded.

"Good, you ignorant jackass, because if we're watchin' out for him, we can all three be waitin' for him," Rufus told his brother.

"Rufus is right," Titus agreed. "He'll be comin' after her. No question. But if we're watchin' for him, we can take him." He sat back in his chair, smiling confidently. "This is our chance, boys, to make one hell of a lot of money and git rid of that half-breed bastard once and for all at the same time."

Titus and his sons exchanged a sly smile and Titus shouted toward the open door:

"Jennie!"

The pretty, ethereal creature who dwelt among them but had never seemed like one of them appeared at the door. Now sixteen, she was delicately beautiful and she knew it—knew it by the way the men's eyes lingered on her on those rare occasions when she accompanied Sarah to St. James. And knew it by the way her brother Luke's eyes followed her as she went about her chores.

"Yes, Pa?" she said softly, her eyes downcast to avoid Luke's stare.

"Fetch me some paper, ink and a pen. And be quick about it!"

The girl withdrew and in a drawer in the other room managed to find the items her father requested. Setting them on the table before him, she disappeared again, as she always did, preferring to spend her days alone than in the company of the people some cruel quirk of fate had given her as family.

"Well, boys, here we go," Titus said as he dipped his pen into the inkwell. "What say we ask for thirty thousand this time?"

His sons laughed, thinking of the days and nights of pleasure such a sum would bring them in the saloons and gambling halls and bawdy houses of the cities on the mainland.

"Thirty thousand," Rufus agreed eagerly.

"Ten thousand each," Luke sighed.

Titus shot his son a ferocious glare. "Twenty for me, boy. Five for each of you."

"But, Pa," Rufus protested.

"Shut up, boy!" Titus silenced his son with a vicious swipe across the face with the back of his hand. "You'll take what you git and be damned grateful for it!"

Luke, sitting across the table, knew enough to say no more.

His sons put into their places, Titus put pen to paper and began to write.

"Is this Mr. Ravenswood's island?" Bridey asked as the *Viorica II* swept into Paradise Bay and prepared to drop anchor.

"No," Aurora replied, standing beside Bridey at the railing. "This is the largest of the islands. Raven's is much smaller. It is off the western shore of this one."

"When will we go there?"

Aurora laughed. "Soon, I should think. Are you really so anxious to get there? I should have thought you'd be sorry to leave the bustle of the city."

"Oh, I don't know. The city didn't seem such a happy place to be anymore, Miss Aurora."

"No, I suppose it didn't," Aurora agreed. "Bridey, don't you think you could call me just plain Aurora now? After all, you won't really be my maid anymore. Can't we just be friends?"

Bridey's pretty face looked troubled. "I don't

know. It would be hard for me to stop thinkin' of you as Miss Aurora."

"Try, won't you?"

"All right." Bridey nodded, her red curls, more orange than Aurora's deep flame-red, bobbing. "I'll try—Aurora."

"There, that didn't hurt, did it?"

They smiled at one another as Raven came to join them at the railing.

"I wrote to someone asking him to meet us," Raven revealed. "He's supposed to be watching for us."

"Wrote?" Aurora repeated. "But when? How could you have written to anyone from the yacht?"

"I sent the letter before we left Chicago. The day before your wedding, in fact."

"You were awfully sure of yourself, weren't you? How did you know I'd come with you?"

"As I recall, I didn't give you much of a choice."

"Come to think of it, I don't recall that you did either."

"Are you sorry?"

Aurora gazed up at him, adoring him. She was nearly recovered from the aftereffects of Electra's "medicine," and their last night aboard the yacht had been one of love, of passion, of beauty given and taken in equal measure.

"Never," she vowed. "How could I ever be sorry?"

Bending his head, Raven's lips met hers in a sweet, tender kiss—a lover's kiss. But the moment was shattered as Bridey exclaimed:

"Here comes somebody in a boat!"

Looking down, they saw a boat being rowed

toward the yacht. Even from the back, Aurora recognized the man who handled the oars so expertly.

"That's Matthew!" she cried. She gave Raven a poke in the ribs. "You knew all along Matthew was meeting us! Why didn't you tell me that first night when I said how nice it would be if—"

She said no more, aware of Bridey standing beside them. Instead she turned to the former maid and told her:

"That is Matthew. He is Raven's cousin. His mother and Raven's mother were sisters."

"Oh."

Bridey studied him as he reached the side of the now-anchored yacht and tossed up a line to secure the smaller boat to the larger. Seeing them standing at the rail, Matthew grinned and waved.

"He's ever so handsome, isn't he?" Bridey mused, more to herself than to them.

Beside her, Aurora glanced up at Raven and grinned. "Don't start on that extra room just yet," she whispered, then giggled as he tugged playfully at one of her long, cascading curls.

38

"Where's Bridey?" Aurora asked as she found Raven chopping wood in the clearing behind their cabin.

Straightening, he leaned his axe against a tree and wiped the sweat from his brow with the back of his hand.

"She went fishing," he told her, grinning.

"Not with Matthew?"

Raven nodded. "I'm beginning to get tired of looking at his face. I swear to you, Aurora, I've never seen so much of him in my life as I have since we brought Bridey back from Chicago."

Aurora laughed. "Have you noticed Bridey lately? She glows. She's in love with him, Raven. I know it."

"Already? She's only been here three weeks."

"It didn't take that long for me to fall in love

with you," she reminded him. "Tell me, do I look as radiant as she does?"

"Even more so. And I take complete credit for it."

"You should." She fell into step with him as he walked toward the edge of the clearing. "I'm writing to your father."

"Send him my best," Raven told her. "If you get it finished in time, I'll take it to St. James when I go."

"When are you going?"

He shrugged. "In a few days. By the end of the week at the latest. Matthew tells me a trunk arrived from my father." He chuckled. "He probably sent us a porcelain service for forty in case we get a sudden urge to hold a formal dinner."

"Raven, be nice," Aurora chided.

He laughed. "I know he means well. But he really has little idea of what life is like here. In any case, I'll go to St. James and get the trunk and whatever is in it."

"Matthew can help you with it."

Raven shook his head. "Matthew will stay here with you and Bridey in case the Oateses get any foolish notions."

"Surely they wouldn't dare—"

"Better to be safe. I don't trust a one of them."

Hand in hand they strolled through the forest. The days were cooler now, the nights positively cold, and the first hints of the magnificent fall colors had already touched the trees. As they walked toward the lake shore, Aurora sighed.

"I wish it was warm enough to swim in the creek," she murmured wistfully.

Raven gazed at her askance, reading her thought as clearly as if they were his own. "That would be nice," he agreed. "But Bridey and Matthew will return on the creek path." He chuckled softly. "Four people on an island of almost six square miles and it seems crowded."

"Well, perhaps after Bridey and Matthew are married and—"

"Married! You're getting a bit ahead of yourself aren't you?"

"I don't think so. They're obviously in love." She pouted prettily. "Although I see that doesn't always mean anything. After all, we're in love and we're not married."

Raven smiled, his blue eyes twinkling with deviltry. "You want me to make an honest woman of you, is that it?" He laughed at the face she made. "I'll marry you whenever you say, my love. But there are arrangements to make. It's not as if we can simply turn up at the corner church, you know. Think about when you want to be married and I'll speak to the people in St. James about it. All Right?"

Dimpling, Aurora slipped into his outstretched arms. "All right," she whispered, and, turning her face up toward his, kissed him.

In Chicago, Graham Hughston boarded the *Sea Mist* accompanied by his Aunt Electra.

"Are you certain you're well enough to go on this trip?" she fussed. "I think you should stay home in bed a little longer."

"Aunt Electra," he said with scant patience. "If I don't get Aurora back, and soon, I'll be resting permanently—in Graveland Cemetery!"

"I still think you should go to the police and tell them—"

"Aunt, the police are not going to do anything. Mike McDonald and Hal Varnell are two of the most powerful men in the city. The city government takes its instructions from them."

"Well! I'd like to give them each a piece of my mind!"

Graham laughed, wincing at the pain of his taped ribs. "I wouldn't recommend it. Contradicting either of those men is detrimental to one's continued good health. As I can attest to."

Electra pursed her lips. "I hope you don't have too much trouble convincing Aurora to leave that . . . that . . . man she's with and come back where she belongs."

"I don't think I'll have too difficult a time," Graham assured her, smiling. "I have people at work convincing her as we speak."

"People? What people? I didn't know you knew anyone up there."

"I made a few acquaintances when I went up to get her the last time. I've contacted those same people, and they assure me they can help remove Aurora from Ravenswood's influence."

"How nice. I'm glad there are honest people around who understand the importance of keeping to one's own class."

Graham thought of the hulking, dirty man he'd thought was Raven. He remembered the crude letter he'd received in answer to his own offer to Titus Oates. Good, honest people indeed. If people such as they so much as appeared on Electra's doorstep, she'd have the butler after them with a shotgun loaded with buckshot.

"I have to be going now, Aunt," he told her, signaling the captain to begin preparations for departure.

"Do you have everything you need?"

He thought of the small leather case containing fifty thousand dollars in cash—the last ready cash he had in the world. Thirty thousand of it was the agreed-upon sum for the capture of Aurora. The other twenty was a bonus for, as he had phrased it in his letter to Titus Oates, "ridding us all of Raven once and for all." The money was aboard. He had seen to that himself. So long as he had the money to meet Titus Oates's price, he needed nothing else.

"I have everything I need," he assured her. "I'll be fine. And I'll have Aurora back here before you know it."

"How wonderful! I only wish that girl could realize how fortunate she is to have you."

Turning a powdered, rouged cheek up for his kiss, Electra left the yacht and went to her open carriage to watch the beautiful white vessel set sail for Beaver Island.

In their small, tumbledown cabin on their speck of an island, the Oates men looked over Graham Hughston's latest letter.

"Fifty thousand," Rufus sighed. "In cash. And all we got to do is catch one scrap of a woman and kill a miserable half-breed."

"I'd have slit that bastard's throat for free," Luke snarled, his bravado far outpacing the limits of his actual courage.

"You'd jump if he said 'boo,'" Titus scoffed. "Yer afeared of him and you always have been."

Luke pouted, but Titus ignored him and went on:

"Here's what we'll do. We'll git the girl and bring her here. When Raven comes to git her back, we'll git him too."

"What if he don't come?" Rufus asked.

"He'll come. He went to Chicago fer her, didn't he? He'll be after her the minute he finds her missin'. He'll be mad—mad and careless. It won't be hard to take him down."

"Then, when Hughston comes to git the girl, we'll git the money," Luke crowed, relishing the prospect of returning to the towns where they'd spent the last "fortune" Graham Hughston had bestowed upon them.

"Wait now, jist a minute," Rufus said. "If we bring that girl here and kill Raven, she'll know we did it. If we give her over to Hughston and he takes her back to Chicago, what's to keep her from goin' to Raven's pa and the two of 'em gittin' the law on us? I got no mind to hang for the sake of that half-breed."

Smiling, Titus sank back into a chair. "Between you, you boys ain't got the brain the Almighty gave a stump. We ain't gonna give the girl to Hughston. And there ain't nobody goin' back to Chicago."

"I don't git it, Pa," Luke said, shaking his head in confusion.

"Look here," Titus told them. "All of 'em— Hughston, the girl, even Raven, got money and connections, rich connections, back in Chicago. If we let any one of 'em go back there, they'd have the law down on us so fast we'd be in a jail cell before we knowed what hit us. If this is goin' to work, they all got to die. All of 'em." He nodded gravely in the face of his sons' amazement. "Raven we'll kill as soon as he comes for the girl. He'll be out of the way. Then, when Hughston gets here, we'll git rid of him and the girl at the same time."

"How're we gonna git rid of Hughston, Pa?" Luke wanted to know.

"Any way we can," Titus answered. "Now, accordin' to his letter, he's expectin' to git here the night of the sixteenth or the mornin' of the seventeenth. If we keep a watch for that big white boat of his, we might git a chance at him before he ever gits to St. James. If he gits here at night, we'll light the light." Titus glanced toward the window. "Supposed to cloud up tomorrow. Hope it stays stormy."

"When're we gonna git the girl?" Rufus asked.

"Soon as we can. Sarah went to town yesterday. She heard tell as there's a trunk came from Raven's father. He's supposed to come git it. We got to watch and see when he does."

"What if he takes her with 'im?" Rufus asked gloomily.

Titus gnashed his teeth. Was ever a man cursed with two more blockheaded sons? "Then we watch for another chance."

"Even if he leaves her behind," Luke pointed out, "he'll likely leave somebody to watch her. Maybe Matthew."

"Are you tellin' me, boy," Titus snarled, "that the three of us ain't more'n a match for Matthew?"

"Hell no, Pa! We could take him!" Luke vowed.

"I surely hope so!" Rufus agreed. The light in his eyes flickered with another emotion. "Pa, after we git that woman here—well, seein' as how we're jist gonna kill her—that is, Luke said she was the

purtiest woman he ever seen and I got a hankerin'
to have a woman like that—"

"I seen her first!" Luke objected. "An' you got
a wife!"

"I ain't fixin' to marry her!" Rufus growled.

"Stop it! Damn yer hides! I said stop it!" Titus
pounded on the table. He had foreseen this. A
beautiful young woman could set his sons at one
another and ruin all his plans. "Ain't nobody
gonna touch 'er! Nobody!"

"But, Pa!" Luke and Rufus protested in unison.

"I said no!" Titus roared. "Somethin' could go
wrong and Hughston could git past us. I don't want
'im sendin' the law down on us fer rapin' his
woman."

"After he's dead then?" Luke asked hopefully.
"After Hughston's dead and Raven too?"

Titus leaned back in his chair thoughtfully.
"Well, mebbe after Hughston and Raven are out of
the way. We jist might have ourselves a time with
that pretty woman before we git rid of her too." He
scowled ferociously at his sons. "But not before,
you hear me! Either one of you lay a hand on that
woman and so help me, I'll geld ya!"

Both Rufus and Luke winced, not doubting for
a moment that their father was capable of anything
he threatened. Their ardor for Aurora was, if not
dampened, at least shelved until they had Titus's
blessing.

Satisfied that he had made an impression on
both his boneheaded offspring, Titus bade them sit
down and help him plot their actions once the
opportunity presented itself.

* * *

The opportunity came two days later when from the deck of their fishing boat they saw Raven climb into his boat and sail off.

"He left Matthew behind," Rufus told his father, nodding toward the shore. "And there's another woman. Should we bring her too?"

"Leave 'er," Titus decided. "I don't want to try and ride herd on two women. One'll be enough trouble."

"They'll tell Raven it was us," Luke worried.

"Think he won't know anyways?" Titus asked. "I said leave 'er and I meant it."

As Bridey, Matthew and Aurora disappeared into the forest, heading back to the cabin, Rufus turned the fishing boat in the direction of the island.

"We're going to walk down along the creek," Bridey told Aurora. "It's so peaceful there."

"Do you want to come?" Matthew asked.

Aurora dimpled. "You two go on ahead. You don't need me along. I think I'll spend a quiet afternoon resting."

Bridey's eyes twinkled. "You'd best tell Raven not to work you so hard durin' the days—or is it the night?"

"Bridey!" Aurora cuffed her playfully. "Don't be wicked!"

Laughing, they parted company, Matthew and Bridey heading for the path in the forest where they had spent so many romantic moments and Aurora entering the cabin, intending to while away the afternoon with a good book.

As she sat on the sofa, her feet propped on a pillow, a shadow fell across her as the sunlight flooding through the open door was suddenly blocked out.

"Did you forget something?" Aurora asked, not glancing up from her book, thinking Bridey and Matthew had returned.

There was no reply, and Aurora looked up curiously. A man stood in the doorway, a short, stocky man with powerful arms and shaggy white hair. A full white moustache drooped over his upper lip.

"Who are you?" she demanded, laying her book aside and rising slowly, cautiously. "What do you want?"

"I'm Titus Oates," he answered, smiling, his gaze running over her admiringly. "And what I want, little lady, is you."

"No," she breathed. She edged across the room, not knowing what to do, panic robbing her of her reason. "Please, just go."

"I will," he assured her genially. "But not alone. Yer comin' with me."

"No!" Her fear was a painful knot in her breast. "Go away! Just get out of here."

"I told you she was bossy, Pa," Luke drawled, stepping into the doorway behind his father. "Didn't I tell you she was bossy?"

"That you did," Titus admitted. "You also said she was the purtiest woman you ever did see. And I kin see you was right about that, too."

Aurora felt faint. Luke! Oh, God! And Matthew was deep in the forest. Perhaps if she screamed—A glimmer of desperate hope flickered inside her, then died. These men were armed, ruthless. If Matthew and Bridey tried to come to Aurora's rescue they might be hurt, or killed.

"Please," she whispered. "I've done nothing to you."

"But yer gonna do somethin' for us," Rufus said from behind her. Having come in through the kitchen, he had cut off that avenue of escape.

With a little, terrified scream, Aurora swung around and found him there—a bigger, older, dirtier version of his brother.

Desperate now, Aurora ran for the bedroom thinking she might be able to crawl out the open window there. But the three men foresaw her plan and trapped her in the corner next to the bedroom door.

With their rough, cruel hands they quickly bound her wrists and ankles with stiff lengths of rope. Laughing, Luke slung her over his shoulder. Then they all left to make their way to the shore where a rowboat waited to carry them out to their anchored fishing boat.

Aurora tried in vain to quell the aching sobs that burned her chest. She could not scream for help—she would not be responsible for Matthew or Bridey being hurt or killed by these fiends. She could only hope and pray that Matthew and Bridey would quickly discover she was missing and Matthew would find Raven. Raven would know who had taken her—he would come for her—he would save her. That was the only hope she had, and only by clinging to it could she maintain her tenuous grip on rationality as she was carried aboard the leaky, stinking fishing boat and dumped onto a roll of rope. Her last conscious thought, before her head struck the iron fitting and the blessed darkness claimed her, was of Raven.

39

Aurora awakened slowly. Her head pounded, her throat was dry, raspy. Sitting up, she wrinkled her nose. Wherever she was, it smelled to the heavens of fish. She looked around. Nets had been piled in the corners of what she now realized must be some kind of shed. There were no windows, only one door, and she knew without even trying the latch that it would be barred.

"Where—" she began, and then remembered. The Oateses had come, had taken her away. This, then, must be their shed on their island. She was a prisoner of those loathsome, hideous men. What could they want from her? What did they expect?

Footsteps approached the shed on the hard-packed earth outside. Aurora tensed, wishing there were more light than the thin slivers that managed to find their way between the warped boards of the walls. Her eyes could not leave the door. When it opened, who would it be? Luke? She shuddered with disgust. There was another—Luke had a brother. Who could have imagined that there were two of them? And their father—Titus. The sire of all that hateful brood.

She pressed herself back against the wall as the door opened. Sunlight flooded the small interior of the cluttered shed. She shielded her eyes with her hand.

"Who is it?" she asked, squinting. "Who is there?"

The door closed and Aurora let her hand fall. Still half-blinded by the light, she saw only that it was a woman who stood before her.

"Sarah? Is that you?" she asked.

"No." The voice that answered her was soft, timid, gentle. "My name is Jennie."

"Jennie?" Her eyes at last adjusting to the darkness once more, Aurora found herself gazing up at the youngest of the clan. Delicate, pretty Jennie with her moonlight blonde hair and finely boned, heart-shaped face. The difference between her and the rest of the family was like the difference between night and day. "Who are you?"

"Jennie," the girl repeated. "Jennie Oates."

"You don't look like Luke or—the other one."

"Rufus," Jennie supplied. "They're my brothers. I have a sister, Sarah. You know her, don't you? Rufus has a wife, Belle. And Pa lives here too."

"It's hard to believe you're their sister," Aurora marveled. "You're so different."

Something in Jennie's pretty face seemed to close then, to shut out Aurora and her words. Aurora, aware of the change, wondered what she had said to so upset this gentle creature.

"I'm sorry, what did I—?"

"It doesn't matter," Jennie assured her. "Pa sent me to see if you was awake yet. He said you hurt yourself on the boat."

"Your brother Luke dumped me onto the deck and I hit my head," Aurora told her. "That's the last I remember until a few minutes ago."

"Do you want to come outside? It's kind of dark in here and—" She pinched her narrow nose with her finger and thumb. "—and smelly, too."

Aurora smiled in spite of herself. "It is both of those things," she agreed. "Won't your father be angry if you let me out of here? I thought I was going to be locked in here until . . . well . . . until they do whatever it is they're planning to do with me."

Jennie shook her head. "You can come out. You don't have to stay in here. We're on an island. There's really no place for you to go."

Aurora sighed. Depressing as it was, there was no denying that what Jennie said was perfectly true. From what Raven had told her, the Oateses' island was some seven miles west of Raven's island. She could hardly swim that distance, nor could she row, even if she managed to steal a boat.

"Do you want to come outside?" Jennie asked. "I'll show you around. I'll show you the well and the privy."

Only too willing to be out in the fresh air after the hot stink of the fishing nets in the shed, Aurora rose and followed Jennie out into the early evening sunshine.

What she saw was not particularly appealing. The cabin stood in a littered clearing dotted with scrubby evergreens. The building itself, not dissimilar from Raven's cabin, was weatherbeaten. Most of the windows had broken panes, some had no glass at all, only shutters that could be closed in foul weather. The roof was patched here and there, clumsily, carelessly. Piles of refuse littered the yard around the cabin and two bony mongrel dogs picked at them. From the way their bones jutted against their mangy hides, it seemed the rotting piles were their only sustenance.

Off to one side, just at the edge of the forest, a tumbledown outhouse leaned toward a half-dead white pine tree. Not far from it, a platform built of scrap lumber covered the open well. Its proximity to the outhouse made Aurora shudder with revulsion.

As they rounded the cabin, Aurora saw Sarah bending over a tin washtub. From it she extracted a dripping shirt. She squeezed the water from it and, shaking it out, reached up to hang it on the washline. Pinning it in place, she turned and noticed Aurora there, standing beside Jennie. Their eyes met and locked. Sarah wiped her hands on her skirt and came toward them.

"From a mansion to a fish shed," Sarah said viciously. "Not so fancy now, are you?"

Aurora's green eyes flashed like emeralds. "You can do what you want with me, Sarah, you and your father and your brothers. But you'll never have Raven back. Not ever. Not now. He never loved you in the first place. You were nothing but his whore."

Sarah's face flushed. Before Aurora could react, Sarah lashed out and caught her across the cheek with the damp palm of her hand. Aurora gasped, her hand raised to her scarlet cheek. A second passed before she returned the blow with one of her own. Then, lifting her skirts with the air of a duchess protecting herself from the dirt of the gutter, she stalked past Sarah.

"You bitch!" she heard Sarah hiss. "No! Maybe I'll never have Raven, but you'll never have him again either! Not ever!"

"He'll come for me," Aurora retorted, not bothering to look back. "You wait and see. He'll come for me."

"My father and brothers will be waiting for him. They're going to kill him. You are the bait."

Aurora's step faltered. Her face went pale with shock. Could it be that her capture was merely a ruse? Was she the bait Titus Oates was using to lure Raven to their island so they could kill him? It seemed only too plausible. And yet she found it hard to believe that Raven would not consider the possibility that Titus and his sons would try to ambush him. He was so much smarter than they, so much more cunning. They would never, ever, be able to outwit him.

She turned, buoyed by that belief, and smiled at Sarah. "They'll never kill Raven," she said confidently. "And if you think they can, you're a fool, just like your disgusting brothers and that ogre of a father of yours."

She saw the crimson flush that suffused Sarah's face and knew her barb had gone home. "Raven will come for me," Aurora went on, twisting the blade she'd plunged into Sarah's already injured pride, "and he'll take me away from this horrible place. And you'll be lucky to have an island left when he's through."

Sarah approached, eyes blazing. "Yes, Raven

will come for you. He might even manage to escape being killed. But the question is, will he want what he finds when he gets here?"

Aurora's eyes narrowed. "What are you babbling about now?" she demanded.

"Don't be stupid." Sarah laughed, enjoying the advantage that Aurora's confusion gave her. "You know that my brother Luke wants you. He tried to rape you once, didn't he? Well, now that he's seen you, Rufus wants you too, and our father. You're so damned pleased with yourself because of your looks and your airs. Well, good for you, you're so beautiful and such a fine lady. So fine that not a one of them can wait to get their hands on you. By the time they're done, Raven won't want to touch you. Think about that, Miss High-and-Mighty."

Turning on her heel, Sarah strode away, leaving Aurora to stare after her, sickened by the thought of any one of those men touching her. And yet what Sarah had said was true—if Luke and Rufus and Titus used her, she couldn't imagine Raven's wanting her. Oh, he would rescue her from them. Certainly he would never leave her in the clutches of people such as they. But be her lover? Her husband? Somehow she couldn't imagine it. What, then, lay before her? A life without Raven? A life lived knowing that he couldn't bear to touch her because she had been touched—and worse—by those filthy, base creatures? She could face anything—anything!—but that.

"Aurora?" Jennie touched her to rouse her from her melancholy thoughts.

"Hmmm? Oh, yes, Jennie. What else is there to see?"

"Not much," Jennie admitted. "There's the old lighthouse on the point. I'm not supposed to go there, but maybe Pa wouldn't mind, if you wanted to see it?"

"Is that the lighthouse your father and brothers use to lure ships onto the reef?" Aurora asked sarcastically.

She saw the fragile creature pale. Biting her lip, Jennie turned her face into the wind, hiding her expression from Aurora.

In spite of herself, in spite of the fact that she loathed Sarah, her brothers and their monster of a father, Aurora sensed that there was something different about Jennie. She seemed like some sort of changeling child. She was gentle, ethereal. Aurora felt that the girl's tender spirit was as much a prisoner in this hellish place as Aurora was herself.

"I'm sorry, Jennie," she said, amazed that she should find herself apologizing to a member of the Oates family for anything. "I shouldn't have asked that question."

"It's all right," Jennie said, her sweet and forgiving nature all too ready to respond to a kindness that was lacking in her life. "You should hear what some of the people on the big island say about Pa and Luke and Rufus."

I can imagine, Aurora thought, but she said nothing.

Together she and Jennie walked down to the beach. With the wind tugging at her skirts and hair, Aurora gazed out at the open water. The waves were breaking with rhythmic regularity, and Aurora watched as Jennie picked up a flat round stone and threw it in such a way that it skipped along the surface several times before it disappeared beneath the waves.

"What're you doin'?" a masculine voice called from behind them.

Aurora breathed a long, disgusted sigh as Rufus approached them. Jennie glanced over her shoulder.

"Nothin'," she answered as her brother came abreast of them.

"Why don't you go and see if Sarah needs help with supper?" he asked her.

She shrugged. "Pa told me to stay with Aurora all the time."

She yelped in pain as Rufus seized the girl's earlobe between his thumb and forefinger and pinched it viciously.

"Well, I'm tellin' you to go and help Sarah!"

Tears glittered in Jennie's eyes. "Pa said—"

"Are you sassin' me, girl?"

Unable to stand by and see Jennie hurt, Aurora slapped Rufus's hand smartly. Taken by surprise, he released his sister's ear and turned his attention to Aurora.

"Don't you hurt her!" Aurora hissed. "She's only doing what she was told! Does it make you a man to bully a young girl?"

"Fiery little thing, ain't you?" he drawled. "I like fire in a woman. And I wouldn't mind showin' you what it is that makes me a man!"

He reached toward her, but Aurora took Jennie's arm and started back toward the trees.

"Come on, Jennie, let's go back. I think I'll go back into the shed." She let her gaze run over Rufus, her nose wrinkled in disgust. "It smells better in there than it does here!"

She saw the quick fire that leapt into Rufus's cruel little eyes and for the first time was grateful for Titus Oates's interest in her. If their father had designs on her himself, neither Luke nor Rufus would dare touch her. Her only problem, then, was how to avoid Titus!

She looked up as they neared the forest's edge and saw a woman standing there. Belle, she assumed, Rufus's wife. She had apparently seen her husband follow Aurora and Jennie out of the clearing and had come to see what he was up to.

So she knows, Aurora thought. She knows that Rufus is as interested in me as his brother and father.

But oddly enough, Belle's hate-filled glare was reserved not for her husband but for the beautiful captive her husband, brother-in-law and father-in-law had brought to the island.

She blames me! Aurora thought. She blames me because her husband is an animal!

As she and Jennie passed Belle, Aurora kept her eyes carefully averted, but she could feel the older woman's glare burning twin holes into her back.

All right, she thought as she returned to the clearing and then to the shed; so perhaps Titus is not my only problem. I'll have to watch out for Belle too. And Sarah.

Sighing, Aurora sat on the hard-packed earthen floor and drew her knees up under her chin.

"I've got to get out of here!" She closed her eyes. "Raven," she whispered, as though invoking an avenging angel to rescue her from this den of devils, "where are you? I need you. Please. Please! Come help me!"

382

She tried to take comfort in her plea, tried to tell herself that as their hearts, their souls were one, he would somehow sense her danger and come to her. But even as she told herself that, her common sense reminded her that he couldn't even know she was gone and might not discover it for days.

40

The morning dawned and in the cold, stinking shed that was at once her prison and her refuge, Aurora huddled beneath the musty, scratchy blanket Jennie had brought to her the night before.

She felt stiff, sore and grimy. Jennie had offered to bring her hot water to bathe in, but she could not bear the thought of taking off her clothes —the chance of Luke or Rufus or Titus spying on her was too great. Their eyes followed her wherever she went as it was. To have them see her in any degree of undress was simply unbearable.

Rising, she shook out the blanket and folded it. As she dragged her fingers through the tangled mass of her hair, she heard footsteps approaching. The steps were swift and light—Jennie.

"Aurora?" She tapped at the cracked, weathered boards of the shed door. "Aurora, are you awake?"

THE WILDER SHORES OF LOVE

Aurora pushed open the door. "Come in, Jennie. What do you have there?"

On a cracked china plate Jennie had several thick slices of homemade bread smeared with blueberry jam.

"It's your breakfast. You're hungry, aren't you? You must be. You didn't eat any supper last night."

Though she hated the notion of taking anything from her captors, Aurora had to admit that she was starving. Taking the plate from Jennie, she ate the bread wordlessly, grudgingly, all the while cursing her empty stomach for its insistent pangs and growls.

"Thank you, Jennie," she said when she'd finished.

The girl smiled shyly. "What do you want to do today?" she asked.

Aurora didn't hesitate. "Go home."

"I'd let you if I could. But it's not that easy." Jennie bit her lip and then hesitantly asked: "Aurora, will you tell me what it's like to be rich?"

"Sometimes," Aurora said, her smile filled with wry irony, "it's more trouble than it's worth. But why do you want to know?"

Jennie lifted a frail shoulder. "Sometimes boats crash on the reef—yachts, Pa calls them. There are storms and they are torn apart. In the morning there are so many beautiful things washed up on the beach. I think it must be wonderful to live with such wonderful things."

"What about the people?" Aurora asked, wondering how many of the yachts had been lured onto the reef by Titus and wondering if Jennie knew what really happened on those tragic, deadly nights.

"They drown," Jennie said softly.

"All of them?"

"It seems so. Some wash up onto the beach, and some they never find. Sarah said they probably got washed away by the lake." She paused and some indefinable emotion passed over her lovely, delicate features before she went on. "Pa makes all of us go down to the beach and pick up the things there. Sometimes there are clothes and dishes and furniture and books. Belle kept some books— books with stories for children. She wanted to read them to her babies but her babies all died. So she read them to me. She taught me to read. Her ma was a teacher on the mainland. That's where Belle lived before she married Rufus."

"And what happened to the rest of the pretty things?" Aurora asked.

"Pa sells 'em. He sells everything that comes from the boats that crash onto the reef. He says they're his 'cause they washed up on his beach. Belle gave me somethin' from one of the boats— don't tell Pa."

"I won't tell him anything," Aurora assured her. "What did Belle give you?"

"Promise you won't tell? Belle said Pa must never know she kept it or that she gave it to me."

"I promise," Aurora said solemnly.

From her pocket Jennie drew a long golden bookchain with a fine stone cameo from which depended an enameled locket.

"It came from a boat that crashed a long time ago. I must have been little because I don't remember it at all."

"It's beautiful," Aurora told her.

"There's a picture inside."

Carefully, Jennie opened the locket and showed Aurora the picture. A beautiful woman in white lace held a tiny baby in her arms.

"The woman," Jennie told her, "was on the boat. They found her on the beach."

"And the baby?"

Jennie shook her head. "They never found the baby."

Aurora closed her eyes, feeling sick. Innocent lives—women, children—taken in Titus Oates's quest for treasure. A tiny baby, so precious, so fragile, left at the mercy of that cold, churning sea.

Suddenly the heat and the stench of the shed was more than she could bear.

"Let's go for a walk, Jennie," she said softly.

As they left the shed, Titus saw them and approached. Aurora chafed, impatient to be away from his lingering gazes and the maddening way he had of looking at her as though she were the main course on his favorite menu. He seemed to have some plan for her—she sensed it every time their paths crossed, and it set her nerves on edge until she felt she wanted to scream.

Moreover, she noticed that Jennie tensed whenever he approached. She was afraid of him— truly afraid. The others seemed merely to respect his authority over them in the same way a pack of dogs respects its leader. But Jennie was very, very frightened.

"The girl treatin' you right?" he demanded of Aurora. "She gives you trouble, you tell me. I'll take care of her."

Aurora's nature rebelled at the malice this

man could direct at so gentle a creature as his younger daughter. There was an underlying air of resentment that showed in his eyes each time he looked at the girl. It astonished and bewildered Aurora. Considering the poor excuses for humanity that were the rest of his children, she would have thought he'd treasure this fragile, golden child.

"Jennie is being kindness itself," Aurora told him. "She is a sweet girl. I cannot imagine what I would do here without her."

"She better be." Titus glared at the younger girl. "I hear one word—one word, girl!—against you and I'll strap you till you can't walk!" One meaty hand closed about Jennie's upper arm and squeezed until his knuckled whitened. "You hear me?"

Aurora felt the girl's trembling, saw the tears well into her eyes. Why was the man such a brute to her? What grudge did he nurse against this sweet young woman?

"Yes, Pa," Jennie whispered. "I hear you."

"Remember what I said!" He looked from Jennie to Aurora and his expression changed from anger and loathing into something Aurora's did not want to see. His eyes glittered and his tongue darted out to wet his lips.

"Jennie and I were going for a walk," Aurora told him coldly. "Excuse us."

Taking Jennie's arm, Aurora pulled her from Titus's grasp and steered her past her father and in the direction of the forest. Jennie stared at her, then ventured a timid glance back at her father who stood where they'd left him watching them go.

"Aren't you afraid of him?" Jennie asked, awed.

"Yes," Aurora admitted. "He's a monster. But somehow I don't believe he'd hurt me. Don't ask me how I know, but it just seems like he won't. At least not yet."

Jennie stopped. "Aurora," she said tremulously, her eyes downcast shyly, "will you be my friend?"

Aurora slipped a finger under the girl's delicate chin and tipped her head back so she could look into her eyes. It was hard to believe that Jennie was only two years younger than she. She seemed in many ways a child—innocent and shy. In other ways, however, she was much more experienced. She'd seen so much that was unpleasant, unbearable for someone with so delicate a nature. She seemed to have taken refuge from the horrors of her life by remaining a child. Aurora could see why Jennie, stuck on the island with those brothers and that father of hers, was so reluctant to grow up.

"Yes," she answered at last. "I'll be your friend. I promise."

Relief was painfully evident on the girl's narrow face. "I'll show you something, if you want. Something I've never shown anyone. Not ever."

"Show me," Aurora urged. She was more than willing to befriend Jennie, for she sensed the girl's desperate loneliness. She was also eager to learn anything she could about the Oateses. Any information she could gather would be useful after she was rescued.

Taking her hand, Jennie led Aurora deep into the forest. They walked on and on, stepping over fallen logs and mossy rocks, stamping down the tangle of undergrowth, startling an occasional rabbit or chipmunk. At last, when Aurora thought they must surely soon reach the other end of the tiny island, they came upon a little clump of evergreens planted in a neat rectangle.

Jennie led Aurora to the opening at one end. Inside, marked with a rough wooden cross and a handful of wilted wildflowers, was a grave.

"What is this?" Aurora asked. "Who planted these trees?"

"I did," Jennie told her. "When I was seven."

"But who is buried here? It's so lonely, so isolated."

"My ma."

Aurora looked around. They were deep in the forest. There was no trail to mark the way to this place. Only Jennie's unerring instinct had brought them. If one didn't know how to get here, one could wander the forest forever and never stumble upon this spot.

"But why is she buried out here?" Aurora asked. "This is such a solitary spot."

Jennie nodded. "Belle's and Rufus's babies are buried in a little graveyard not far from the cabin. Belle made a little fence for it. It's ever so nice."

"Then why wasn't your mother buried there?"

"I can't tell you," Jennie whispered.

"Yes, you can. We're friends, aren't we? You can tell me."

Jennie bit her lip. She was obviously torn between fear of revealing her secret and her desire to share it with her new friend. At last she took a deep breath and said:

"She's here 'cause she's not supposed to be

dead. Nobody knows it. Not Luke or Rufus or Belle. Not even Sarah. Only Pa and me—and now you. But Pa doesn't know I know."

"Jennie, I don't understand this at all."

"I didn't either. Not for a long time." Leaving the grave, Jennie went to a fallen log and sat down. She patted the log beside her, and Aurora joined her there. "I never told it to anybody. Not Belle or Sarah. Nobody at all." She shivered, though not with the cold. "It happened a long time ago when I was only five.

"There was a celebration in St. James. We were all gonna go. But at the last minute, Ma said she didn't want to go. She told Pa to go ahead with the rest. He told her to keep me here—that I was too little to go. She didn't want to, but he made her.

"She put me to bed as soon as they left and told me to go to sleep. I didn't, but I pretended so Ma wouldn't be mad at me. She went outside and pretty soon I heard her talkin' to somebody. I thought Pa was back, but when I looked out the window I saw her talking to a man I never saw before. He kissed her. They went to the shed—the one where you're stayin'. I wondered why, so I got out of bed. But I only got to the door when I saw Pa comin' from the shore. He must have come back—I guess maybe he knew the man was comin' to see Ma. Anyway, he opened the door to the shed. Ma screamed and so did the man. Pa cussed somethin' awful. There was a gunshot, then another. I went back to bed and pretended I was asleep, but when I looked out the window again I saw Pa carryin' Ma toward the woods. He came back and got a shovel. When he went back into the woods I followed him. He came here."

"He murdered his wife and buried her here," Aurora breathed.

Jennie nodded. "I don't know what he did with the man. When he was almost finished with Ma, I ran back to the cabin and got back into bed. I didn't want him to know I saw him. I was afraid."

"Oh, Jennie!" Aurora was filled with compassion for the girl. To see her father murder her mother and then bury her in this lonely place . . . .No wonder she was terrified of the man!

"He told Luke and Rufus and the rest that Ma had run off with the man. I never said anything 'cause I didn't want Pa to know I saw what he did."

"Jennie," Aurora said, taking the girl's cold, trembling hand. "When I leave here, I want you to come with me. You must not stay here. This is no place for you."

"Pa would never let me go," Jennie whispered.

"If I have anything to say about it, he wouldn't have a choice. Will you come? You don't want to live here forever, do you?"

"No," Jennie breathed. "I don't want to live here." She turned toward Aurora, her eyes filled with tears. "Will you take me away from here? Truly?"

Smiling, Aurora gently brushed a strand of hair out of the girl's eyes. "Truly," she promised.

Her eyes went back to the rectangle of evergreens that surrounded the lonely grave of Titus's victim. That was one more crime for which he would pay, she thought to herself. And unlike the yachts where nothing could be proven against him, this crime was undeniable. There was a body and an eyewitness.

Filled with fresh determination, Aurora rose

and took Jennie by the hand. She would see Titus Oates pay the ultimate price for this crime if no other. But first, she and Jennie must be rescued from this dreadful place.

Raven, she thought to herself. Do you know that I'm gone yet? If you do, please, please hurry! And bring help!

41

"Raven!" Matthew argued. "You can't simply go to Gull Island by yourself and free Aurora from the Oateses."

"I can't leave her there! Christ, Matthew! When I think of her there, at the mercy of those animals ..." His knuckles were white and strained on his clenched fists. "If any one of them has so much as touched her—"

"The Godless devils," Bridey wailed, burrowing deeper into Matthew's embrace. "Why did we leave her alone!"

Raven gazed at them, clinging to one another in their anguish and guilt. He sighed. "Don't blame yourselves. If I know Aurora, she probably didn't even try to call for help."

"If only we'd stayed with her," Matthew said.

"They must have planned this very carefully," Raven muttered. "And perhaps it's better you didn't stumble upon them. No doubt they were armed and ready to fight."

"They wouldn't hurt her, though, would they?" Bridey whispered, pleading for reassurances that neither man, in honesty, could give her. "They wouldn't!"

"You don't know these people," Raven told her bluntly. "They're no better than animals. I'm surprised they haven't tried something like this before."

"They have," Matthew said softly.

Raven stared at him. "What are you talking about? When?"

Matthew took a deep breath, anticipating Raven's fury. "When she was here before. It didn't come to anything, so I never told you. The day I met Aurora, remember, when you found the newspaper article in St. James about Graham Hughston and the reward. When I got here that day, I found Luke Oates trying to rape her."

Raven trembled, his bronzed face darkened with the hot blood of his rage. "And you didn't tell me?" he hissed.

"I tried!" Matthew defended. "When I followed you down to the lake after you confronted Aurora. I tried. But you wouldn't listen to me. You were so furious about Graham Hughston that you told me to go away. Don't you remember?"

"Yes," Raven admitted, "I remember. Sarah was supposed to stay with Aurora while I was away."

"She never came. Luke came instead. But I stopped him before he could do her any real harm. She was frightened and bruised, but that's all."

Raven breathed deeply, trying in vain to control the blood-lust raging inside him. He wanted to go to the Oateses' island and kill them, all of them, lay waste to every foul reminder of their very existence.

"I have to get her back," he snarled between gritted teeth. "I have to go there, Matthew. Every moment that passes with her there, in their power—" He slammed his fist on the table in anguish.

"You can't go alone," Matthew told him sternly. "It's suicide and you know it. You must realize they'll be expecting you—waiting for you. It's a trap, Raven. It's their chance to kill you. Then, with you out of the way, Aurora will be truly at their mercy."

"So you want me to stand by and do nothing! God knows how they're treating her! Abusing her! They're nothing but animals—they're no better than mad dogs. They have to be destroyed, once and for all!"

"Yes, you're right. But do it right! If you go in there yourself, you'll be lucky to escape with your life. It would be a miracle if you got Aurora out unharmed. If you're very fortunate, you might kill one, perhaps two of them. But not all of them—not by yourself. So you wouldn't have stopped them. Not completely. Do it right, Raven, and finish it forever."

"Through the proper channels?" Raven muttered. "Contact the authorities? How long will that take? What will happen to Aurora while she's waiting there for me? How will she feel when the days pass and I don't come to help her?"

Matthew laid a comforting hand on his cousin's arm. "It's the only way, and you know it."

Raven gazed at him, his blue eyes smoldering

with the glow of his murderous anger. He felt helpless, maddeningly, frustratingly helpless. But in his heart, he knew that what Matthew said was true. He could not simply storm the Oateses' island himself. Even with Matthew's help there was too much chance of Aurora's being harmed—even killed—before they could find her and free her. And Titus Oates was certain to be expecting him. There could be no doubt he and his sons would lie in wait for him. If Raven were killed, Aurora would be at the mercy of those animals. Matthew was right. Strength was needed here, and strength lay in numbers.

"All right," he acquiesced softly, reluctantly. "We'll get help."

"We can go to St. James and send word to the post commandant at Fort Mackinac asking him to come and help us—"

"Send word?" Raven asked. "No, that would take too long. It would be too simple for them to dismiss the matter. I'm going there. I'm going to make sure they realize how urgent this is. Are you coming with me?"

"I'm coming," Matthew replied. "Let's go."

It was late afternoon on the sixteenth of October when Raven and Matthew were ushered into the office of the young, newly promoted captain who was acting as post commander in the absence of the commandant who had been called away.

The captain rose as they entered. "Gentlemen," he said. "I am Captain Braxton. Kyle Braxton. Please sit down and tell me what I can do for you."

Sitting across the desk from him, Raven related the events of Aurora's abduction. He spoke briefly, forcefully, but when he was finished, the captain shook his head.

"Frankly, sir, I think this might be a matter for the police. Kidnapping, after all—"

"The police can't help us where these people are concerned," Raven told him. "This goes far beyond mere kidnapping. These people have, over many years, lured ships onto the reef that surrounds their island. They've deliberately wrecked them and murdered any survivors in order to claim the salvage."

"I've heard of them," Kyle admitted. "But nothing could be proven."

"Well, something can damned well be proven now," Raven snarled.

Kyle hesitated. "To be honest, Mr. Ravenswood, I'm not certain this is a matter for the Army. Perhaps the Navy would be better contacted. It is a matter of jurisdiction, you see, and I would not want to overstep myself by committing men and a ship—"

"To be honest, Captain Braxton," Raven interrupted, "I think you're afraid of committing yourself to anything without your commandant's approval."

"Well, of course I will lay the matter before him when he returns. If he thinks it is wise—"

"And when will he return?"

"A week, perhaps sooner."

Raven thrust himself out of his chair. "Good Christ, man! We're talking about a young woman alone on an island with a pack of murderers! One of these bastards has already tried to rape her once!"

"Mr. Ravenswood—"

"Never mind! Come on, Matthew, we'll get her out of that hellhole ourselves."

He stormed toward the door, pausing with his hand on the latch. "And I'll tell you something, Captain Braxton. When the newspapers discover that you refused to help rescue Aurora Jephson from her kidnappers, you'll be lucky to be put in charge of shoveling up after the horses!"

"Wait!" Kyle shouted as Raven left the room. "Please! Wait! Come back!"

Angrily, Raven returned to the office and stood, glowering, near the door. "What is it, captain? Be brief, if you please, I have important business to attend to even if you haven't."

"You said Aurora Jephson. Surely . . . that is . . . she wouldn't be from New York, would she? With relations in Chicago? An aunt and an uncle?"

Raven and Matthew exchanged a curious glance.

"Her uncle, Carlisle Jephson, died recently," Raven told him. "He and Aurora's aunt are from Chicago. And yes, she is originally from New York. But how do you know her?"

The scene in the forest on Mackinac Island replayed itself in Kyle's mind. He had never forgiven himself for what he had done. He could only blame it on the wounds done to his masculine pride when he'd realized that Aurora's aunt considered him far beneath her niece. Though he'd intended to take the money Graham had given him and enter business or, perhaps, study the law, he had found he could not bring himself to touch it. When his tour of duty had expired, he had stayed on rather than face the decision of what to do with his ill-gotten gains.

"We met here on Mackinac Island months ago," Kyle told Raven. "Aurora was traveling to Chicago with her uncle and aunt. They stayed for a short while at their cottage here before going on. But I thought . . . that is to say, I understood . . . that she was engaged to marry a man named Graham Hughston."

"She was," Raven confirmed. "But that is over now. She is going to be my wife." His eyes flashed like sapphires. "If, that is, we can ever manage to get around to rescuing her from Titus Oates!"

Responding to the impatience and anger in Raven's voice, Kyle called for maps and charts of the area to be brought, and soon the three men were deep in discussion of the best way and the safest time to invade Titus Oates's lair.

42

The bank of fog approached the island from the northwest, rolling along the surface of the lake like a great grey wall moving to envelope them. Standing on the shore, Aurora watched it coming, fascinated.

"We won't be able to see a thing once it gets dark," she told Jennie who had come to stand beside her.

"No, I suppose not," Jennie agreed. She seemed subdued, strangely preoccupied.

"Is something wrong?" Aurora asked. "Has something happened to you?"

Jennie shook her head. "No, not to me," she replied cryptically. "Come on, let's not look at the fog any more."

Taking one last look, Aurora followed Jennie into the forest, walking toward the opposite side of the island where the horizon was still clear and the glow of the setting sun turned the clouds to crimson and orange. In the distance she could see the emerald-green mound that was High Island.

"Do you think he's come back yet?" Jennie asked.

"Who?" Aurora countered.

"Raven. That's who you were thinking about just now while you were looking at High Island, wasn't it?"

Aurora nodded. "Yes, I was thinking about him," she admitted. "And yes, I was wondering if he'd gotten back yet and if he's even now planning a way to get me out of here."

"You know that my Pa and my brothers are plannin' to kill him if he comes here after you, do you?"

"I know. But I believe that Raven will outsmart them, Jennie. He'll know that they're lying in wait for him and he'll figure a way to escape their trap. I truly believe that we were meant to be together, and no one, not your father, not your brothers, not anyone, will keep us apart forever."

"Aurora," Jennie said softly, "there is something you don't know. I wasn't supposed to tell you, but—"

"What is it, Jennie? Something about Raven? Has someone heard something about him?"

"No, it's not about Raven. It's about that other man. He wrote Pa a letter."

"Other man? What other man?"

"The man who came to take you away before."

A chill ran up Aurora's spine. "Graham Hughston? The man from Chicago?"

Jennie nodded. "After you came back with Raven, he wrote Pa a letter. He said he'd give him a lot of money if Pa could get you away from Raven and keep you until he could get here from Chicago."

"Is that what all this is about? Is Graham Hughston coming up here to get me again?"

"I guess so. Pa wrote back and said he'd do it, and that man wrote to tell him he was coming. I think . . . I'm not sure, but I think part of the money was for killing Raven."

"Oh, my God. Did he say when he was supposed to be here?"

"I'm not sure but—"

"Think, Jennie, please think!"

"I think he said the night of the sixteenth or the morning of the seventeenth."

Aurora tried to remember what the date had been on the day she'd been taken from High Island. Counting on her fingers, she added the days she'd been the Oateses' prisoner.

"The sixteenth! That's tonight! This is the night of the sixteenth!"

"I know."

Aurora leaned back against a tree and willed her pounding heart to slow. "If Graham comes and takes me away, then Raven could come for me and find only Titus and your brothers waiting for him." She pressed a hand to her lips. "Oh, Jennie, we've got to warn him! We've got to!"

"But how?"

"I don't know. I only know that—"

"Jennie!" Rufus appeared walking along the beach coming toward them. "Jennie! Sarah wants you. You'd best git yer skinny ass over there and see what she needs."

Afraid to question her brother, Jennie only

nodded and disappeared, running in the direction of the cabin in the clearing.

Aurora pressed herself back against the tree and eyed Rufus warily as he approached. She glanced around, looking for a branch or stone, some weapon she could use against him. There was nothing within reach.

"Afternoon," Rufus said. His eyes slid over her, lingering here and there before returning to her face.

"I do believe yer even prettier than Luke said you was," he drawled, moving close enough that she could smell the musty, stale sweat that emanated from his grimy clothes and unwashed body.

"Jennie told me your father sent for Graham Hughston," Aurora hissed.

"Jennie's got a big mouth."

"I won't go with him! I won't go back to Chicago! You can't force me to!"

Rufus smirked. "You couldn't hardly stop us if we meant to send you, an' you know it. But it don't matter none. 'Cause you ain't goin' nowheres."

Aurora stared at him, nonplussed. "But Jennie said Graham was coming—"

"He is comin'. He sent a letter to Pa sayin' he was leavin' Chicago days ago. But you ain't goin' back there with him."

"I don't understand."

Rufus's smile exposed a mouthful of blackening teeth. "Pa jist sent for that damned fool Hughston to git him out of the way. He'll take his money, but that's all. Pa's got other plans for you, woman."

"What other plans?" Aurora demanded, uneasy and suspicious.

Rufus stroked her cheek with his finger, chuckling when she jerked her head away. "Luke was right, you know. Yer skin's softer than—"

"What plans!" Aurora shouted.

"Pa's decided he might like to git married again. He'd like a pretty young thing—like you."

Horrified, Aurora felt her knees threaten to buckle.

"No! Never! I'd rather die!"

"Aw, hell, it won't be so bad. I know Pa's a old man but Luke an' me, we'll be around if you git lonesome." He moved closer so that he loomed over her. "I know how to keep a pretty woman happy."

"Get away from me!" Aurora snarled. "Keep your filthy hands off me! And that goes for your brother and your father and your whole disgusting family!"

Rufus's eyes narrowed, his face flushed with temper. "You think yer too good fer us or somethin'?"

"I know I'm too good for you!" she shot back. "You're not good enough to be called people! You're nothing but filthy, dirty animals!"

"You little bitch!" Rufus growled. Taking her shoulders in a punishing grip, he pressed her back against the tree until the bark dug into her back through the limp linen of her blouse. "I'll show you what yer good enough for!"

Aurora twisted her head this way and that trying to avoid his searching mouth. His body pushed against hers, crushing her, revolting her, sickening her.

"Let me go, damn you!" she screamed. "Get your dirty hands off me!"

"Before I'm done with you, you'll beg for me like I bet you beg for that damned half-breed that you been—"

There was a sudden, jarring thud and Rufus stared, dumbfounded, at Aurora before sliding to the ground, unconscious. Standing behind him, Jennie grasped a thick branch in her hands.

"Are you all right?" she asked Aurora, her eyes filled with concern, her hands trembling.

"I'm all right. Thank you! Thank you, I—"

"What in the hell have you done!" Titus appeared out of the forest. "You goddamned, ignorant little bitch!" With a vicious swipe of one hand, he knocked the branch out of Jennie's hands and nearly knocked her off her feet.

Kneeling beside his son, Titus turned him over. "Rufus! Rufus, wake up, damn you!"

"He attacked me," Aurora spat. "Jennie was only trying to—"

"I don't give a damn what Jennie was trying to do! I need him tonight! I need him and Luke and—" He looked down at his unconscious son. From the look of the bloody lump forming on the back of his head, it was apparent that Rufus was not going to regain consciousness any time soon.

"I'm sorry, Pa," Jennie whispered, backing away as her father rose to his feet.

"You stupid little bitch!" he hissed. "I should've knowed you'd turn against us and side with her! I should've knowed you'd have no loyalty to the people who raised you and put food in your whinin' mouth and kept clothes on your good-for-nothin' back all these years! I shouldn't have listened when that cheatin' wife of mine wanted to keep you! I should've let you drown with yer ma and pa and the rest of 'em!"

Both Aurora and Jennie stared at Titus, trying to comprehend his tirade. What did it mean? Jennie wasn't his? But that would have to mean that she—

"Pa! Hey, Pa!" Luke skidded to a halt near them. "We got to—" For the first time he noticed his brother's body. "What happened to Rufus?"

"He couldn't keep his hands to hisself and Jennie cracked his head for 'im."

"He was after that skinny runt?" Luke glared at Jennie, forgetting that before Aurora's arrival on the island, he had often eyed his youngest "sister" with more than a brotherly interest.

"Course he wasn't, ya numbskull! Christ! I got idiots instead of sons! Grab his arms, fool, and help me git 'im back to the cabin."

"But, Pa, the fog's comin' in thick and it's startin' to git dark! We got to get out to the point and light in case Hughston—"

"Shut yer yappin' mouth, boy!" Titus roared. "Help me with yer brother afore I give you a lump on the head like the lump on yer brother's head!"

Between them, the two men took Rufus's limp body and dragged him off in the direction of the cabin. As they disappeared into the forest, Aurora took Jennie into her arms and hugged her joyfully.

"Do you realize what this means?" she asked. "It means Titus isn't your father! And Luke and Rufus aren't your brothers! You're not an Oates, Jennie. Maybe you have another family some-where."

"He said he should've let me drown with my

pa and ma," Jennie reminded her. "So they must be dead."

"I suppose they were in one of the shipwrecks on the reef and—" Aurora caught her breath. "The locket! Jennie, the locket!"

"What about it?"

"You said that Belle gave it to you—that it came from a ship that had crashed on the reef when you were too little to remember."

"That's right. But what about—?"

"The lady in the picture could be your mother, Jennie. The baby could be you! Maybe that's why Belle gave it to you—so you would have something of hers even if you didn't know it. Oh, Jennie! The little girl in the picture—the baby—she could be you! Don't you see?"

"Do you think so?" Jennie asked, clearly dazzled by the prospect. "The lady was so very pretty —like an angel. I'd like for her to be my mother, Aurora, but I don't suppose we'll ever know."

"But we might be able to find out. When we get off this damned island, we can have the records searched and find out what yacht was wrecked on this reef when you were a baby. There can't have been too many—and the fact that a baby was lost and presumed drowned will narrow down the list even more. We could find out who you truly are, Jennie. It's not impossible. You might have relatives living somewhere who have mourned your loss for years. Wouldn't it be wonderful to find them and learn about who you are and where you came from?"

"But first we have to get off the island," Jennie reminded her.

"Well, when Raven comes. Or—Graham! Graham is supposed to be coming for me! We'll tell him and he can take us away from here. I never thought I would actually welcome the sight of him!"

"Aurora," Jennie said softly. "I don't think so. We can't leave the island with Graham."

"But we can! Jennie, don't look so frightened. Things are going to be all right. Trust me! Graham will take us—"

"Aurora! Will you listen to me? We can't go with Graham because Graham is never going to leave!"

Aurora eyed her curiously. "Never going to leave? What are you talking about? Of course he's going to leave! He certainly wouldn't want to stay—" The realization struck her with the force of a thunderbolt. The light! Luke said something about lighting the light!

"Oh, my God," she breathed. "Jennie—Titus isn't planning to—" Catching her breath, she looked out over the lake. Night was falling quickly and the fog had thickened until it obscured all sight of High Island. They might as well be surrounded by an eternity of open water. She noticed that Jennie was looking out along the beach toward the point of the island.

There, atop a tumbledown tower, the beam of the searchlight glowed dimly in the fog.

"He's going to lure Graham's ship onto the reef, isn't he?" she asked dully.

Jennie nodded. "He said only Graham Hughston could prove that you'd been taken away from Raven by force. He said that Graham had to die."

"Oh, no. Oh, dear Lord, no!" Aurora lifted a

trembling hand to her forehead. She felt giddy, dizzy. But she couldn't take refuge in the sweet forgetfulness of a faint. She had to stay awake—she had to try to warn Graham—to save Graham and the innocent lives of the crewmen aboard his ship. She had to try to destroy that damned, cursed light once and for all.

Taking her skirts into her hands, Aurora ran through the forest toward the point and the lighthouse that beamed its invitation into the night, beckoning the unwary to a grinding death and a watery grave.

43

Aboard the *Sea Mist*, Graham Hughston paced the bridge. The fog had descended upon them, enveloped them, until there was nothing to be seen around them but the thick, grey, writhing mist. Even the water was invisible.

"We should drop anchor and wait it out," the captain told him.

"Drop anchor?" Graham stared at him, clearly appalled by the suggestion. "We're nearly there! You have your charts and your maps to guide you. What kind of a captain are you to let a little fog frighten you into dropping anchor a few miles from your destination?"

Captain Winston glared at him. "I know enough to use care, Mr. Hughston. I know enough not to endanger my crew and my vessel—" His eyes swept disdainfully over Graham. "—and my passengers."

"Oh, for Christ's sake, I wasn't impugning your abilities, it's just that—" He glanced out the window. "There! A light! It must be the lighthouse at the harbor entrance."

Captain Winston checked his compass and gauges. "It can't be. The coordinates are all wrong."

"Damn your coordinates, man! It's the light-house, I tell you. Steer for it!"

On the island, Aurora ran on and on, her every breath aching, burning in her lungs. The heavy, wet, mist-laden air swirled in the trees, turning the forest into a place of mystery, a place of ominous, grey-shrouded silence.

She screamed as a branch of a fallen tree tripped her. She fell, her palms scraping on the rocks that littered the forest floor. One hand crushed a spreading half-rotted fungus and slid out from beneath her.

For a long moment she lay where she had fallen. She was frightened, desperate, horrified by the sheer barbarity of what the Oateses were about to do. Then, as she lay there, she heard Luke shouting to his father:

"There she is, Pa! She's comin' straight for the reef!"

"Oh God, no!" Aurora moaned. She pushed herself to her feet and ran on, through the forest toward the point. If she could somehow put out the light, perhaps it would warn the captain to turn away. Perhaps he would realize that he was making a grave, a deadly, mistake.

She pressed a hand to the ache in her side as she emerged from the forest. Her heart pounded with fear and exertion. Her feet dug deeply into the wet, shifting sand as she started across the beach. And then she heard it, even before Luke cried out:

"There it is, Pa! Here it comes!"

Aurora could not force herself to look out over the rolling black water as she heard the first grinding, splintering sound of wood on rock. She could not shut out the screams of terrified crewmen as they realized they were riding their doomed ship to its death.

She felt Jennie's hand, ice-cold and trembling, on her arm.

"Oh, Aurora," she breathed. "It's terrible! It's—"

Aurora raised her head and looked. In the glow of the lighthouse beacon, the Sea Mist loomed over the reef like an enormous white shadow, a ghost ship out of legend, pounding its hull to splinters on the jagged rocks. The water crashed against it, lifting it, then slamming it down, opening huge, gaping wounds in its once sleek and flawless sides. The masts that had ridden so straight and proud toppled, crashing into the water, the yardarms snapping like twigs, the rigging lashing, the white canvas of the sails dragging the pieces down into the churning water.

Over the din of the turgid water, the splintering of the hull and the grinding of wood on the reef came the screams of the crewmen, the shrieks of agony, of fear.

Overcome with the horror of it all, Aurora sank to her knees in the sand, Jennie's comforting arms around her, and stared, helpless, as the Sea Mist died.

"Jennie," a woman's voice said from behind

Aurora as she knelt there in Jennie's arms. "Take Aurora back to the cabin. She shouldn't see—"

"No!" Aurora looked up and found Belle standing there. The woman, Rufus's wife, who had seemed so hostile to her when she'd first been brought to the island now gazed down at her with a look of genuine, if surprising, compassion. "I want to stay," Aurora told her. "I have to—"

"But there's nothing you can do," Belle insisted. "You can't help the men aboard that ship and you can't stop Titus and Luke from doing what they're bound to do. I learned that long ago."

With Jennie's help, Aurora rose. She gazed out toward the lake. It was nearly over. The pounding waves were destroying the yacht, driving it further up onto the rocks, shattering it as if it were merely a child's balsa wood toy. As the lighthouse beacon swept the water, she saw the first of the bodies riding lifelessly on the undulating waves.

Sour bile rose in her throat. Murder! This was murder, cold-blooded and premeditated, just as surely as if Luke and Titus had held guns to the men's heads and pulled the triggers.

Yanking away from Jennie, Aurora stumbled into the edge of the forest and tried in vain to control the violent spasms that wracked her.

Jennie was beside her again. "Aurora, come back to the cabin. You shouldn't be here. You shouldn't see this. It will do no one any good."

"I have to see it," Aurora told her stubbornly, turning once more toward the ghastly, nightmarish scene. "I have to see it because I'm going to tell everyone what went on here tonight. They're going to pay for this! Titus and Luke! They're both going to pay!" She saw Belle standing a short distance

414

away, watching and listening. "I'm sorry, but I have to see them punished for this and for—" She felt the gentle pressure of Jennie's hand on her arm and glanced toward her. In spite of everything that had happened, Jennie entreated her to keep the secret of Titus's wife's death. "For everything they've done," she finished.

Belle glanced over her shoulder as an explosion ripped through what remained of the *Sea Mist*. The boilers had exploded and the fractured hull was on fire, its blaze dimmed to an eerie glow by the swirling fog.

"When I first married Rufus," Belle said softly, as if gazing back through the mists of passing years to a happier place and time, "I didn't know what he was. I prayed for a child, but I lost my babies, one after another. Now, I'm not sorry. I wouldn't have wanted to raise a child here, with them—a child who might grow up to be like them." She looked at Aurora. "If we get out of here and you go to the police, I'll tell them what I know."

"You don't have to. They cannot force you to speak against your husband," Aurora reminded her.

Belle shook her head. "I won't protect him after what he's done. But I ask you for one thing: Look after Jennie. It's not her fault she was raised here."

"The woman in the locket is her mother, isn't she?" Aurora asked. "Jennie is the baby in the woman's arms."

Belle nodded. "When she was washed ashore in her cradle, Titus wanted to kill her. His wife convinced him to keep her, to raise her as his own."

"I'll take care of her," Aurora promised. "And we'll try to find out who she is—if she has any family. I—"

Her words were drowned by the splintering of the yacht's hull as it split in two, shattering like porcelain, its teakwood decks turning to kindling, its beautiful furnishings slipping into the water along with the bodies of its crew.

She pressed a hand to her mouth as Luke seized the limp arm of a white-uniformed crewman and pulled him up onto the beach. With his toe he rolled him over. Then, bending, he peered into the man's face. After a moment, he straightened, shrugging, and turned away. Another victim for whose lost life he would answer.

Aurora's sickened gaze scanned the beach. The black water was dotted with fragments of wood, ragged pieces of sail, a gaily striped cushion from a wicker deck chair, a body, white-uniformed, drifting toward shore on the crest of a wave.

It seemed that everywhere she looked, she saw them—the dead and the dying. She held her breath every time Luke or Titus bent over a body. It was almost a relief when she saw Luke or Titus examine them and shrug, walking away. For she knew they meant there to be no survivors, and she couldn't have borne seeing them murder a man after the Fates had been kind enough to deliver him from the explosion and fire and water of the shipwreck.

"Pa!" Luke shouted. "It's him! It's Hughston! Over here!"

"Graham," Aurora breathed, rising.

Leaving Jennie and Belle behind, she ran to

the place where Luke stood, gazing down at a dark-suited prone body lying on the sand.

"Graham," she whispered, dropping to her knees beside him. "Oh, Graham, please! Please, don't be dead! Don't be—"

Reaching down, Titus seized Graham's arm and yanked him over onto his back. Through sightless eyes Graham stared up at the night sky where the moon and stars were concealed by the veil of thick, grey fog.

"Oh, no," Aurora murmured. "Graham." She brushed the sand from his face. His skin was starkly white, damp, cold and clammy to her touch. The wet chill of the water had stolen the last vestiges of warmth from his lifeless form.

"Did you see the money anywhere?" Titus asked, glancing around at the debris and wreckage that was beginning to litter the beach.

"Not yet," Luke replied. "I was hopin' he'd have it on him—a money belt or somethin'. But it'll likely turn up. The water's too rough for much to sink before it gets to the shallows."

"Damn you!" Aurora hissed, rising. "God damn you all straight to hell! I hope the money sinks to the deepest pit of the whole damned lake! I hope it rots there just like you're all going to rot in prison for what you've done! I hope—"

"Shut yer mouth!" Titus roared. "Shut yer mouth, woman, before you end up like him!" He pointed to Graham. "If it wasn't that I kin get money out of you, you'd be dead right now! By God, you will be dead! As soon as I git what's comin' to me, you'll be dead! I swear it!"

"You'll get what's coming to you, all right," Aurora snarled. "But it won't be money—not mine nor anyone else's. You'll get what you deserve—you'll spend the rest of your miserable days in a prison cell! You and your foul sons, too! I only wish to hell they still hung murderers in this state!"

"Get out of here!" Titus growled, his eyes burning with hate. "Get out of here or money or not, I'll throw you into that water and hold you down till you drown!"

Rising, Aurora backed away from him. She could see in his eyes that he meant every word he said. The sight of the death and destruction he had caused by the simple act of lighting the beacon seemed to have unleashed in him a blood-lust that went far beyond the ordinary craving for wealth and power that seemed such a primary facet of his personality.

Surrounded by misery, the pain, the death, the destruction of the *Sea Mist* and her crew, Aurora suddenly reached the limit of her nerve, her emotions. Lifting her sodden skirts, she stumbled away down the beach, away from the lighthouse and the glow of its beacon, into the darkness.

She had not gone far when she heard Jennie calling to her, begging her to wait, pleading with her not to go far. But she ran on and on. She wanted only to get away from the horror, the sickening, mind-boggling, repulsive barbarity of it all.

She didn't see the body lying in her path, washed ashore by the relentlessly pounding waves that swept the sandy beaches. She didn't see it as she ran blindly into the darkness until she tripped over it and fell, sprawling onto the sand beside the supine, white-uniformed corpse.

Something brushed her bare foot. She heard a sound—soft, mewling, a groan. Pushing herself up onto her hands and knees, she turned to see the cold, wet fingers of the man's hand move once, then again, clutching spasmodically.

He was alive! The knowledge at once thrilled and terrified her. Moving to his side, she brushed back the dark, dripping hair that lay over his pale, cold face. He turned his head toward her. His eyelids fluttered, opening, closing, revealing dark eyes that were dazed, unseeing, blinded by shock and pain.

"Geoffrey," Aurora breathed wonderingly. A familiar face. Alive . . . alive! Not frozen in death as Graham's had been.

She heard Luke shouting to Titus and her heart stood still in her bosom. If they knew there was a survivor, however close to death he might be, they would surely kill him.

She scanned Geoffrey's body. The left leg of his trousers was torn and bloody. He was injured, though how badly she could not tell. But he was alive and she had to keep him that way.

His lips moved, trying to form words. Aurora pressed a finger to them, trying to quiet him.

"Hush, Geoffrey," she said softly. "Don't say a word."

"The light," he whispered, then turned his head and coughed up a mixture of water and sand. "The light—"

"Hush now," she told him again. "You must be quiet. I'm going to help you."

Inwardly she rejoiced. Here was a witness from the ship itself. He had seen the lighthouse beacon! He could testify that the ship had been deliberately lured onto the reef, beckoned to its doom in the most cold-blooded of ways.

She looked around desperately, wondering how she could get him to safety. He was not a large man but he was too heavy for her to carry and the forest was no place to try to drag an injured body.

Leaving him for a moment, she ran back along the beach to where Jennie was standing.

"You have to help me," she said urgently. "Come with me, Jennie. I need you."

Together the two women managed to lift the injured sailor and get him to the relative safety of the shed in the clearing. It was risky, Aurora knew, to keep him so close to the cabin. She could only pray that the shipwreck would keep Titus and Luke occupied until help arrived.

44

Weary, sickened, head aching from lack of sleep and the exhausting tension under which she had lived since her abduction, Aurora sat in the cool half-darkness of the shed waiting for the sun to rise.

She glanced at Geoffrey as he slept restlessly, tossing and writhing. His leg was bandaged. Only a small crimson stain marred the whiteness of the linen wrappings. Silently, she blessed Belle who had come to them and cleansed Geoffrey's wound, stitched it closed, applied a salve of her own making, and bound the wound. She had brought a bottle of Rufus's whiskey and together they had poured enough of it down Geoffrey's throat to quiet him and lull him into a drunken slumber. He still slept even as the morning came, and for that Aurora was thankful. The longer he slept, the less chance there would be of his making enough noise to attract any unwanted attention.

She would have to leave him alone sooner or later, she knew. She could not remain in the shed all day. It would look too suspicious and one of the men might decide to come and see why she was secluding herself.

"Please, please," she prayed. "Let them be too busy with their ghoulish robbing of the wreckage and the victims of the *Sea Mist* to wonder where I've gone. Let them—"

She gasped as the door opened and the dim light of the misty dawn flooded the shed.

"I'm sorry," Jennie said, her voice hushed so as not to awaken their sleeping patient. "I didn't mean to frighten you. I've brought you something to eat."

Aurora shook her head. "Thank you, Jennie, but I couldn't. After last night—" She took a deep breath, remembering against her will the hell-on-earth scenes she had witnessed the night before.

"You have to," Jennie persisted. "Please, try to take a few bites at least. You'll make yourself sick."

"I couldn't, really. But leave the bread and jam there. Perhaps when Geoffrey awakens we'll be able to get a little of it into him."

"He's so pale," the girl remarked.

"Yes," Aurora agreed. "I just pray that he lives. I remember him so well from my trips aboard the yacht."

She sighed, remembering the sleekly beautiful yacht she had seen destroyed with such utter finality in the foggy darkness of the previous night.

"Aurora," Jennie murmured, her eyes downcast shyly. "What will become of us?"

"Don't you worry about that!" Aurora said firmly. "We are going to be fine. Raven will come—I know it. He'll come and bring help and we'll leave this awful place. We'll never, never have to see Titus or Luke or Rufus again. I promise you that."

There was a knock on the shed door and both women gasped. But when it opened, it revealed only Belle holding a small brown bottle in her hand.

"Did he wake up?" she asked, nodding toward Geoffrey who lay quietly now, snoring softly. "I brought some laudanum just in case he was in pain."

"Not yet," Aurora replied. "I hope when he does, his pain won't be too bad. I wouldn't want him to cry out. Someone might hear him."

Belle nodded. "Rufus is up and about this morning. He has one hell of a headache and I think he'd as soon shoot any one of us as look at us."

"What are they doing?" Aurora asked. "Titus and Luke and Rufus and Sarah?"

Belle exchanged a look with Jennie before she answered. "They're burying the dead," she said softly. "They're—"

"Hiding their victims," Aurora finished for her. "What of the wreckage of the ship?"

"Most of it sank, as they knew it would. They've gathered most of what could be salvaged and sold and piled it up on the beach."

"Did they find the money?" Aurora hoped Titus's greed had been thwarted.

"Yes," Belle answered, almost apologetically. "It was in a sealed case. It washed ashore this morning."

"Damn!" Aurora hissed. "I wish it had gone to the bottom. I wish—"

"Belle!" Rufus's voice seemed to shake the weathered and warped timbers of the shed. "Where in the hell are you!"

Scrambling for the door, Belle left the shed before her husband had a chance to get there.

"Here I am," Aurora and Jennie heard her saying. "What do you want?"

"Go on down to the shore and help Sarah roll up the riggin' from those masts. We can use the rope on the boat." There was a pause before he went on: "What were you doin' in that shed? Is that lazy bitch Jennie in there?"

"She's with Aurora," Belle answered. "Titus told her to stay with Aurora."

"Well, they kin both git their dead asses out here and earn their keep."

"I'll tell them," Belle said hurriedly. "I'll—"

"Git on down to the beach like I told you, woman!" Rufus snarled. "I got a score to settle with those two."

"But Rufus!" Belle's voice was tinged with panic. "Titus needs you down there too, doesn't he?"

"I'll be there in a minute. Don't you be tellin' me what to do. Now git!"

There was a thud and a groan as Rufus shoved Belle, who lost her balance and fell in a heap on the ground. Almost at the same moment, the shed door was jerked open and the newly risen morning sun streamed in.

Rufus's grizzled head appeared around the doorjamb.

"What're you two doin' layin' around in here

and doin' noth—'' He stopped as his eyes came to rest on Geoffrey lying on a cushion of nets, half covered with Aurora's blanket.

"Sweet God Almighty!" Rufus breathed. "You brought one of 'em back here. Good Christ! Is he alive?"

"No thanks to your brother and your father!" Aurora snarled. "And I mean to keep him that way."

"The hell you will! I'm gonna git my gun and put 'im with the rest of 'em."

The shed door slammed and Rufus's footsteps faded in the distance as he headed for the cabin. Aurora and Jennie stared at one another, paralyzed with fear. What could they do? It was all they had been able to manage just to bring Geoffrey to the shed in the first place. They couldn't possibly move him to safety in the time it would take Rufus to fetch his gun.

Shoving herself to her feet, Aurora left the shed. She would try to stop Rufus in any way she could. She would throw herself in front of him if need be.

But when she saw him emerge from the cabin, his rifle in his hands, she saw the futility of what she was attempting to do.

"Stay away from here!" she shouted, knowing her efforts were useless but unwilling to give up without some kind of fight. "Leave him alone! I won't let you kill him!"

"You try and stop me," Rufus growled. "Jist try it and I'll put you in the ground with your little sailor-boy in there!"

"No!" Rushing at him, Aurora seized the gun and tried to wrench it out of his hands.

As easily as if she were no more than a bothersome insect, Rufus jerked her off her feet and sent her sprawling in the dirt. Reaching out, his hand fell on the latch of the door as Aurora lay there helpless, despairing.

At that moment Sarah appeared, running breathless from the direction of the point.

"Rufus! You've got to come! Bring your gun! Hurry!"

"I got somethin' to do here first," he growled, pulling at the door as Jennie held it shut from the inside.

"No! Come now! It's soldiers! They've come ashore from a sloop anchored beyond the reef. Soldiers! From the fort!"

Rufus looked at her as if she were speaking some foreign language. "Soldiers?" he breathed uncomprehendingly, incredulously.

"Hurry! You've got to help! Luke ran away. I can't find him! Pa needs you!"

Without another word, Rufus ran into the forest, followed by Sarah. Aurora, pushing herself to her feet, stared at Jennie, who had opened the shed door when she'd heard Rufus run off.

"Soldiers," she murmured, a mixture of awe and relief dancing in her eyes and in the hushed tone of her voice. "Soldiers—from the fort!"

Aurora felt a wave of purest joy washing over her. Soldiers! It could mean only one thing to her—Raven!

Catching up her skirts, she fled into the forest, running toward the point—toward the sounds of the shouts and the sounds of gunfire. Jennie followed at her heels.

And then, without warning, she was falling,

tumbling on the damp leaves and the fallen branches that littered the forest floor.

Jennie gave a little frightened scream and Aurora looked up to find Luke standing over her. A pistol glimmered in one hand.

"They've come, Luke," Aurora told him. "Raven and the soldiers. It's over."

"Not quite," he rasped. Reaching down, he jerked her to her feet. "There's somethin' that ain't finished. Somethin' between me and you."

A sick foreboding knotted in Aurora's stomach. From the corner of her eye she saw Jennie poised in the mist.

"Run, Jennie!" she hissed. "Run, get help!"

With the grace of a deer, Jennie was off. Luke raised his arm, the gun barrel glinted, but Aurora threw herself against him and the bullet went far wide of its mark.

"You'll pay for that," Luke snarled.

But as his meaty hands closed painfully on her shoulders, Aurora knew only the relief that Jennie had escaped and the desperate hope that she would find Raven.

The beach, when Jennie reached it, seemed to be a swarm with blue-uniformed soldiers dashing from the shallow-bottomed boats that had ferried them from the sloop that lay at anchor in the distance. They ran from their boats to the edge of the forest, skittering around the shots of Titus and Rufus and Sarah, who had taken positions behind the piles of salvaged goods they had gathered on the beach.

Jennie scanned the scene eagerly. She had seen Raven on many occasions, both in St. James and when he'd come to their island to see Sarah. Her desperate gaze went from man to man. He had to be there! He had to! Aurora's life would depend— And then at last she found him. He was with another man, a soldier, an officer. He and the officer and another man she recognized as Matthew lay in wait behind an upturned boat near the water's edge.

"Raven!" she screamed, her voice frustratingly muffled by the continuous cracking of gunfire. "Raven!"

At that moment his head turned; his miraculous blue eyes found her there, at the edge of the forest.

"Luke has Aurora! You've got to come!"

Heedless of the danger, Raven rose and, as he did, Rufus raised his rifle and took aim.

"No!" Sarah's shriek split the air. She darted from her hiding place and ran toward Raven.

She was nearly halfway across the clearing when Rufus's shot rang out and she fell lifeless to the ground.

Kyle caught at Raven's arm. "I'll come with you," he said.

"No." Raven shook his head, already moving away. "This is personal. See if there's anything you can do for her." He nodded regretfully at Sarah's prone form.

He followed Jennie through the forest to the place where Luke had caught them. Raven's rage boiled in his veins as he saw them, Aurora pinioned against the thick trunk of an ancient oak, struggling with Luke. Her blouse hanging in shreds from her shoulders, she writhed, trying to escape the searching, punishing hands that sought to drag up her trailing skirts.

Raven knew he could not simply shoot Luke, there was too much danger to Aurora. But as he ran toward them, Luke whirled. One arm snaked about Aurora and pulled her in front of him. He pressed the cold barrel of the gun to her temple.

"Take one more step, half-breed, and she's dead," he growled. He laughed cruelly as Raven halted. "That's right. Now throw that gun away."

"Raven, no!" Aurora moaned, gasping as Luke's fingers dug into her bruised flesh.

"I said throw it!" Luke ordered.

"Let her go," Raven demanded. "It's me you want to kill. I'll throw the gun if you let her go."

"I do want to kill you," Luke agreed. "And I will. But I'll kill her first if you don't throw down the damned gun!" The click of the hammer was like thunder in Aurora's ear as Luke drew it back.

Raven knew Luke was desperate. He knew he was lost. If he left the island alive, it would only be as a prisoner. He had nothing to lose by killing Aurora.

Holding his gun in plain sight, Raven tossed it aside. It fell in the misty darkness, lost in the thick carpet of leaves. His hands at his sides, Raven faced Luke.

"Raven," Aurora breathed, tears smarting her eyes. She heard Luke's sadistic laughter, saw the gun in his hand as he raised it.

"Watch yer half-breed lover die," Luke hissed, taking aim.

Through her tears Aurora saw the single, swift movement of Raven's arm as it snaked behind him.

The deafening blast of Luke's gun almost masked the hiss of Raven's knife as it flew past Aurora's ear and embedded itself in Luke's throat.

Blood spurted onto Aurora's shoulder as Luke fell back. His blood stained the leaves on which he lay. He was dead by the time Raven reached Aurora's side.

He gathered her into his arms and held her until her trembling body quieted, until her sobs became soft and gentle tears that slid silently, unheeded, down her cheeks.

"I knew you'd come," she told him. "I knew it!"

With both hands, Raven swept back her tangled hair. He gazed down into her eyes, his look a mixture of love and concern.

"Are you hurt?" he asked gently, touching her cheek as though to reassure himself that she was real—that she was truly back in his arms once more.

She shook her head, knowing what he meant. "No, they didn't hurt me," she assured him. "They didn't harm me—in any way."

Stripping off his shirt, he helped her pull off her tattered blouse and cover herself. Holding her close, he led her back toward the shore.

The battle was finished by the time they reached the forest's edge. Rufus, stunned by the sight of his sister falling mortally wounded by his bullet, had himself been felled by a bullet from a young soldier's gun. Titus, though seriously wounded, had been captured alive and was even then being clapped into irons. He would face a trial and imprisonment.

Aurora and Raven looked around as a band of

the soldiers who had swarmed over the tiny island appeared, leading Belle and Jennie.

"They're innocent," Aurora told Raven. "Belle is Rufus's wife, but she did nothing—I swear it. And Jennie—Jennie is as much a victim as any of the sailors who died in the wreck of the *Sea Mist*. As much a victim as Graham Hughston himself."

"Graham?" Raven asked.

"Dead," Aurora told him. "In the shipwreck last night."

Holding Raven tightly by the hand as though afraid to let go, Aurora went to the young officer in charge.

"These two women had nothing to do with—" She stopped when her eyes met those of the blue-uniformed captain. "Kyle," she whispered. "Kyle Braxton."

He pulled off his hat. "Hello, Aurora. I'd like to talk with you later if you feel well enough. There is something that I need to explain. Something I think you should know."

"All right," she agreed. "But for now . . . this woman," she pointed to Belle, "was Rufus Oates's wife. But she did not help them with the shipwrecks. And this girl," she motioned toward Jennie, "was a survivor of one of the wrecks years ago. Can't they go free? They're innocent, I assure you."

"I'm sure they are," Kyle agreed. "But I'll have to take them back to Mackinac Island to make their statements and so they can testify at Titus Oates's trial." His eyes went to Jennie's pale, delicate face and his gaze softened as she blushed and cast down her eyes demurely. "You won't mind coming back with us, will you, miss?"

Jennie shook her head, and when she dared

lift her gaze, her eyes seemed filled with dazzled admiration for the handsome young officer who spoke to her with such kindness.

Matthew approached and took Aurora into his arms.

"Is Bridey all right?" she asked anxiously. "I've been so worried about her."

"Worried about her! She was worried about you! She felt guilty that she was not there to help you when you needed her."

"I'm glad she wasn't there. I know she would have tried to stop them and she would only have gotten hurt."

"She'll be glad to know you're safe and sound." Matthew exchanged a look with Raven, then said: "She'll be especially glad to know that you'll be back in time to be a witness at our wedding."

"Wedding?" She looked at Raven, who smiled and nodded.

With a little cry of happiness she flung herself into Matthew's arms. She was free and safe and back with Raven, and the two dearest friends she had were going to be married. The day had turned out far, far better than she could have hoped.

45

The celebrations that went on far into the night on High Island had a dual purpose. First, and more important, it was the day of Bridey's and Matthew's wedding. Second, the news had come that Titus Oates had been sentenced to spend the rest of his life in prison. No more would ships unlucky enough to be passing his island on dark, stormy or foggy nights be in mortal danger; no more innocent lives would be taken to satisfy one man's lust for wealth.

Aurora and Raven strolled along the shore in the moonlight listening to the music and the laughter coming from the clearing near Raven's cabin. The day had been filled with joy, but Aurora could not help longing for her own wedding day, still a month away.

"I've been thinking," Raven said as they

paused and gazed out over the gently undulating, seemingly endless expanse of night-dark water that stretched before them. "I've been thinking that perhaps we should go to Chicago on our honeymoon."

"Chicago?" Aurora looked up at him surprised. "I should have thought you'd never want to see Chicago again."

"It isn't so much Chicago I want to see as my father."

Aurora's eyes were warm with tenderness. "I'm so glad the two of you have found one another again. So many years were wasted while you both nursed your private grudges."

"We owe a lot of it to you, my darling," he said softly.

He felt the loss of the years when he and his father had been estranged. He wondered now, having learned that Sarah had systematically intercepted and destroyed dozens of letters from his father, if it would have made any difference if he had received them. He thought it might have. With the passing of the years, he had come to realize that his father was not at fault for his mother's dying alone in the forest, nor for Raven's living the life of the scion of a wealthy house in Pittsburgh. That was the life she had wanted for him, and she had been happy that he'd had the opportunity to go. She had been happy to know that he was there, accepted, cherished as the son of the man she had loved until the last moment of her life.

Aurora sighed contentedly and slid her arms about Raven's waist. "Everything's turned out so perfectly. Even for Jennie." The smile she turned up toward Raven was teasing, flirtatious. "And you told me not to play matchmaker! I think I did rather well. Bridey and Matthew are married. Kyle and Jennie are courting."

"How do you know they're courting?" Raven wanted to know.

"I got a letter from Jennie. I didn't show it to you because you were off with Matthew doing whatever it is that bridegrooms and their best men do the night before the wedding." She leaned back in his arms and looked up at him. "What *did* you do last night?"

Raven's smile was maddeningly inscrutable. "Never mind. You were saying? About Jennie and her letter?"

"Oh!" She slapped him lightly. "You wretch! Anyway—Jennie said that Kyle found her a position as a companion to an elderly lady on Mackinac Island. Apparently this lady and her husband came from Detroit. They used to spend their summers on the island. When the husband died, the lady sold her house in Detroit and moved to the island. But it's hard to find a companion who wants to live there year round. It's so isolated and quiet there in the winter.

"After Titus's trial, Kyle took Jennie to meet this lady and she was hired to be her companion— to read to her and walk with her . . . just to keep her company. And—" Aurora paused to give her next words their proper significance. "—Kyle arranged it so his free day coincides with Jennie's day off. What do you think of that?"

"Could be a coincidence," Raven said, knowing how it would exasperate her.

"Raven! You haven't got a romantic bone in your body!"

"You don't think so?" he challenged.

"No! I don't think so!"

Aurora squealed as he seized her, as easily as if she were a child, and slung her over his shoulder.

"Raven!" she protested, giggling as he headed for the welcoming, concealing darkness of the forest where autumn had carpeted the floor with a thick cushion of brightly colored leaves. "There are other people around!"

"They're busy," he said, "they won't bother us."

"Raven!" She gasped as he laid her down on the crisp, fragrant bed of leaves. "It's cold out here!"

He lay down beside her, one hand caressing her arm through the thin silk of her gown. "We'll warm it up," he promised, his lips at her throat.

"Raven!" She stared up at him as he loomed above her.

"Aurora!" he shot back as his hands pinioned her wrists to the forest floor on either side of her head.

Her smile was half-amusement, half-seduction. "Yes?"

"Shut up."

A little giggle escaped her lips, then slid into a sigh as his mouth stilled her protests.

Spring had come to the islands after the long, deep, bitter winter. The delicate, pale green of the newly formed leaves seemed to glow with some inner brilliance all their own in the yellow light of

436

the nurturing sun. The first wildflowers were beginning to appear among the brown, withered leaves of the summer before on the floor of the forest.

Aurora, now happily Raven's wife and carrying their first child—conceived, so she steadfastly believed, on the night of Bridey's and Matthew's wedding—sat on the bank of the pond, her bare feet dangling in the cool water. She was reading a letter from her attorneys in New York.

"Well?" Raven asked, coming to sit behind her, his long legs braced on either side of her, his chin on her shoulder. "Have they found anything?"

She nodded. "They say that a yacht called the *Jacintha* sank in the summer of 1877. Among those lost was a Mary Clemmons and her eighteen-month-old daughter, Jennifer. Mrs. Clemmons was a widow with no known living relatives. She was lady's maid and companion to Mrs. Leonie Halleck, wife of Robert Halleck, the yacht's owner. They were from Philadelphia." She sighed. "It would have been so much more romantic if Jennie had been the Hallecks' daughter. Don't you think so?"

Raven smiled. "Every girl can't be Cinderella, you know, darling. Besides, think of all the trouble your fortune caused you."

"That's true," she laughed. "The letter goes on to say that Jennie's father had been the chauffeur for the Hallecks, much older than Jennie's mother, and he died within months of Jennie's birth. He is also not known to have had any near relations living." She looked up at Raven. "I had hoped she would have lots and lots of relatives who would

437

have been so glad to see her restored to them after all these years."

"She'll have Kyle's family," Raven reminded her. "After all, they are going to be married this summer."

Aurora's smile was at once triumphant and teasing. "I told you he was courting her, didn't I?"

"'I told you so,'" Raven mimicked. "Yes, you told me so. And you were right. I admit it."

"Jennie says that when Kyle is through with the Army, he'd like to study the law. Perhaps I'll write to the attorneys in New York and ask them to make him a clerk in their offices until he's ready to practice. What do you think?"

"I think you enjoy playing Lady Bountiful," Raven said, "dispensing happiness to the people you love."

"I like making people happy," she admitted. "Most of all, I like making you happy."

He drew her back until she lay against him and his hands spread over her belly where the child of their love grew.

"I'm going to have to build that bigger cabin after all," he told her gently, nibbling at her ear.

"As long as there's room in it for me, I'll love it," she replied, caressing his cheek as it lay against her own.

"Oh, you can share my room."

"Forever?" she asked, turning in his arms and twining her own arms about his neck.

He kissed her with heartbreaking tenderness. "And always," he promised.

All around them the island was awakening from its long winter slumber. The warming winds rustled among the tender young leaves, the animals nursed their newborn babes in fur-lined nests, the sun-kissed waves sparkled and danced as they made their inevitable way to the shore. But for Raven and Aurora, there was only the two of them, in their eyes, in their hearts, in their souls . . .

Forever . . . and always.

AUTOGRAPHED BOOKMARK EDITIONS

Each book contains a signed message from the author and a removable gold foiled and embossed bookmark.

SCARLET SURRENDER
Sandra DuBay

"Wonderful escapist fiction. It fulfills all her readers' fantasies!" —**Romantic Times**

Young Victoria traveled from war-torn New Orleans to the shores of France in search of her husband, a man she didn't love. But the innocent beauty would find love en route to her destination—in the strong arms of the handsome captain, Grey Verreaux.

_____2555-8 $3.95 US/$4.95 CAN

LEISURE BOOKS
ATTN: Customer Service Dept.
6 East 39th Street, New York, N.Y. 10016

Please send me the book(s) checked above. I have enclosed $_____
Add $1.00 for shipping and handling for the first book; $ .25 for each book thereafter. No cash, stamps, or C.O.D.s. Allow 4 to 6 weeks for delivery.

Name _____

Address _____

City_____State_____Zip_____

Canadian orders must be paid in U.S. dollars payable through a New York banking facility.   ☐ Please send a free catalogue.